I WASH MY HANDS

The "Autobiography" of Pontius Pilate

I WASH MY HANDS

P. DREW WARREN

Contents

This book is dedicated to my children and to everyone who struggles to find their purpose and destiny in a broken world. May you find peace with your past, forgiveness in your heart, love in your soul, and joy wherever your path may lead.

Acknowledgements

In an instant, I felt dramatically compelled to write this story. What could have been a fleeting moment of inspiration gave way to the full outline of this book within fifteen minutes. For that, I thank God.

I knew little about Pontius Pilate beyond what everyone knows. He was the man who ordered the death of Jesus. I knew nothing of his life before that moment and nothing about what happened after. Setting out to research, I read, watched, and listened to sources far more knowledgeable than I am. The research not only provided detail and context to the story, but it also served to confirm the authenticity of the initial outline that flowed from a divine spark of inspiration. It was as if Pontius himself was whispering in my ear. For that, I thank Pontius Pilate.

Every free moment for months became time for research and writing. Time spent with my family was also spent with Pontius, Claudia, Cornelius, Abigail, Cassius, Lulit, Atticus, Corea, and many others. They became part of the extended family. My wife and children did not invite them, but they accepted them, and I think they grew to love them. For that, I thank my family, especially my patient and loving wife, Cameron.

I knew that Pontius was telling his story through me, but like Thomas, I had my doubts. I turned to my most trusted friends to read the story and give me insights.

- This story contains sensitive religious content, so I chose a former Catholic Priest and two protestant pastors, and a learned agnostic, all close and beloved friends, to review my words.

- The story is about finding and living one's purpose. I chose close friends and confidants who exemplify this to read, critique, and advise.
- I flew through the writing of this book because it flew through me like a mountain stream on its way to the sea. I knew I would need professionals to fix my mistakes. For this, I chose friends with academic and literary backgrounds.

Each of these people provided wisdom and guidance. Like sculptors, they smoothed my edges, knocked away my imperfections, and chiseled this story into something ready for publication. For this, I thank Sean, Jeff, David, Nicole, Rosa, Rob, Linda, Andrea, Tara, and Deborah.

I would be remiss if I failed to mention authors who inspired me, but there are too many to list. I will call out Dean Koontz in particular, though. His writing taught me to try to create a tapestry through my words - weaving threads of meaning into every sentence, a strand of light through every dark fiber, something new to see on every page, and pulling it all together so the reader gets the big picture. I do not know if I accomplished that, but Dean inspired the effort.

Most of all, I thank you for taking the time to read this book. I hope that each of you will find some aspect of Pontius Pilate's journey that will help you on your own.

Dramatis Personae

Whatever significance my story has is largely due to the people with whom my life was entwined. The most impactful of these was Jesus Bar Joseph, and most of you already know much about him. I am providing this list of people important to my journey to help you keep the cast of characters straight.

As you read, you can reference this list if you have trouble remembering names and relations. To be honest, the convoluted relationships, especially in the bloodlines of Caesar, are difficult for even me...and I knew them all! Add to that the Herodian dynasty and its incestuous branches as well as the tendency for people to change names, and you will thank me for this list later.

Those already present in the historical record are underlined in case you wish to do more research. Others may not be known to history, but their impact is no less significant to me or my life's work. May they inspire hope and love in your life as they did mine.

Pontius Pilatus

Abbanes: A friend of Joseph of Arimathea and a fellow merchant, involved in the spice trade with India.

Abigail: Of Jewish background, Abigail was a slave who served as Claudia's maid servant. Later, she married Cornelius and is the mother of Hannah.

Agrippina the Elder: Wife of Germanicus, mother of Caligula, granddaughter of Augustus, grandmother of Nero through her daughter Agrippina the Younger.

Agrippina the Younger: The daughter of Germanicus and Agrippina the Elder. The sister and occasional lover of Emperor Caligula. The mother of Emperor Nero.

Alicia: Daughter of Alucio and Maya and mother of Sapio and Sophia.

Alucio and Maya: A couple of Iberian descent who took part in the revolt of Judas the Galilean and were subsequently enslaved and separated by Herod Agrippa. Their daughter is Alecia, and their grandchildren are Sapio and Sophia.

Angitia: Goddess associated with healing, snakes, and magic.

Appius Claudius Caecus (fl. c. 312–279 BC): A Roman statesman and writer best known for major building projects, including the Appian Way, the first major Roman road.

Aurelia and Aeneas: My aunt and uncle. Sister and brother in law of my mother

Aurora Gratus: Wife of prefect Valerius Gratus.

Barabbas: The prisoner, a murderer and terrorist, the crowd, led by the temple priests, chose to free rather than Jesus.

Caesar Augustus: Originally named Octavian, Augustus was the emperor at the time of by birth and throughout my childhood. He was also the biological grandfather of my wife Claudia Procula.

Caligula (AKAGaius Caesar Augustus Germanicus): The son of the Roman general Germanicus and Augustus' granddaughter Agrippina the Elder. He eventually became Roman Emperor. Nicknamed "Little Boots" (Caligula) by his father's soldiers, whom he accompanied on military campaigns.

Cassius: A Roman soldier proceeding to the rank of centurion in the Praetorian Guard. Along with Cornelius, one of my two closest confidants.

Claudia Procula: My beautiful wife, the biological daughter of Julia, granddaughter of Augustus. As with others in my time, she was known by her first name in intimate settings and her maiden name in more formal settings.

<u>Claudius (AKA Tiberius Claudius Caesar Augustus Germanicus)</u>: Roman Emperor after his nephew Caligula and before his grand-nephew Nero. He stuttered, limped, and was hard of hearing, conditions which made him the object of bullying and rejection among his family members.

Dagrun and Alba: Household slaves at my family villa.

<u>Drusilla (AKA Julia Drusilla)</u>: The daughter of Germanicus and Agrippina the Elder. She was the favorite sister of Caligula and was known to be his lover. When she died, Caligula named her a goddess.

Gaius and Joanna Proculeius: The adoptive parents of my wife, Claudia Procula. Other than the last name, little is available in the historical record.

<u>Germanicus Julius Caesar</u>: Roman General and Politician known for his military campaigns in Germania. The great-nephew of Caesar Augustus, father of Caligula, and the older brother of Claudius Caesar.

<u>Gnaeus Calpurnius Piso</u>: A Roman aristocrat and politician who took over as Prefect of Syria for Quintus Silanus during my time as an officer in the legion. Later, he engaged in a power struggle with Germanicus and was arrested for his murder.

<u>Gnaeus Lucius Pilatus</u>: My father. Herein referred to as either father or its Latin equivalent, Pater.

<u>Herod Agrippa (AKA Marcus Julius Agrippa or Agrippa I)</u>: The grandson of Herod the Great, nephew of Herod Antipas, and brother of Herodias (wife of Herod Antipas). He was a lifelong friend of Claudius Caesar and the last known king of Judea.

<u>Herod Antipas</u>: Ruler (Tetrach) of Galilee and Perea, He is referred to as both "Herod the Tetrarch" and "King Herod" in the Bible. He was the son of Herod the Great, brother of Philip the Tetrarch, husband and uncle of Herodias, and stepfather and great-uncle of Salome.

<u>James the Great</u>: One of the twelve apostles of Jesus. Together with his brother, John, he is called one of the "Sons of Thunder" for their argumentative and aggressive personalities. His moniker, "the great," refers to him being the older brother as well as the eldest James among the followers of Jesus, rather than his size. The brothers were fishermen in Galilee along with their father Zebedee.

James the Just: The half-brother of Jesus. He was not a disciple during the ministry of Jesus but became one after His crucifixion. He was the first Jewish bishop of Jerusalem and supported maintaining more Jewish tradition and ritual within the new Christian faith.

Joanna and Chuza: Joanna was a wealthy supporter of Jesus. She was the wife of Chuza, the steward/most trusted employee of Herod Antipas.

John the Baptizer (AKA John the Baptist):

John, son of Zebedee: One of the twelve apostles of Jesus. Together with his brother, James the Great, he is called one of the "Sons of Thunder" for their argumentative and aggressive personalities. The brothers were fishermen in Galilee along with their father Zebedee.

Joseph Ben Caiaphas: High Priest of Israel during the first century who opposed Jesus, calling for His execution.

Joseph of Arimathea: A wealthy man and member of the Sanhedrin who arranged for the burial of Jesus in his family tomb. In this book, I explore his relationship to Jesus and his role in spreading Christianity.

Joses, Simon, and Salome: Half-siblings of Jesus and children of Mary. They were among the followers of Jesus during his ministry in Judea.

Judas the Galilean: A revolutionary in Judea who led a significant revolt against Roman authority in the early years of the first century, more than ten years before my arrival. He is the founder of the "fourth philosophy" of Judaism, the Zealots.

Julia, (AKA Julia the Elder): Birth mother of Claudia Procula. She died in Gual, where she had been exiled by her father, Augustus, in response to her alleged sexual indiscretions.

__King Herod the Great__: The Roman-appointed king of Judaea (37–4 bc). Known as the Great because of his major building projects, including the Port of Caesaria, fortresses, aqueducts, and the rebuilding of the Jewish Temple in Jerusalem. The father of Herod Antipas, who I was to work with during my time as prefect, Herod the Great, was also known for killing family members, committing atrocities, and being a generally vile human.

__Lathraíos__: A young Jewish priest, apprentice of Nicodemus, and follower of Jesus.

__Lavilla__: The youngest daughter of Germanicus and Agrippina the Elder. The sister and occasional lover of Emperor Caligula.

__Livia Drusilla__: The second wife of Caesar Augustus and empress from 27 BC to AD 14. She was the step-grandmother of my wife, Claudia, and the original evil stepmother.

__Lucius Aelius Sejanus (commonly known as Sejanus)__: The mentor of my youth. An ambitious and power-hungry soldier prefect of the Praetorian Guard.

__Lucius Vitellius__: Prefect of Syria in the last year of my time in Judea. He was a favorite of Tiberius, who sent him

__Marcus Arrecinus Clemens__: Prefect of the Praetorian Guard during the reign of Emperor Caligula.

__Marcus Vesuvius__: The defendant in one of my first trials, accused of murder in a Roman street.

__Mariamne__: A Hasmonean princess and wife of Herod the Great. She was known for her great beauty. Herod loved his honey to death.

__Mary Magdalene (AKA Mary of Magdala)__: A female disciple of Jesus who witnessed His crucifixion and was the first to see Him resurrected. She was known to be very close to Jesus.

__Mary__: The mother of Jesus and James the Just.

__Matthew__: One of the twelve apostles of Jesus. He was highly educated and likely of the priestly lineage of Levi; however, he made his living as a much-reviled tax collector. He was key in documenting the life of Jesus and the rise of the early church.

Nicodemus: A Pharisee and a member of the Sanhedrin who is drawn to hear Jesus' teachings. Nicodemus is considered in both Catholic and Eastern Orthodox traditions to have secretly been a disciple of Jesus.

Octavia Camilla Pilatus: My mother. Herein referred to as either mother or its Latin equivalent, Mater.

Paul (AKA Saul): A key apostle who, along with Peter, is considered one of the two most influential leaders in founding the Christian church and faith. He was not a disciple of the living Jesus and initially persecuted Christians; however, he converted after a dramatic encounter with the resurrected Jesus left him blinded on the side of a road.

Peter (AKA Simon, Peter the Apostle, Simon Peter, or Cephas): One of the Twelve Apostles of Jesus. Despite being known as hotheaded, his leadership skills made him a key leader in the early church. He was the brother of the apostle Andrew.

Philip the Essene: A leader of the Essene sect promoting the revolutionary belief that slavery was against God's law. This character is fictional but based on a series of real revolutionaries undermining Roman rule of Judea.

Philip the Tetrarch (AKA Herod Philip II): Son of Herod the Great and half-brother of Herod Antipas. He ruled over the northeast part of his father's kingdom between 4 BC and 34 AD after Herod the Great's death.

Philip, Matthias, Thaddeus, and Bartholomew: The other Apostles, not specifically discussed in detail in this book. Matthias took over as one of the twelve after the betrayal and subsequent death of Judas.

Philo of Alexandria: A Hellenistic Jewish philosopher who lived in Alexandria, Egypt, a Roman Province at the time.

Protogenes: Assistant to Caligula, known to carry two books, one titled Sword and the other Dagger, veiled threats to anyone whose name may be listed therein.

Quintus Caecilius Metellus Creticus Silanus: The prefect of Syria during my early years in the Roman Legion.

Sapio: Son of Alicia, grandson of Alucio and Maya, and the brother of Sophia.

Sarah and Tavi: A slave couple, eventually freed, who served me and my family at our villa in Abruzzo.

Simon (AKA Simon the Zealot): One of the twelve apostles of Jesus, Simon was from Canaan. He came from "the fourth tradition" of Judaism, the Zealots, believing in the violent overthrow of Roman rule to establish the Kingdom of God.

Sophia and Turibas: Young Iberian couple. Sophia is the daughter of Alicia and granddaughter of Alucio and Maya.

Stephen: A leader of the early church in Jerusalem. He angered members of various synagogues with his teachings and was tried for blasphemy. As a result, he became the first Christian Martyr.

Thomas (AKA Doubting Thomas): One of the twelve apostles of Jesus, Thomas was known for his dubious nature but was the first to recognize Jesus as divine when he shouted, "My Lord and my God."

Tiberius Gemelus: The grandson of the Emperor Tiberius and the cousin of the Emperor Caligula. After his other family members were systematically eliminated by either Sejanus or Livia, he was named joint heir by Tiberius. Caligula had him assassinated.

Valerius Gratus: The prefect of Judea just before my term in that office.

Volisios: A Celtic tribal leader based on stories of such leaders in the historical record.

Prologue

For the past two thousand years, I have been able to monitor the unfolding of the history of humanity. From my vantage point, I can see everything from "In the beginning" to your current headlines like "Russia Attacks Ukrainian Electrical Power Facilities." I can even see what, to you, appears to be the future, all the way through "The Revelation".

From this timeless perspective, I feel uniquely positioned to write this story, the story of my life, how it intersects with history, and how episodes of my life impact you.

I have no need to correct the record regarding my own life. I do so now, not for myself but for you. If only the full history of my life were known and understood, then so much of the pain of your last two millennia could have been averted. You could have avoided civil wars, world wars, assassinations, slavery, genocides...all the many manifestations that evil assumes in the world brought into existence through the weakness of human nature. This weakness, known to many of you as "sin", is not evil itself; it is the condition that separates you from God and allows evil to occur, but I digress. The most important thing, as you will see, is not what happened in the past; it is how you use your past to shape the future, free of shame or any other form of self-obsession.

The purpose of this book is to correct the historical record, give the world the rest of the story, provide an example of how you can overcome your burdens, and "wash your hands" of the dirt of the world. For context, I will start from the beginning of my life, which I will call the "Old Testament." That phase of my life ended on the 6th of April, in the year you consider A.D. thirty-three, while looking up the hill of Golgotha. Little is known about me after that well-documented penultimate moment, but I will fill in those blanks in the second portion of this narrative, which I refer to as the "New Testament."

I want to tell you what this story is...and what it is not. My memory of things that happened over thousands of years may not be perfect, and, from my current perspective, details are not all that important. Therefore, it is not a history book, but it is frequently historical. It is not a theology book, but it has theological facets. It is not meant to be religious, but for some of you, it may have religious implications. It is certainly not a myth but references some mythology. While it IS a love story in every sense, I think the way I would describe this book is as an allegorical brew of historical fact, steeped in theology, but, like a cup-o-decaf, it is religiosity free. Parts of this story are sad, parts are scary, parts are gruesome, and many parts are very funny. That is just the nature of life and reflects the truth of our existence. I hope you can take this story seriously, but don't take yourself so seriously that these elements seem "sacrilegious". Remember that the most sacrilegious person in my time was Jesus Himself.

As for me, in the beginning, you may find me to be... well, in your current vernacular... somewhat of an A-Hole. I hope you will give me a bit of grace, for I am, like all humans, a reflection of the zeitgeist in which I existed. Besides, in the end, I clean up fairly well. Obviously, I am writing from a post-mortem perspective, but even after death, I have retained the core of my personality and the background that makes me who I am. As such, I have found that I occasionally slip back into the Latin vernacular of my childhood...well, actually, of my entire carnal existence. After trying to edit these things out, I ultimately decided to keep them. They help align my story with my former reality.

I pray that my story makes its way to you and strikes a sacred chord that will bring you peace and harmony. I pray that it is not too late.

The Grace of the Lord Jesus be with all. Amen

Pontius Pilatus

The Old Testament

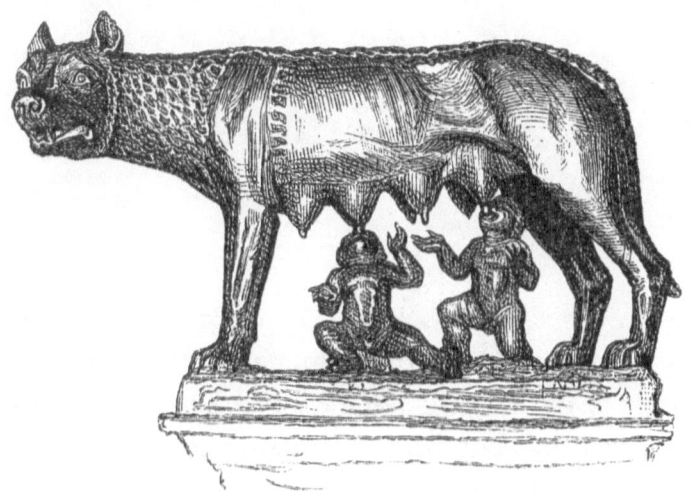

Capitoline Wolf Breastfeeding Romulus and Remus
Grafissimo, 2021, istockphoto.com

I

My Genesis

In an area known as the greenest region of Europe, bordered to the west by soaring, snowcapped mountains and on the east by the Adriatic Sea, I made my entry into the world. There are some who say I was born in Scotland, but that is fake news, a conspiracy theory promoted by Scottish tourism officials... or is it????

I was born in shadows... both those of the Apennine Mountains and of Romulus and Remus, the mythological founders of Rome. The twin brothers were set afloat in the Tiber River by their mother to avoid infanticide by King Amulius. They were the offspring of a human mother and Mars, the god of war. Adopted, nursed, and raised by wolves, they understood the nature of the world as a wolf would – be the predator or become the prey, be the alpha or have an unpleasant panorama, never stray from the pack, or deign to express divergent ideas. Perhaps it is not surprising that Romulus murdered Remus to seize all the power and become the first Roman Governor.

I was born on April 21st, the birth date of Rome itself. In many ways, I was the perfect representative of Rome. As I was descended from Gaius Pontius, the Samnite general who defeated the Roman Legion in a battle three centuries before my birth, this may seem somewhat counterintuitive. However, Rome itself was born of violence, formed by luring and uniting people who you might categorize as criminals or thugs. If you want a notable example of early Roman behavior, look further into the incident with the Sabine women, without whom there may have been no progeny at all. For those who may not have the motivation to look the story up, I will summarize – Roman men invade another city to kidnap and rape their women. The progeny of this atrocity are the ancestors of all Romans.

Over time, the sharper edges of these warring factions were worn down and the layer of grime spawned by the murders and rapes that brought us into existence were washed away. However, at our core, we Romans remained true to our ancestry. Then this has been true for all human civilization.

Since the dawn of time, the human race has evolved from being more animalistic and hedonistic to being more aligned with God. Rape, murder, slavery, and every form of evil behavior still occur in your time but, thankfully, almost no one sees these things as normal or acceptable. Somehow, it took you thousands of years to get to that level of piety – congratulations.

∞

I was born into privilege, a member of the Equestrian class, one of the two ruling classes of the Roman Empire, along with the Senatorial class.

My father had served as a high-ranking officer in the Roman Legion before assuming the role of gentleman farmer and political leader, advocating for our region in Rome. He married my mother through an arranged marriage after his time in the Legion. The two of them were the quintessential power couple with both economic resources and social standing. That said, they loved one another and were devoted parents to my younger siblings and me.

My mother had a midwife and slaves attending to her rather than shepherds, wisemen, and farm animals. My entry into the world was facilitated with the most expensive and finest of oils. While thanks to Eve and her manipulation by the serpent, childbirth is never easy, my mother was made as comfortable as possible, as opposed to Mary, the

"Blessed" Virgin, who, 10 years later, would endure childbirth covered in hay and donkey excrement.

You could say I had it made. Being raised in what is now known as the Abruzzo region meant that I was surrounded by beauty reflecting the glory of the gods, or at least that is how I saw it from my youthful perspective.

Neptune kept watch over our waterfront while blessing our horses with strength, speed, and stamina. We knew we had crossed him when storms washed in from the sea, our fishermen's nets came up empty, or our horses would not breed. Since both the bounty of the oceans and the health of our horses were integral to our prosperity, we gave thanks to Neptune often and sacrificed to him on regular occasions.

Ceres made our crops and wombs bear good fruit and ensured that our harvest was plentiful. We knew that she was angry when our grape vines withered, or a mother miscarried. We were being punished and needed to get back into her good graces. Agriculture, particularly grapes, olives, and wheat, was the fuel for our bodies as well as the economic engine of our family. Accordingly, we graciously sacrificed to Ceres as well.

All of this happened under the watchful eye of Jupiter, king of the gods, who kept order among the often-conflicting pantheon of deities. After all, how could we humans, who lived in constant wars and threats of war, believe that our gods were at peace or that displeasing them could result in anything but punishment? We held feasts in honor of Jupiter and went to his temple to offer sacrifices at least once a year.

My personal favorite god at the time was Bacchus. You may know him from Mardi Grawe Krewe and Parade named after him, where half-naked ladies drink in excess and show their breasts in supplication, earning beads and tokens with his likeness. Like his Greek predecessor, Dionysus, Bacchus was the god of fertility but also represented excess, gluttony, and debauchery. These were my best friends for the first three decades of my life. After that, the love of my wife Claudia eroded those ties. Then they were forever severed on a Hill called Golgotha. You will hear more about that later.

∞

Our house could not compare to that of Caesar Augustus, who ruled at the time of my birth. It did not even have what you would call necessities, like hot running water and air conditioning.

It did have a great deal of marble, soaring Doric columns, pools and fountains, and exquisite works of art, including paintings and statues, mostly reflecting the gods. One statue in particular, standing in a fountain at the center of our home, was of the goddess Angitia holding a snake. The people of my region had worshipped Angitia for centuries, even before we were absorbed into the Roman Empire.

In both grandeur and function, though not in style (we could not be rivaled in style!), our home might have paralleled some of the beautiful plantations of the American Antebellum period. We kept livestock and, true to our Equestrian social class, bred horses fit for the highest-ranking Roman officers. Our fields produced the finest crops; not cotton or tobacco, but grapes, olives, vegetables, and wheat.

Best of all, at least from my childhood perspective, is that most of the work was done by slaves. Anything not done by free slave labor was done by lower-class "plebians" who were paid very little.

My parents' labor was confined to overseeing estate operations, socializing with others of the Equestrian or Senatorial classes, procreating to spread our illustrious lineage, conducting warfare to take over other parts of the world, settling petty territorial squabbles, or assuaging perceived slights to our egos.

My parents were a product of the time and culture in which they were born. They believed that their privileged positions were ordained by the gods. They did not treat their slaves with cruelty; they saw them as people who had the misfortune of having been born into their role. They even freed many of them over the years. Freed men could become farmers or merchants; however, of course, they could never become our equal.

I was born into the Equestrian class, a child of privilege. However, we were not of the highest class; that position atop our Roman social pyramid belonged to the Senatorial class. My CLASS-mates and I were, like underclassmen in an elite University, still elite but looked down upon by the Senatorial class. On the other hand, unlike those underclassmen, we had no hope of advancing to the upper class; we were forever the target of their condescension. This is based on history and having once been conquered by the Romans.

At least we were not like the plebians or freed men who had little social standing or the slaves who had none. We made the rules and benefited handsomely from them. Thank the gods that this social stratification and power structure have changed in the past two thousand years! An amused wink and shaking of my head are implied for those who do not get sarcasm.

II

⚜

Snakes!

I woke up to the sound of a rooster crowing twice on May 1ˢᵗ of my twelfth year. I excitedly jumped out of bed, threw on my best toga, which was, of course, my only clean and non-stained toga – I was, after all, a very healthy, active, and mischievous twelve-year-old boy.

I joined my family downstairs in the wide-open foyer surrounding the statue of Angitia, holding snakes above her head and casting her shadow on the still waters of the shallow pool in which she stood. Once per year, we made the journey to the temple in Cocullo for the Festival of the aforementioned goddess.

As with any twelve-year-old, adventures like this assuaged my need for action. As with any 12-year-old, things were starting to change for me, and suddenly I found myself looking forward to the vast array of breasts that would surely be on display on this momentous occasion.

Since before Romulus killed Remus and the founding of Rome, Angitia was worshipped by my ancestors. Sister to Ceres, Angitia was known to have the power to overcome poison and heal snakebites. Our local culture valued what you may call witchcraft, fortune-telling, sorcery, and spiritual healing. These things you consider occult helped us to understand the world and feel a sense of control, even though, as I now know, no human really has control.

∞

The ride to Cocullo took about two hours, so we woke early to make the journey by horse-drawn carriage. Our entourage of slaves went with us, of course. We would need people to kneel down so pater could climb onto his horse or to help mater in and out of her bath. Of course, my siblings and I needed our nannies so my parents could focus on their business dealings or social obligations.

We traversed the bumpy, winding roads through the lush landscape of the Apennine foothills. The journey was a sensory overload. The landscape around us alternated in brightness as we passed through forests and foothills filled with all the hues of nature. The sounds of hoofbeats, wheels, and my sisters' annoying voices filled my ears. The smells of my mother's scented body oils merged with the natural scents of pine, magnolia, horse dung, and my brother, who seemed to forget mater's instruction to bathe.

Despite head bobbing, butt bumping, and brotherly B.O., I enjoyed the ride. It made me feel alive, activated all of my senses, and entertained me in an interactive and immersive manner unknown to most children in your era.

∞

Just outside of town, our family found a grove of Beech trees under which to rest and prepare ourselves for the celebration. The huge trees, hundreds of years old, formed a canopy, sheltering us from the sun. A small stream gurgled past us, conveying clean, fresh, chilly water from the heights of the mountains just beyond town to the lush valley in which Cocullo was nestled.

The tops of the mountains, just a month ago white with snow and apparently dead foliage, were now green and teeming with renewed life. The gods had blessed us once again, rewarding our worship and sacrifices.

At my mother's insistence, I, along with my siblings, washed my hands in the stream before sitting down to picnic in the grove. My father and mother reclined on an ornate rug while drinking wine and feasting on figs, grapes, and cheese. Normally, being of significant wealth, we would have had meat or fish with our meal, but lamb and seabass do not travel well without the luxury of Yeti coolers.

I recalled from prior festivals that the action normally started at midday and lasted throughout the night, with many people sleeping off the party the next day. We would be staying that evening with my mother's sister and her family, who resided just outside of Cocullo. My parents would have us in bed before the night became too wild, but my friends and I had heard tales of the debauchery in which the people partook, and I longed to witness it.

May first was the largest and final day of the festival, but many activities had been going on since March when the charmers began catching the stars of the show – thousands of snakes. Mostly, these snakes were grass snakes and other harmless species. While not without its "charm," the Festival of Angitia did not equal the larger Roman festivals like those of Lupercalia or Saturnalia.

Lupercalia celebrated Romulus and Remus and the founding of Rome. It entailed men picking women's names from jars to engage in sexual trysts, likely in "honor" of the kidnapping and rape of the Sabine women, the genomic foundation of Rome. Rebranded and enduring even in your time, this festival of lovers pays tribute to Cupid, the son of Venus, goddess of Love, and takes place in mid-February of each year.

The Festival of Saturnalia honored the god Saturn and occurred in late December. Everything shut down for 7 days during this festival, masters served their slaves, loud and familiar music rang from every corner, candles were lit, and gifts were given. These traditions remain in your time but have been absorbed into the Christian Christmas celebrations. Thankfully, the X-rated aspects of these Roman festivals were not adopted by the followers of Christ.

In retrospect, I understand why the Christian priests and leaders of the early church incorporated these "pagan" rituals. In the earliest days, this allowed them to celebrate their beliefs in secret, blending into the festivities of a culture in which they risked ostracism and even death for practicing their beliefs. It further served to help non-believers integrate into Christianity. Now, however, I see this as an example, as I have witnessed over and over through countless eras, of man attempting to use human understanding and tactics such as manipulation, coercion, and deception to bring people to God. Using ignoble means to accomplish noble ends is never God's way.

∞

Much to my parents' chagrin, my siblings and I played and soiled our togas while they tried to have a short nap after lunch. My two sisters made mud pies while my younger brother and I engaged in "warfare", sparring with sticks as if they were short swords and throwing branches we had fashioned into javelins.

We were proving to be quite true to our hereditary name, Pilatus, which literally means "skilled with a javelin." When I placed a javelin perfectly in a grassy noll ten feet from my mother's head, my father jumped up to punish me. Thankfully, realizing my skillful throw from twenty-five paces away, his demeanor softened, and he urged me to be more careful. This seemed inadequate for my mother, who gave him a sideways glance and me a glare, reminding me that the women ruled the Roman roost, at least for all things on the home front.

Washing up in the stream once more, we prepared ourselves for our grand entrance. We rolled into town with Sol, formerly known as Helios, directly overhead and radiating his glory down upon us. The elevation and the Mediterranean breezes modulated the effect of the sun and made the day perfect for an outdoor festival: the breezes carried the assorted aromas of the festival; the sound of music echoed off of the mountains surrounding the small village; and people seemed to absorb sun's warmth which radiated from their smiles and laughter.

The aromatic streets were pulsating with vendors offering Arrosticini Abruzzesi, skewers of meat preferred in the region, as well as a wide variety of fruits, nuts, and vegetables. They also sold mementos of the festival, including toy snakes fashioned of leather, Angitia straw dolls, and icons of blessed Angitia, ranging from pocket coins with her likeness to small statues to adorn home or garden.

As we shopped, we met up with my aunt Aurelia, uncle Aeneas, and their three children. My aunt was a younger and, do not tell my mother I said this, more beautiful version of my mother. She had married a man of noble senatorial lineage and even more resources than my father. Perhaps having servants to take care of all of her needs, including the heavier burdens of parenthood, allowed her a stress-free existence where she could be pampered and focus on aspirations to rival Venus. While her heart, mind, and soul may have been somewhat lacking, I did see many men turn their heads as she walked by, worshipping her figure with reverence most often reserved for a goddess. My mother, by contrast, maintained a natural beauty but also emanated a strength that served her well in running our country estate and being an equal partner in my parents' union, well, as equal as our time and place allowed. In retrospect, perhaps the fall of Rome may have been averted if the coming centuries had bred more of my mother's strength and less of my aunt's narcissism.

As we shopped, I slowly became aware of the low beat of drums. The sound of the cornu, a horn that wrapped around the musician's body like a constrictor, rose above the din of the crowd. I noticed the masses begin to shift and move in the direction of music like snakes under the spell of their charmer. Knowing what was coming, my aunt sent her children and my little sisters with her slaves back to their summer villa outside of town. My brother and I, at eleven and twelve (almost thirteen!) respectively, were almost adults and allowed to stay for the main event.

Drawing closer to the commotion, I could see that the music was coming from the steps of the temple of Angitia, where several musicians beat drums, blew horns, or plucked a lyre. As people assembled around the temple, my brother and I made our way to the front, sitting at the edge of the steps with the adults a few feet away.

The music started slowly, almost inaudibly. The crowd began to sway in unison to the low rhythmic tones. If people were still talking, the rest of the crowd seemed oblivious, lost in the beating of the drums and the reverie of the occasion.

The sun, once glaringly bright, had transformed into a deep blood orange as it descended behind the mountains, looming above the temple roof, giving the impression that one could walk up the stairs of the temple and continue to ascend all the way to Mount Olympus.

The skies were painted by the gods' glorious shades of red, pink, and purple, matching the royal purple blaze on the collars of my parents' white togas.

The music escalated in both tempo and volume over the next several minutes, ending at the crescendo that suddenly stopped in an abyss of silence. The absence of noise was timed to the setting of the sun, creating the impression of having fallen into a dark hole under the earth. I gripped my brother's hand in a combination of fear and anticipation.

Suddenly, men clad only in leather subligaculum (fancy Roman underwear) emerged from the temple carrying torches. They ignited fires in great bowls strategically placed at the edges of the temple steps.

The music resumed in a low, quiet throbbing. We sat enthralled, and I could feel the anticipation of the crowd behind me and an energy I could not adequately define but later came to understand as sexual tension.

Two young women then emerged from the temple, also topless, and carrying dozens of snakes. They did not walk, they undulated to the music, twisting their bodies like the snakes writhing in their hands and around their shoulders. As they danced, other snakes emerged from the temple, hundreds of them slithering about on the steps of the temple. I knew these to be harmless species and no one in the crowd panicked; we were all too enthralled at the spectacle before us.

The music grew even quieter, a hissing whisper, signaling the imminent entrance of the temple priestess. The seconds felt like an eternity, and when she emerged, the priestess did not disappoint. Her skin glowed with the oil in which she had been anointed in preparation for this "holy" day. Her hair was pinned up with a golden pin shaped like a snake and reflecting the firelight, a shimmering, reptilian Prometheus.

Unlike the rest of her shimmering figure, her shoulders were clothed, a snake draped over them, a living scarf. I immediately recognized the snake as an Egyptian cobra like the one that had killed Cleopatra forty years ago after her failed coup attempt with her lover Mark Anthony. Some may have thought the death of these conspiratorial lovers to be tragic and worthy of admiration. This snake was a reminder that this was not a tragic tale of star-crossed lovers but one of power lust and blasphemy against the gods – if they had been in the favor of the gods, Angitia would have spared Cleopatra death from the snake bite.

This sinuous serpent was at least six feet long and, unlike the one that had just slithered over my foot, was deadly. As the priestess danced, the imported reptile seemed to dance with her, a deadly dance partner taking turns leading and being led in sensuous, salacious swaying.

I was not sure what the feeling was under my toga. Much like the dance of the priestess, it was confusing, exciting, and almost painful. As the music got louder and louder, the dancing duo moved more rapidly, and you could see the snake becoming more agitated. Twice I saw it strike out and bite its sacred handler, but she continued to dance, seemingly oblivious to the pain and unfazed by fear – clearly, unlike Cleopatra, she was favored by Angitia.

For several minutes, the priestess danced, contorting in ways that seemed more serpentine than human. Then the music came to a sudden end with the priestess coiled on the ground holding the snake high overhead, a symbol of Angitia's power to be adored like a living idol of our great goddess and protector. The Priestess uncoiled her oily body, rose to a standing position, kissed the snake on the lips, and, giving a slight bow, turned, seductively swaying her hips as she returned to the temple with her serpentine lover, a testament to Angitia's power.

∞

I did not want to leave but I knew my parents would drag me out before the drunken orgies started. I felt my mother pull my tunic, and we turned back toward the edge of town to start our carriage ride back to my aunt and uncle's villa. However, I soon found myself separated from the rest of the family by throngs of overly excited spectators. I just could not find my way back to them or to our carriage, so I did what I thought was best, heading back to the temple. While I was excited by watching the crowd, they also scared me as they became more out of control and, somehow, less human.

Seeing the door to the temple slightly cracked, I went inside. There, I saw the priestess, now fully clothed, placing her snake companion into a large basket, which was hauled off by some of the temple guards who were apparently too busy to notice me. I sat and listened while the Priestess spoke with the two other snake charmers, unfortunately also clothed at this point. She asked, "Did you not feed the cobra? That monster bit me...TWICE. Thank Angitia that we had its fangs removed." The young priestesses both said that the snake had been well fed and pled for mercy at their leader's feet.

The angry, hard expression of the lead priestess softened. She caressed the cheeks of her apprentices, verbally expressing her forgiveness. She then unfastened the toga of the one closest to me, and I watched as the white garment slipped over her breasts and fell to the floor. Then I felt...

My father's rough hand on my shoulder with a grip that could crush a bronze urn. He spun me around, and we were nose to nose. He whisper-yelled in that way only a parent can, "Your mother is going to kill you...and me too!"

That night, I learned a few things. One – my father's wrath is painful. Two – it is nothing compared to that of my mother. Three – never blindly trust your own eyes. And finally, the gods are not real.

III

A Truly Momentous
Occasion

Upon our return from Cocullo, life resumed as normal for my siblings, though mine was starting to change. I still joined with them for much of our typical routine, including our daily tutoring. We grumbled at our lessons like children have for time immemorial. No child wants to give up free play time, but I will say our education would be the envy of most modern children.

We learned in the real world, taking our lessons about nature out in nature, learning about astronomy under the stars, observing math in action through the engineering feats of aqueducts and colosseums. We were not taught what the answers were, but how to derive them.

In fairness, the subsequent millennia have made the world more complex. There is more history to be taught. More is understood about science and mathematics. Engineering has gone from simple mechanics to nanotechnology. The immersive, real-world education that my siblings and I enjoyed may not be possible in modern education. I feel a level of sadness for children of your era who, even at the youngest ages, are taught to keep their bottoms in seats of classrooms full of far too many children and far too little freedom to explore.

I am not sure I would be a good student in your time – I doubt teachers in your warehouse schools would be as understanding or impressed with my javelin skills as was my father. I would likely end up being referred for evaluation and medication. Circa year 3 AD (CE for the irreligious among you), though I was the exemplar pupil. My keen intellect, sharp senses, and "quick eyes" caught the attention of my teacher, my father, and other civic leaders of our community. These were considered hallmarks of future military and civic leadership. Therefore, while my siblings got free time once they completed chores and tutoring, my time was occupied with a new vocation – preparing for leadership. This meant much time with my father, who became more and more the center of my life.

∞

The day of my thirteenth birthday began as usual, with the crowing of roosters greeting the sun. Like most spring days in Abruzzo, it was cool, but the sun, rising over the distant sea, glinted off the dew-covered leaves while casting long arborous shadows over the fields I surveyed beyond my window.

These lands were my birthright. I guess I had always known that, but looking out the window, this realization came over me with a sharpness and salience I had never experienced. Somewhere deep down, I also recognized the great burden of responsibility this laid on my shoulders, but the invincibility of youth kept it in at bay in the shadows of my consciousness.

Mother and Father had been arranging this day for months, and visitors began arriving before the sun reached its peak. Of course, my aunt, uncle, and cousins came, but so did neighbors and a few of the leaders of the region. I watched the children play, but I knew I could not, as this was a celebration of my entering adulthood.

Instead, I felt equally out of place sitting beside my father as he engaged in conversation with the other men on the expansive portico that ran most of the circumference of our villa. I mimicked their behavior the best I could and even participated at times, but I felt like an impostor. Servants milled about, ensuring that the wine selected for this occasion flowed generously into each mug as soon as it was empty. Platters of olives, figs, stuffed grape leaves, and other finger foods were circulated.

One of our household slaves, an attractive young woman of about eighteen, saw my empty wine mug and leaned down to refill it. Grateful for both the visual distraction and the anxiolytic properties of the wine, I smiled broadly and said, "Thank you."

My father said, "Yes, thank you, Alba." Then he gave me a look that reminded me that I was not quite a man yet. Apparently, one glass of wine was enough, and I should keep my eyes in my head.

Alba's husband, Dagrun, also a slave, gave a sideways glance with a slight smirk as he delivered a platter to his beautiful wife. While our divergent social status precluded friendship, we shared the normal desires of young males. Showing maturity well beyond my own, Dagrun did not seem to be angered at my natural attraction to his bride. I felt conflicting emotions at that moment – pride at my station in life, the sadness of isolation, and a desire for friendship. Social stratification creates loneliness, lack of connection, and inequity that harm all people, higher and lower classes alike.

∞

Besides my father, one man stood out from the others. As he approached, accompanied by two other soldiers from the local garrison, Sejanus could be recognized at a distance. The red tunic of a Roman Cavalry Officer, the cockaded helmet, and his unmistakable self-assurance gave him away. When he arrived, I saw he was also accompanied by a young lady barely older than me.

Sejanus, who appeared to be in his mid-twenties, dismounted and helped the young lady from the carriage in which she had been riding. She radiated beauty and caught my attention immediately, and I could tell others around me were equally enthralled. Sejanus sauntered to the base of the stairs leading up to the portico, greeted my father and the other men, and said, "This is Apicata, my betrothed. We are to be married in Rome in the summer. I would like to invite you all to the ceremony."

With that, Apicata nodded like a woman who knew her place and demurely said, "Hello." She walked past, avoiding eye contact, escorted by one of the servant girls, to join the women inside. My father gave Sejanus a knowing look that harkened me back to the proud look he gave me while simultaneously scolding me for launching my javelin near Mater nearly a year prior. I was starting to understand and decipher these looks.

Sejanus was impressive. Strong, handsome, and self-assured, he was a man to be emulated. For the next few years, I felt privileged to have many opportunities to do so. Perhaps, were I more mature and wise, I would have paid more attention to how Sejanus interacted with Apicata: how she appeared to be in his control and under his thumb, how his smile reflected more the pride of ownership than the joy of love.

Another man sitting on that portico did not particularly stand out. He was clearly known and admired by others, but to me, he just seemed to fade into the background. If I had known he was to be my father-in-law, I probably would have paid more attention.

∞

As the sun started making its journey down toward the summit of the mountains, my mother came out and said, "Pontius, it is time to get ready."

In my era, birthdays, "dies natalis" as they were called, entailed several rituals and traditions, the first of which was ritual cleaning. In many ways, this was a religious event, celebrating the god of the self. The "genius" ("Juno" for females), your personal god, associated with just oneself, was to be exalted, worshipped, and sacrificed to on this day.

I bathed and was anointed with oil. I donned a snow-white robe and made my way outside to a grassy mound upon which there was an altar and a fire pit ready to be lit.

My father emerged from a wooden shed. With one hand, he was leading the lamb that I had personally selected for this sacrifice. The other hand gripped the knife with which he expected me to conduct the slaughter. A strange déjà vu overcame me as I watched the lamb walking up the mound on which he would be sacrificed and burnt as an offering to the gods.

I felt as if time both accelerated and stopped, as if all of time was captured in this one moment. I was in my body, yet I looked at myself and the gathered party from overhead. I have heard this referred to as an out-of-body experience, and it is most often associated with death. I now recognize this as the feeling of being connected with the divine, with everything in the universe, with God. It is but a fleeting glimpse for mortals, and most fail to recognize its significance – I certainly did.

Standing atop the mound, I watched myself hold the knife high above my head as I had rehearsed, showing my command and intentionally evoking images of Jupiter. I watched myself pull the blade in my right hand along the jugular vein of the lamb. I watched the lamb's lifeforce burst out in waves with the last throbbing of its heart. I could tell it was bleating - calling out to its own mother - pleading for the pain to stop – pleading for its life to be spared. The lamb's voice, though, would go unheard as its vocal cords had been severed.

I had lived on a farm my entire life and had seen and participated in slaughtering livestock many times. Generally, up to this point, I did not form relationships with the animals; I did not name them; I did not cuddle with them. I ate them. However, something about this slaughter kicked me in the belly and made me feel something I could not explain.

I was a 13-year-old boy, so identifying complex feelings was not my forte. Now I can say it was a mix of sadness, repulsion, regret, guilt, and even anger – anger that my parents, my society, and the time and place into which I was born made this event predestined. I had no choice. It was not up to me. I had a role to play, a role I would reprise.

My father took the lamb from me and proceeded to skin it and prepare it for the fire. Mere moments later, I was handed the bloody carcass to put on the fire.

Covered in the blood of the lamb, the wave of divinity I had experienced was washed out by the wave of nausea and regret that was just as incomprehensible to me. Both of these waves passed and left my internal sea of feelings flat, not a calm, peaceful sea but a vast, flat ocean devoid of life. There were no robots in my time, but for the rest of the evening, I felt like an automaton going through the motions, a preprogrammed script not of my own authorship.

I was not fully myself, which is especially strange as birthdays in my culture were, after all, a celebration of the self. The term genius originated in my time, but it did not mean to be of great intelligence, aptitude, or wisdom. Instead, it was the name we gave the god of self, a god to be worshipped and sacrificed to along with Bacchus, Neptune, Jupiter, Ceres, Venus, or even Angitia.

While the lamb roasted, I recited a prayer to my genius for blessings upon my future. I prayed that my genius would guide my steps. I poured my cup of wine (I was allowed one now) into the fire in honor of my genius. Others at the party followed, pouring out libations in my honor and in the honor of the birth of Rome.

IV

In My Father's Shadow

In many ways, I was born again on the day of my thirteenth birthday. In my era, the legal age of adulthood was fifteen. Military recruits started their basic training at fourteen. My thirteenth year would be spent in the shadow of my father. He became a godlike figure to me, molding me in his image to take the mantle of leadership in our family, our community, and our empire. To my young mind, the possibilities were endless.

I was not only expected to be a soldier. I was expected to be an officer; to learn how to command other soldiers and learn the management skills that would allow me to assume my place in government and the administrative state that made the Roman Empire so transformative. Rome had conquered the world based partly on military strength but mostly on efficient business practices, establishing a transportation infrastructure with Rome as its center and assimilating varied cultures through mutually beneficial alliances. The continuation and expansion of this empire relied on kids, I mean men, like me, who had the skills, knowledge, and wisdom to make decisions and lead others.

The day after my dies natalis, my father woke me before the rooster crowed. The sun's orb had not yet crossed the horizon, but I could see soft pastel colors starting to brighten the sky to the east.

Pater said, "Get up, young man, it is time to start your training."
I replied, "Can't I sleep a little longer?" still feeling out of sorts from
my experience of the night before. My father was having none of it.
"Today you are mine, not your mother's."

And that was my experience over the next couple of years. My life
to this time had been very mater-centered as the running of the home
was very much matriarchal. My mother was not a homemaker in the
rather demeaning way some in your generation think of it.

She ran the house like an enterprise. She managed a large staff.
Kitchen servants, cleaning staff, personal attendants, even our esteemed tutor, all reported to her. I had always reported to her as well.
My chores, academic lessons, bedtime, personal hygiene, and behavior
were all policed by my mother. She was affectionate but demanding,
and I always wanted to please her.

Now I found myself with a new master. Pater managed my life
now. He supervised my exercise and training routine, including long
marches, runs, horseback riding, and weapons training etc. He worked
specifically with my tutor to make sure I had lessons in accounting
and finance, military history, engineering, horticulture, and other
practical knowledge I would need in order to ascend to my rightful
position in the Roman social hierarchy.

What I enjoyed most, though, was acting as an assistant to my
father. This took the form of administration of matters of both our
estate and the state. I would go to meetings with the other local leaders. I traveled with him to Rome, where we sold and arranged the
distribution of produce and livestock. We also met with senators and
Roman officials, rubbing elbows with the rich and powerful, as one
point even dining with Caesar Augustus.

On the home-front, I would ride the fields with my father, monitoring the cultivation of olives and wheat, overseeing the herding of
sheep and the care of our horses. At first, I was a bit nonplussed when
he taught me how to do menial and manual farm tasks. I was surprised

that he would ever perform these tasks at all, much less that he would want his son to do so. After all, these tasks were meant for the help.

Then he went even further, actually having me work for the servants, practicing these skills, which I found utterly humiliating at the time. After all, in my culture, these people were beneath me, to be looked down upon.

Then he had me teach these skills to my brother under his guidance. As strange as all of this seemed, after just a few months, I felt an astonishing level of mastery and a sense of, not just self-esteem but also self-efficacy. I knew I could do anything to which I set my mind.

In retrospect, I think my father was more divergent and free-thinking than I gave him credit for. He did not categorize people as worthy or unworthy, at least not to the extent common in my times. He was certainly part of his corrupting culture, but at his core, how he treated people had less to do with their station than their character. I wonder if he would have been open to the changes to come had he been around to see them.

∞

That year went by quickly, and by my fourteenth year under the sun, I felt ready to face the world on my own. I was fit, strong, and educated, but not so well educated that I embraced my own mortality or fallibility. That level of wisdom comes with more experience, and I was about to get more of that than I wanted in Caesar's service.

Shortly after my much more sedate 14th birthday celebration, I saw a Roman cavalry rider approaching the villa. On the portico with my father, we watched Sejanus dismount from his imposing steed. He sauntered to my father and gripped his wrist in a hearty Roman handshake and said, "Greetings, Pilatus. May I join you and your family for lunch and conversation?"

He then turned to me and greeted me in the same manner. "Greetings, young Pilatus. I see the past year has treated you well," he said, looking me in the eye and gripping my shoulder. I was still second to my father but had leveled up sufficiently, at least in the estimation of Sejanus, to warrant the adult treatment.

V

In Caesar's Service

As it turns out, I was the topic of conversation. We drank wine and ate a fine lunch while discussing my future in the Roman Legion. It was customary for those of our equestrian class to start in the officer ranks, but not all were as prepared as I was, thanks to my father. Regardless, the first step was to complete basic training at the local garrison where Sejanus had recently been promoted from Centurian to Prefect over the full post.

My father negotiated my position, and Sejanus agreed that I would start as a centurion, most likely in a Cavalry unit stationed in Syria... "That is if you successfully navigate basic training," Sejanus said, smiling at me and nodding at my father.

At the mention of Syria, my mother gasped. My father assured her that the great wars in Syria were a thing of the past, the last one having ended two centuries before. "Now," he said, "the most action he is likely to see is a dust-up between competing religious factions."

Sejanus chimed in, "Since Pompey annexed Syria almost eighty years ago, we have been trying to cultivate logic and civilization in those tribalistic factions, but they have proven to be very reluctant pupils. However, they are a rich province that provides a large tax base to Rome. There is much opportunity for advancement for young Pilatus there!"

I was eager for the opportunity to strike out on my own and to get out from under the shadow of my father. Though I knew I would miss his strength and the safety of my mother's home, I was ready to spread my wings. The next two years of training would give me that opportunity while keeping me relatively close to home.

Sejanus and his entourage left. I sat with my parents and planned my departure. For the next month, I would teach my brother to assume many of the duties I had taken on over the past year. I would finish some last lessons with my father and with my tutor. And I would say goodbye to friends and family.

We took another trip to visit family in Cocullo, where I enjoyed watching the snake show. It no longer held any religious meaning to me, but I remained a fan of the extravagant theatrical toplessness of the temple priestesses and their oiled-up leader. I enjoy knowing that the "Festival of the Snake Catchers" continues in your day but has morphed to celebrate St. Dominic of Sora, a leader of the Catholic Church in Medieval times. It is certainly a positive change that your culture no longer conflates hedonism and Godliness. On the other hand, even from my current vantage point, I miss those oiled-up breasts.

∞

After saying goodbye and settling my affairs at home, I rode alone, for the first time, to the Cavalry Post. For the next year, I learned and relearned the use of weapons, horseback riding skills and techniques, hand-to-hand combat, and all the behavioral expectations and habits of a soldier. I learned how to live as a part of a military unit. I marched over one hundred miles every week. Most of all, I was inculcated with Roman propaganda. Everything I did, everything I read, everything lesson learned, revolved around serving Rome and Rome's godlike leader, Caesar Augustus.

While I no longer believed in Rome's gods, I fully believed that their stories were foundational to the understanding of Rome and our place in the world. Romulus and Remus founded the great City on the Hill. Rome had grown from an enclave of outcasts and immigrants into the world's greatest power, uniting warring tribes into one cohesive empire where logic and intellect reigned supreme and were embodied in the personage of Caesar.

After the death of Julius Caesar, his great-nephew and chosen successor, Caesar Augustus, along with the great general Marcus Agrippa, defeated Mark Antony at the battle of Actium to unite the Empire.

That was fifty years prior, and the empire has grown larger and stronger each day, week, month, and year since. Rome was destined to rule the world, and Augustus was clearly, from my immature perspective, the instrument to fulfil this destiny.

In turn, I was to be his instrument, carrying out whatever task I was given and providing the brilliance of Roman rule to the unwashed masses. To quote a future poet, well, past poet to you, "Theirs not to reason why, theirs is but to do and die." Tennyson captured what you want from an effective fighting force: unquestioned loyalty and obedience. That is what Caesar had in me. In turn, I found my purpose.

After completing my training (and indoctrination), I was given my first chance at formal leadership, having command over a contubernium, a group of eight soldiers in the making while they went through their training. This gave me a fantastic opportunity to build my leadership skills while still under the tutelage of our Battalion (we called it a Cohort) Commander, Sejanus. He had been promoted from Centurian and now commanded all six "Centuries" of troops at our post. While Sejanus was no longer my direct commander, he seemed to have taken a special interest in me and my development.

Throughout this time, I was able to go home once per month. I looked forward to this trip. I got to spend time with my parents, recounting stories of my training and life in the barracks. I got to horse around with my brother and tease my sisters. Best of all, I got to eat tasty food, have my clothes washed, and be pampered by Mater and our servants. I also enjoyed rides, surveying *my* land, *my* livestock, *my* crops, and *my* workers.

∞

Soon, I received my orders to ship out to Syria and made my final trip to the family villa. As you have surely noted, dealing with mixed emotions was not my strength. Sadness, fear, excitement, anxiety, and joy battled one another in my psyche, and it manifested in my gut. I spent more time in the bathroom during that brief visit than I had in at least six months.

One day before my departure to the great unknown, my father came to me as I saddled my horse for my final daily property survey. "I have a great surprise for you, son! Meet me at the house after your ride."

Life was already so full of changes that the idea of a "surprise" had me ruminating more than the cows I encountered on my rounds. By the time I got back to the villa, my stomach was in knots – good thing that, unlike our cows, I did not have two of them.

VI

⁊⊗⊷

My Betrothed

My parents were sitting outside with another couple as I arrived. I recognized the man as having attended my Dies Natalis. Pater said, "Pontius, I would like to introduce you once again to Gaius Proculeius and his wife Joanna. And this is their daughter, Claudia. We have arranged for your marriage."

I looked down at this snot-covered toddler and wondered what my parents were drinking. Thankfully, it would be a LONG engagement.

As it turned out, Claudia Proculeius (formally referred to as Procula) was adopted and being raised by the Proculeii. Her biological family tree is as intertwined, complicated, and painfully poisonous as bougainvillea. For the sake of your sanity, I have included a family tree to help you visualize these convoluted family relationships in the back of this book.

Claudia Procula was, in fact, the biological daughter of Julia the Elder. Julia had died delivering Claudia on the frontiers of Gaul, where she had been exiled by her father, the one and only Caesar Augustus! In fact, Julia was the only biological offspring of Augustus. That is right, my future wife was the granddaughter of the Emperor of Rome.

After her second husband died in battle, Julia had been married to Augustus's stepson, Tiberius. She had five children by her prior husband, but never gave Tiberius an heir. Rumor has it that she became quite wild and indiscreet in her sexuality, which resulted in her divorce and exile.

Luckily, I knew nothing of these connections at the time. I had, of course, heard the rumors about Julia. In first-century Rome, we had no reality television, but scandalous sexual stories certainly made the rounds, especially among adolescent boys.

Our arranged marriage would return young Procula to an approximation of the social status of her heritage, while not placing her in the direct social sphere of her birth family, something her parents seemed to be trying to avoid. It would, however, provide a link for my family and me to the highest echelons of Roman leadership. I am not a fan of arranged marriages, but I guess my parents were more sober than I thought, and the little ankle-biter turned out okay after all.

Several years later, I would learn the rest of the story from Procula herself, but I will give you a preview of the woman who would grow to be the light in my life when I was surrounded by darkness.

∞

Claudia Procula's birth mother, Julia, having been exiled for her sexual immorality, stood in contrast to the purity of Procula's nature. It is thought by many that tales of her immorality may have been magnified, exaggerated, and spread by her stepmother Livia. As the only biological heir of Augustus, Julia was a natural target of Livia's well-known manipulations and power plays in her quest to make herself and her progeny the rulers of Rome. It is quite likely that young Claudia would have been poisoned or otherwise murdered if Julia had not been in exile. In fact, two of Julia's other children died unexpectedly in childhood, and the others also found themselves exiled and ostracized. It could be said that Claudia was *passed over* for infanticide because she had a destiny to fulfil.

Her adopted father, Gaius Proculeus, was named after his own father, who had been a trusted officer and military advisor of Augustus. Gaius commanded the guard who both protected and isolated Julia during her exile. His wife, Joanna, was Julia's only friend. Her confidant, without whom Julia would have died alone, far from family, in a strange and cold land nestled in the Alps.

For the difficult months of her pregnancy, Julia confided in her friend, bearing her soul, and sharing the story of her own life and the twisted, vile, cruel, and corrupt family to which she was born.

Her father, Augustus aka Octavian, had been a reluctant emperor and a flawed man. His younger years were marked by military conflict born of ego and avarice as much as national defense or interest.

According to Julia's memoirs, "Much fuel was added to the fire by women who had power only to the extent that they could wield the men around them as if they were their own sword and shield. The alliance of Cleopatra with my father's nemesis, Mark Antony, is one such example.

"My father and Mark Antony were close friends separated by their own narcissism and the manipulation of women. Cleopatra, though born into Egyptian Royalty, still felt the need to use seduction and her feminine wiles to gain power within the Roman Empire. She thought she had chosen the ultimate victor in bedding Marc Antony. Her misjudgment led to her suicide by snake.

"Instead, my father, Augustus, defeated Mark Antony, taking control of all of Rome. However, he had his own Cleopatra, my stepmother Livia, who was even more cunning and repugnant than her Egyptian counterpart.

"Livia is conniving and murderous. She and my father were both married during the wars with Mark Antony. However, she sensed that Augustus would prevail and, given his lineage from Julius Caesar, he could easily take the role of emperor. Therefore, she seduced my father, ended both of their marriages, and insinuated herself into affairs of the state. Once Augustus was Emperor, she was the de facto ruler.

"My father's efforts to return Rome to its roots as a republic were thwarted left and right by the scheming of his power-mad wife. Worse, there was no limit to what she would do to ensure that her own children, my stepsiblings, were the heirs to the power. She even had my father marry me to my stepbrother, Tiberius, so there was no question that he would inherit the empire.

"Livia murdered two of my children and other family members and had me exiled to keep make sure Tiberius had no competition for the throne."

Joanna was there for the birth of my beloved Claudia Procula. Julia knew that she was not going to survive childbirth. Her hard life had caught up with her, but she was at peace. The forced somnolence of her hard pregnancy had allowed her to reflect on her life, come to terms with her own choices, and to let go of the hate she had harbored in her heart.

"My dearest friend, I pray that you will keep these stories confidential. You need not be caught up in Livia's vindictive paranoia. I need you to love my daughter, keep her safe, and raise her to be better than the world into which I bring her. I pray that you will help her become an example for all people, especially women. They can stand up for what is right. They can be an equal partner with their husbands. They must speak their minds. They must do all of this to change the world. My little Claudia can be a model for other women."

Julia's friend and confessor became Procula's adopted mother. She wrote Julia's memoirs, passing them to Procula when she was old enough to understand and cope with her familial history. However, this is not Livia, or even Julia's story.

This is my story, and Procula is my wife and partner. She IS my story and warrants my reader's prolonged attention, while her evil step-grandmother certainly does not. I will say that Livia's evil ways did not stop with Julia's passing. She continued to poison the world around her, both figuratively and literally, until the day she died. After that, I know not where she went.

VII

A Strange and Dusty Land

No one cruises the Mediterranean between October and May as the weather becomes treacherous in the winter months. Accordingly, my cohort set sail in early June for the trip from Ostia, about twenty miles southwest of Rome, to Caesaria in Judea.

I had never been on a ship and had never seen a port city; the closest experience I had had was fishing from a rowboat on the calm Adriatic side of the Roman boot. We had marched the south banks of the Tiber to enter the port of Ostia, which we could see, hear, and smell long before we stepped foot in the city. We could see several ships at sea and others in port. Ostia, as the port city for Rome, was a bustling and cosmopolitan city dominated by the import and export trade.

We stayed overnight in the city, ready to ship out first thing in the morning. I had seen much of city life in Rome, which many of my compatriots had not. They were taken in by the architecture, art, and culture of the town, but what fascinated me was the port itself.

These ships had been around the world, or at least the world as we knew it. Roman roads connected the far reaches of the empire and allowed travel by land, but the lifeblood of the empire flowed around the Mediterranean, reaching its extremities and ensuring a healthy corpus Romana. The heart of the Empire was Rome itself, but its veins were the sea routes, and its arteries the ports.

Standing on the shore at the port, I could feel the very beating of the Empire's heart. I felt and smelled the breeze off the water like the warm, salty, copper smell of blood. I could not wait to sail upon the waters and explore the empire; an irresistible urge like that of a lover called by the sirens.

Then again, I had never sailed the choppy Mediterranean aboard an actuaria with thirty smelly Roman soldiers. Aboard four such vessels, we bobbed, pitched, rolled, and yawed our way around the Roman Peninsula, to Crete, between Cyprus and the Greek mainland, and south to Caesaria. All the while, I swayed back and forth with my comrades, a bunch of young adults dancing to tidal tones and occasionally regurgitating over the rails like, well, a bunch of drunken sailors.

The twenty-three-day journey was not always that bad. There were many calm days, some lovely ports, and sunrises and sunsets that almost made you forget the lack of personal hygiene by which you were surrounded.

All said, though, when we saw Caesaria looming in the distance, we were all ready for terra firma. All four ships in the armada broke out into cheers. I felt as buoyant as our ship, but as we approached the shoreline, my trepidation grew.

I had left "the greenest region in Europe" and was arriving in a strange and dusty land. My spirit of adventure won out, keeping any fear I had at bay, but I could tell this would be a period of adjustment.

We disembarked and stayed in Caesaria for several days before making the northward trek through Judea to Syria. I was loath to leave the opulent comfort of the city built by Herod the Great in honor of Caesar Augustus. The port accommodated large ships bringing in not just soldiers but also merchants and immeasurable wealth. This wealth was hoarded, transferred, and spent in Caesaria, making the city itself a treasure.

When the time did come to set out to Syria, I was grateful to be a cavalry officer rather than an infantry legionnaire; traversing roads through barren landscapes of rolling rocky and sandy hills on our way to Damascus was much easier on horseback. Little did I know how big a role this road to Damascus would play in my personal history and the history of the world as you know it.

This particular trip totaled 153 miles, which would take us nine days. We were to join up with a cohort whose purpose was peacekeeping and support of our imperial interests in Syria.

As I was riding along the road, through one of the few thickets of woods we encountered, my horse suddenly reared up, and I found myself face down in the grass. I heard what sounded like an angel speak with a strangely powerful tone, an octave too high to be typically masculine: "Do not move if you want to live."

Thankfully, I listened. The next thing I saw was the shimmer of a sword out of the corner of my eye as it arced through the air to land inches from my face. I jumped up, ready to battle the sword-wielding giant next to me. Before I could draw my own sword, I noticed the unmistakable death throes of a decapitated horned viper at my feet.

My angel-voiced Angitia, who saved me from the bite of the snake, stood beside me, his sword glistening with snake blood as it hung by his giant frame. Cassius said, "I am glad you listened. I would rather kill a snake than bury a friend." And friends we were to be from that day forward until the end of our days.

When Cassius spoke, he did so in a quiet, high-pitched, almost angelic voice that escaped his lips like a song. This seemed incompatible with his tall and muscular build and the lethal weapons he carried. He looked like Ares but sounded like Bellona, the male god and female goddess of war, respectively. Whether you looked at him or heard him, he somehow commanded your attention and compliance; however, it was confusing if you looked and listened simultaneously. His rugged good looks were only accentuated by a scar that ran from his forehead down his right cheek. A latter-day warrior, Theodore Roosevelt, may have had him in mind when he said, "Speak softly and carry a big stick."

As we traveled, we exchanged stories of childhood. I told him of growing up in the lush land between the Apennines and the Sea. I told him about my siblings and parents. Of course, I told him about the Festival of Angitia. I teased him and called him Angitia since he saved me from a snakebite. Enduring my teasing with grace tinged with the discomfort of someone who had been taunted before, he laughed and called me Lupus Catulus (wolf cub) since I was born on the birthday of Rome. He asked me what wolf milk tasted like and accused me of fratricide for killing my brother Remus.

Cassius told me about his childhood in Rome. He had seen some THINGS...chariot races, games, processions, speeches, and executions at the Forum. He had seen Emperor Augustus multiple times and had even played with his great-grandson Claudius once at a public trial and execution.

As he described it, "Claudius was a couple of years older than me, but seemed to have no friends his own age. In fact, he seemed to have no friends at all. Neither of us really wanted to watch someone being strangled or decapitated, their body thrown down the Gemonian Stairs," referring to the infamous stairs of mourning.

"Instead, we played hide and seek in the gardens outside the forum. I was surprised he was allowed outside of the view of the Praetorian Guard, but I do not think anyone particularly cared about Claudius. He was nice but a bit odd and had trouble talking. You could tell there were great thoughts in his head, but they were lost on their way to his lips. Even with his family, he was an outcast. I felt sorry for him."

"You felt sorry for him! He is a member of Caesar's family. He is too far above you for you to look down upon," I laughed. Cassius replied, "Caesar is just a man, and his family is no better than ours. In fact, I have heard rumors of murder, incest, and sexual depravity among them. His wife, Livia, strikes me as evil incarnate; a she-wolf willing to eat her own cubs to advance her ambitions. If these things are true, they should not be allowed to live, much less rule."

"Keep those thoughts to yourself, my friend. That is, unless you want to be executed yourself." We changed the topic, but some of Caesar's brilliance was tarnished in my eyes.

When my commanding officer was not around, I let Cassius ride as I hiked like an infantry soldier. At night, we sat around a campfire drinking beer and sharing jokes. Maybe there is something about saving someone's life because, even separated by time and space, Cassius and I shared a permanent bond.

∞

After our long journey through the arid wilderness, our first view of Damascus seemed to be a mirage. Cresting a large hillside, the landscape suddenly changed from every monotonous brown to a painter's palette with all the tones of nature; blue skies, green grass and trees, and every color of wildflower lay before us while the dry brown of death was all that could be seen behind us. It felt we were stepping out of death and back into life. I could just make out the city on the horizon. It seemed to shimmer in and out of existence as it radiated out into the vast blue of the cloudless sky.

Our new home was a Roman castrum (fort) located in the countryside outside Damascus. Large wooden walls surrounded the castrum, a permanent version of a Roman camp. Inside, thousands of smelly soldiers took up residence and had all their basic needs met. From there, we went out on patrol in small groups, quelled occasional riots and minor uprisings, and ensured the smooth conduct of commerce in this Syrian citadel of wealth and prosperity. We did not collect the taxes but made sure the tax collectors were unmolested. We did not try to enforce Roman lifestyle or beliefs, but we made sure that locals paid tribute, both in deference and wealth to Caesar.

I spent years getting to understand the people and their strange ways. I grew to appreciate and even admire many of their customs and values. I rose in rank and was soon in charge of a Century (80 men), which made me Centurion. As Sejanus had promised my mother, for the most part, my time in Syria was free of serious danger. However, there was that one time...

VIII

That One Time

The biggest threats to the peace in the east, especially neighboring Judea, at the time of my service in the Eastern Legions, were Jewish uprisings. The Jews were an especially intransigent culture whose deeply ingrained religious beliefs made them extremely difficult to manage, much less fully integrate into "higher" Roman values. While I had given up my childish belief in the literal existence of a pantheon of gods, they held what seemed an intractable adherence to the belief in their one "true god." Therefore, these uprisings were not simply political, they were conducted with religious fervor.

Being in Syria, we heard of minor uprisings, but none rose to the level of the last major revolt about twelve years before I arrived in country. On that occasion, a man named Judas, hailing from a region called Galilee, fancied himself to be a Messiah sent to free his people from the oppression of outsiders – from Rome. He led his followers in a series of minor skirmishes and riots. He then had the audacity to steal weapons from Herod's armory.

Judas and his followers were dealt with very harshly by Rome, their crucified bodies lining the roads between Nazareth and Jerusalem. Any known supporter of this radical sect that was not executed was sold into slavery by my Roman predecessors or the family of King

Herod, setting in motion a plot that I will address in more detail later in this story.

Anyone going to the Passover festivities at the Temple would have had to pass hundreds of men dead or dying on crosses, a reminder to keep religion out of politics. Three such known pilgrims at the time were a very young child named Jesus, his mother, and his adoptive father. They and hundreds of thousands of other Jewish pilgrims received a stark reminder that the only god to be followed was Caesar.

As I said, that was years before my arrival in the region, and the lessons learned seem to have tempered such zealotry. The people of Judea had learned consequences, the contorted bodies and anguished faces of their crucified brethren, along with the smell of their rotting flesh, seared into their memories. Rome had learned to cut down any such political movements with maximum haste and force. It was in everyone's best interest to make such behavior too costly to contemplate.

∞

Toward the end of my time in Syria, we received word from Valerius Gratus, Governor (aka Prefect) of Judea, that he needed assistance in crushing a potential insurrection. The Prefect of Syria, Quintus Caecilius Metellus Creticus Silanus (try saying that fast), ordered that I lead a full cohort of soldiers from Damascus to Jerusalem. As it turned out, this was one of Silanus's last official acts as he was to be replaced by Gnaeus Calpurnius Piso the next year at the request of Tiberius Caesar. Piso was an atrocious little man with whom my path would cross down the line, but more on that in a future chapter. Suffice it to say, he was a Piso something for sure.

We arrived in Jerusalem seven days later, about two weeks before the Passover festivities. Having never spent time in Jerusalem, my knowledge of these traditions was limited and second-hand. I had no idea of the scale or intensity of the festival, which gathered the most devoted Jews from around the world. The Jews in Damascus celebrated Passover, including a special meal and sacrifices to their God. The most devout of them and those with the means to do so made the arduous annual pilgrimage to Jerusalem for Passover. This made Damascus quieter and more peaceful during that time, but had quite the opposite effect in Jerusalem.

We passed pilgrims on our way and found that the hillsides outside of the city were already starting to fill with the faithful camping in preparation for Passover, which, as it was explained to me, is a full week of religious activity including ritual bathing, feasts, prayers, and sacrifices.

Upon arriving in the city, I met with Prefect Gratus and the commanders of his Judean troops at the lavish palace of King Herod the *Great*, the last true King of Judea who had rebuilt the *great* Temple next door to the Palace as well as the *great* port City of Caesaria. These *great* building projects were Herod's lasting legacy, while his behavior on the throne would certainly not have given him the Moniker of *The Great*.

It was Herod's Palace in which Judean Governors resided and conducted business while in Jerusalem. It seemed that there was a sect of the Jewish faithful called the Essenes who, while normally peaceful, were now causing issues. They believed, much like all other Jews, in loving and worshipping their "one true god" and following his laws. However, they also believed in the resurrection of the dead, the immortality of the soul, and, most troublesome, a coming apocalypse in which the Jews would overthrow their rulers and usher in a literal Kingdom of God on earth. This is the type of messianic and seditious belief that led to the revolt of Judas the Galilean, who established "the fourth Philosophy" of Judaism, the Zealots.

Essenes, though, typically sequestered themselves away from cities, preferring their own company in the countryside where they could live a clean life. While Zealots invited and instigated conflict with Rome, Essenes normally lived in peaceful separation.

In this case, however, an Essene named Philip was preaching for the abolition of slavery, a belief held tightly by the Essenes but roundly rejected by most Jews and almost every society during the first century, especially the Romans. Slaves made up between thirty and seventy-five percent of the population, depending on the region. Slavery was essential to conducting business, especially tasks that required intensive labor. Agriculture, before tractors and manufacturing before machines, required a large and inexpensive workforce. While we can now see the tragic and horrific implications of thinking one can own a human, to people in the first century, it was the expected norm. If somehow the slaves united against their masters, the world as we knew it would end. Rome would certainly not allow that type of sedition to gain traction.

Philip had the ear of all the Essenes, the vast population of slaves and lowly freedmen servants, and even a few higher-class locals who had sympathy with slaves. This was a problem. Philip was a messianic Jew before there was a Messiah. As such, he was a predecessor of what you, in your time, call Christianity. Now I see it as poetic and profound that Christian tradition was built on the fundamental belief that the "meek will inherit the Kingdom of God." At the time, I just thought it to be another insane fringe belief that needed to be subdued.

Meeting privately in his office overlooking the temple below, Gratus grumbled, "Under normal circumstances, I could deal with Philip and his followers. I would quietly round them up and purge Judea of their poisonous preaching before it could spread. The big problem, though, is that we are two weeks from Passover, and this place is a tinderbox ready to burn with the smallest spark. We must extinguish this ember quickly. My men are spread too thin, just putting out the typical fires of the festival. I expect you to hunt down Philip and his followers and make an example of them before we have an inferno on our hands. I need this done in the next week!"

∞

I divided my cohort into six centuries of eighty men, and each centurion was given local guides. Each group was assigned a five-square-mile section of the city and the surrounding landscape. We would use a logical grid search, find, and pull out this invasive weed at its roots – or so I thought at the time.

My men took their task very seriously. They found people preaching or supporting this insane belief - all people were created equal and had a fundamental right to freedom - absurd! They gathered dozens over the next two days. They were camping in the hills surrounding the city, gathered around campfires sharing their philosophy, or preaching to small groups of pilgrims on the roads into Jerusalem. They did not find any within the walls of the city as this group seemed to believe that large cities, especially Jerusalem, were a source of impurity. While others bathed to become clean enough to enter the temple in Jerusalem, they bathed upon leaving.

After my men rounded up the followers of Philip, they brought them to the dank, dark cells under the Antonia Fortress, where they would await their judgement. They were unable to locate Philip himself, though. It was reported that he had left the city heading east toward the Dead Sea. There were tales of a community of Essenes living in caves near the banks of the Dead Sea, but this was technically outside of the jurisdiction of the Gratus, and no one seemed eager to follow.

Two days before the start of the holy week, Gratus conducted a very short trial from the steps of Herod's Palace. The prisoners, filthy and bloodied, were chained together in the courtyard surrounded by my men as Gratus pronounced his sentence.

They were to be put to death by means of crucifixion and hanged from crosses along the roads into the city. Normally, this sentence was carried out by professional executioners within the city, but Gratus wanted a warning to those coming for Passover. He also said that the rules of the temple would require that the dead within the city be removed before Passover to ensure that the Temple is ritually clean. He wanted to maximize the impact of the slaughter by leaving the corpses on crosses to decay. This meant that my men would carry out the sentences as we left Jerusalem and returned to Damascus.

∞

The next morning, my cohort once again split into its six centuries, and each group was assigned a road or pathway into the city. Each Centurion was to supervise his men carrying out the crucifixions as conspicuous, carnal warning signs to any possible rebels. We established a meeting point where we would camp the next evening after carrying out the punishment. I would ride between the roadways, along with the most trusted man in my command, to oversee the work of my charges.

My cohort rode out of the city and split once outside of the gates. We were a commanding, imposing, and inspiring vision mounted on powerful horses, dressed in our red Roman tunics, and carrying javelins, swords, and shields. The visual impact this must have had on the citizens gathered for their "silly" religious festivities must have inspired awe. It also stirred fear and intense apprehension, especially as they saw their countrymen and women chained and marching out to their deaths.

Riding next to the young officer whom I had groomed to be my trusted second, I escorted the prisoners to meet their fate. As we rode through the shadow of an olive-covered hill just beyond the city walls, a young lady in chains looked up at me. She had tears in her eyes - I expected that she was going to beg me for her life. She did not. Instead, she looked me in the eye and said, "I am sorry for the painful path you are on. One day you will meet the Anointed One, and I pray He will bring you peace."

Something about the look in her eye told me that she sincerely believed the truth of what she was saying. Something about her resonated with something inside me, like iron in the presence of a magnet. She reached out and touched my foot, and I felt a small jolt, surely just static electricity. Whatever her "truth" may be, I was not ready to face it. I spurred my steed, perhaps a bit harder than needed, suppressed the churning sea of irrational emotions welling up within me, and rode forward toward my destiny.

∞

Each century led a group of eight to ten people, consisting of rabbis and the rabble they roused with their inflammatory speeches about freedom and the coming kingdom of God. I had never shrunk from my duty. I was, as I was trained to be, an efficient and rational Roman officer carrying out my assigned functions. I knew the necessity of keeping order. I was doing my job, and I embraced it. My men did as well. In fact, they took it a step further, seeming to enjoy it.

Women were raped before being nailed to the cross, suffering one indignation before another.

Some of my men did not know the proper placement of nails, so more than one person had to be mounted twice after the flesh and bone of their hands ripped apart.

One group decided to mercifully shorten the process of death by cutting open those hanging on the crosses, resulting in waterfalls of intestines flowing from their owners who remained alive long enough to see and smell their own glistening bowels.

The worst, though, was a woman hanged from the cross while pregnant. As I rode by her lifeless form, I could see the fetus struggling for life within her, its tiny foot kicking the uterine wall, a prisoner trying to escape captivity. I could not allow the suffering and stabbed the baby in the womb that was supposed to nurture and protect it from the harshness of this world. While I know this spared the child hours of suffering, I would forevermore be haunted by having taken the life of an innocent.

These moments were forever ingrained in me. They challenged my core beliefs about myself about the goodness of Rome. I could no longer see myself as a valiant crusader for Roman ideals. I could no longer see Rome as idyllic at all.

IX

The End of Days

I spent several long years in Syria. I missed home and family, but was kept up to date with frequent letters, especially from my mother. I learned that my brother had also joined the Roman Legion and had been sent to Gaul to serve under a young general named Germanicus, grandnephew of Augustus.

My younger sisters each married into influential families and were living in Rome. Mother also frequently updated me on my betrothed, Procula, who she said had matured into a stunning beauty who "shines as bright as the sun." This was hard for me to believe, as I still saw her as a toddler who was not fully potty trained. However, I was hopeful; she had now turned sixteen.

I too matured, growing as a leader and a man. By the time I left, I was no longer the immature and invincible young man who set out from Rome as a teenager. I had to learn many lessons in life through experience, and not all my experience was virtuous. I do not want to recount the various times I was forced to act against foolish people who did not know their place or thought they could get away with breaking the law. Likewise, I do not kiss and tell, but many lovely women came into my life during those years, a necessary step to understanding oneself and how to manage relationships.

As I was advancing, so were two of the men with whom my life seemed forever entwined, Cassius and Sejanus. Sejanus was called back to Rome, where he assumed a high-ranking civil post. Before he left, Sejanus sat down with me in his office and said, "I would like to stay in touch. I am sure we will be working together again, and it would help me to have your eyes and ears on things here."

The ambitions of Sejanus appeared unlimited. We did correspond often after his departure. While dealing with the religious and cultural issues of the region, Sejanus developed an adamant animus toward all things Jewish. This did not dissipate with his relocation. Admittedly, between the influence of Sejanus and the natural condescension of youth, I too harbored some negative perspectives that would come back to haunt me.

The career of Cassius paralleled my own advancements, and we ended up commanding our respective Infantry and cavalry centuries. However, while I would eventually be the camp prefect, commanding all stationed at our castrum, he would be sent with his infantry cohort to the front lines in Gaul, fighting to expand and strengthen the empire against the "barbarians."

∞

While my days continued, three people who had great influence on my life saw the end of their days. I say it this way because I have a different appreciation for life and death now. There have always been apocalyptic predictions and fears of the grand "end of days." I find this concept to be a distraction that often keeps people from personal and spiritual growth.

Forgive me for going out of order for a moment, but I recall that when asked when such a day would come, Jesus said it would be within our lifetime. Now I understand. It is not necessarily that some all-consuming day of judgement will fall upon the world with corresponding cataclysms; rather, there are literally trillions of "end of days." These occur for each of us at our appointed time. Any day can be our own end of days, whether this corresponds with a mass extinction event or not. It is our perpetual challenge to be ready. From the perspective of the human soul, "judgement day" for all of humanity is irrelevant – it is identical to judgment day for that single soul. We all face our day of judgement, our own end of days.

My three losses happened in quick succession within a four-year period. The first of these transformative End of Days came for Caesar Augustus. He died in what you consider the year fourteen AD, when I had been in country for eight years. News of his death in Rome traveled fast! It only took a month for it to reach us in Syria – ah, for the good old days when the news cycle was longer than a sneeze.

The death of Augustus caused much anxiety and unrest in both the troops and the masses. The former questioned who would be in command and how this would impact careers. The latter prayed that this would be the dawn of a new era, free of Roman rule.

The unrest was quickly tamped with the announcement that Augustus had named Tiberius his successor. Tiberius was the stepson of Augustus, and his mother was Livia. Cassius and I had many very private conversations about this and how we were now being ruled by evil Livia and her progeny.

∞

The second end of days was more personal. When the mail arrived, I expected the usual updates on life in Abruzzo and was excited to open it. The first thing I read was "I am sorry to tell you..." and I knew. Mater went on to tell of Pater's passing, which had been quiet. He was still a relatively young man by your standards, in his mid-fifties, but he had started to decline rather suddenly a few months prior. He had trouble getting out of bed, complained of pain in "my bones", and eventually lost his appetite. One morning, he simply did not wake up. We did not have the dreaded C word then, but cancer comes anyway, regardless of whether we called it by name.

I requested leave to help my mother, see to the estate, and mourn the man who, more than anyone, had loved me and made me who I am. I spent five months on leave, two of which were traveling to and from home. The other three months were full of family time, tears, and togetherness. Everyone shared stories of my father and how he had impacted their lives. Father was much beloved and admired. As I said, my family was not perfect and was a product of our culture and times, but we had a solid foundation of love.

Mother and I spent much time together. At first, we cried together, neither of us having words to express the complicated mix of loss, fear, regret, and love swirling through our hearts.

Then we focused on family business matters; after all, as the oldest male, I was now the presumptive leader of the family. With me otherwise occupied in Caesar's service, I was blessed to have a young and capable mother who had been an active partner in the Pilatus family business dealings.

Mother also had trusted servants and staff who, despite the social ills of the Roman caste system, were loyal to her. Little did I know how much deeper and more significant these relationships would become.

It was natural that Mother would continue to run the family business as I focused on career matters beyond the estate. I was, after all, an ambitious young man in my mid-twenties, not yet ready to settle into the role of family patriarch.

X

Silver Linings and Veins of Gold

The silver lining around the dark cloud of Pater's Passing was getting to know the newer and much-improved version of Claudia Procula. She was every bit as stunning as my mother had indicated. The first time I saw her was at the large family gathering held at the villa in my father's honor. Everyone, from our immediate family, most of our extended family, and many esteemed guests, attended. Despite over 150 people at the gathering, Claudia immediately caught my attention when she walked into the room. She wore a toga pulled off one simultaneously dainty and well-muscled shoulder. Her long, dark hair was a stark contrast to the bright white of her toga and spilled over her breasts like curtains I desperately wanted to look behind.

I asked my brother, "Who is that goddess who just walked into the room?"

He laughed heartily and said, "Why, that is your lovely future wife." When he added "You lucky bastard," his own, also beautiful, wife slapped his arm with an audible thwack, catching the attention and familiar sideways glare of our mother.

Claudia Procula was a mesmerizing vision. She seemed to float through the room like an angel blessing anyone in her vicinity. From a distance, I saw shimmers of light reflecting from her dark hair, which, when she got closer, were revealed to emanate from strands of red woven by nature into her mahogany mane, like veins of gold running through rock. When she took my hand, I felt an electrical surge flow through me, both familiar and unique. It felt as if my soul recognized hers, and I could see that somehow, her soul, reflected in her glimmering green eyes, also recognized mine. This time, I would not gallop away from this soul connection in fear but gallop toward it in awe.

Thankfully, somehow my soul too met with this angel's approval, and, in the far too distant future, her body would accept mine as well. I would come to recognize that Claudia Procula was of two natures, both of which I would love deeply. I fell in love with her spirit nature that first day, seeing the brightness of her soul in her eyes. Later, I would fall in love with her human nature, the nature I would know in the dark, when spirit could be felt but not seen and spiritual electricity gave way to bodily chemistry. The truth of Claudia was not one of these natures or the other. The truth of Claudia could only be found in the perpetual, graceful dance of her duality.

Over the three months that I was in Abruzzo, I got to know Claudia Procula and was shocked, over and over, to find that her internal glow matched and even exceeded her external radiance. It was as if I discovered her anew in each moment. We spoke, often diving to great depth, discussing human nature, politics, and philosophy. She had a keen understanding of the world and an intense desire to make a difference in it.

Other times, our conversation floated gracefully on the surface like leaves languishing on a deep lake. She was witty and at times a bit satirical, somehow making the world, even at its most atrocious, something to observe with humor rather than suffer with sorrow.

One day, riding through the grounds of the villa together, she told me her story. She recounted how her mother had passed during childbirth and how she felt inescapably tied to her family tree and Roman royalty. Instead of saying this in a boastful way, her countenance dimmed, and her head lowered, but she maintained eye contact. She had no shame over what she could not control, yet it was clear that she regarded her family history as a horror story, not a fairy tale.

She then said, "My family is my adopted parents and my siblings. They have raised me to stand on my own and have my own thoughts, but to love others and see everyone as equals. We must live in and adapt to an unjust world; a world in which those born into a high class rule over and make slaves of others, forcing their will upon the rest of the world like Jupiter raping Europa. However, we most certainly do not have to support such a world. We can make change, sometimes seemingly slight change, and other times, earthshattering revolutions. We do what is in our control."

Joanna and Gaius Procula had obviously adhered to the instructions of Procula's biological mother, Julia. Procula then turned to me, looked me in the eye, and said, "I will only marry you if we are to be equal partners. In public, I will follow the rules and adhere to the customs expected of us. I will defer to your position in matters of business, but always expect you to listen to my opinion. And in our home, we are either equal partners or you are on your own."

I looked at her, once again shocked at the courage of her audacity. My mother was always strong, but she knew better than ever to talk to my father in such a manner. They rarely argued and I had certainly never seen them fight, but I had never heard my mother express herself so boldly to her husband, the man of the home, the head of the household. Words and tone such as this would have come to blows in most Roman homes, though unlikely in my more "progressive" home. That said, I am pretty sure there would have been a war of words.

We kept riding in silence for a bit as I let Procula's words percolate. I already knew her well enough to know these were her terms, and she would not back down. This equality of the masculine and feminine, entwined circular power, was vastly different than the linear power structure of my day. It would take me some time to fully accept these terms, and Procula was patient with me. However, we understood one another, and that is a great cornerstone from which to build a relationship.

Way too soon, it was time to take leave of the family and head back to my duties in Syria. My mother assured me that she could handle the home and that her sister and brother-in-law would be close by if needed. I was sorry to have to leave Mater and was equally sad to leave Procula. Thankfully, my time in Syria was nearing its completion.

∞

Unlike the passing of my father, the final end of days of this period was not peaceful or natural. The murder mystery about to ensue marked a time of transition for me and for my friend Cassius.

XI

⊙⊗⊙

Germanicus

I returned to life in Syria feeling a higher level of responsibility than ever before. There is something about the passing of a man's father that places the weight of the world more squarely upon his shoulders. This is, to some degree, a burden but it is simultaneously empowering. Knowing that the safety net is gone makes choices clearer and less ambiguous.

In my personal time, I still enjoyed the finer things in Damascus. Having grown up in the country, I had never really experienced cosmopolitan life until Damascus, where fine wine flowed freely, the smell of food and spices filled the air, and beautiful women performed sultry dances in dark taverns. While most of the locals were of the Jewish faith and thereby more conservative, Damascus was a center of trade and finance, attracting merchants from far and wide, and money knows no morality.

Of course, Romans ruled, and I ruled the Romans, at least the ones serving under me in the Syrian Legion. I was what you might call "kind of a big deal", fitting in perfectly in an age of narcissism and hedonism. What others may call sins, most of our culture considered virtues.

We modeled ourselves after our Roman idols, our gods, whose lustful exploits with whoever and whatever they wanted were legendary.

The gods thought nothing of executing or murdering mortals on a whim; you never want to trigger the wrath of a god.

The gods could have anything they wanted at any time they wanted, so, of course, gluttony was not a sin; rather, it was an art form complete with vomitoriums to make room for further consumption.

People did not see hoarding gold and silver as greed, they just believed it to be their birthright.

We took sloth to an extreme as well, with people literally carried about Rome on "litters;" why expend the energy on walking when slaves can do that for you?

You might accuse Caesar or those of us who followed him of being prideful. Clearly, though, we were too good for that.

Naturally, Romans were to be looked up to, admired, and emulated. Envy was an expectation, not a flaw.

Why should I be any different? Except I knew that I was. I went out of my way to avoid having to flog people in an age when others looked for opportunities to do so. I drank my share of wine but never liked to feel out of control, so I stopped well short of slurring and stumbling. I loved women, but after my trip to Abruzzo, I was even starting to feel guilty for that. My bride-to-be had somehow infiltrated my psyche like a beautiful parasite.

A year or so after my return to Syria, I received a letter from my angel-voiced friend Cassius. He told about fighting under Germanicus, who had promoted him to tribune, working directly under him to oversee the infantry units in Gaul. Now Germanicus had been appointed Consul and had been given supreme command over the eastern provinces, including Judea, and yes, Syria!

Cassius would be sailing with him to Antioch, so I started to make plans to spend time with him and meet Germanicus. However, these plans, as many of you may understand, kept getting delayed. Why do today what you can put off until tomorrow, right? Days turned to weeks and then to months, and I had still not made the trip.

Then I received a letter from Sejanus that would accelerate my travel plans. He was now the Prefect of the Praetorian Guard for Tiberius. For those who do not know what this means, think of this as the head of the Secret Service, the Secretary of State, and the Chief of Staff all rolled into one. In his letter, Sejanus said:

"Pilate, I am recalling you to Rome to serve as Tribune and to work with me directly. I need someone I trust with your leadership ability and discernment. I also need someone who understands the dynamics and political issues of the eastern provinces. You are the natural choice. Please make plans as soon as possible for your travels. I would like you to be back in Rome before the end of the fall."

I had already known that my time in Syria would soon come to an end, and I had started making plans to return home. Sejanus kept me from further procrastination and spurred me into action and toward my future.

I decided to take the longer overland route home rather than sail. With it being summer, this route would be navigable. While it would be a hard trip, it would not take much longer than sailing once you factor in the trip to Caesaria. There were easy Roman roads to follow the entire way. There were stops strategically placed along the way where one could stay at a nice inn and have someone tend to the needs of their horse. Best of all, I could go through Antioch and visit Cassius. Well, maybe the best thing is that the overland route kept me from spending a month on a ship with the Roman ranks (in both meanings of the word).

Two weeks later, I embarked on my journey with a fresh horse, my meager belongings, and a trusted escort from my base. Cornelius was the young officer who had been by my side as I witnessed the atrocities my men committed in Jerusalem. He, too, had heard the young woman pray for my forgiveness. He, too, had heard the tortured screams of people whose flesh and bones were ripped apart in flawed crucifixions. He had witnessed as I pierced the pregnant belly, ending the suffering of the child within.

In many ways, Cornelius was a younger version of me. This was interesting since we had very different backgrounds, mine being more privileged. He was tall, with broad shoulders and a commanding presence. He was of keen intellect and depth of thought. Like Cassius, Cornelius, and I had come to share a bond that would last to the end of our days.

Cornelius had been with me since he first arrived in Syria six years ago. Without him as a sounding board after leading men to conduct rapes, torture, and butchered crucifixions, I am not sure I could have gotten through my first Jerusalem incident. He always spoke the truth, even when he disagreed with me, but did so with warmth and empathy. You always knew that what he said came from his heart.

Cornelius and I would make this journey together, then he would return via ship to Caesaria in the spring. Cornelius was one of the few actual Roman soldiers in my command, as most were locals who had sworn an oath to Caesar, an action that made pariahs of the soldiers among the locals who almost universally hated Romans, especially in the eastern provinces. However, the wages of service were enticing, not just in remuneration but in the opportunity to gain Roman citizenship. The motivations of these soldiers and the conflicted feelings they had toward Rome typically made them more difficult to command and less trustworthy.

I am sure that Cornelius's Roman heritage was part of the reason he had become my right-hand man, but his good-natured amiability, calm temperament, and wise problem-solving made him perfect to retain this role. I was fortunate to have him helping me settle into my new role in Rome while he awaited return to the eastern provinces.

The road to Antioch was shorter and more pleasant than the road to Damascus. We were able to find lodging each night of the four-day ride. Antioch was a sprawling city with over 250,000 inhabitants and made Damascus look like a small town. With its location on the

Mediterranean, it was a major hub for commerce, specializing in the trade of spices and silk from the East. Upon arriving, I presented myself to the local garrison and asked for Cassius. We were pointed to the imperial palace! Cassius had indeed moved up the ladder.

We navigated the busy streets of Antioch, the hooves of our horses rhythmically ringing as we crossed the bridge over the Orontes River, which split to form an island before converging once again to make its way to the sea. This island was the center of culture in Antioch, hosting homes of the wealthy, a hippodrome for chariot races, a theater, and the aforementioned imperial palace. As we crossed the bridge and the scale of the palace became clear, Cornelius turned to me and asked, "Can we just stay here?"

"Unfortunately not, my friend," I said. "Sejanus awaits our arrival, but on a more positive note, so does Claudia Procula." Cornelius gave me the slightly nauseated look men give one another when their comrade is under the influence of a woman. Little did I know that Claudia would have to wait a slightly longer...we would extend our stay a bit beyond the few days I had envisioned.

Cassius greeted us with great enthusiasm at the gates of the palace, a rider having been dispatched to forewarn him of our arrival. After hearty Roman handshakes and introductions, Cassius exclaimed, "Come, Pontius, I want you to meet the great Germanicus!" His admiration for his mentor was clear in both words and expression. Given how difficult it must have been for him to overcome his distaste for the royal family, I knew that Germanicus must be both powerful and magnanimous.

"I do not want to disappoint you, my friend, but it has been a long ride from Damascus. I need an evening to freshen up and prepare myself for such an honor." Cornelius looked at me with a palpable sigh of relieved gratitude. Even in the prime of our lives, long journeys were exhausting. I did not know that they were also preparing us for future adventures well into our older years.

Servants showed us through the courtyards of the palace to the stables, where our horses were immediately tended to. We then entered the palace itself. We walked what seemed like another mile before reaching a suite of rooms that were assigned to us. The palace had dining rooms, baths, and much to see; however, on this night, I cleaned up the best I could, fell asleep at sunset, and did not wake until the sun rose again.

After spending much of the next morning walking about the island and the palace grounds, Cornelius and I met up with Cassius.

It was almost surreal to see how easily Cassius and Cornelius formed a bond. These two men had both saved my life, one from a literal serpent and one from the coils of serpentine self-loathing that gripped me after the Jerusalem incident.

I listened to them banter and share stories of their own lives. These stories often included me, and they frequently laughed at my expense. Cassius told us war stories and tales of heroism from his time in Gaul. I told him of my father's death, Procula, and events in Syria since his departure. It was as if we had never been apart.

A lesser man than Cornelius may have felt like a third wheel during these conversations, but he joined in seamlessly. We immediately morphed from a couple of old friends to the three amigos.

For dinner, we joined Germanicus for a feast made for a king...or at least a supreme Commander and Consul. My mouth still waters at the thought of the food and wine we consumed that evening. Germanicus was a gracious host who regaled us with stories, lit up the room with his personality, smiled, and laughed frequently along with his guests, and treated everyone as a guest of honor.

It was easy to see what Cassius saw in this man. It was also easy to see that Germanicus was a man people would follow. He was a natural-born leader. He seemed destined to rule Rome one day.

Germanicus even introduced us to his young son, carrying him around the room on his shoulders. He said, "My dear friends, let me introduce Gaius Julius Caesar Augustus Germanicus." The other soldiers in the room laughed, clapped, and shouted "Caligula!" meaning "little boots," the nickname their young mascot had earned as he toured through the blood and carnage of Gaul. The soldiers clearly adored him, but I sensed, even then, something was off. I thought to myself, "Caesar's bloodline and 'little boots' stomping through blood puddles is not a good combination."

XII

Murder

Over the next few days, I spent time enjoying the beauty of the palace, luxuriating in the baths, eating like a king, relaxing, and pampering myself; something I had not been able to do in many years.

Occasionally, however, a strange sense of foreboding crept its way into the recesses of my mind like a spider spinning its web in an attic corner. Perhaps it crawled out from somewhere deep inside my psyche... perhaps from some external source trying to communicate and warn me. Either way, it was incompatible with such opulence; surrounded by wealth and the finest treasures of man, how could there be anything to worry about? Listening to soul or spirit whispering in the form of intuition was not something to which my mind was open at the time.

On the third day, Cornelius and I encountered an omen that certainly did not alleviate this strange anxiety. In fact, it put a spotlight on it, forcing me to pay attention to the warnings from below the surface of consciousness.

Strolling a riverside path, Cornelius stopped and glanced toward the shore. "Is that a cat?" he asked.

"I think it used to be," I responded. Finding a dead animal is not so strange, except that its blank eyes were staring at us from the sand while its body was twisted to face the opposite direction. Worse, upon closer inspection, we would see that it had been sliced open from scrotum to chin, leaving nothing but a hollow cavity. All the organs were just...gone. There was no blood surrounding the cat, so it must have been killed elsewhere. Its neck heinously broken, and its organs harvested, someone or something had discarded the poor creature upon the shore. We saw no trail of blood or evidence of a kill site, so we surmised that someone must have killed the poor animal on a boat and tossed it out. No natural predator would kill in such a manner, but what would motivate a human to do so?

That evening, we were to join Germanicus once again for dinner, but while the food and wine were delicious, our gracious host was not to be found. His servant let us know that he had become ill and was recuperating in his rooms. Cassius sat with us at dinner and was perplexed at what could have caused this sudden onset of illness. "I met with him this morning, before breakfast. He was his normal, robust, and hardy self. Germanicus is more fit than a champion gladiator. He will be back up in the morning."

He was not.

Nor was he the next morning.

Nor the next week....

Cassius frequently checked on his mentor and gave us reports. It would seem that he was getting better, but then he would take a turn for the worse. There was also a terrible smell in his rooms that just would not dissipate, no matter how much they were aired out or how much incense was burned.

Cassius asked if Cornelius and I could stay longer, saying, "I am thankful to have your friendship at this hour." I assured him that I had a few weeks before I had to move on.

∞

One morning, Cassius sent a man to retrieve us from our quarters. The soldier took us to Germanicus's suites, which occupied the far end of the northern wing of the second floor of the palace. There we found Cassius, sitting in the atrium, looking white as a ghost. He showed us through the large apartment to the general's room. There, the great man lay looking to be half the man he was a mere month before. He was awake but seemed incoherent, mumbling and barely audible. I was able to discern the words "poison" and "Piso," referring to his rival in a power struggle for control over Syria.

By his side, and clearly distraught, sat Agrippina, his beautiful wife. Scrawled on the wall above his head were letters written in what looked to be blood! The letters M...O...R...S/E...S...T spelled out "death comes."

Not long after, death did come. The young, vibrant leader, destined for even more greatness, succumbed to the grave at age thirty-three.

No one could understand or explain, but Cassius said, "This was poisoning! Even Germanicus said so. Maybe Piso was involved, but I wager it was Livia making sure her baby boy Tiberius stays in power."

"Hush!" I exclaimed, "Talk in my quarters."

We retreated away from possible prying eyes and ears. In the privacy of the sitting room of our suites, we broke out the wine to settle the nerves and spoke among ourselves. The three of us trusted one another even with words that could get us executed for treason.

Trying to be the voice of reason, I said, "There is no proof; even the writing on the wall could have come from anyone, not as a threat or curse but as a warning." Even as I said the words, I did not believe them.

Cornelius chimed in, "We have no proof of wrongdoing."

I agreed.

Cassius said, "Then let's find the proof!"

We concocted a plan to investigate Germanicus's suites. Agrippina, Caligula, and the servants had been moved to another wing of the palace under these horrific circumstances, leaving the rooms empty for us. Still, we decided to go in at night when we could work in privacy. There was no need to raise suspicions at this point.

That evening, we walked the halls in silence and lit our candles only upon entering the suites. The golden glow undulated, throwing homunculus-like shadows of nude statues about the room. The shadows alternately penetrated and retreated, fading from dark corners and recesses as we explored the living quarters.

With Germanicus gone and the windows open, the stench dulled to mere malodor, but there remained a haunted heaviness that made me feel like I was wading through a flooded crypt.

First, we examined the writing on the wall, which was indeed blood. Looking closely, Cornelius said, "This was smeared on by hand. See, there are prints from small fingers, perhaps those of a woman."

I nodded and said, "Those prints certainly did not come from a soldier. Perhaps it was a mistreated household slave?"

Cassius sounded offended when he replied, "Germanicus was a fair man who treated everyone well – even his slaves."

I gripped my friend's shoulder and said, "I am sorry, Cassius. I know this is hard for you. I just want to consider all possibilities."

We separated and each took a room. After a few minutes, Cornelius called out in that same "whisper-yell" I first encountered with my father in the temple of Angitia - whisper-yells are never a good thing.

Cassius and I joined him in the atrium, where he had found a small lead tablet rolled up and secured on the top of the door frame. In my earthly days, lead was easily beaten into almost paper-thin sheets onto which one could easily etch words or simple art, making it an easy surface on which to write or draw before the availability of paper and pencil. Think of it as first-century Etch-A-Sketch.

This particular tablet had several small symbols and the words "Germanicus, cursed to suffer and die." People in the first century were more inclined to superstition and what a modern psychiatrist might call magical thinking. Perhaps that pendulum has swung too far; in your times, to believe in anything unseen is considered, by many, to be delusional. That is, unless, of course, scientists propose a theory of unseen and unknowable multiple universes to explain impossible math and scientific observations. Why insert a creator when random chance can produce "miracles" if given infinite universes in which to do so?

In my time, such objects were not abnormal. People who ask gods for blessings in exchange for sacrifices are just as likely to request curses. However, to find such an item in Germanicus's living quarters with his name upon it was unusual to say the least, especially on the night of his death.

Upon further exploration, I discovered the source of the foul smell. It was a clay vase adorned with imagery of warriors wielding swords, shields, and javelins. Inside was what appeared to be the blood-soaked organs of a small animal teeming with maggots. I thought back to the cat carcass on the shore and the writing on the wall above the bed of Germanicus. It appeared that someone who had access to these rooms had placed curses upon Germanicus, sealing an ungodly request to the gods with the sacrifice of the cat and using it blood to write upon the wall.

Unfortunately, the list of suspects was long since servants and visitors had frequent access. Piso had been in these quarters for meetings with Germanicus prior to his falling ill, but had not had direct access since. Could he have enlisted a servant to carry out the writing on the wall or to administer more poison when the first dose proved not to be lethal?

We retired with more questions than we had before our sleuthing. We still did not know that Germanicus had been poisoned, but it was clear that someone had motive and opportunity.

∞

The next day, we learned that Piso, who had been staying at his Antioch home, left upon learning of Germanicus's death, returning to his main home further inland. Cornelius said, "Running away sure makes Piso look guilty."

"But that does not prove that he did it, much less that he did it on his own. Livia or Tiberius could have enlisted him," Cassius said, his quiet angel's voice incongruent with the underlying accusatory tone of his words.

"Since Piso has left town, let's go see what we can find at his home," I said. "Perhaps we can find the answers there."

The walk to Piso's home took but fifteen minutes. It was on the other side of the island where the homes of the rich aristocracy lined the shore. The peaceful quiet of these streets contrasted starkly with the chaotic clamor of the streets just on the other side of the bridge. The money was made on the east side of the bridge; it was enjoyed on this side. There was a social order that built these homes and made this lifestyle possible. I was struck by the lengths to which people enjoying the money might go to keep that social order.

Outside of Piso's home, we encountered a groundskeeper who was willing to admit us. Our Roman uniforms made compliance highly likely. His countenance when he uttered his master's name made it clear that it would please him to help prosecute a case against Piso. The scars snaking up onto his shoulders from under his shirt were evidence of Piso's management style and character. You can force subjugation and servitude, but you cannot win loyalty through brutality.

Roaming Piso's palatial premises was like an Easter egg hunt, but no one would want the eggs we found. There were three more lead tablets with curses aimed at Germanicus. More shockingly, we found several human body parts, including a severed head, several fingers, and male genitalia. Such items were used in magical rituals in my era, though this was certainly the first time I had encountered anything of this nature.

We left the villa through the back and found ourselves looking over a beautiful river vista. The sun was starting to creep down in the west. Shadows of tree canopies cast upon the water, which appeared deceptively still. The servant we met earlier now turned his attention to the rear of the villa. I asked if he had any knowledge of the magical items we found in the house. He told us of a witch named Martina who was friends with the wife of Piso. She frequented the home, and he assumed she had been hired to cast spells on Piso's behalf.

I noticed a small rowboat tied to a tree on the riverbank and set out to investigate. Even before we got the little craft, I heard flies swarming. The interior of the boat looked like the scene of a decapitation, with blood pooled at the bottom and spattered all over. A closer examination of the oar yielded a small bloody handprint consistent with the prints in the blood above the bed of Germanicus. Perhaps Martina was a very petite woman and had rowed this waterway between the villa and the palace, leaving her curses and delivering poison. However, I doubt she could have accessed the palace. Enquiring with the servant, he indicated that the handprint was much too small to belong to the witch, who he said was "as physically imposing as she is creepy."

One way or the other, it appeared that Piso had, most likely, conspired to murder Germanicus, either by poison or "dark magic." We returned to the palace with the intent of reporting what we had found to Germanicus's widow.

Agrippina was outside when we approached, watching young Caligula play happily in the garden, slicing at the bushes with a wooden sword. His youthful indifference to the loss of his father was initially refreshing; life moves forward even in the darkest times. However, there was something about his laugh and excitement that exacerbated rather than abated the darkness.

We told Agrippina what we had found. Anger, outrage, and profound sadness all slowly gave way to vengeful resolution. "I will be returning to Rome to meet with Tiberius and get justice for Germanicus. Come, Caligula, it is time for dinner."

With that, she turned and walked back toward the palace. Caligula smiled and waved as he walked by, following Agrippina. His hands and wrists were lined with fine cuts and puncture wounds, as if he had recently strangled a cat.

Cassius and I looked at each other knowingly. We both knew that pursuing this new line of inquiry would enrage Agrippina, put our lives in danger, and would not change the outcome. If Caligula participated in his father's murder, his fate was not up to us. We washed our hands of the matter.

XIII

The Long Engagement

The long journey from Antioch to Rome was arduous and might be considered just the first leg of a westward adventure that lasted the rest of my days. Cornelius and I rode for hours each day, but thanks to the greatness of Rome, the roads were well maintained and had rest stops, or "mansiones," built in every few miles, places for weary travelers to recuperate from the rigors of the road. These stops always had places to shop, dine, bathe, sleep, and enjoy libations. We stayed at an inn each night. Some were quite lovely, others less so, but there was always room at the inn for a Roman officer.

Travel by land also gave me an effective way to survey much of the Roman eastern provinces in person rather than just reading or hearing the stories of others. I felt this was important for my career. I knew I was destined for remarkable things.

We traveled through Greece and up into Germanica before traveling down the Iberian Peninsula toward Rome. We met many travelers giving me insights into their cultures, which, given the greatness of Rome, were surprisingly diverse. I saw it as a testament to the greatness of Rome that we could herd these cats into a cohesive Roman Empire. We met Colossians, Thessalonians, Philippians, Galatians, Ephesians, and Corinthians. I "knew" that one day, it would become my job to convert all of these "heathen" masses to good and loyal Romans.

Over the last two years, I had exchanged many letters with Claudia Procula and had found myself yearning to see her face again. As we travelled down the Apennines, we reached a point where we could complete our journey by heading west to Rome. Instead, we headed east toward home.

Riding the familiar road down from the mountain toward my land, my villa, my family, and my future wife, I felt strong and blessed. I was blessed by my family heritage. I was blessed by my upbringing. I was blessed by my social station. I was blessed to be a son of the bloodline of Romulus and Remus. Over the years, I had lost my belief in the Roman gods, though they still told important stories of who we were as a culture. In more recent years, I had even lost faith in the godliness and goodness of our current emperor and his predecessors. They were just men, fallible men, most were even evil men. They did not represent the power and intrinsic goodness of being ROMAN. However, Tiberius was my employer, and to rise to the station to which I was destined, I had to placate him and navigate his treacherous waters. This was the logical approach...I still had faith in Logos.

Riding the path to our villa, my "deep" thoughts and a silent reflection turned to excitement as I shared reminiscences with Cornelius. I told him about each of my family members and our home life. I told him about growing up as an equestrian. I told him of the beautiful and hardheaded Procula.

Cornelius grew up as a plebeian but aspired to higher rank through his service in the Legion. He could never rise to the aristocracy, but he could hold high administrative or military office. He was quite worthy of ascension, and I would use my power to assist. I felt no guilt in sharing stories of my privilege; however, it was my birthright to have such advantages.

As we approached my childhood home, wearing our Roman military uniforms, I recalled watching the approach of Sejanus and his comrade as a child. Our paths were not just parallel but intertwined. Sejanus saw my potential and nurtured my growth. I had looked up to him, even idolized him, since childhood. Now I was returning to work directly with him again in Rome. But first, I would see my family.

∞

My mother watched our approach from the steps of the villa. I could see the moment that she realized that it was me. Even from 150 yards, I could see joy overcome her. She waved enthusiastically and jumped down the steps as I dismounted. The next two weeks would be filled with the contented happiness that defines home, at least for those of us who had loving childhoods.

I also introduced Cornelius to Procula, and he immediately understood why I was smitten with her. In an arranged marriage, such attraction and connection are rare. It was clear that Cornelius and Procula also shared a connection. I had not fully recognized the strength of character and values that attracted me to Cornelius as a friend and pupil. Now that I saw them reflected in Procula, I appreciated them even more. Time would reveal just how important both of these people were to me and to my purpose in the world.

Procula and I had spent very little time together since our introduction and engagement more than fourteen years prior. She was now a grown woman of eighteen. I was a battle-tested and mature man ten years her senior. Yet, despite my efforts at hiding it, she made me weak. She had the potential to be my Ancile, the mythical shield sent from heaven to protect Rome. She could just as easily be my Sword of Damocles, hanging over my head by a hair, making me nervous and unable to rule. Little did I know that she was both. Little did I know that this vulnerability was not weakness but was the essence of strength.

∞

One afternoon, Procula and I picnicked near the stream that meandered through the valley in which our cattle and sheep grazed. Lying on a blanket in the grass near the stream, we looked at the clouds. The clouds formed objects, animals, and people, providing prompts that launched much discussion.

She pointed out a dog. We both laughed when I countered that it looked like two dogs with one sniffing the other's rear.

Then she pointed to a cloud that was the perfect profile of Caesar Augustus as seen on the older coins of the realm. This brought forth much discussion of family, both past and future.

We agreed we wanted children. "Our children will have all of my love and attention," she said. "They will know they are loved for who they are instead of who their parents want them to be."

Not recognizing either the paradoxical truth and error inherent in my words, I replied, "We will have many children. We will keep them safe, allow them to grow strong and wise, and make this world a better place."

A cloud camel led me to recount my experiences in the Eastern Provinces and my horror regarding the events in Jerusalem a few months prior. I told her everything, hoping she would accept me and what I had done. Telling her of the torture of crucifixion and the atrocities my men committed, I could not look her in the eyes. Despite my efforts to restrain emotion, I watched as my tears fell into the soil below. Procula lifted my chin. As she looked into my eyes, she said, "You are not responsible for the choices others make. There is little, if anything, you could have done differently in those circumstances. Your tears wash away your guilt, watering the seeds of new growth." We lay in silent comfort for several minutes.

Then I pointed out a cloud in the shape of Poseidon's trident. We agreed of the absurdity of a god ruling the seas and causing shipwrecks. Then Claudia Procula surprised me by saying, "Yes, the gods are silly. They are just our way of making sense of the universe from a human perspective. But what about God's perspective?"

"What do you mean, a god's perspective?" I queried.

Claudia corrected me, "Not a god, the GOD! I do not believe that there is a goddess of snakes, or a god of the sea, or a god of war...There is no man up in the clouds sending down lightning bolts to smite people who make him mad. But there must be something that organized all of creation, the Creator God. We simply cannot exist without one. There are too many miracles. There are too many coincidences to be explained by circumstance. When my mother died giving birth to me, she expressed feeling forgiven, redeemed, and healed even though her body was dying."

"That is not proof of some magical orchestrator of the universe now, is it?" I asked, trying to sound both erudite and commanding. "It is wonderful, but can just as easily be her acceptance of the end of her life and letting go of her earthly struggles."

"That is true, but what about the moon perfectly covering the sun in an eclipse?"

"One of nature's weird but trivial anomalies," I counter.

"What about the miracle of childbirth?" asked Claudia.

"Biology," I said a bit too coarsely.

Claudia looked at me with pity. "There is so much more in this universe than can be explained by your philosophy."

Claudia became more animated, her voice rising in volume and speed, her face lighting up with emotion and passion, as she threw out question after question. "What about the universe providing exactly what you need when you need it..."

She went on... "What about everyday miracles of creation like the earthworm? Having the ability to eat or defecate from either end, it exists to make our gardens fertile. I have even heard rumors of a creature called a narwhal, a whale with a long horn. That makes no sense except that its horn enables it to break up ice, allowing life to continue under frozen seas."

"I don't know, but there must be a logical explanation," was my rebuttal, not yet knowing the evolutionary theory. I was starting to regret debating Claudia. I am sure that if I had argued evolution, she would have said that evolution alone could not explain such biodiversity.

"Then there are the things completely beyond nature, like the bright flying shields people report in the night skies. What about the miraculous healings of people written off by our best physicians? None of these things make any sense in our rational thinking. We are like the people chained in the cave in Plato's allegory. All we see are the shadow puppets of reality happening beyond the mouth of the cave. Speaking of shadows, what about people who see or hear spirits? Are they all lying or crazy?"

Before I could respond, she answered for me, "No, these things are beyond our understanding, but they are part of a fabric of creation, God's creation."

I started to mumble, but Claudia Procula gave me no window to protest.

"What about the fact that I sometimes have dreams that perfectly predict events before they happen?"

That one hit home, and I was silenced for a moment. "Really? I have had dreams like that, but you are the only person I have ever told. I did not want anyone to think I was crazy. In dreams, I have experienced things that happened to a friend before they ever told me. I have dreamed of things that have yet to happen to me...then they happen. I have no explanation. I just kind of forget about them, like we do most dreams. I must admit, though, it does feel like someone is trying to tell me something while I sleep."

I told Claudia about the murder of Germanicus and my intuitive sense of foreboding. At the mention of her family of origin, I watched darkness cross her face, a shadow emanating from within. She reminded me that Germanicus, too, was family. "I never knew him, but I am sure Livia had some hand in this. Another family member assassinated in the name of political power and control!"

After processing the story and sharing her unique perspective on the evils of Tiberius and Livia, she returned to the topic of precognitive dreams: "See, you are starting to recognize that something beyond yourself communicates with you, in your dreams and through intuition."

I responded with an almost inaudible, "Hmm."

Filling the void left by my perplexed thoughts, Claudia added... "And what about love? Love connects everything, yet makes no logical sense. What about the fact that I can look in your eyes and know that you want me, that you are scared that you might lose me, and that you want to spend your life with me?"

She was right, and that scared me in a way foreign to me, despite my time as a soldier. Having no words, I leaned over and kissed her. It felt like I was me, but was outside of my body and beyond the confines of time. For that moment, I felt that I was in perfect harmony with the universe.

After a moment of bliss, I was smacked back into reality - literally. Claudia Procula slapped the back of my shoulder...HARD...and said "Enough, Loverboy! That is a great prologue, but if you want the rest of that story, you need to marry me."

And just like that, Claudia and I started planning our wedding.

We agreed that she would go to stay in Rome with family as often as possible while I started my new position as a tribune. This would allow us to spend time together and begin planning our future. While she agreed that this would be best, she expressed some worry. "I have family and resources in Rome, but I will also have my new adoptive father watching over me."

"What are you talking about?" I asked, bewildered by this new wrinkle in the already rumpled and dirty fabric of her family history.

"When Tiberius found that his ex-wife had given birth while in exile, he sought me out and found that I was being raised by my adoptive parents. Thankfully, that horrid man is not my natural father, but he chose to 'adopt' me in part for appearances, but I think largely to keep an eye on me and make sure I am not a threat to him politically. After all, I am the granddaughter of Augustus."

I shook my head and sighed. "Just when I thought the family tree of the Caesars could not get more complicated. And now I am to be a branch of it."

"More like a little leaf," Claudia teased.

"I guess I'd better perform well in my new position," I countered. I certainly do not want to make Dad angry -we know what happens to people who do."

"Too soon!" she shouted giving me a glare reminiscent of my mother. Then she laughed... but I could still sense repulsion and rejection of her connection to the tree of Tiberius.

Claudia Procula stood on her own and was not defined by her heritage: not her mother's allegedly scandalous behavior, not her illegitimacy, and not her "royal" blood. She would certainly not be defined by me. Clearly, her adoptive parents, Gaius and Joanna, had lived up to their promise to her dying mother.

∞

My duties under Sejanus called, and I had to depart from my home and my wife-to-be to serve the emperor once again, a position that was transitioning, in my mind, into more of a career move than a true calling. Slowly but surely, whether I recognized it or not at the time, my belief in the sanctity of Rome was becoming diluted by the growing evidence that Rome was a governing system of, by, and for man, specifically a man, as well as those in the highest classes, most enmeshed with Caesar.

It was not ruled by an infallible god in the form of Tiberius or any of his ancestors or progeny. It was not the glorious empire founded by Romulus and Remus. It was certainly not presided over by a pantheon of gods intent on spreading their virtue along with their seed, producing demigod offspring throughout the world, through the power of the Roman Empire.

Instead, now I recognized, at least on a subconscious level, that I had to support myself and my family and that my success depended on pleasing Sejanus and his immediate superior, Tiberius himself. This was adequate for me at the time. I had a job to do, and I would do it well.

XIV

The Appian Way

Three hundred years before I was born, Appius Claudius Caecus, a prominent senator and leader of the Roman Republic, started work on the world's first superhighway. Later named in his honor, the Via Appia was to become the prototype for other roads connecting the world as we knew it. The expression, all roads lead to Rome, was true and remains an homage to Appius Claudius Caecus.

Another common expression, "when in Rome," alludes to the vast diversity of the Roman Empire. While there were many cultures comprising the Empire, there was one city that exemplified all things truly Roman. The city of Rome itself was built on seven hills, comprised of public entertainment venues, government buildings, temples to the gods, and people "doing as Romans do." In many ways, the Via Appia, also known as the Appian Way, made this life possible. The Appian Way is an apt symbol of all things Roman.

Over the next few years, I would be getting a thorough education in the "Appian Way." My professor would be Sejanus, my mentor and benefactor. He was the Prefect of the Praetorian Guard, and Tiberius Caesar took no official action without consulting him. This put me in the center of Roman circles of power, at least as long as I remained in the orbit of Sejanus.

Cornelius and I took rooms at a building near the Forum, the complex of government buildings that would be my true home in this new phase of my life. Cornelius would stay through the winter as my assistant, helping me acclimate to the Appian Way before returning to Syria. This apartment would serve well for now, and there was no need to invest in a domus until Claudia Procula and I were wed. Besides, my real home was still my Country Villa. What the apartment lacked in refinement, it made up for in convenience.

My new digs were also relatively affordable, to the extent that Rome had affordable housing. It was not as affordable as the large and crowded apartment-style buildings one could find in the slums. These were occupied primarily by Jews, who were relegated to the fringes of Roman society. The Appian Way was full of discrimination and prejudice, and no other group was quite as maligned as the Jews. Our culture, exemplified by my mentor Sejanus, took antisemitism to the extreme. I would have much cultural programming to overcome in the future.

∞

Fittingly, I began my position as tribune shadowing Sejanus, the man in whose shadow my professional career had sprouted. For three months, I observed him directing his troops, interacting with senators, supervising other tribunes, and even meeting with Caesar Tiberius himself.

Much of the life of Sejanus was a book open before me from which to read, research, learn, and model my career. We worked together and reviewed administrative issues while taking meals. We spent time in taverns drinking, watching, observing, and discussing what we observed. As was the custom in Rome, we even bathed together as we talked about his current role and his ambitions.

There were, however, chapters in the book of Sejanus that I could not read. Frequently, he dismissed me so he could have private meetings with other leaders and officers...and then there were those less savory looking characters. Clothes blotted with stains, poorly groomed, and always armed, many had the appearance of criminals or mercenaries. I could not understand why he would associate with such people, though I assumed he justified it as a matter of gathering information or conducting clandestine operations. However, wondered how much bathing it would take to cleanse some of these people of the things they had done.

Sejanus largely kept me out of this side of his work, though I saw more than I wanted to. His mentorship was integral to my success, but I felt the darkness of his dealings seeping into my psyche.

∞

One evening, Sejanus and I went to the Temple of Hercules Victor after dinner. Ships carrying Egyptian grain and treasure had been frequent targets of pirates, and we Romans were experiencing a serious food supply shortage. He said, "I want to pray to the gods that they bless our shipments and end the scourge of piracy that is leaving our people hungry."

I suspected that his concern had less to do with gold grain than with gold bars, but I accompanied him and echoed his concern. I was not above placating my superior. Admittedly, my deferential attitude, even beyond the good manners Mater had taught me, was initially aimed at gaining wealth and power. Now it was becoming increasingly clear that it was also required to ensure my health and well-being.

We walked the streets of the Palatine Hill toward the temple that had been restored to its former glory by Tiberius seven years prior. The tall white columns surrounding the circular temple were bathed in the rose gold light of the dying sun. Entering the temple, the heavenly gold of nature and nature's god was supplanted with the red glow and black smoke of oil lamps lit by the temple priest, giving the ambience of the underworld.

Sejanus kneeled at the altar, and I followed his lead. He prayed for the arrival of the first grain ships of the season. He prayed for the strength of Rome and the health of its people. Then he prayed for a curse upon the pirates, that they may suffer excruciating pain before death, that they be forced to witness the rape of their wives and the murder of their children.

The evil vindictiveness of Sejanus's words made me nauseous; the realization that they reflected his heart made me shudder. I let it go. When in Rome...Besides, what could I do about it? I could not control Sejanus. I washed my hands of it.

As we stood up from the altar, a man rushed in carrying a bag. He took Sejanus by the shoulder, and, out of breath, he said, "It is done." Handing the bag, Sejanus bowed, turned, and walked out of the temple, retracing the path of glistening drops left by the bag, which I now noticed was drenched.

Sejanus, a broad smile upon his face, reached into the bag like a starving man reaching into a bag of honey cakes, but instead of a sweet treat, he pulled out a severed head. As he held the head up by its hair, I could almost imagine the man still to be alive. His eyes were open, his skin still contained the suppleness of life, I swear I saw his lips twitch! Sejanus threw the head on the altar, spit on it, and said, "Thank the gods. One less pirate!"

∞

That night, as with most nights during this season of my life, I went home to my apartment and the company of Cornelius. In those first few months in Rome, Claudia was still in Abruzzi, and we were living the bachelor's life. Cornelius, a few years younger than me and completely uncommitted, was more amorously adventurous, but I enjoyed the wing man role.

Haunted by the horror of severed heads and fallen idols, I was not up for nightlife. I needed to escape the darkness, not venture further into it. I found myself profoundly questioning all I had ever held sacred. One by one, my heroes were proving themselves to be idols of clay. I even questioned my own "Genius", my god of self. After all, how could I so revere a man like Sejanus, who was clearly devoid of humanitas – kindness, courtesy, altruism, or empathy?

After swearing him to secrecy, I told Cornelius of the events at the Temple. I described the alleged pirate's face and the gory blood, bone, and sinew in the detached neck. If I could not get the image out of my head, Cornelius would have to hear about it.

"The worst part for me was Sejanus's prayer," I said. "His hatred knew no limits. Piracy is a scourge on our people and needs to be dealt with harshly no doubt, but to curse his family, to wish rape and murder upon them, was...dark."

My subconscious mind was starting to put things together. "Somehow this reminds me of our time in Antioch with Germanicus," I said.

Cornelis responded, "I do not believe in the power of curses. The curses placed on Germanicus in Antioch did not cause his death; someone poisoned him."

"True," I said, "it was hatred that killed the great general, not some supernatural phenomenon. However, the curses showed the mental depravity of the person or people involved in his murder. I doubt that young Caligula actually murdered his father, or at least that he knew he was doing so. However, the evidence suggests that someone hated Germanicus so much that they encouraged his own precious Caligula to kill animals and use their blood to fingerpaint graffiti curses over his father's bed."

"Such is the nature of hatred and its consequences," said Cornelius. He then asked, "Do you think that Sejanus may have had something to do with the death of Germanicus?"

My mind was blown. "I had not thought of that, but he is the right hand of Tiberius. Tiberius was certainly on my list of suspects, along with his mother Livia. They could certainly have used Piso to carry it out."

Piso was subsequently tried for the murder and conveniently "committed suicide" before he could put on a defense. "Surely Sejanus would have been in on such a conspiracy."

"Yes, he could have been in on it...or he could have manufactured it," Cornelius countered. "Would Sejanus have a motive to kill Germanicus?"

"Actually, now that you mention it, Sejanus told me just the other day that he is going to entreat Tiberius to name him his successor. With Germanicus out of the way, Sejanus has a path to becoming the next emperor of Rome."

Cornelius just looked down and shook his head. "What does it say about our Roman leaders that such an atrocious act could easily be attributed to any of them?"

"Correction," I said – "it could be attributed to any of them or ALL of them. And, it is not just our leaders, the preponderance of our people will stop at nothing for personal advancement or to get what they desire."

Cornelius argued, "I think you are too cynical, or at least I hope you are. I believe most people are good but are afraid to stand up to the evil around them, especially the evil of those in powerful positions. They have their own lives to consider, not to mention the lives of loved ones. We have created a climate where people are afraid to speak up. They can literally be killed for doing so. Perhaps even worse than death, they can lose their livelihoods and their reputation. Differences of opinion, divergent ideas, and critical thinking are dangerous."

XV

❦

Trials and Tribulations

Winter passed into spring, and with the changing of the season came the sad departure of Cornelius. Admittedly, that sadness faded quickly since I now had more time with Claudia Procula warming me as the sun warmed the cobblestone under my feet. She was staying with an aunt and uncle, and we were able to dine together, take in shows at the theatre, stroll the city streets, shop in the markets, and otherwise enjoy the brighter side of the city. My personal time was much happier and healthier than was living the bachelor life with Cornelius, serving as wingman as we toured the Roman taverns and houses of ill repute.

The time had come for me to step out from behind the shadow of Sejanus. We would continue meeting regularly, but I was to assume my new role independently. Despite my misgivings, I was thankful for the role Sejanus played in my advancement and would continue to benefit from his mentorship. On the other hand, I was happy to keep a greater distance.

As a tribune, I was to settle disputes and conduct trials. My courtroom was outside where everyone could watch, engage, and learn. Since there were no broadcast or social media in those days, public observation and the grapevine accomplished this function. Most of the issues that came before me were trivial - vendor disputes and petty crime. There were, however, some significant cases with larger implications for Rome...and for me.

One morning, Claudia met me for breakfast before court and walked with me to work as she often did. She liked to watch me conduct trials and then talk about the cases after the fact. She held true to her word and never interjected her own ideas into my trials, supporting me in my public duties. However, I valued her wisdom and the insights she had as an objective observer. This served to help us grow as a couple, learning from one another and building the mutual respect and trust that formed the foundation of our relationship and of any healthy marriage.

On that day, I heard the custody dispute between two women. One was the wife of a prosperous merchant. Her husband conducted a great deal of business with the ruling elite. The other was a former slave in their household. She and her husband had served the merchant until the merchant granted their pleas and set them free. They still worked for the merchant and lived on the family's estate. Both women became pregnant around the same time and had daughters who shared a nursery during the day. Unfortunately, one of the infants died in her sleep, and both women claimed the remaining infant as their own.

After listening to both sides and their witnesses, I could not be sure of the truth. However, I could be sure that the wealthy parents could better provide for the child and that the child would gain an inheritance. With this in mind, I ruled in favor of the child, granting custody to the merchant's wife.

That evening Claudia and I debated the decision. "I had no way of knowing the truth, so I did what I thought best for the child."

"I see your point, Pontius, but what you fail to consider is that wealth is not the best predictor of happiness and a good life; love is. The love of the true parents is much more valuable than money."

"But it is a 50% chance that I got that right. What else could I do?"

"I do not know my love. I just pray, for the sake of the child, that you are correct. Maybe, the mothers will see the value of working together and giving the child the benefit of both of their love and attention."

"Well, they do live in the same household. Perhaps I should have made that a stipulation. It is up to them now."

∞

On another occasion, I was to decide on a case involving the murder of a senator. This was a big story in my time, as it certainly would be in your current age, however, it was not as uncommon as one might think. I lived in a violent time, and people were murdered at much higher rates than in your day. Add to that the specter of political intrigue, and the life of a senator was rife with risk. However, most politicians were killed by legally sanctioned executions for crimes like treason – a euphemism for disagreeing with Caesar Tiberius.

This murder was not a sanctioned execution. In this case, the senator was found dead outside a tavern that also served as a brothel and gambling house. The rumors were that he had frequented the tavern, enjoyed the company of the young ladies of the night, and also engaged in gambling. Such behavior, in times ancient and modern, put one on the precipice of tragedy and my guess was that this time the senator went over the edge.

The defendant, now before me in a cage, had been seen stabbing the senator, opening his belly from groin to sternum. He clearly wanted no chance that the senator would recover from his wounds. The scoundrel, Marcus Vesuvius, was still covered in the blood of the victim, making him a magnet for the flies now swarming in the cage. In my day, speedy trials were the norm rather than the exception.

As the prosecutor began to describe the crime, something about the defendant caught my attention, but I could not quite make out his face from the recesses of the cage. I asked the soldier guarding him to have him stand so I could see him. Upon seeing his face, I was instantly back in Temple Hercules Victor, watching as Sejanus held the dripping head up by the hair. Marcus Vesuvius was a henchman and was, at least on one prior occasion, hired by Sejanus. I sensed trouble brewing.

Hearing the prosecutor's case, there was little doubt that the man in the cage was also the man seen in the alley gutting the senator like a pig for a feast. Given my prior experience with the man, that little doubt was completely washed away. But if I found him guilty, was I putting Sejanus at risk? In doing so was I also putting myself at risk?

The defense put forth their best arguments. It was dark in the alley. The witnesses were drunk and disreputable. The senator had many enemies. The blood on his clothes was from an animal he had slaughtered in sacrifice to a god, a sacrifice no one had witnessed.

When they were done, I adjourned for lunch to buy time before issuing my decision. Claudia had not come to court that day or I would have asked for her input. Thankfully, she was not there. I had not told her about that night in the Temple. I felt dirty enough, it seemed my job to help her keep her hands clean. Besides, I did not want to take any chance that Claudia Procula would think less of me.

Returning to the dais, the court was called to order once again. I had spent the lunch hour considering all options and ended up at only one that was viable. Marcus Vesuvius stood before me, and I looked him in the eye as I pronounced him...

"Not guilty." In my head and in conversation with the attorneys, I defended my choice, saying, "The evidence was circumstantial, and the witnesses were unreliable."

I later heard that Marcus Vesuvius had been murdered that afternoon. I was told that his throat was slit, practically beheading him. He was left kneeling before the altar of Hercules Victor with blood spewing like the eruption of a volcano, blood like lava flowing to the floor.

∞

Not long after my ruling in the Vesuvius trial, Sejanus asked me to join him for dinner. Plopping a juicy nugget of lamb in his mouth and washing it down with a hearty swill of red wine, Sejanus congratulated me on the wisdom of my recent rulings. He said, "I may have another opportunity for you. I believe you know Valerius Gratus, Prefect of Judea."

"We have met, yes. What of him?"

"He is preparing to retire. He seems to be burned out, trying to keep those people in line." Yes, he said "those people" with all the intended disparaging overtones. "The Jews are the people we find hardest to govern, but are clearly those most in need of Rome's guidance. They are so entrenched in their superstitions and traditions that they simply cannot behave rationally. You have experience dealing with them from your time in Syria, do you not?"

"I do... and you are right. They base all their decisions on their religious beliefs instead of rational thought. I am happy to go and support the new prefect if you see that as the best way I can serve you and Rome."

"I was thinking something different," Sejanus said with a serpentine smile. "You would make a perfect prefect. You have good judgment, intelligence, knowledge of the people, and understand the needs of Rome."

I knew that he meant that I understood the needs of Sejanus, but I left that unsaid.

"If you are agreeable," he continued, "I will recommend you to Tiberius."

"Let me speak with Procula, and I will get back to you in the next couple of days."

∞

...And speak with Claudia Procula, I did. She was all in favor of escaping Rome. The Via Appia was wearing thin, especially knowing that she was so close to Tiberius. She said she would miss the food, shopping, and theater, but looked forward to being in a "less corrupt" place.

We agreed that, before making any such move, we would finally tie the knot. We were done planning and ready to start making babies... I mean a life together.

I went back to Sejanus with our decision, and he congratulated me on the pending nuptials. He insisted that he would pay for a great wedding banquet to be held at the Palace of Tiberius on the Palatine Hill.

The look on my face must have made my distaste obvious. "Tiberius will not be there. He has been staying at his villa in Sperlonga. It seems that he considers Rome to be a toxic environment." I unconsciously nodded in agreement.

"When he is away, I oversee the Palace. Also, you might consider working on your non-verbal communication, especially when we meet with Tiberius to finalize your appointment."

I was not sure if my sense of foreboding was about having to discuss the new Tiberian wrinkle in our wedding plans with Claudia, having to supplicate myself to Tiberius for my new job, or the very idea of having to try to govern the ungovernable Jews.

XVI

⚬⚭⚬

Caving In

Claudia and I were wed on June 6, in the year you would call 25 AD (or CE for the more secular of you). June was the favored month for weddings, placing the favor of the gods on the marriage. I do not think anyone ever researched the divorce rates of other indicators of marital success related to June weddings, but I find it ironic that Romans looked down on Jews for being superstitious.

One way or the other, we gave in to social mores and to the invitation to use the Emperor's Palace. Claudia overcame her reluctance because Tiberius would not be there, and the palace would accommodate all our family and friends. It was a lovely venue and a night to remember, especially the end of the night.

The week after the wedding, Claudia and I set about packing our important belongings while I set off to meet with Tiberius Caesar for the final appointment to Judea. Aptly, I traveled with Sejanus down the Appian Way from Rome to the Villa of Tiberius in Sperlonga. This gave us time to talk strategy and make governing plans.

The hoofbeats of our horses and those of the eight-man contingent accompanying us formed the soundtrack of our 79-mile, three-day journey. Accentuated by the occasional horse whinny, soldier laugh, or bird call, and combined with swaying in the saddle, this made the periods of silence between conversation almost hypnotic.

Sejanus and I talked about how to govern Judea. To him, the Jews were a difficult people who needed to be put in their place and kept in line. He clearly disdained the Jews and looked upon them as inferior, but the Eastern Provinces were key to the well-being of all Romans, supplying much of the wealth and produce that fueled the empire. My position was key to the success of the empire, but it would not be easy.

"Sejanus," I said, "I will do whatever is needed, but I know I can bring these people in line without violence. I truly respect how devout they are, but they need to balance that with rationality."

"Respect how devout they are?" Sejanus huffed sarcastically.

Recognizing his skepticism, I took a more condescending approach - "I may not be able to convert them from their absurd beliefs, but I can help them see the benefit of embracing our secular systems. They just need to see what is in it for them."

Giving me a look of incredulity, Sejanus said, "You will have no problem with their rulers or even their priests. They have found ways to benefit themselves by fleecing their own flock in addition to receiving payments and bribes from us. Herod the Great saw the wisdom of collaborating with Rome fifty years ago. Now his family continues to rule. These Jewish figureheads satisfy the masses but are bankrolled by us 'Roman Infidels.'

"The priests," he continued, "run the Great Temple in Jerusalem where all believers are expected to congregate on holy days. The people must make sacrifices, but the only worthy sacrifices are those sold to them by the priests themselves. To buy the lambs or doves for sacrifice, they can only use the temple coins. Standard coins bear images of Caesar, which makes them idolatrous and sacrilegious. Therefore, the people must exchange their money for temple coins at a ridiculous exchange rate."

Sejanus laughed as he said, "The piety of the people holds them hostage to the most impious people of Judea. You will have to collaborate with crooked priests to keep the people straight. I believe you have already seen an example of the kind of events that can transpire when the priests fail to keep their flock in line."

"I have indeed witnessed that," I responded, "and I have heard stories of much worse. Instead of a couple of dozen crucified extremists, there were thousands. In my term, I plan to have no such incidents. I can balance the carrot and the stick. I will make people see the benefit of adherence to Roman law."

"You have done a great job for me so far, and I do not doubt you, my friend," said Sejanus. "However, these Jews are a different kind of horse, one that does not like carrots and does not respond to the stick. I hope you prove me wrong."

∞

The last leg of our trip was the shortest, as we made good time and Sejanus wanted to make sure we arrived early in the day and had time to prepare for dinner with Tiberius. We stayed our final night of the trip in a small seaside village that primarily served travelers and visitors to the temple of Jupiter Anxur, a glorious Temple overlooking the Mediterranean.

Despite my firm non-believer status, I felt drawn to this temple. After dinner, I walked up the hill alone to explore the massive stone building and its grounds. Out of breath, approaching the magnificent structures that made up the Temple, I took a moment to collect myself. The air was filled with a briny smell carried in by gusty breezes off the sea. The smell of wildflowers accented the salty air, creating a sweet and salty aroma that I could almost taste.

What struck me as I walked around the temple was that, while it held no religious value to me, it still felt holy. The deep desire of man to understand the universe and the glory of creation was the very mortar that held this building together. One could feel the dedication and determination of the builders and the devotion of the worshippers who came to this site. I certainly would not be leaving a sacrifice or saying a prayer to Jupiter, but I fully appreciated the desire to feel connected to something larger than myself, something to provide meaning and purpose in this broken world.

∞

Ambling down the last miles of Via Appia to see Tiberius, I could start to make out the outlines of his grand villa. I was struck by the fact that it must dwarf the temple that still seemed to call to me, echoing off the walls of an empty chamber in my mind, my heart...my soul?

In contrast, despite its astounding architecture, the villa did not call to me. In fact, I felt somewhat repulsed. Now I understand that this too was a temple, but a temple to ego, to self, to the "greatness" of man, a man. There is nothing holy in humanism; though one can certainly learn much by studying humanity, the mortar that ties creation together cannot be found in man.

I was told that dinner would be served in the grotto. It seemed strange, given the palatial estate in which I was rooming for the evening, that we would be dining in a cave. After settling in, cleaning up, and mentally preparing to meet Tiberius, I rejoined Sejanus in the vast courtyard, and we set out down the cliffside to the shore. Approaching the grotto, I started to understand why we were to dine within its walls.

The cave was more like an amphitheater hollowed out by the tides over millennia. The sea breeze, water, and shade within the grotto gave it natural air conditioning, which was certainly "cool" this time of the year. A large tidal pool at the center of the cave had been enclosed with stone, creating a fishpond teeming with life. In the center of the pond was a platform on which stood a great marble statue showing a scene from the Odyssey. Surrounding the pond were more statues depicting Homer's epic tale.

Tiberius was seated at the far end of the grotto, surrounded by other diners who fanned out along the edge of the pool. I found it fascinating that the very much mortal man in front of me felt it necessary to improve upon nature with mythical tales of a man overcoming the challenges of gods.

Hors d'oeuvres of shrimp and scallops were passed to guests by barely clad young slaves, boys and girls having barely reached adulthood. Sejanus and I sat next to Tiberius and discussed all the most recent events in Rome and issues in the provinces as reported by each Roman Prefect. This, of course, brought us to the discussion of Judea and the imminent retirement of Gratus. Sejanus introduced me and gave Tiberius my work history, singing my praises and recommending me for the job.

As we spoke, a succulent dinner of sea bass and Mediterranean vegetables was served, and the dinner entertainment of exotic dancing ensued. Tiberius glanced away from the lithe lady in front of us long enough to look at me and say, "I am sure that Sejanus has fully vetted you. Good luck with the Jews." So much for my interview.

We finished our dinner, and dessert was starting to be served when I first sensed a small rumble. The low rumble grew, and someone yelled, "earthquake!" An arm fell from the statue in the middle of the pond, splashing loudly as people started to run out of the grotto. The small stones dropped all around and splashed in the pool like rain from the heavens. The splashes were starting to get larger before we could even get to our feet. Tiberius, forty years my senior and quite intoxicated, was terribly slow to get up. I grabbed one arm while Sejanus grabbed the other, hoisting him just before a boulder would have crushed him. We hurried out of the cave, but not before Sejanus, shielding a drunken dictator, took a large blow on his back from a falling stone.

We got out in time, but there were six others who did not. The young slaves were all huddled on the shore, their youth and athleticism spared all of them. This was not so for some of the guests who enjoyed the good life so much that it brought death down upon them.

Tiberius mumbled frantically, "Thank you, Sejanus...you saved my life...it seems that even the gods are conspiring against me...no matter where I go, I am a target...I will go to my villa in Crete...I am trusting you will take care of this mess and all of the messes in Rome."

In fact, Tiberius spent the next ten years of his reign in Crete running the empire at a distance with Sejanus in charge. His paranoia, perhaps a chemical imbalance but more likely the projections of an evil mind, became more pronounced as he slithered down into a life of even more pronounced debauchery and mortal pleasures. He filled his last years alternating between his two favorite activities - throwing people who displeased him or triggered his paranoia from the cliffs and partaking in sexual practices the likes of which I shall not describe.

Tiberius went to Crete, and Sejanus to Rome. I was off to Judea.

XVII

⟨✦⟩

The Imperfect Prefect

Arriving in Caesaria, I found a much-diminished Valerius Gratus. Time and the strain of his position had clearly taken their toll on him since he commanded me to find and crucify the followers of Philip the Essene. Claudia and I dined with Valerius and his wife on the first night of our arrival in what was to become my new home for the next ten years.

"I am honored to see you again, Pilate, and even more so to see your stunning new bride. I cannot imagine how you landed such a catch."

"I cannot imagine either," said Procula, eliciting laughs all around.

"I agree with you both," I said, "but wait until you get to know her. You will be utterly incredulous."

Gratus' wife, Aurora, chimed in, addressing Procula, "I look forward to taking you out of all this politics and showing you around your new hometown. I think you will find it rivals Rome in all the right ways but lacks all the crime and grime."

"The only problem with this city is the people," Gratus huffed.

Aurora countered, "And yet murder, rape, and theft rates among these people are lower than anywhere else in the Empire. They are peaceful and loving people."

Gratus huffed, "Low crime rates... that is, unless you count treason as a crime. Forgive me, Pilate, I am a tired old man, and these people have been the bane of my existence for eleven years. I cannot wait to pass the baton to you, my friend."

As we were speaking, a centurion entered the room, whispering some news to Gratus. The centurion then turned to me with a smile and said, "Greetings, Dominus."

When I saw him out of place, years later, and in a centurion's uniform, I was caught unprepared for the rush of recognition and emotion. "Cornelius, my friend!" I shouted. "I am so happy to see you." We took a moment to greet one another, and he hugged Claudia. "We will have to catch up very soon, my friend," I said.

As Cornelius left the room, Gratus said, "I see you know the head of my guard. He has been sent by the gods, making my last few years in this place tolerable. If you keep him on, I am sure he will serve you equally well."

I spent the next two weeks with Gratus, hearing his stories and training for my new job. As would be the case for any new job, there were basic policies and procedures to review and offices and infrastructure with which to become acclimated.

My first week in country was dedicated primarily to these more menial onboarding issues. However, the key to success in any position is personnel. Of course, Cornelius and I had breakfast together daily, catching up and sharing war stories. Gratus introduced me to the rest of the staff I was inheriting, from household staff to key administrators. These people would report directly to me, and I would have full authority to hire and fire as I wish. This was not the case with the four other positions that I was to supervise.

First, I had the "pleasure" of being introduced to Joseph Ben Caiaphas, the High Priest of the Jews. Prior to the meeting, Gratus and I discussed that I had the authority to appoint a high priest, but that doing so was mired in a religious and political quagmire. Gratus said Caiaphas was the leader of the Sadducees, giving him a "holy" lineage; all Jewish priests were descendants of Levi. Being the son-in-law of the prior High Priest Ananas, Caiaphas and his family controlled the

Temple in Jerusalem, ruling over the riotous Jews while picking their pockets.

In introducing the high priest of the Jews, I could see a slight smirk on the face of Gratus that said, "I have not even told you the half of it." However, I found Caiaphas to be a reasonable man who came to me with an appropriately deferential attitude. I had the upper hand in this relationship, and he clearly knew it. The High Priest, physically perfect for his role as a "wise" elder, even bowed his grey-bearded head to me before departing.

Less deferential were the brothers I met at a feast held to honor my arrival. The sons of Herod the Great, the King of Israel, who had built the great seaport and city of Caesarea in which we gathered, each ruled over parts of Israel. Their father had navigated the treacherous waters of Roman intrigue and civil war as a friend and benefactor of Mark Antony, yet somehow remained in power after Caesar Augustus won the war. This great port city, one of the wonders of the world at the time, was testament to why Herod kept his dominion, whether that be his architectural skill or his obsequiousness in naming it to honor Caesar.

Neither of these "kings," really tetrarchs serving at the whim of Rome, lived up to the "greatness" of their father. On the other hand, neither of them was ordering the wholesale slaughter of children under two years of age or having their own children executed to keep power.

Philip, a slender and tall man with patrician features, controlled the northeast regions of Judea. Antipas, heavy-jowled and stocky, controlled the regions of Galilea and Perea. As they stood before me, I could sense that these two had taken normal brotherly rivalry to abnormal extremes.

There was a third brother who had controlled the rest of Israel, but he had been banished several years before, leaving Antipas and Philip to squabble while I would maintain direct control over these sections, including Judea and, of course, the great secular hub of commerce, Caesaria.

The divisions and infighting between these brothers and their spouses were quite evident at the feast. Each wanted what the other had and each lacked appreciation of their own blessings. This became even more evident when I was introduced to Herodias, the wife of the third brother who had been exiled.

Herodias was quite beautiful, and both of her brothers-in-law looked upon her like a pork chop. This was strange enough since she was still married to their exiled brother. However, it became positively bizarre when one considered that she was also their niece. Herodias was the daughter of their half-brother Aristobulus IV, who had been murdered by his father (and theirs), Herod the Great.

While lust accounted for some of the tetrarch's clear coveting of their brother's wife, ambition was another facet of their desire. The brother who could claim Herodias had an upper hand in reclaiming the portion of Israel that had been controlled by the exiled third brother.

Looking at Philip and Antipas, it was clear that ambition was more of a key motive for Herodias. She was a princess whose father had been murdered before she could take the throne. Then she had a seat on her royal throne until her first husband/uncle fell out of favor with Rome and was exiled. She wanted power and control back, and, like other women at the time, her avenue to gain power and control was through manipulating the patriarchy.

∞

Of course, Claudia and I shared our thoughts and opinions on this dinner and the other first impressions of Judea. "Caiaphas," I said, "seemed malleable and easily controlled."

She had not had the chance to spend time with Caiaphas beyond a brief introduction but, true to her nature, she shared her opinion that I was wrong. "My first impression of Caiaphas was that he was a snake, coiled, slippery, and ready to strike. The household staff verified my impression."

Continuing she explained, "Caiaphas is the head priest and leader of the Sadducees. They are one of four main branches of the Jewish religion with the Pharisees, the Zealots, and the Essenes."

I told her, "I have encountered Essenes before. Their stubborn refusal to renounce their rhetoric about freeing all the slaves is what led to the crucifixions outside of Jerusalem that still haunt my dreams."

"For them, it is not rhetoric. Essenes are, according to my sources, true believers who hold firm to the original teachings of Judaism and live their lives accordingly. They not only refuse to keep slaves, but they also eschew any corrupt political or religious practice, including the management of the temple. They do not eat meat and focus on the health and wellness of the body. They believe in resurrection and that a messiah will bring a new kingdom of heaven. The Essenes are well known for baptizing people to cleanse their sins and even performing miracles."

Continuing, she said, "The Zealots share most of the same beliefs and traditions of the Essenes but believe they must take a more active, aggressive, and militant role in establishing the kingdom of Heaven. In their estimation, the Messiah will lead an army to rise up against Rome and any other earthly power in the way of such a kingdom."

"The Pharisees," she said, "also believe a messiah will come and that people will be resurrected from the dead. They embrace the original Jewish teachings and traditions, but they add many rules and regulations on Jewish behavior based on oral tradition and priestly interpretations. They are very legalistic and literal in adherence to the rules of their faith, rules they themselves wrote, and are adamant about keeping people compliant."

"What does any of this have to do with Caiaphas?" I asked.

"Well, Caiaphas is of the fourth group of Jewish believers, the Sadducees. They do not believe in resurrection, or a God anointed messiah. Their belief is more social, societal, and practical in nature. They enforce the social structure...and make sure it benefits them most. In many ways, Caiaphas' beliefs are mostly self-serving. From what my friends have told me, he is quite good at playing all the angles and cannot be trusted."

"I will watch my back with him," I said. "Speaking of watching my back, what did you think of our new Herodian friends?"

"Did you see the way Herod Antipas was leering at Herodias?" Claudia asked.

Sarcastically, I responded, "I feel like an Essene... compelled to bathe and cleanse myself after spending time with him."

"It was not just Antipas," Claudia reminded me. "Both brothers were literally flirting with their sister-in-law."

"Who also happens to be their niece," I added.

Claudia visibly cringed as I continued, "And it seemed pretty clear to me that both brothers inherited their father's willingness to stab anyone in the back for their own gain."

Claudia said, "Well, I do not envy you having to work with these people, they are not a reflection of the Jewish people I have met so far. Then again, I suppose Tiberius and others in my natural family are poor reflections of most decent Romans.

∞

After our two-week whirlwind tour of Judean life and politics, we said goodbye to our tour guides, seeing Gratus and Aurora off into the sunset. I learned a great deal from Gratus in that brief time, but I knew I could do the job better. I knew "these people" would not wear me down. I knew I could make Judea Roman!

Claudia and I were left to process what we had learned. Claudia loved the city of Caesarea and its people, as she said, "At least the non-Romans," she laughed. I had a different perspective.

There were things I admired about the people (though certainly not their rulers!). They had great faith and lived by it. They were clearly not perfect. They had their petty squabbles. They committed crimes. They got drunk and made poor choices. Their people were just people. However, their overall society made Romans seem, well, dirty in comparison. On a subconscious level, I know now that I felt some shame as well.

Over time, Claudia grew even closer to the people, having an almost completely Jewish household staff. She grew to love them and treat our servants as friends and family. I even noticed some Jewish habits and behaviors creeping into her daily routines. This led to a feeling of jealousy and misplaced anger.

At the time, I dealt with these feelings as most do, I pushed them down, and projected my shame onto others. I actively put down the Jewish people as inferiors to be criticized, belittled, and at times punished.

This, of course, led to arguments between me and my beautiful wife. To her never-ending credit, she put up with me and tolerated my bad behavior more than any woman should have. I think she saw the seeds of growth that had been planted in me and viewed my occasional bad behavior as symptomatic of the struggle for these seeds to sprout in the infertile ground of my heart.

While trying to grow as a man, I was also struggling to grow as a governor. In many ways, my growth as a governor conflicted with my growth as a man. It is as if I were of two natures locked in a balance for supremacy: one a great tree taking root and growing toward the light, the other a mushroom thriving in darkness and dung. This battle, unbeknownst to me, was reaching its penultimate moment, a conflicting crescendo of battle drums beating faster and louder.

Now I see that this was not unique to me; it is the essence of the struggle to be human, to be an immortal soul living in a carnal shell. We were designed intentionally to fight this battle. In so doing, we grow stronger and into an ever-closer approximation of the "image of God."

My first few years as Prefect were the manifestation of this conflict acted out on the Judean stage. It was comic, tragic, and always dramatic. Within the first few weeks of my administration, I got my opportunity to show my prowess as governor. You could say I set a high standard.

∞

Less than a month into my administration, Caiaphas came to me with concern. There was a Zealot stirring the masses and sowing dissent in Jerusalem. The Sadducees wanted to quash any issues that may arise well ahead of the next holy day, that of Sukkot.

I was tempted to tell him to deal with it himself; the priests had their own guards, and my legions were stretched as it was. I was not in Judea to act as security for Sadducean business operations. On the other hand, any rebellion in Jerusalem would have consequences for my Governorship and Roman tax collection. I agreed to send an extra cohort to Jerusalem. This placated the sniveling Sadducee and got him out of my palace.

The next week, crowds started to amass in Caesarea like clouds gathering for a storm. It was Claudia who brought this to my attention upon returning from the market with her handmaid. Despite my embarrassment, having a wife who cavorted with the locals could be helpful. Her sources said that I had offended Jewish believers, breaking their admonition against graven images.

I naturally asked, "What in the hell are they talking about?"

Claudia explained, "The troops you sent to Jerusalem carried standards with the image of Tiberius."

"Of course they did. They are Roman soldiers and fight for Tiberius Caesar."

Patiently Claudia responded, "Remember, my love, what we have learned about this culture and the Jewish religion. They absolutely reject any graven images. They consider this idolatry and your troops going into the city of the Temple holding an idol, violated the sanctity of their God."

"What kind of foolishness is that?" I responded. "They did not actually go into the temple. They only carried the standards of the realm. It was not a religious statement!"

"They will not even allow Roman coins in the Temple because they carry images of the emperor," Claudia reminded me.

"That is right, Claudia," I said a bit too snarky. "Therefore, the faithful exchange these 'heathen' coins at a significant loss to the Sadducees for coins that also bear images, just ones of which the priests approve. This is lunacy. We shall just wait it out and let them know that such triviality is beneath us."

∞

And wait, we did...

And wait...

And wait...

And wait...

And wait...

After five days, we had not dozens, not even hundreds, but thousands of protesters in the city. We were no longer able to enjoy our peaceful palace. I had to do something. I drew upon my vast logic, wisdom, and intelligence to make a plan.

Emerging from my palace into the courtyard, I sat upon the judgement seat, my thronelike chair, overlooking the masses. They would listen to my reason. They would get past this senselessness. They would come to embrace Roman values, including respect for the emperor. I had my soldiers waiting in the wings in case the Jews needed a bit more convincing.

I put forth my best arguments for why the Roman standards did not violate Jewish legal standards. I left no room for argument. The case was settled...in my mind. Not so much in the minds of the protestors.

Finally, I had to go to my last resort, one that I was sure would dispatch the crowd. On my signal, my soldiers surrounded the courtyard. They drew their swords, and I commanded that they use them on anyone who remained in my courtyard beyond five minutes.

No one left. After three minutes, I asked, "Are you really willing to die over this issue? None of you were injured, and the sanctity of your temple was not violated."

Finally, I saw some movement and murmuring in the crowd. One by one, people were...not leaving but kneeling and baring their throats.

When the final moment arrived, it was not the Jews who gave in, it was me. I had not come to Judea to continue massacring people. My predecessors' history showed that this did not work, and while I was not against the death penalty when deserved, killing people for staying true to their beliefs was not in my job description.

The protesters went on their way, and my legions used non-offensive standards when entering their holy city.

I would like to say that this was the only miscalculation I made in my early years as prefect, but it surely was not. I made many, not the least of which was the construction of an aqueduct carrying water to the holy city of Jerusalem.

This should have been an incredible win for me. The city was parched and in need of a water source, and this amazing feat of engineering deserved accolades, not criticism. Unfortunately, I decided that providing water to the priestly city should be paid for by priestly proceeds. No matter how I tried to explain it, the people saw taking money from the temple as yet another sacrilege. I was beginning to understand why Gratus looked so tired.

XVIII

❧

Epistles

A few years after my governorship, letters would start being exchanged by Jewish believers in new communities. Through these letters, including one written to "the Romans", the people were trying to establish consensus on how to govern themselves. What were the expectations of conduct? How do they deal with problems that arise? Who should be in leadership roles? These letters would form the foundation of a new faith, despite being aggravatingly ambiguous at times and at other times completely contradictory. Sometimes they even seemed to be written in code!

Likewise, during my time in Judea, I received a great deal of direction from Sejanus and Tiberius. These letters were at times ambiguous, contradictory, and encrypted. They advised, suggested, requested, and intimidated. They did not pick up the phone and call or send me a text. They sent me letters, especially Sejanus.

My position naturally attracted enemies who would not hesitate to complain. If they could, they would have gone beyond figuratively stabbing me in the back. I wondered if Julius Caesar had felt this way and whether I had my own Ides of March on the horizon. I waited.

Every time a letter arrived, I opened it like you might open a letter from the IRS. Sometimes I was elated to find it was from my mother or brother telling me about happenings in their lives or the lives of other family members. Other times, I was happy to get word from Cassius letting me know how he was doing or sharing gossip from Rome. More often than not, though, my trepidation was legitimate.

Shortly after the Standards Incident, I received a letter from Sejanus. After a gratuitous salutation and expressions of "friendship", he got to the point:

> "I have been made aware of a situation that caused upset in Jerusalem. You were unwise in having troops fly standards with the image of Caesar in the Holy City. This mistake is forgivable given that you have much to learn in your new role. However, when faced with protests, you must not show weakness or give room for protest to turn to insurgency. If you are willing to draw the sword, you must be willing to use it. Let us make sure that such an incident does not occur again."

After the Aqueduct issue, Tiberius himself wrote to me:

> "Today, I met with a contingent sent by the Sanhedrin in Jerusalem with concerns about your leadership. They recounted multiple episodes in which you failed to heed my admonition to stay out of the affairs of Jewish religion. This pattern culminated in your confiscation of funds from the temple treasury to build an aqueduct. I admire both your ingenuity and your frugality, but these attributes are overshadowed by your lack of wisdom in these matters. The Jews are the most devout of our subjects, and failure to honor their religious principles will have consequences. Those consequences will fall on your shoulders, not mine."

It seemed that Sejanus and Tiberius had conflicting perspectives, making my job nearly impossible. The thing that they seemed to agree on was that I was dispensable and that perhaps I was in danger of more than just my job being cut.

This sentiment was born out in letters from Cassius, who cryptically alluded to watching my back as incidents like that in Antioch were becoming frequent. He was, of course, alluding to Germanicus, but was unwilling to use that name or elucidate his meaning to others who would intercept and read his words.

Mother's correspondence about an old family friend being found guilty of treason added more context to the words of Cassius. He had allegedly conspired with other senators to dethrone Tiberius. Being found guilty, he was executed, and his body thrown down the Gemonian Stairs to rot along with those of his wife, fifteen-year-old son, and ten-year-old daughter.

I was thankful to be far away from the epicenter of intrigue, but I knew that there was no escaping the hands of the empire should they turn against me. For my sake and for Claudia, I kept my head down and did my best to keep my hands clean.

XIX

Dinner Party

After the aqueduct incident, a courier brought communication from Herod Antipas. The fall Jewish holidays were approaching, and he was offering an olive branch, a gesture of friendship and forgiveness in the spirit of Yom Kippur, the day of atonement, two weeks before Rosh Hashana, the signaling of the new year, calling the faithful back before Yom Kippur.

This year, Herod's own birthday fell on Yom Kippur, giving him a chance to symbolically insinuate himself into the holy celebration. He invited all the most influential and important people from the region to better place himself at the top of the social pyramid. He was also symbolically offering me a chance to start over, and, of course, I had to honor that symbolism, even if I could not bring myself to honor the man.

Actually, Antipas had several homes and three main residences. His original palace in the Galilean capital of Sepphoris was built by local craftsmen and artisans from the town of Nazareth and the surrounding area, starting twenty years earlier. Any Jewish tradesmen, especially stonemasons and carpenters living in Nazaeth, would have spent much of their time laboring for Herod Antipas, holding their noses while earning a living.

A child growing up in this atmosphere would have been inundated with anger and hostility toward the Jewish Tetrarch and his Roman puppeteers. A child growing up in Nazareth would have learned and honed a trade to serve both his family and, begrudgingly, the Roman Empire. Any child growing up in Nazareth was part of a branch of the family tree of King David, born to defeat Goliath and making the practice of Judaism even more sacred and profound. Any child growing up in Nazareth would have to learn to balance their deep Jewish faith with the harsh geopolitics of a first-century Roman colony.

Taking a cue from his father, Herod Antipas had also recently completed a palace and the surrounding city of Tiberias, in honor of the current Emperor. The gleaming city on the Sea of Galilee would eventually be considered a holy city to Jews; however, Antipas had trouble finding people to live there as it was built on sites of ancient tombs. Given the cleanliness laws, Antipas had to incentivize foreigners and undesirables to relocate there.

However, I was not going to Tiberius or to Sepphoris. Claudia and I were being summoned to his fortress, Masada, high on a plateau overlooking the Dead Sea. The fortress was imposing and virtually impenetrable, a place for Herod Antipas to escape to avoid the next uprising that threatened his rule and his life. Such thoughts were not paranoia to a man like Antipas; they were the natural consequence of his choices, his lifestyle, his own treatment of others.

∞

Claudia and I settled into rooms in the fortress and were provided with servants to tend to our every need. Antipas treated his guests well, at least those in a position to advance his own interests. Little did we know that he had another guest at the time who was not treated with such magnanimity.

Of course, Claudia made instant friends with the servants; despite my admonitions about cavorting with slaves, she continued to treat them as if they were worthy of our friendship. The morning after our first night at the fortress, the slaves brought breakfast, and Claudia brought information. "Herod has a prisoner in the cells below the fortress. It is the one they call John the Baptizer. The servants say he is the anointed priest who came to proclaim the coming kingdom of God. They claim he has great power and is heralding the coming of the Messiah."

"I have heard of this man," I replied. "He is insane, lives in the wilderness, eats nothing but honey and locusts, and dunks people in the river, claiming to have washed away their sins. Why would Herod bother with such a madman?"

"I am told that John had publicly denounced Herod's new marriage as an affront to God and a violation of Jewish law. John also has many followers, and they believe he has come to announce the rise of a new kingdom. Antipas sees this as a threat to his rule."

"New marriage, what new marriage?" I asked.

Not waiting for an answer, I sneered and impatiently added, "Besides, Antipas is a puppet. He has no real rule, just palaces, fortresses, and a meaningless title. If John the Baptizer is threatening any rule, it is the rule of Rome. If at some point, this madman poses a real threat, I will deal with him. Herod has no authority to act on this without my approval."

∞

That night, we gathered for a feast with "great king" Herod, along with many other guests, including his brother Philip and his wife, as well as many local dignitaries. The Jewish New Year was approaching, and they had gathered to prepare. Like Procula and I, many of those in attendance would leave here to make the pilgrimage to Jerusalem. They were the faithful traveling to the center of their religion in reverence. My pilgrimage was a less religious but still reverent mission, ensuring "Pax Romana," a peace secured by aggression and forced subjugation to Roman rule, the Appian Way.

As we prepared to dine, the host entered the room, literally with fanfare, though not from a ram's horn. That traditional call to the people of Israel to come home was still several days away. Antipas went to his seat overlooking the room, welcomed us as his guests of honor, and said, "I have a joyous and important announcement to make!"

Waiting to make sure all eyes and ears were on him, he continued, "Joining me tonight is my beautiful new wife, Herodias!"

With that, his new wife/sister-in-law/niece entered the room. For what felt like an eternity, you could have heard a pin drop. The face of Philip went from shock to horror to disgust, even though he, too, would eagerly welcome Herodias to his bed. His attempts to hide his lustful envy were inadequate for both his own wife and Antipas; the former glared at him with contempt, and the latter smiled at him with the mocking "grace" of a poor winner.

Claudia and I looked at each other, and I said, "Well, at least this night is entertaining."

She smiled and replied, "These people are nothing if not entertaining."

As we ate, I spoke with Herod Antipas, trying to keep my judgements to myself. I enquired about John the Baptizer. He told me with a nervous laugh that he intended to let him go after Passover.

"He was positioned at a point in the Jordan where most pilgrims pass on the way to the Temple in Jerusalem. His preaching undermines the Sanhedrin, and I feel it best to keep him out of site during the Holy Days. Of course, part of my bringing you here was to let you know that I took this action to ensure the safety of Jerusalem for the New Year."

"Of course," I said, relieved, though I knew there were always many levels of motivation with Herod. "As long as he is to be released after Yom Kippur."

Dinner continued, and Claudia and I enjoyed our own company as much as possible. People watching in this crowd was entertainment enough, but as dessert was being served, Herod announced that his new stepdaughter/niece, Salome, had been practicing a dance as entertainment for the party.

Soon, a strikingly beautiful young lady, very young lady, was prancing lithely about the room. Scantily clad, her gyrations and contortions were provocative to all; to some in a nauseating way, but clearly to Antipas in a seductive way.

Salome seemed to relish the attention and the power her salacious movements had over Herod and others in the room. Attention-seeking is normal for a young teen, but I wondered about who would ask for such a performance and, even more disturbing, what kind of mother would allow it.

While these people were completely responsible for their choices, what kind of world did they grow up in that allowed them to perceive such a performance as normal or acceptable? I felt pity, anger, and indignation at the display and at its purveyors. I could not make eye contact with Procula, but from the corner of my eye, I saw tears streaming down her cheeks.

When Salome completed her dance, she sat upon her stepfather's lap and asked if he liked her dance. Whether from wine or a loss of blood flow to his brain, Herod's words were almost incomprehensible. "Yes, yes, my dear! How can I reward you for such a beautiful performance? Anything you want is yours!"

Salome looked at her mother, who was smiling at her like a cat that had caught a mouse. Salome said, "Let me ask Mother what I should do."

Salome sauntered to her mother, whose expression conveyed a foreknowledge that filled me with foreboding. Young Salome stretched upward on tip toes to put her ear to her mother's mouth. It was clear the child was but a puppet in her mother's game. Herodias whispered in her ear, and Salome turned, first with a perplexed expression but then a sly smile. Her mother patted her on the bottom and sent her back to Antipas, who squirmed in his seat.

Lithely crossing the room to face the flustered fornicator, Salome smiled and said, "Give me the Baptizer's head on a platter."

Everyone in the room gasped, both at the request itself and the shocking juxtaposition of innocence and evil. Herod's jaw (all four of them) hit the floor. He looked at me with a look of horror, letting me know that this was unexpected. "Child! I will give you ANYTHING – a new horse, a crown of jewels, a chest of gold... half of my kingdom! Surely, those things are of more value to you."

"My mother is of the most value to me, and she wants the Baptizer's head."

Red-faced and sweating, Antipas said, "This is not what is best for anyone, my dear. Please pick something different."

"I want his head, and I want it now!" Salome cried, stomping her feet and glowering at her stepfather.

Aggravated and defeated, Antipas slumped on his throne and glanced at his new wife. I wondered if he now felt any regret for his recent nuptials. It was clear that his hands were now just as tied as his tongue had been upon Salome's request. Turning to the head of his guard, Antipas said in exasperation, "Let it be so."

I gave my best "don't you dare" look to Antipas, but his guard departed the room on a mission. He looked back with a look that asked, "What could I do?" I started to stand up to put an end to the insanity, but, recognizing the political overtones of trying to assert my dominance in this crowd and within Herod's own fortress, I hesitated.

Before I could fully weigh my options, we heard yelling from below the floor. From somewhere in the depths of the catacombs beneath the fortress, a man's voice screamed but was instantly silenced.

Mere moments later, the guard, spattered with blood, returned. He carried a covered silver platter that he presented to Antipas. Removing the lid with shaking hands, Antipas said, "It is done." Looking at me, he uttered the words, "I am innocent of this man's blood. I had no choice."

Herod and I both knew that only Rome had the authority to carry out capital punishment and that he was not acting on behalf of

Rome in carrying out this execution. He had committed a despicable crime...in my presence!

I did nothing. I washed my hands of it.

XX

⟨⟩⟨⟩⟨⟩

A Change in Management

About a year after that memorable dinner party with Herod Antipas, I received a letter from Cassius in Rome that hit me like a
gut punch. Sejanus had been arrested for treason! From his pleasure
palace perched atop Capri, Tiberius had sent Sejanus a letter to be
read to the Senate. Sejanus expected that the letter would praise his
work as Prefect and award him greater authority, perhaps even name
him as the successor of Tiberius. It did not...

Instead, the letter accused him of conspiring to usurp the power
of the emperor, committing treason, and even assassinating Tiberius's
son and others in the line of succession. While all of that was true, Sejanus thought he had the emperor's stamp of approval on his exploits,
at least the ones known to his boss.

Cassius wrote, "The shock and horror on the face of Sejanus as
the messenger publicly read Caesar's accusations was as pronounced as
the glee on the faces of the senators whom he had victimized, plotted
against, and bullied for the past ten years."

His letter continued, "The senators already hated Sejanus for the
trials and executions of those who deigned to question his authority.
They had no misgivings about arresting him. They also had none about
ordering his execution. He was strangled to death the same day, his
body mutilated and dragged around the city before being cast down

the Gemonian Stairs into the Tiber River. His wife and children were then similarly dispatched.

The letter concluded with a word of caution. "Tiberius is starting a campaign to rout out any people who supported Sejanus. You need to distance yourself and keep your head down." In a postscript, he said: "Burn after reading."

I had lived with the threat of death over my household for the past several years. Since my time as Tribune in Rome, I had been keenly aware of the treacherous path I had to walk and the consequences of a single misstep. Every time I failed to satisfy Sejanus or Tiberius, there was a chance that I would be removed from my position; that may well correspond to the removal of my head from *its* position. Now this threat had been amplified. Every decision I was to make for the remainder of my time as prefect was filtered through the lens of potential lethality, for myself and Claudia.

Over the next year, I received other correspondence from Cassius and family members giving me updates. The news was never good. Invariably, Tiberius had those connected to Sejanus removed from office and, most often, sent to the afterlife. As Sejanus's hand-picked governor of Judea and protégé since childhood, it seemed not a matter of if my arrest was coming but when.

Claudia, of course, was my rock, steadying me and reminding me to focus on things within my control. While I did not want to burden her with my issues and anxieties, it was not fair to withhold the information. Our marriage, per Claudia's insistence, was based on full partnership. Never had I been more grateful for this arrangement and for the strong and wise woman who somehow fell into my life.

XXI

⟨✦⟩

Darkness and Light

The next couple of chapters of my life are the hardest for me to write. They represent my greatest failure and my greatest victory, my greatest shame and my greatest pride, my most haunting nightmare and most breathtaking dream. I have heard such moments referred to as one's "Big Dark" or "Dark Night of the Soul", but such semantics often ignore, or at least diminish, the subsequent "Big Light" and "New Dawn of the Soul."

By focusing excessive attention on the dark, one places darkness in a position of power, putting it on a pedestal to be revered, making darkness a permanent part of one's identity. My experience is that the dark is transformative only in that it refocuses you on the light, a light that has always surrounded you, that is always within you.

By the fourth year of my decade in Judea, the fortieth year of my life overall, I had survived the Standards Incident and ducked the aqueduct debacle. I stood out as generally acceptable in my leadership, especially in a time when so many leaders appeared expendable.

I felt I had turned the corner with my subjects and was starting to build a reputation as an efficient and wise governor. The anti-Jewish policies and pressures of Sejanus had abated with his death and made it easier for me to govern fairly. I had managed to keep my job and my own head as Tiberius and Sejanus used me as a pawn in their power struggles. I had survived the past year when many of my peers with less direct connection to Sejanus had not been so fortunate.

Despite my growth as a leader and good fortune to still be in my position, the Sword of Damocles was ever-present. If you fell on the wrong side of Tiberius's list, you and your family were in mortal danger. Making decisions with a sword hanging by a hair over your exposed neck is challenging to say the least.

Given this atmosphere, facing the biggest Jewish festival of the year was enough to give one ulcers. Procula prepared me for Passover with her usual love and support. She made sure we had everything prepared for our journey to Jerusalem and allowed me the luxury of focusing on the affairs of state.

Claudia, much more connected to the Jewish people, also gave me scouting reports on issues I may have to face during our two-week stay in the holy city. I had been hearing talk about a Jewish teacher named Jesus, so I was not surprised when she brought him to my attention. I was surprised to find that she had actually seen him in person. She had gone with her handmaid and some other household staff to see him preach in Capernaum while I had been away in Syria.

I scolded her for taking such a dangerous trip without me. To which she at once scolded me for daring to scold her. "Besides" she said, "we were perfectly safe and were accompanied by a Centurion and several guards."

"One of my Centurions led troops outside of Caesaria without my knowledge or direction!"

"You were not here to ask, dear. He only followed my orders."

I thought about telling her that she did not have the authority to issue orders to Roman soldiers. Then I thought better of it.

"Are you going to keep arguing with me or do you want to hear about Jesus?"

I relented. There is no point in arguing with Claudia Procula!

"Jesus has quite a following and for good reason. People come from all over Judea and beyond to hear his wisdom. He spoke about the kingdom of God and asked why we humans should worry about our food or clothing when even the lilies of the field and birds of the air have all they need. He compared the Kingdom of God to a mustard seed, saying it is the smallest of seeds, yet it grows and spreads quickly to provide sustenance, shade, and shelter."

"What is he, a Pharisee, Sadducee, Zealot, Essene...?"

"I really do not think He fits into any of the main branches of Judaism. The Pharisees and Sadducees seem to treat Him with disdain. He is certainly no Zealot; His principles and methods are too peaceful and pacifistic. The teachings of the Essenes line up better, but He does not seem to be formally associated with them. More important than what kind of Jew He is, is what He can do. At a wedding in Capernaum, He turned water into wine. He has healed the sick and lame, even bringing two people back from the dead. I myself saw Him feed five thousand people with just five loaves of bread and two fish."

"Five thousand people! Where was he preaching, the forum? And what is this horse manure about loaves and fishes feeding that many people? That is impossible."

"Are you calling me a LIAR, Sir?"

"Of course not, my dear," I backpedaled, trying to maintain my dignity. "I just meant that you must be mistaken."

"So, are you now calling me intellectually challenged or mentally disturbed?"

"Neither of course!" I exclaimed, my dignity quickly dissolving. "I just meant that he must have done a magic trick, a sleight of hand. After all, no one can be brought back from death, and water does not magically turn into wine. There are charlatans all around who pull the wool over people's eyes in order to pull the change from their pockets."

"If you met Him, you would know better," Claudia said with a strange mix of light sweetness and a tinge of pity.

"Well then, let's hope I do not have to meet him," I grumbled darkly in return.

XXII

Death of Innocence

Arriving again at Herod's palace in Jerusalem, one week before Passover, I recalled my first visit here with prior Governor Gratus. I thought of the horrifying outcome of our mission to silence Philip the Essene, just days ahead of Passover, but a decade prior.

In my state of mind, there was a powerful and palpable juxtaposition as I stood in my haunted mansion full of wickedness and looked over the courtyard of the Temple where the "Holy of Holies" supposedly rested, where God resided, where one had to be purified to even enter. It made me feel corrupt, a shiny apple with a rotten core.

I shared this thought with Claudia, who reframed it for me. "My love, it is not you that is corrupt, it is a corrupt system set up to glorify man but pretending to glorify God. The priests enrich themselves selling salvation while ignoring that their real ruler is Tiberius rather than God. You are a great man, but ultimately a cog in a wheel built around a debauched hub. That cog has no choice but to travel a wicked path as long as it is part of that wheel."

"Thank you for the words of comfort and support, my angel," I laughed. "How exactly am I to break away from this corrupt wheel when I was born into it and when my life, and yours, depend on my playing by the wicked rules. I wish there was a way to separate ourselves from that wicked wheel, from the Roman chariot of corruption."

"We must find a way to see beyond this moment, beyond this place, and recognize that we are just in training for an eternity that is *beyond* time and space. Your body is mortal and dies, but your soul is energy that transforms; energy does not die. God is spirit, energy, which is likewise endless and connected to all of creation. Our souls can commune with God if we can overcome the weakness of our carnal nature."

"There you go with that mystical mumbo jumbo."

"One day, that mystical mumbo jumbo will be embraced by the most scientific of minds. For now, we are to face our daily battles knowing that they are preparing us."

"I am not sure what they are preparing us for, but I hope my battles this Passover season are not as trying as some of the past."

With that, a servant knocked on my door announcing that I had a visitor waiting outside.

∞

Within an hour of arriving at my home away from home, Caiaphas had slithered to my doorstep. He could not enter the residence; that would make him "unclean"; entering a Roman residence would make him impure for Passover and unable to enter the Holly of Holies. I found this just a little too ironic.

We sat in the courtyard and discussed his "urgent" concern about Jesus of Nazareth. "He is undermining Roman rule and is clearly treasonous in his speech," he hissed.

"I have never met this man or heard him speak, but I have heard reports. I am told that he speaks of a Kingdom in Heaven and has even supported paying taxes, saying, 'Give unto Caesar what is Caesar's.' It seems to me that his preaching threatens not Caesar but you and your control of the people."

Caiaphas countered, "He is very slippery in his wording, but he is an insurrectionary and is fomenting a revolt as surely as the Maccabees revolted against the Greek Seleucid empire two hundred years ago. Where is that empire now?"

Laughing, I mocked, "YOU speak to me of slippery words." However, his warning hit home. Rome was built on the back of the infrastructure left by the Greeks. We incorporated Greece just as much as we had Judea and Egypt. Keeping these disparate groups in one cohesive empire was beyond challenging. These Judeans were known to be the most difficult group and had been the downfall of empires; before the Seleucid Empire, there were the Ptolemaic, Macedonian, Persian, Babylonian, and Assyrian Empires.

"If you want to keep your position (and by implication, your life), you need to heed my warning and work with me to prevent further escalation of this movement," Caiaphas sputtered, clearly feeling snubbed, as I had intended.

"Funny, I am pretty sure it is you who works at my discretion. I am sure there are others in line to be the high priest. They would probably know better than to speak to me about my own job security. For now, please keep me apprised of any real threats. I am sure you have more important and divine matters to deal with today."

∞

Claudia and I settled in and had a relatively uneventful end to a long week of travel. Saturday being the Jewish Sabbath, no business was being conducted, keeping eruptions to a minimum. However, unbeknownst to me, storm clouds were gathering along with the hundreds of thousands of visitors starting to flood through the city gates. This storm would be far worse than the one I experienced during the Standards Incident. In fact, it would be the storm of the century, of countless centuries.

The bleating of lambs and the cooing of doves coming from the temple was a constant reminder of the sacrifices with which this week would culminate. There was an unmistakable tension in the air.

Claudia and I walked the expansive palace grounds on Saturday evening. We had, of course, been here before, but the palace was huge and there was much of it that we had yet to explore. This gave us time to talk about everything from current events to household management. She particularly liked to regale me with stories of her staff, whom she clearly regarded as friends and not the slaves that they were in reality.

We set out to explore the second wing, which was separated from our residence by more than a hundred yards. A plaza paved with marble separated the buildings. High walls protected the sides of the plaza and were lined with fruit trees that provided both shade and sustenance, bringing to mind Claudia's stories of "the birds of the air" and "mustard seeds." I dared not mention these thoughts for fear of another sermon.

Herod the Great's palace was not as much a residence as it was a fortified compound where the long-deceased king could safely retreat from the hatred of his subjects. The buildings on either side of the plaza were mirror images, built to exacting standards; each was able to house a small army.

By the time we had returned to the building in which we were quartered, Herod the Great's original living suites, our conversation had turned to one becoming more frequent... children. Walking the wide hallways, we talked about the children we wanted. We longed for a son to become a greater man than I; to teach and raise in the ways I was raised...but better. We longed for a daughter to inherit her mother's beauty and indomitable spirit. We longed for a baby, boy or girl, to bring into the world, innocent and uncorrupted, a fresh start with a chance to renew goodness in a world in which we had both seen so much evil. We had now been married for five years and had not been blessed with a child.

Entering the grand foyer at the front of the palace, Claudia paused and looked stricken.

Looking over my shoulder at her, I knew something was wrong. I turned and took her in my arms as she went limp, knocking over a bowl of fruit that sat on a table at the foot of the magnificent marble stairs leading to our rooms. We sat at the base of the stairs, her head resting on my chest as she regained her bearings.

"Walking into this room, I was overcome by sadness, an overwhelming sense of grief and loss."

One of Claudia's maid servants scurried into the room after hearing the commotion. Genuinely upset at seeing Claudia in this condition, the woman fell at her feet, "What happened, my lady? What can I do for you?"

"A glass of water would be helpful, my dear," Claudia whispered, barely audible as tears rolled down her cheeks.

Returning to the room with the water, the young woman said, "Sometimes I am also overcome walking into this room. Knowing the evil perpetrated by King Herod, right here, makes me ill."

"What evil?" Claudia asked.

"Oh, I assumed that you knew that story, and that is why you became upset."

"No, I have no explanation, just a feeling. It felt like someone beloved and cherished was being ripped from me, taken away, never to come home."

"That makes sense ma'am," the slave said, despite looking stunned. "Shortly before King Herod's death more than thirty years ago, he ordered exactly such evil right from the base of these stairs, an evil I do not even want to want to speak of and do not want you to have to carry with you around this palace."

"You must tell me, my friend. I have to understand what came over me."

The maidservant, whose name I did not even know, looked at me with beseeching brown eyes. I responded with a nod, and she started the story.

"One late night, the silence of this palace was disturbed by loud and persistent knocking at these very doors. Herod's guards opened the doors to find three men dressed in royal clothing. They insisted on meeting with Herod."

"It turned out that these were wise men, kings from faraway regions. They came to Jerusalem following a bright star in the sky. They believed this to be an omen announcing the birth of the Messiah. They believed that they would find the baby somewhere near Bethlehem and had come to share this good news with Herod.

"Herod, hobbling from the ravages of age, came down these very stairs, angry to have been disturbed, his wickedness as virulent as the diseases that ate away at his body. I am told that when he died, he had no scrotum as it had been eaten away by rot and maggots...Sorry for bringing up something so revolting...I guess I just like telling that part of the story. A fitting end to an evil life."

"Just finish the story," I replied with exasperation.

"Yes, Dominus, as you wish," she replied with due deference, though she looked me in the eye as if an equal. "The wise men had been following the star for several weeks, travelling at night, saying it was the fulfillment of ancient prophecy, announcing the birth of the King of the Jews, born to change the world."

"We Jews know of these prophesies of a coming Messiah, an anointed one, a great prophet and King. Some say it is two different people, one a prophet and one a king, in the tradition of Aaron and Moses. Others believe it will be just one man coming once. Still others say it is one man who will come twice, as a mortal, then as a resurrected immortal.

"One way or the other, this was highly threatening to Herod. He was only half Jewish and was beholden to his benefactor, Caesar Augustus. Given those factors and his villainous nature, the people had never embraced him as King. That is why he rebuilt the temple with such grandeur, hoping to buy popularity and affection. That is also why this palace overlooks the Temple... so people in the Temple always see and remember him. It also allowed him to spy on activity in the Temple, a place in which he would never be allowed due to his impure lineage.

"Herod placated the visitors and sent them on their way with a request that they return to him to tell him where he could go to worship the new King of the Jews.

"Once they left, he sent a spy to follow them, but the spy never returned, and neither did the wise men.

"With malice and hubris in his heart and evil in his soul, Herod sent soldiers to kill every child under two years old in or around Bethlehem.

"They followed his orders, ripping infants from their mothers' breasts and slicing their necks, chasing down toddlers and cutting them in half. Innocent blood soaked the soil of Bethlehem, 'the house of Bread.' Babies' cries were silenced, but their mothers' cries still echo through Judea. Everyone knows of someone whose baby was murdered. My own mother lost her first son and still cries thinking of him. I cannot help but think of her when I walk into this room."

Claudia responded to her maidservant, "I am so sorry, my love. I did not even know the story, yet, to the very depths of my soul, I felt your mother's pain and the terror of these children. It feels as though those children were ripped from my own breast." Tears streamed down Claudia's beautiful face as she sat on the stairs. I put my arm around Claudia's shoulders as the slave girl knelt next to her, both of Claudia's hands in her own, crying in unison.

Looking into Claudia's emerald green eyes, the girl said, "My Lady, do not despair. While we all still feel the pain of this atrocity, I know the Messiah escaped the slaughter. He walks Judea as we speak. I feel it in my body. I feel it as my blood flows through my veins. I feel His presence in my soul."

"Thank you for telling us this story," I said, in genuine gratitude but also to avoid further religiosity. Then I felt oddly compelled to ask, "What is your name, young lady?"

"I am Abigail," she replied.

XXIII

◇⥤⥦◇

My Dreams Haunt Me

Sunday morning, I received another report from Caiaphas. The Sanhedrin had issued an arrest warrant for Jesus of Nazareth for violation of Jewish law. This was within their purview, and they could carry out discipline for such violations, but capital punishment was not an option.

I counseled him that he was to inform me of any further development. Jesus had yet to be seen in the city. I hoped he would not.

Speaking to Claudia of these developments, she expressed anger and disgust. "Jesus preaches peace and love, and these men respond with hostility and hatred. Jesus preaches freedom, and they respond with oppression. Jesus speaks of God's power, and these people use God's name in vain. These men are not really priests of the One True God. Jesus said, 'you will know them by their fruit' - the fruits of the temple priests are rotten."

Trying to lighten the mood and brighten the sorrow that still haunted Claudia's eyes while still speaking truth, I said, "Clearly the Sanhedrin comes from a vine, just not DI-vine."

This elicited a smile from Claudia that conveyed minor amusement with a touch of pity.

"Seriously, though, watch how you speak of the 'One True God', my love. Remember that there are eyes and ears of the Empire all around us. Such talk might be seen as undermining Roman gods, including our deified emperor and his lineage of gods."

"Thank you, dear. I will try to keep my communication more private, but remember that I told you from the beginning that I would not be kept silent. I will speak my mind, especially when it is truth."

∞

By Sunday evening, things had escalated even further. Claudia was the bearer of the bad news. Having been in the city during the day, she witnessed Jesus coming into town, an event that was apparently quite a spectacle and had been the topic of both hushed whispers and angry outbursts throughout the day. Beloved or reviled, Jesus was a hot topic to all.

"I was at the Antonia Fortress and saw him and his entourage entering the city," I told Claudia. "I cannot believe that fool actually came to Jerusalem. Does he not know that his enemies wait and conspire against him? I could hardly get a word in edgewise with Caiaphas earlier. He has spies watching every move and listening to every word from the mouth of this Jesus. I wish Jesus would leave the city before things get out of hand."

"He is no fool, but I don't think He will be leaving Jerusalem before Passover. He does seem to be intentionally playing out a scenario that must end in confronting those who conspire against Him. He rode into town on an ass with people laying clothes and palm fronds before Him. It was a direct reference to a Hebrew prophet who, five hundred years ago, said, 'Behold: your king is coming to you, a just savior is he, humble, and riding on a donkey'. They were waving palm fronds and olive branches, a triumphal entry to the city."

"So, he *is* at least alluding to being a king."

"He is not threatening Rome in the political sense but is sending a clear spiritual message to the people about God and God's Kingdom."

"I can see how this would enflame Jesus's enemies at the Sanhedrin. There are many who would say it is treasonous, but his slings and arrows seem aimed at the Temple priests, not Rome itself. I am sure I will get the privilege of speaking more with Caiaphas again tomorrow," I sighed.

∞

The next day, my trials would escalate, literally. I conducted the first few of several trials I would oversee, as was always the case when I came to Jerusalem. They saved serious infractions for my visits since these were regular throughout the year. Some of these I ruled to be innocent, yet others I sentenced to time served plus flogging. However, those guilty of serious infractions I sentenced to death, and the most egregious warranted crucifixion. While I found this punishment to be horrific, so did the people. This was intended to be a warning against such actions as murder or sedition, things that set off sparks in our tinderbox world.

The first significant trial was that of Barabbas. He was the leader of an insurrection in which multiple people had been killed. He was a known criminal with what you would call a long rap sheet, and many people had witnessed his crimes. This case was a slam dunk for the prosecution. His crimes were the types of terroristic acts that had to result in public and painful punishment. He would be thrown back into the cell to await crucifixion later in the week.

At midday, as I prepared to take a break from my dais, I heard quite a commotion coming from the direction of the Temple. Cornelius and a detachment of soldiers rushed out of the courtyard that served as my tribunal. I went back into the palace and to my rooms overlooking the temple courts. Whatever had transpired appeared to have settled down, but I was amused to see merchants and ministers alike scrambling on the ground, fetching coins and scurrying after doves and lambs.

Cornelius came to me before I resumed court. He told me that Jesus had overturned the merchant tables, dumping the money changers' coins, setting the sacrificial animals free, and chasing the merchants and tax collectors with a whip.

Initially, I could not help smiling, thinking "those snakes have it coming." Instantly, though, I was overcome by nausea, recognizing that this action made it nearly impossible for me to stay neutral.

"Why was Jesus not arrested at the scene?" I asked.

"Well, I was not sure you would want to interfere in Temple business, and he left without any further violence," Cornelius said.

"No," I responded, shaking my head, "your inaction was definitely the best action. This was a crime against the Temple... on *Temple* grounds! It is the jurisdiction of the Temple Guard. Why did they not arrest him?"

"There were hundreds of people all around, many or most of them followers of Jesus. I think they were afraid to take action. I also saw, in the faces of a few of the Temple Guards, that even they harbored some affection toward Jesus. His teaching resonates with the people and is starting to undermine the Sanhedrin at the highest levels. Not only do some of the guards seem to have mixed allegiances, but I also know that at least a couple of the priests admire Jesus."

"So now I am to be the enforcer for the corrupt criminal enterprise running the temple?"

"It is a difficult situation. Not all the priests are corrupt, but they must follow their leaders. I imagine you may understand this."

I stared angrily at Cornelius, but he continued. "Jesus resonates with the Jewish faithful who believe in the one true God and the teachings of the Jewish religion, but see that there are men who have seized the religion, using it for their own earthly gain. Roman rule is hated, but the bastardization of the faith is the target of this 'insurrection'. If it is possible to let this play out in the Temple, I think that would be best."

"Thank you, Cornelius. I value your insights and will try to follow them. It just seems that this is like a herd of elephants rampaging toward a destination that cannot be averted. Oh, and one more thing, did you know that one of our men took Claudia to see this Jesus in Capernaum?"

"Um, uh"...Cornelius sputtered, looking at the ground.

More amused than angry, I asked, "Et tu, Cornelius?"

∞

Claudia and I had dinner brought to our suite later that evening and spoke of the day. She had watched the trial of Barabbas and agreed with the guilty verdict, though she would never approve of crucifixion.

"Better to place him in a bag filled with scorpions and throw him in the river", she said, referencing another punishment used on occasion. "Even that is more humane."

"Being humane is not the goal. Preventing future terrorism is."

"You missed quite the scene at the temple today," Claudia said, changing the topic.

"I saw the aftermath and heard all about it from Cornelius. You were actually there? Why do you insist on putting yourself in danger?!"

"You should have seen it. Jesus is always such a powerful but peaceful presence. Today, though, we saw His wrath."

"Yes, and so did the priests. This is getting out of control, and I am afraid of where it is leading."

∞

Waking before dawn on Tuesday, my mood was as black as the sky outside my window. Clouds blanketed the moonless sky, leaving not one visible star to cast hope upon the landscape. Haunted dreams slipped just beyond the limit of my consciousness, and I dared not try to retrieve them.

Trying not to wake Claudia, I rose from the bed, dressed, and walked to the atrium at the center of our wing of the palace. There, surrounded by ghostly statues of the gods and the dark forms of small trees and plants, I sat on the edge of the impluvium, the rainwater pool at the center of the atrium. I prayed but knew not to whom I was praying or even what I was praying for. I felt like I was caught in circumstances beyond my control. "Please take this burden from me,"

I cried. The only response to my pleas was the mocking echo of my words from the atrium walls set to the rhythm of faint splashes as water dropped from the roof into the dark pool at my back.

In the privacy of the dark atrium, I let down my mask of invulnerability and cried, giving in to the hopelessness of my situation. Something needed to change, and I was starting to recognize that I was powerless to change it.

XXIV

≈

What is Truth?

I struggled through the next couple of days, watching the city sim-
mer, knowing that the boiling point was coming. My only hope was
to keep this cauldron of corrupt priests, violent soldiers, oppressed
natives, and weary pilgrims from boiling over, burning anyone in the
vicinity, the virtuous along with the depraved.

This damage control mentality colored my decisions and may give
some insight, though not justification, into my actions. Justification is
not mine to expect nor yours to give, but insight and understanding
are key to growth. Damage control may have even been the wisest approach in this untenable situation, at least given the limits of human
wisdom and understanding.

I can now see that there was a plan that had to be carried out and
that I had a role to play. Nothing is predestined, but everything un-
folds to reveal God's plan. That does not make retelling this easier.

Early Friday morning, the sun barely on the horizon, my slumber
was disturbed by loud and persistent pounding on the palace doors,
echoing throughout the residence. One of my servants came to fetch
me and informed me that the Temple Guard, accompanied by several
priests, had a prisoner outside. He went on to say, "He is quite a sight.
You may wish to keep Lady Claudia inside."

I had the servant summon Cornelius to accompany me, knowing that this would be a tense scene and that I would need his calming presence and wise counsel. Walking down the stairs, I was reminded of Claudia's fainting spell while passing through the foyer below. Scenes of Herod the Great staggering down these stairs, greeting wise men, and ordering the murder of innocent children flashed through my mind.

I was thankful to see Cornelius and ten of his men already waiting for me at the base of the stairs. Those pounding on my doors were not "wise men" and were not coming to celebrate the birth of the Messiah. Facing these vile vigilante priests and their venomous leader, Caiaphas, was easier with Cornelius at my side.

The large doors standing between me and the courtyard were triple a man's height and thicker than my forearm. Two guards standing on either side added to the sense of security. Herod the Great's paranoia made this compound seem impenetrable. Part of me wanted to stay behind these doors and the safety of these walls. However, I was certainly not going to hide from Caiaphas and his mob.

The guards pulled the doors open, and Cornelius and I walked through, taking our position at the top of the stairs, looking down upon Caiaphas, as it should be. Our soldiers fanned out on either side of the portico surrounding the courtyard below. I was thankful that, with Passover officially underway, these unholy men could not enter and further corrupt my residence.

Caiaphas was accompanied by several other priests, which I found strange since they would be needed in the Temple; sacrifices started in just a couple of hours – killing thousands of living creatures takes manpower. They were also accompanied by twenty or more armed Temple guards escorting one prisoner, Jesus of Nazareth.

Jesus was bruised and bloodied but was standing upright, looking directly at me with a gaze that was strangely powerful for one so physically broken. Beyond the power of his gaze, his eyes conveyed a stoic acceptance, wisdom, and even love. This was the first time I had actually seen Jesus in person, and I found him utterly disconcerting. This was even more salient in his current condition, but I suspected I would always find him to be so.

"Good morning, Pilate," said Caiaphas. "We apologize for the early hour, but this is an emergency. We have been able to execute the arrest warrant on this prisoner, Jesus of Nazareth. It is imperative that his trial be conducted and concluded early today. It is against our law to allow a man to remain on a tree during the Passover," he said, referring to crucifixion.

"So, you have already tried and convicted this man in your mind and assume fate will have him dying on the cross. That is very presumptuous. Your emergency is not mine. Get this man out of here. He can be tried after the Passover, or you can try him yourself!"

"You know we have no authority to carry out capital punishment!" cried one of Caiaphas' Temple Priests.

"What crime has this man committed that would warrant the death penalty?"

"He has broken our most sacred laws, violating the Sabbath and is inciting our people against us with sacrilege and blasphemy," said Caiaphas.

I looked at him with contempt and started to turn. Another of his entourage shouted, He dares to call himself Son of David, Messiah, King of the Jews in direct defiance of Caesar. This cannot be put on the back burner."

Feeling trapped by this last allegation, I paused to collect my thoughts and consider options. "Guard, bring the prisoner to me," I said as I started to stand and return to Great King Herod's haunted foyer, feeling the weight of history on my shoulders; all of history to this point as well as everything to come from this point forward. It was my burden to bear, but I prayed it be lifted. I fervently hoped for Jesus to say something, anything that would give me a way out.

An impatient priest, not recognizing his error, yelled, "We have the Galilean and must try him before the Passover."

"Galilean, you say?" I enquired, seizing the opportunity as I returned to my seat. I glanced at Cornelius, who, oddly, had a tear in his eye. "Why would I be the judge of a Galilean? He is a subject of Herod Antipas, who is even in Jerusalem himself for Passover. Take him to the Hasmonaean Palace and let Antipas judge him."

Caiaphas looked at me with contempt, knowing I had won this round. "I will do as you say, Pilate." Turning on his heel in frustration, he marched out of my courtyard. His guard yanked Jesus by the chain that bound his wrists, almost pulling him off his feet. The level of hatred on display by the priests was inconsistent and incompatible with the countenance of the prisoner they led like a lamb to the slaughter: a sacrifice not to the God they proclaimed with their mouths but to the gods in their hearts – vanity, greed, and power.

Cornelius and I went inside. We agreed to meet up again in thirty minutes to eat and strategize after we had time to fully dress and ready ourselves for this day.

∞

Cornelius and I sat in the atrium, taking our sustenance from the breakfast platter before us as well as the comfort that nature provided in this open-air refuge. "I suspect they will be back," I said, my words punctuated by drops of morning dew splashing in the impluvium.

Nodding in agreement, Cornelius said, "Indeed, they will. I cannot see Herod conducting a trial when he will be blamed by one side or the other for an unpopular outcome. Besides, he cannot order an execution without your approval, and the Sanhedrin will accept nothing less. He is still loathed by the people for the death of John the Baptist, and he will not put himself in further disfavor with Rome due to another unsanctioned execution.

"I see that this situation is unusually upsetting to you," I said, referring to his public tears next to my dais, though I did not want to embarrass him by calling that out.

"Yes, sir. As you know, I was asked to accompany Procula to see Jesus speak. I found Him to be utterly spellbinding and can find no earthly explanation for the miracles He is reported to have performed, and certainly not the feeding of the multitudes that I myself witnessed.

"Also, over the past couple of years, you may have noticed, I have grown quite fond of the people of Judea, particularly those on your household staff. They are so different than what we grew up with in Rome. They have deeply held convictions and live by standards to which we should all aspire. I would gravitate toward them one way or the other, but I must admit a special fondness for one of Claudia's maid servants."

"Let me guess," I said, "does this young lady go by the name of Abigail?"

"Yes, she does," said Cornelius, looking me directly in the eye as if daring me to look down upon his choice of women. "I feel that we were brought together for a purpose. That I am closer to who I am meant to be in her presence...and she in mine. Actually, it is even bigger than that. I feel that the universe has set my feet on a path that has brought me to this moment and prepared me for my next choice."

"I can see that you and Claudia have much in common," I said with a hint of sarcasm, though I envied his faith.

As if hearing my thoughts, Cornelius said, "And so do you. You are at this moment because you have been prepared for it. I am by your side because God intended it."

"I do not know about that, my friend, but I do know this day is going to get out of hand. How do we deal with it?"

"You stand by your convictions and make the decisions that are being laid upon your heart. You know that there is a greater purpose to all of this. You accept that not everything is in your control."

"I am the governor. What is beyond my control in these decisions? I can choose whether or not to convict Jesus. I can choose whether or not to execute him. It is all in my hands."

"That is true, but every choice has consequences, some good, some bad, but all part of God's plan. The priests are fanning the flames in a tinder box. The resulting fire could consume all of us around it. On the other hand, Jesus is a good man, and I have come to believe He is even more. Whatever happens, God will use your actions for His purpose."

"I do not want to be used...even by God."

"God does not use people. He uses their actions, even those that are sinful."

"Perhaps I should wake Claudia," I said.

The knock came.

∞

Cornelius stood beside me as I took up position on my judgement seat. I looked at Jesus, who was an even more shocking visage now. Though now ironically adorned in a robe of royal purple, it was clear that he had been further beaten. Blood ran down his face from a cut on his brow, his brown beard now glistened red in the morning sun, his nose was swollen and twisted from its natural position...yet those eyes.

The crowd surrounding Jesus had now grown. The priests and their guards were now joined by people they had picked up on their trek to and from the Hasmonaean Palace. They represented Herod's court, city residents, pilgrims, men, women, young, and old. This was big news and big news traveled, especially among those looking for entertainment, and in my day, entertainment was not reality TV, it was blood sport.

On top of the natural tendency for people of lower moral fabric to be attracted to the atrocious, it was apparent that the priests had intentionally stacked the deck in their favor, bringing people who, for one reason or another, would support their wishes. Thus is the nature of those to whom earthly gain is god - people are treated as soulless subjects to be manipulated and used as pawns in the all-important crusade for power and control.

The jeering, sneering crowd filtered into the courtyard, filling it to capacity as I observed from my seat. I saw some faces mixed in the crowd with haunted expressions of horror and sadness, but they were far outnumbered, adrift in a sea of hostility. I did not recognize any of these faces, but I would see several of them in the future.

I waited for silence. When Caiaphas started to speak, I cut him off with a sense of pleasure, saying, "I will not compete to be heard over this crowd. If you want to move forward, I suggest you quiet your followers." Unfortunately, they complied, and I asked, "Why is Jesus back before my tribunal?"

"Herod says he defers to your judgement."

Sure, I thought to myself. He is still dealing with the consequences of silencing the voice in the wilderness, that of the beloved John the Baptizer. He would not make that mistake again. I was on my own.

"Herod found this man not to have committed a crime. I concur! Set him free!"

The crowd below erupted with angry chants. Several skirmishes between those loyal to the Sanhedrin and my soldiers broke out on the periphery of the courtyard. The people were testing the boundaries, ready to surge forth after Jesus, after me, after blood.

"Silence!" I shouted, my soldiers drawing their swords. "I shall have the man scourged and punished, but I will not crucify him. Whatever crime He committed is not against Rome and does not warrant death!" With that, I motioned to the guard, and they took Jesus out of the courtyard, parting a sea of humanity with each step He took.

∞

It was clear to me as my men took custody of Jesus and walked him out to the post at which he would be whipped that I was punishing an innocent man. I could tell there was something more, though.

The gravity of this seemed to be beyond typical crime and punishment, but I could not wrap my head around it. This was certainly not the first time I had a man scourged, and I am sure there were others undeserving of their punishment. "Heavy is the head that wears the crown," so they say...but this burden felt much heavier, infinitely heavier.

Going inside, I climbed the stairs, away from the mob at my doorstep, out of Herod's haunted hall, to the one person I trusted most in this world. Claudia waited, looking out the window at the front of the long hallway, the one overlooking the courtyard. She stood straight and strong, but her red eyes and wet cheeks conveyed her vulnerability. Being her husband, I wanted to protect her, to keep her from pain. The love in her eyes and the welcome warmth of her arms told me that Claudia wanted to protect me as well.

"My love," I said, "I wish you had not watched that."

"*My* love," she replied, "how could I not? Your pain is my pain. I certainly cannot turn my back on you in this time. I am here for you."

"And I for you. I just wish I could think of another solution. If I did not punish him, there would be blood in the streets, and it would be on my hands. That would be tragic, but the consequences of such a revolt, even short-lived, would be my own execution, and yours. Tiberius is ordering executions of entire families, not just the offending official."

"You made the decision you believed best, but I do not think it will be enough. Watching the priests, listening to their mob, this is not over. You will be forced to choose life or death for Jesus. I dreamed of this moment last night. I pray that the outcome from my dream can be changed. I wish you could have nothing to do with this innocent man. In my dream, I saw Herod the Great as he tried to prevent the coming of Jesus by murdering innocent children. Now you are in the same judgement seat, fulfilling Herod's wishes. Now, though, the world has had an opportunity to meet this man, the only truly guiltless man to ever walk the earth. Man's response is murder. They will have His blood, like that of a lamb in the Temple."

Consciously ignoring the fact that my wife just alluded to Jesus as the Messiah, I said, "If they will not be satisfied with the punishment ordered, I have one more idea to prevent that end. I will find a way out of executing this man."

"I am not sure that will be up to you, my love. At the sermon I witnessed, Jesus taught a prayer. I have been praying it daily since that time. I will share it now with you: 'Our Father in Heaven, Holy is your name. Your kingdom come. Your will be done on earth as it is in heaven. Give us today our daily bread and forgive us our sins as we forgive those who sin against us. Lead us not into temptation, but deliver us from evil, for Yours is the kingdom, the power, and the glory forever'."

"It is not your will that will be done. It is not your Kingdom but God's. Do what is right, but know that you are not in control. He is."

With that, I went to the atrium. Sitting alone by the impluvium, I saw my reflection in the silent and calm water. I saw myself more clearly than ever in my life, the goodness and the sinfulness, the light and the shadow, and the strength and weakness. I sat in stillness...in reflection.

∞

I could not let the people see my anguish and my tears as Jesus was brought back to me after the soldiers had their way with him. He now wore a crown of thorns, its barbs tearing the skin of his forehead, which bled profusely with streams flowing down his face. His entire body was covered with open wounds, muscle and sinew glistening under ripped flesh. I had Cornelius bring him inside, away from the crowd, where I could hear his voice, now almost inaudible with pain and thirst.

"Where do you come from?" I asked, truly astonished at the man before me. He endured torture and ridicule without breaking, without cursing his captors, without uttering a single word of anger at me. He remained silent.

"Do you refuse to speak to me?" I asked. "Don't you realize I have power either to free you or to crucify you?"

"You would have no power over me if it were not given to you from above. The one who handed me over to you is guilty of a greater sin."

Time stopped, and I nearly fell to my knees. This beaten and broken man before me just showed me, his likely executioner, grace. Throughout the ages, people would judge me for what was to happen on this day. Jesus forgave me.

I took a moment to recover. Somewhat disoriented and shaken, I said, "Your own people, the priests, handed you over to me. What have you done?"

Jesus replied, "My kingdom is not of this world...it is from another place."

"So you are saying you are a king?" I asked.

Jesus answered, "You say that I am a king. In fact, I was born into this world to testify to the truth. Everyone on the side of truth listens to me."

Listening and trying to understand, I asked, "What is Truth?" My inquiry met with only silence. "Are you the Messiah, the anointed one, the king of the Jews?"

His last utterance to me was simple and profound. "I am."

XXV

The Place of the Skull

S tanding outside, I now addressed the crowd below. "See now the King of the Jews," I said, hoping they would see His suffering and clear mortality as evidence that He was no longer a threat. "He has endured punishment and will be set free."

"No!" Cried Caiaphas, "Crucify him!"

The crowd responded with chants of "Crucify! Crucify! Crucify!"

Looking over the bloodthirsty crowd, I said, "As you wish. I sentence Jesus Bar Joseph to hang on the cross until He is dead."

The crowd cheered and literally jumped with joy.

I let the celebration continue for a few moments. Then I had Cornelius bring out the other prisoners to be crucified.

Three ragged and roughed-up prisoners joined us at the top of the stairs. Two were convicted of theft. The third was Barabas, the murdering terrorist.

Giving the crowd the starkest choice possible, I said, "As is the custom on Passover, I am to release one of these men and forgive their crimes. Standing before you now is Jesus Bar Joseph, guilty of preaching a message unpopular with the Sanhedrim. Also standing here is Barabas, guilty of murder, rape, and insurrection. Which of these men will you spare?"

To my shock and disgust, chants of "Barabas, Barabas, Barabas" started - at first coming from a priest but soon echoing around the courtyard.

Exhausted and unable to further control the situation, I looked at Jesus. His eyes showed love, not the hate I deserved for what was to come next. I whispered to Cornelius, who, I could tell, was equally drained. He then whispered to one of his men, who turned and entered the residence.

Moments later, Abigail brought a bowl of water, handing it to Cornelius. Abigail was joined in the doorway by my beloved Claudia. They embraced and looked on as I washed my hands.

"I am innocent of this man's blood."

∞

Cornelius put his hand on my shoulder, and we turned our backs on the priests and their mob. Without knowing how I got there, I found myself in the foyer in Claudia's embrace. I cried silently. I heard Cornelius ordering his soldiers and the staff away. When I looked up, it was just me, Claudia, Cornelius, and Abigail. They were the only people in the world who understood what I had been through, what I had done to try to change the evil outcome, that I had no control and was not to blame. What they did not yet know, that maybe I did not yet understand, is that one can be without blame and still bear responsibility.

I looked at each of them, kissed Claudia, and said, "I must be alone." Upstairs, I watched through the window as the cross was placed on Jesus's shoulder. I too felt its weight bearing down on me. Changing into street clothes and covering my head, I slipped out of the palace through the servants' entrance.

Golgotha, "place of the skull", skull mount...I would follow Jesus up that hill. If only I could, I would make a deal with God and get Him to swap our places. If only my body could be broken for His, if only my blood could be spilled.

∞

Following the sea of humanity in the wake of Jesus, closing back in on Him like a tsunami, I now saw sublime symbolism that could not be created by the most gifted writer. We were ALL following Him up a hill named for death. Golgotha, so named for looking like a skull, was now also a literal place of death, not only because we Romans executed people here but also because, for centuries, people had buried their family members in small caves all around this mound.

His blood drizzled the path in front of me like morbid breadcrumbs leading me home. A few yards ahead of me, He fell to the ground, unable to bear the weight of the cross in His weakened state. A large African man was summoned to help him carry the cross; the executioners did not want their prisoner to die before they could nail him to the cross.

Along the path some were crying. Others were cheering. Still others looked away in disgust. Some were Judean. Others were Romans. Still others were pilgrims from remote regions. Some were men, others women. Many, sadly, were children. Jesus was leading ALL of us, unifying all of us.

At the top of the mount, Jesus dropped his cross and fell to His knees. Two of the death squad grabbed Him and laid Him down forcefully on the cross. Two other squad members grabbed one of His arms, pulling it straight while a third member positioned a nine-inch nail on his wrist, the perfect spot between the bones, allowing His arm to bear the weight of His body on the cross. The hammer dropped, and Jesus cried out in agony. They repeated this process on the other arm. Then they pulled His legs, positioning them heel over heel, slightly bent. The hammer fell again; He cried out again.

The death squad worked in practiced unison, lifting the cross into position in a pre-dug hole. Death was assured and could not come soon enough. It could be hours, but it would not be allowed to be days, as was the case with some crucifixion victims; the priest would not allow Him to remain on the cross when Passover officially began at sunset. If He were still alive, His legs would be broken, expediting death through suffocation.

∞

At last, he shouted, "My God! My God! Why have you forsaken me?" I thought, with great sadness and regret, "They have finally broken Him." Then I noticed that several of those around me muttered His words: "My God! My God..."

I thought they were sharing His brokenness and His pain, but they went on muttering in unison even as He fell silent. I could not make out all of what they said, just catching snippets:

"My God, I cry out by day, but you do not answer....
.... Yet you... the Holy One...the one Israel praises...
...our ancestors.... you delivered them...
.... To you they cried out and were saved...
...in you they trusted and were not put to shame...
...All who see me mock me...hurl insults...
...Do not be far from me...trouble is near...
...My mouth is dried...my tongue sticks to the roof of my mouth...
...Dogs surround me...a pack of villains...
...they pierce my hands and my feet...people stare and gloat...
... Lord...You are my strength...help me...
...The poor will eat and be satisfied......All... will...turn to the Lord...
...future generations will be told about the Lord...
...They will proclaim his righteousness...He has done it!"

It was as if they had all been given the same script to read. It was eerie and disturbing. Yet, it was utterly sacred and moving as well. I found myself overwhelmed, not knowing at the time that they were reciting the writings of King David from centuries before. Psalm 22, written by David a thousand years before, perfectly predicted this very moment. It was as if Jesus orchestrated His death based on this Psalm, and yet no director but God could have done so.

∞

Uttering one last mortal howl, Jesus slumped on the cross, His body pulling away from the wood, arms stretched backward in a grotesque and seemingly impossible manner. I started to feel electricity in the air.

A soldier pierced His side with a spear, making sure that He was dead. An arterial spray of blood mixed with water erupted from His skin, spraying the soldier and those of us at His feet. It formed a fine mist that was carried by gusts of wind from the black clouds suddenly forming overhead.

Day turned to night; a black veil of clouds blocked out the sun. Lightning crashed all around and thunder roared in rolling waves, drowning out all other sound. Gusts of wind grew into a tempest, picking up dust and debris, yet no rain fell, as if nature herself refused to cleanse this scene.

I felt a low rumble in my feet, which intensified to a throb, the heartbeat of an angry earth in mourning. Stones began to slide down Golgotha, some were large, round stones that had concealed bones in ossuaries dotting the hillside.

As lightning illuminated the sky, I looked down the hill at my palace, praying for the safety of Claudia and our friends. As I did so, I glimpsed the temple. There, I saw the great veil that separated the people from the innermost part of the temple, accessible only to the high priest. The veil was swaying and filling with wind, as if filled with the breath of God. Suddenly, unable to withstand the wind, the veil tore from top to bottom, exposing the Holy of Holies. No longer were the people sheltering in the courtyard separated from the seat of God.

I was overcome. My mind felt as torn as the Temple veil. Outside of myself and outside of time, I was thrown back to other times I had experienced such feelings:

There I was, covered with the blood of a sacrificed lamb on my 13th birthday.

There I was with Claudia under the Abruzzi sky in a brief kiss that lasted forever.

There I was, locked in the gravitational pull of the woman my men would crucify, in the orbit of her eyes, full of love and pity, as she said, "One day you will meet the anointed one, and I pray He will bring you peace."

A bridge connected these disparate points in time. Then I recognized that it was not just these moments between my youthful self and current self that were connected by this bridge. Everything, everyone, and every time are here and now, all of creation interconnected. We mortals recognize this only on rare occasions, considering it an anomaly, something abnormal and strange. In reality, it is only our own imperfection that keeps this state from being routine. Perhaps, this is good – these moments help us understand God from a human perspective.

I cannot tell you how long this moment of sacred reverie lasted; I had no experience of time at all. The clouds began to part, and the ground stabilized under my feet, but upon return to my body, I found that my mind remained black and unsettled. It seemed that the world beyond my eyelids ceased to exist, and I felt compelled to sleep. I have no further memory of the events of that horrendously miraculous day, and I have no memory of getting to the place I ended up.

∞

I slept. I dreamed. And in that sleep...what dreams came.

I cannot tell you any specific content of the dreams. I can only describe the feeling. It was emptiness, separation, and utter despair.

Emptiness – I found myself in a vast, vacuous void, barren of any meaning or purpose;

Separation – I was separated from anything good. Separation from family. Separation from friends. Separation from anything beautiful. Separation from love.

Despair – I felt the deepest sense of loss imaginable. My heart cried out for whatever was lost, not even knowing what was gone.

I wailed, I clawed, I cried, I flailed.

My screams echoed back to me, a persistent reminder of my pain–no, of *all* pain–I was pain and pain was me. My efforts to reach out, touch something, gain any traction, a foothold in what I knew as reality were all thwarted...

All this flailing was like that of a fish out of water, separated from oxygen, unable to breathe but unable to die... suffering without end.

The dreams did not have a beginning. They did not have an end. It was as if they were timeless, eternal.

Part Two: The New Testament

Spreading the Word
Duncan1890, 2021, istockphotos.com

XXVI

⟨❦⟩

Out of Darkness

LIGHT!! Out of the blackness of my mind came a pure light. It pierced the horror of my dreams, vanquishing the emptiness and despair. Replacing the separation with unity. Filling the corners of my soul with love.

Waking, at first, I thought, this must be heaven. The gods...no God has brought me home. Then my eyes adjusted. A beam of light shone through the opening in the rocks. Dust particles floated through the light, a reminder that I was still earthbound, where all things decay.

Looking around, I saw that I was in a cave surrounded on all sides by stone. Looking behind me, away from the light, I saw a box and recognized it as a reliquary holding the bones of someone's beloved family member.

I got to my knees and crawled through the mouth of the cave and found myself on the slopes of Golgotha, overlooking the temple and the palace. I rose to my feet, stretched my arms, and filled my lungs with air. Life had returned.

I walked the path back to the city gate. Entering the city, I saw people working, cleaning debris that had fallen when the earth shook. I saw that people were putting things back in place. Nothing to see here. Earthquakes happen. Storms happen. Crucifixions happen. It is all natural... nothing supernatural here.

I walked past the temple. The priests were supervising their slaves and servants as they began to assess and make repairs. The temple would recover its former glory, at least until the Romans finally destroyed it 30 years in the future.

As I walked through the courtyard where I had given in to the High Priest and his minions, a member of the Sanhedrin ran up behind me, shouting my name. I turned to face him, ready to put him in his place, physically, if necessary, but I quickly saw something different on his face. He looked sad and agitated as if in mourning. His face was well-lined with fissures of age and experience, yet there was something preternaturally ageless about him. There was also something familiar about his deep brown eyes that I could not quite place.

"Dominus, my name is Joseph. I am the great-uncle of Jesus of Nazareth, His mother's uncle. I helped raise Mary, his mother, when her father died. When her husband later died as well, I helped raise Jesus. It is in this capacity, not my role in the Sanhedrin, that I come to you. I pray that you will allow me the traditional family honor of burying my kinsman."

Still taken aback by both the boldness and countenance of Joseph of Arimathea, I stood silent for a moment before responding, "It is my honor to allow this, and I am pleased to see that not all in the Temple march in lockstep with Caiaphas. Please accept my condolences for your loss and express my deep sorrow to your daughter."

Joseph looked at me in equally stunned silence. We both saw in each other, men trapped by circumstance and both powerless to control those circumstances. We saw something more though...We saw kindred spirits no longer willing to be victim of evil around us, people who did not accept that lack of control absolved responsibility. I was beginning to realize that I had awoken to a new version of myself, one with a new purpose and destiny.

Even as Joseph walked away, I knew our paths would cross again. Our destinies were intertwined by supernatural forces that I could not yet name.

I walked to my palace, where Claudia sat outside with Abigail and Cornelius. Claudia ran to me, tears streaming down her face. She jumped into my arms, nearly knocking me over. "I was so worried. Thank God you are home! Where have you been? Never mind. You are a mess. Let's get you cleaned up, and you can tell me all about it."

We went inside and I cleaned up, washing away the dirt of the tomb. I changed, not into my Roman uniform but again into street clothes. I knew that I would have to don my uniform again, that I would have to remain an officer of the Roman government, but I now recognized this as a role I would have to play, not the person I was.

For some time, I sat on the bed next to Claudia. It was good to have her close. It was good that she recognized my need for silence at that moment. Like a man facing the end of his life, scenes from my own life flashed before me, as if my brain were reorganizing, putting things into perspective, processing my past, and preparing me... The question is - for what?

I could now see that my whole life had prepared me for the past twenty-four hours. My hike up Golgotha started in Abruzzi and every event since my birth was a step up that hill. The changes to come in my life may seem drastic but not when one considers that, even before my literal "come to Jesus" moment, I had washed away the hedonism, idol worship, and self-absorption into which I had been born.

Finally, I told Claudia the details of the past 24 hours. I was hardly able to put my experience into words, but I wept and did the best I could.

When I was done, she just lay beside me in our bed and let me recover, saying only, "I love you and am here for you."

"I allowed the crucifixion of the Messiah. He stood before me, and I knew He was... different...special. I could see that, but I had no idea the nature or degree of His divergence. He knew what was coming. He accepted it. He had to endure it – for us, the very people who tortured Him, humiliated Him, and executed Him. On the Cross, he said, 'Forgive them, Father, they know not what they do.' You saw what happened when He died!"

"Of course, EVERYONE saw, heard, and felt what happened when He died," said Claudia. "You did not cause His death, even if you did allow it. Even the vile Caiaphas himself did not cause it. It was part of a divine plan, the end of which we do not know. I have, however, been learning from Abigail and some of the other staff. To them, it is the fulfillment of centuries of prophecy. They told me the predictions of the prophets. They even quoted parts of a song written by King David that read like a script of yesterday's events."

"My God! My God! Why have you forsaken me?" we said simultaneously.

I shivered from head to toe.

"I may not have caused the death of Jesus, but I am responsible. I could not control it. I could not change it. I washed my hands of control yesterday. That does not mean I bear no responsibility. I can NOT wash my hands of changing myself, changing my way of interacting in the world, or making what change I can in this corrupt and wicked world."

"Let's take a walk," said Claudia, recognizing a growing agitation in me. I knew I had work to do, but I had no idea what I was to do or where to start. She continued, "Let's just take the next step together. We do not need to know where we will end up to know the next right step."

∞

We encountered Cornelius in the foyer. He seemed to be waiting for me - my bodyguard, my companion, my friend, and more.

As we walked through the doors of the palace, we encountered a very disheveled Caiaphas and his not-so-merry band of bootlicking priests. It seemed that they were still feeling the effects of the events of the preceding afternoon; the blackness of the skies and quaking of the earth manifested as palpable psychic darkness and anxiety.

"May I trouble you, Pilate? We need to secure the tomb of Jesus. As you probably know, Joseph of Arimathea took the body and placed it in his family tomb. I am...I mean, people are afraid the followers of Jesus will steal the body and claim he rose from the dead. Can you imagine the unrest that such deceit could cause?"

"Make it so," I told Cornelius, who then ordered that one of his units ensure round-the-clock guards.

Then I looked at Caiaphas and said, "We would certainly not want anyone to lie to or exploit the people."

"Certainly not," said Caiaphas, not even recognizing the mocking nature of my comment.

∞

Over the next two days, I spent a great deal of time in solitary contemplation, but balanced this in the loving companionship of Claudia or in deep discussion with Cornelius. The second half of my life would have a whole new cast of characters, but the camaraderie of Cornelius and the love of Claudia were to be constant and consistent.

For the next two nights, Claudia and I ate together with Abigail, Cornelius, and others in the household. My relationships with the "staff" were forever changed by the events of the past Friday. Each of us maintained our individual personalities, strengths, weaknesses, free will, and the other things that made us unique and human. However, we no longer saw each other in a hierarchy of worthiness. We were all spiritual beings of equal and immeasurable value, trying to make our way home while negotiating this carnal life.

Claudia and I found these dinner parties, which would become a regular occurrence moving forward, to be much more enjoyable than prior experiences with Herod Antipas or Tiberius. None of us felt the need to mask who we were, watch what we said, or look over our shoulders. This model of coming together for meals, sharing perspectives on how to live in this broken world while loving and supporting one another, worked for us.

∞

Monday morning, I awoke compelled to move, to get out of the palace, to walk.

"Where will you go?" asked Claudia, as I finished dressing and kissed her goodbye.

"I am not sure. I just need to take the next right step."

In the foyer downstairs, I came across Cornelius, who seemed to be waiting for me. He was also dressed in civilian clothes and asked, "May I walk with you?"

How he knew I would be setting out, I do not know. "I had intended on going alone, and I am not sure how good my company will be."

"I understand. We can walk in silence, but these roads are treacherous. It is better that we walk together." And so, we did just that, from that point forth, covering more miles and more years than I could imagine at that point. We walked.

XXVII

❦

The Road to Emmaus

At first, Cornelius and I walked in silence, taking in the sights, listening to nature around us, processing the events of the past three days. We approached a hill covered with olive trees and noticed a small group gathered around a tree at the base of the hill. They were dressed in the traditional black garments of Jewish mourners, and we suspected that they may be friends and family of Jesus. We started walking in the opposite direction. While my personal experience with Jesus left me feeling that He had forgiven me of my sins, I was not so sure His followers would agree.

Not wanting to encounter Caiaphas, his priests, or, for that matter, anyone we may know, we went around the city and started heading west toward the Mediterranean coast. There was a sign on the road indicating that we were headed to Emmaus, twenty-one miles ahead.

After traveling the road for about an hour, we stopped at a stream to drink and clean up a bit. I splashed my face in the cool water and began washing my hands when I saw a fellow traveler sitting by the stream a few yards ahead of us. Sitting on a stone and hanging his feet in the water, he appeared oblivious to our presence.

Not wanting to startle him, I said, "Hello, friend."

He looked in our direction, smiled, and waved in a welcoming manner. Cornelius and I approached him. He indicated that he was traveling in our direction and asked if he could join us. It was always safer to walk in groups, so we agreed.

As we walked together, we shared nuts, figs, and grapes while we talked about the past few days in Jerusalem. He said he had seen Jesus coming into town on a donkey and had been there when he was crucified.

Desiring an outsider's perspective but not wanting to give away my identity, I said, "The High Priest and the rest of the Sanhedrin sure seemed to want him dead. They got their way."

The traveler said, "The Temple priests have become rich and powerful through their positions. It is human nature for them to try to hold onto that power. Everyone has dual natures - human and spirit. Priests are supposed to be models for how to live according to the spirit nature. Love of money and power corrupted them. However, God wants them back, too. It is harder for them to enter heaven because they must put down their possessions and their high status to crawl through the gate. I pray that one day they will be able to do so."

Something about the man seemed familiar, but I could not place it. "You are very wise and much more forgiving than I am. Caiaphas and his brood of vipers put Jesus to death for no reason other than to protect their status and maintain control of the people."

"Everyone wants control but paradoxically, the only way to gain control is to give it up."

Then I recognized Him. I had seen Jesus beaten, bloody, swollen, and slaughtered. Never had I seen Him clean, healthy, and whole. Cornelius had seen Him before, surely, he must have known. I glanced over at Cornelius who gave me that knowing look my father had given me many times growing up. I looked back at Jesus who smiled and answered my previously unanswered query of Him, "I am Truth."

I almost fell over, but Cornelius put an arm around me, steadying me. Jesus continued, "From now on, you will be my gardener. I am prepared to scatter seeds throughout the world. From the furthest western shores of the empire to the eastern frontiers. From the ice-covered northern regions to the sand covered African Sahara. Eventually my garden will encompass the planet, and all people will be welcome back within it."

He spoke of His disciples, describing each as would a proud and loving father. He told us where each of the eleven other disciples would go and the struggles they would face. "You will till the soil of the empire making sure my seeds can grow. You will root out weeds and guard against vermin. My other disciples will do the planting, and I will reap the harvest. Thanks to the Roman empire, there is now the infrastructure needed to carry my message throughout the world. Roman soil needs a Roman gardener."

"How will I know what to do? I was raised as a Roman not a Jew. I know nothing about the expectations of Judaism."

"Precisely. Just listen for my voice. Now it is time for you to return to Jerusalem to meet the others."

"They will hate me for what I did," I started to protest, but when I looked over at Him, He was gone.

In dismay and questioning my own sanity, I started our march back to the city, Cornelius at my side, my tether to reality.

XXVIII

Close Encounters

Making our way back into the city, Cornelius and I encountered many new faces among the crowd. Pilgrims should be leaving the city after Passover, not just now arriving. We saw people embracing and rejoicing as if celebrating a family reunion. The snippets of conversation we heard made little sense.

I saw a young man embracing an older woman and telling her, with tears in his eyes, that he loved her and was "so proud of my beautiful little girl."

We passed a boy, about eight years of age, comforting a couple I assume were his parents. He was saying, "See, I am fine now! You don't need to cry anymore. There was nothing you could have done. Now swing me, daddy!" With that, his father held him by the wrists and twirled him around, nearly hitting the mother and several people passing by.

A young couple walked hand-in-hand. As they passed, I heard the young man say, "I am sorry I could not make it to our wedding."

We kept walking, though we did not know where we were to go. We were told to come back to the city, but beyond that, we were clueless. We started making our way toward the palace. There, standing atop the highest parapet, we looked for a sign, listened for His voice. Nothing came.

As we gave up and started inside, we noticed a group of pilgrims heading toward the city from the east. It appeared to be the same group we had encountered under the olive tree.

"I believe these are our new friends," said Cornelius.

"I am not ready to see them, but let's follow and see where they go."

"You stay here, Dominus, I will follow and report back to you," Cornelius replied.

"Thank you, Cornelius, but please do not call me dominus anymore. First of all, you are my friend, not my servant. Secondly, I am not worthy of being called 'Lord.' Besides, I am not THAT much older than you," I added, trying to lighten the tone, humor being one of my go-to coping skills.

∞

When Cornelius returned, he said, "After they entered the city gate, I was able to follow at a short distance. They came to the home of a wealthy family and knocked on the door. They were greeted by a well-adorned woman with the enthusiastic hugs of a loved one.

"Please monitor them and make sure we know where they go. If I am told that I must meet with them, I need to know where they are."

"Dominus, I mean Pontius, don't you think we should go ahead and introduce ourselves now? That is what we were told to do. I think you are just avoiding and procrastinating."

"You are right, Cornelius, but I am not ready. I need to prepare myself. I ordered the death of their leader, friend, and family member. How can I face them?"

It took me three more days to work up the courage and, then it was only after Claudia pushed me. On that morning, Claudia woke me and told me of her dream. She said she had met with Jesus in her dream. He had come to her as she walked through the city, walking beside her as she came to a house. He pointed and said, they are waiting for you. When she asked who was waiting, Jesus said, "My friends."

∞

Claudia accompanied Cornelius and me as we walked through the city later that morning. We were just three friends out for a stroll, dressed as peasants and wearing head coverings, not wanting to draw the attention of the Jews who hated me or the Roman soldiers who would simply not understand.

We found the house and proceeded to knock. A servant came to the door, cautiously opening it just wide enough to see my face. At first, she had the look of recognition without context, seeing me without my uniform. Then she looked at Claudia, who was always more memorable than I, and I saw panic overcome her.

"Please," I said, "I am not here to cause trouble." She continued to look at me dubiously and with thinly veiled scorn.

"I am with the government; I am here to help," Cornelius said, and we both laughed. The servant snickered, lowering her guard.

"Seriously," I said, "we want to talk about Jesus."

My initial introduction to the group went as I expected. There were looks of horror, sadness, and anger when I entered the room. It was as if my presence opened up still festering wounds, ripping stitches, and tearing flesh.

A muscular and stocky man named Peter, AKA Simon (names were strangely fleeting in my time), jumped up and started to charge at me. Others held him back. He took a deep breath, and his countenance changed as if breathing in not just fresh air but a fresh spirit. Shaking off the hands that had held him back, he opened his arms and welcomed me with a hug. Being a Roman, a soldier, and a nobleman, hugs, especially with strange men, were new to me, but I just went with it.

"I have stories to share with you," I said. I told them about my perspective on the trial and execution of Jesus, asking their forgiveness for my role. Some faces softened and showed signs of empathy, while others remained hard and cold. I recognized two women standing in the corner, arms around one another. They were at the trial, and I had been with them at the foot of the cross. They nodded as I told the group of my experience at the feet of Jesus and on Golgotha. I told them of the sky going black… the temple veil being torn…of waking in the tomb…of my apocalypse.

"I am certainly not an expert in your ways, customs, or beliefs, but what I saw was definitely an apocalypse. From what I understand, many Jews have an apocalyptic philosophy and religion, believing that God will destroy earthly power and establish His kingdom."

"Yes, we know what apocalyptic means," said the largest man in the room, one called John, as he scowled at me, his arms crossed and biceps twitching as if they were preparing for battle.

"Well, the word actually means the lifting of the veil, revelation of a new truth," I said.

"Again, we know what it means," said John.

One named Matthew said, "Let him finish John", his tone conveying the amiable hostility usually shared only by brothers.

"I was actually on top of that hill with Jesus, and most of you were not", I said, making eye contact with everyone in the room before proceeding. "What I saw certainly revealed a new truth to me. The veil of the Temple was literally torn. You all may be waiting for something that has already happened. The Truth has already been revealed."

Cornelius and I then told them of our experience on the road to Emmaus. The group was surprised at the revelation we had of Jesus on the road to Emmaus, but not as much as I would have expected.

Peter said, "I am stunned that Jesus would choose to reveal Himself to you, a gentile, a ROMAN, and the very man who sentenced Him to death. However, He revealed Himself to us as well, in this very room. There were also two others who, like you, Jesus met on the road to Emmaus. You are clearly not lying, but I cannot fathom why you are here and why Jesus would have spoken to you."

The younger of the two women to whom I had still not been introduced, emerged from the corner. She spoke about having watched Jesus draw His last painful breath and then being the first to see Him alive again outside of His tomb. She began to cry.

Claudia went to comfort her. Putting her arms around the Woman, Claudia said, "I am here for you, Mary." Mary's tears continued but were counteracted by a bright smile. It was as if I were looking at a sun shower, her eyes were all the vivid colors of the heavenly sunshine reflected and refracted by her tears like wet surfaces of the earth washed clean by the rain.

It was clear that Claudia and Mary had a pre-existing acquaintance. I wondered about that for a fleeting moment. I experienced a strange mix of vindication and sadness. I was not crazy, and these people knew it but that meant I was not the only one to have seen Jesus. He was not here just for me. I started to speak but was interrupted by another man sulking into the room.

John shouted "Thomas, where have you been?! You will never believe what happened."

Thomas said, "I had to take some time for myself. I am lost. Jesus did not keep his promise. I had finally begun to believe that Jesus would end Roman rule; that he had come to establish God's Kingdom. Seeing Him on the cross ended that delusion."

"Wait. You have not seen Him?" asked Peter.

We all shared our encounter stories, but no one had seen Him in the past week. Cornelius spoke of finding Him washing his feet in the river and walking for miles with us before I recognized Jesus. Cornelius laughed at my expense.

Mary Magdalene said, "At first I thought He was a gardener tending to the grounds outside the tomb."

One called Simon, but not the one Jesus renamed Peter (I met all these people, and the names are still confusing), still seemingly in a state of shock, said, "He ate fish with us right here in this room. It was as if nothing had ever happened and we were back in Capernaum, me, a bunch of rowdy fishermen, and our rabbi."

Thomas said, "I do not know what happened while I was gone, but I think you have been drinking a bit too much wine. Until I can touch

Jesus myself and put my hands in his wounds, I can not believe he has returned.

∞

I told them of my assignment - that I was to make Jerusalem and the rest of my territory safe, well safer, for them over the coming years. However, I told them that they would have to move on from Judea and take the message to every corner of the empire. "James will be going to Hispania, Peter to Britannia, and Thomas, you will go to India. Your journeys will be dangerous and sometimes deadly. I know the empire, its leaders, its roads, its communications channels, and its ways. I will help you get your message out despite the peril."

Thomas said, "India? I am not going anywhere until Jesus comes back and tells me to himself. Besides, how can I go to India? I know nothing of India. I do not know the language. Who in India would even listen to me anyway?"

Almost in unison, several others murmured and mockingly asked, "Still you doubt, Thomas?"

Out of the corner of my eye, I saw Matthew sitting and writing at a table on the other side of the room. I said, "Matthew, what are you writing?"

He responded, "Someday, we will not be here to tell the story of what we saw and heard, who was here to witness these things, or how we worked together to spread the news. I have seen how the Romans usurped Greek history, philosophy, and religion and used it to their purpose. We need to write history so it cannot be written for us."

"I understand, and you are correct," I said. "However, I have seen how letters are intercepted and taken out of context, providing Roman authorities with grounds for all forms of atrocity. We must be careful with what we write and how we communicate. I would say, at least for now, we should commit as little as possible to writing and take care not to write anything that can be used as a reason for persecution. Most people do not read anyway, so much of what we will share will be in oral form. When we do write things, we should use code words, change names, and otherwise make it difficult for an out-sider to know specifics. Once you have read a letter containing any-thing that may put our people in danger or cause conflict with either Roman authorities or the Temple, you will need to commit it to mem-ory and burn it."

"That will make it difficult to share the words of Jesus, and people desperately need His wisdom," said Matthew.

"You are right, Matthew," said Peter grudgingly, as if those words caused him physical pain. "However, any day now, Jesus will come again, and there will be no more need for secrecy."

I did not tell him that I thought this was not the case. I got the sense that time to God was not as we understood it, nor was the con-cept of revelation or apocalypse. The disciples took my warning seri-ously, though, and many years would pass before the stories of Jesus were put into written form. Even when this did happen, care was taken to convey necessary messages without easily incriminating those still alive or endangering the followers of Christ.

Matthew was right once again. Over the centuries, this intentional obfuscation has certainly sewn some skepticism, but it also led to de-bate, discussion, and intense efforts to better understand God and His message. More people have now come to understand God through Christ than, *cumulatively*, had ever even been born by my time. It seems we somehow got the message out despite the ambiguity.

∞

Cornelius and I left the disciples in that room. They had much to think about and, while I felt a connection to them, their bonds had become familial. They required time to process the events of the past week and their implications for their lives. I would later find out that Jesus had joined them again later that evening. He resolved the doubts of Thomas. Thomas was the first to truly recognize the divin-ity of Jesus, exclaiming, "My Lord and my God!" after literally putting his fingers in Jesus' wounds.

XXIX

Baby Steps

All of this was new to me. I felt like a child just entering the world, at first unable to hold up my head, then learning to sit up, and then to walk. My first steps were cautious, but like a child, I always felt a parental presence guiding and keeping me safe. Of course, from the baby's perspective, these steps are terrifying.

Not long after my first meeting with the disciples, I received a letter from Cassius. The persecution and prosecution of the friends of Sejanus had continued, and more blood had been spilled down the Gemonian Stairs. It seemed, though, that there was a decreasing appetite for such retribution. Perhaps the lascivious appetites of Tiberius, while utterly disgusting, provided distraction, allowing the senators to regroup and rule the roost, even if only temporarily.

The new Prefect of the Praetorian Guard, Naevius Sutorius Macro, had continued the persecutions but was now spending more time in Capri, where Tiberius had brought two of his potential heirs to train in the ways of Caesar.

The letter concluded: "While things may be starting to cool off, I urge you to remain cautious. With deep admiration and friendship, Cassius. Postscript - Burn after reading."

The letter was a reminder that, as always, Rome was a violent place in which one could never be assured of safety. Death or imprisonment could come for me at any time at the hands of Tiberius or his hench-men. However, death could come for me, for any of us, at any time. We do not know the day or hour, but death comes for us all. I just no longer feared it.

Things were different now. My work had a different purpose. It was no longer about me. I knew I had to keep my position as prefect of Judea, at least for now, so I continued my usual administrative duties. Perhaps because I no longer felt the pressure to advance myself, my career went more smoothly. I did not make such glaring errors in judgement. I gave Tiberius no cause to doubt my loyalty or my aptitude. In fact, I gave Tiberius very little, including my attention.

Home life was also different. My family was not just Claudia and me. It now included everyone in the household. They were not blood relations, but we grew closer and loved one another.

Cornelius and Abigail married and soon were expecting a new addition to the family. Their wedding, on the shores of the Mediterranean in Caesaria, was officiated by Simon Peter. Hanna was born nine months to the day from the day Abigail and Cornelius were married. I teased Cornelius that God did this so he could remember his anniversary.

Claudia and I were never to be graced with a child of our own, perhaps because of the turmoil and danger of my new mission, but we cared for baby Hannah as if she were our own.

Most of the initial work I did on behalf of the coming Kingdom during these early years in Judea was clandestine. It was imperative that I maintain my image as a Roman Prefect. Public awareness of my conversion to Judaism and following Jesus would result in harsh punishment for me and severe consequences to our rising faith movement. Of course, as a result, I had no opportunity to publicly repent of my role in the crucifixion. History would forever portray me harshly, but my soul is at peace.

I followed all the usual Roman customs, only celebrating Jewish holidays or speaking of God's Kingdom within my very small household circle. I even kept icons of Roman gods in the house. While this was a violation of Jewish Law, Jesus told me that these laws were secondary to our overall mission – to love God and love our neighbors as ourselves. My work was done to support this mission.

Oh yeah, I guess I forgot to mention that Jesus still spoke with me. He gave me direction, helped me understand perplexing things, and kept me moving forward. He did not come to dinner, though I felt His spirit with me at all times. Instead, He came to me in my dreams. These dreams were not like the others, which made little sense and seemed trivial. These dreams were lucid, logical, and illuminating. Sometimes I would just hear His voice, but my favorite dreams were those like the one where He gave me my first mission.

XXX

The Spanish Mission

Over the weeks immediately following our meeting in the upper room in Jerusalem, the disciples traveled back to Capernaum. They reported multiple encounters with Jesus, who pushed them to begin their outreach and mission work to spread His message. I, on the other hand, traveled back to Caesarea, but Jesus came to me as well.

He sat across from me at a tavern. I dreamed that I entered the tavern and sat by myself at a table, sipping beer, deep in thought. Jesus walked over, beer in hand, and sat down with me. We communed, talking through the myriad of thoughts and worries on my mind.

We spoke of Claudia and the sadness she felt, we felt, at not having a child. I asked if, and when, we would have such a blessing. It was breaking Claudia's heart, and that was breaking mine. I said, "I know that compared to yours, such suffering is trivial, and I should not ask about such things."

He responded that no suffering is trivial, but that it all has a purpose. In typical Jesus fashion, He did not directly answer the question, but said, "Love is not from the body, it is from the spirit."

We then spoke of my first mission. "Your love has grown to include those in your household, even though you are not related to any of them. I brought you and Claudia together for a purpose, and your love for her knows no bounds. However, you need to learn more about the others in your household. They all have stories, and I brought them to you for a reason. You will find one who was made a slave by Rome after the revolt of Judas the Galilean. He has served you and your predecessors in this very palace. His heart was stolen from him and lives elsewhere. You will reunite him with his heart while it still beats."

With that, He got up from the table, laying a hand on my shoulder and favoring me with a smile as He walked out.

∞

I awoke and at once shared my dream with Claudia, who lay next to me. When I opened my eyes, I was startled to see her looking at me expectantly.

"I heard you talking in your sleep, my love. I could not understand much, but you were having an intimate conversation with someone. Thank God for your sake, it was not a woman," she said, laughing and holding a pretend knife to my throat. As usual, we found laughter, love, and joy in our time together.

I told her of the dream. She cried a little in talking about having children and said, "I am sad that our love has not produced a child, but it makes me even more sad that you grieve for me. Whether we have a child or not, I love you. We will find many ways to bring love into the world."

She went on, "As for the person in the household that Jesus spoke of, I am fairly certain that it is Alucio. He was born in a far-off land but came here as a young man. I do not know all the circumstances, but he was imprisoned and forced into slavery along with his wife. She was pregnant at the time. He has not seen her or his child since."

I had, of course, gotten to know Alucio over the past months, but I had not heard his whole story. Claudia agreed to bring him to me and was thrilled to be part of the mission to return Alucio to his family.

∞

"Dominus, I am thankful for how you have begun to change the way things are run in the palace," Alucio said when I sat down with him over lunch that day. "You and Procula have been very generous and accommodating. Claudia, I mean Procula, feels like the daughter I never knew."

"Thank you, Alucio," I responded. "Perhaps you will find it in your heart to forgive me for having never been as gracious and accepting of you as my dear Claudia. She was much further along on her spiritual journey, while I needed some divine intervention."

"You have always treated me fairly. I have grown to expect mistreatment and being relegated to the shadows. This has never been the case with you."

"No one should expect any such thing, and I am sorry for not seeing the injustice sooner. Being born into darkness makes it difficult to recognize the lack of light. My work now is to allow the light to shine. Now, please tell me your story."

"Thank you. Before I came to Judea, I had converted to Judaism. My wife and I journeyed here to escape Roman persecution in our homeland of Hispania. Actually, that is the Roman name for our land, but the ancestral name of our land is Iberia."

"For the past three hundred years, our people have worked in silver and copper mines for the Romans. We built their roads. We provided grapes and olives. Rome enriched itself on the backs of our people.

"Judas the Galilean was the first of what they now call Zealots, so named for his zeal to overthrow Rome and re-establish a Jewish kingdom. His message resonated with me, and I followed him, as did many others from my homeland. When he was killed over twenty years ago, many of our band were also executed. My wife and I were fortunate to keep our lives, but we lost our freedom. We were taken to Rome by the grandson of King Herod, Herod Agrippa."

Yet another poisonous leaf on the family tree of Herod the Great, I thought to myself, not yet knowing that I would have further encounters with the man.

"Agrippa," he continued, spitting forth the name as if it were toxic, "sold us into slavery. I believe my wife and many of the others returned to Hispania to work the mines or homes of their Roman overseers. I was purchased by Gaius and came with him and his wife here when he became prefect."

"That is terrible, my friend," I responded. "I am so sorry for the years you have lost with your family. I cannot take away all you have suffered, but I will do all I can to make things better."

"Perhaps it is not too much to wish I could be set free and have a chance to reunite with my family before passing from this earth."

"It is NOT too much to ask! I do ask for your patience, though. If I grant your freedom, it will raise alarms and prematurely end my work. However, I do have someone in mind who may be able to help."

∞

James was referred to as James the Great among the disciples, as there was another among them also named James. James the Great was the older of the two named James. Through quite a large personality, he was not nearly as physically imposing as his brother John, who had threatened me in my first meeting with the disciples.

James and I met in private when we returned to Jerusalem for the Holy Days in September. I sent Cornelius on a clandestine mission to bring him to me. Despite our earlier meeting just after the death of Jesus, James was happy to have been escorted from his room to the Herodian Palace by an armed centurion.

They came through the back entrance in the dead of night. Candlelight flickered in his eyes, along with what seemed like occasional flames of hate, as he sat across from me. He clearly struggled to balance his human nature and God nature as he listened to the man who allowed the death of his Rabbi, his Messiah, his cousin, his friend. I understood.

James, though not as large as his brother, was still a force to be reckoned with, and his hostility palpable. Accepting his reaction to me was part of accepting responsibility. I had faith, well, at least hope, that love would dispel hatred and keep James from attacking me.

As I told the story of Alucio, James listened and recalled his own interactions with Judas the Galilean. He had, of course, known of and interacted with Judas and his followers when he was younger. Judas had two sons about the same age as James and his brother John. They had carried on their father's message. They were all from the same region, and the message of revolution was a popular one to the Jewish people. All the disciples had interactions with Judas the Galilean and his sons. The odd exception being another Judas, Judas Iscariot, who was now dead because he could not accept that Jesus had another way to build the Kingdom without warfare.

I had Claudia bring in Alucio. "James, please meet my beautiful wife, Claudia, and our friend Alucio. Claudia will help you come and go in the house to meet. I will find a way to arrange 'escape' after the winter, and you can sail from Caesarea to Hispania under aliases in the spring. That will give you time to plan and learn some of the ancient Iberian and Celtic languages. Latin is now the main language of Hispania, but some natives still speak Iberian or at least a version of Iberian mixed with Celtic that emerged over centuries of trade. This will allow you to converse en route with little chance of being understood even if overheard. It will also give you a way to minister to the Jews of Hispania while remaining undetected by Roman leaders.

This will be challenging and dangerous. However, it will plant the seed of Christ's message firmly in the soil of Hispania and will re-plant Alucio where he belongs.

∞

Over the next several months, I watched at a distance as Alucio learned more of Jesus, and James learned more of Hispania. I marveled at watching God's plan unfolding in front of me. It was as if God was winking at me and saying, "See my miracles."

I remembered back to an early discussion with Claudia where I had scoffed at her belief in such things as miracles. Now I laughed out loud at the recollection. The soldiers guarding the door gave me a sideways glance, perhaps questioning my sanity, but I was not there to win their approval. Like Alucio, I too was starting to enjoy my newfound freedom.

That freedom, though, came at a price. In order to enjoy my freedom, I had to maintain a lifestyle in which I no longer believed. I had to keep good relations with Tiberius even though I no longer felt any allegiance, alliance, or connection. I even had to play nice with Caiaphas and the rest of the Temple leadership.

In some ways, this was easier. They no longer made my blood boil. I saw them as weak, misled, and symptomatic of human sinfulness. Their behavior was evil, but their hearts were sick. As Jesus Himself had said, "They know not what they do." These words changed the way I perceived them and dealt with them. Frankly, they changed the way I dealt with everyone. That change of perspective made me much more patient and tolerant, not of the terrible things that people do, but of the people who do terrible things.

In other ways, though, dealing with the Jewish leadership was even more treacherous and fraught with risk. They were like cornered animals, and nothing is more dangerous. They would do anything to keep their power, and the followers of Jesus were growing in popularity and influence.

While the other disciples were solidifying and expanding their ministry in and around Jerusalem, James was residing in Caesarea, on the grounds of the Palace. During the day, he helped to maintain the buildings and grounds. At night, he would meet with Alucio.

I had two highly significant meetings during these months, the first of which was with my old friend Herod Antipas.

∞

One day, Antipas came unannounced to meet with me about a variety of issues. After talking aqueducts, taxation, legal issues and other standard matters of governance, he spoke about the growing influence of the followers of Jesus. He did not know how Rome would want them to be dealt with. Antipas was not, by any means, a religious fanatic or theologian. He was very content to accept my edict that they should be left in peace. They were not a threat to Rome and had not broken any Roman law. He added, though, "That will not satisfy the Temple priests."

I replied with our time's equivalent of "screw them." "They are to be left to their own business as are the rest of the Jews. Their religion is for them to handle. Rome will only deal with Roman matters."

As Antipas was preparing to leave, one of his men pointed at a man on the grounds and whispered in his ear. Antipas turned to look and then looked at me. "Is the man tending your gardens one of the followers of Jesus? He looks very much like one of the fishermen, one of the twelve core followers of Jesus."

Knowing that word would spread to the Sanhedrin and then to Rome, I could not admit the identity of James. This could result in tragedy for all involved. "He is one of my staff and has been in my service for some time. Many people look alike."

My answer, while misleading, was not technically a lie, and it satisfied Herod Antipas. I prayed that would be adequate. I had never before felt an internal admonition about telling a lie, except now that I really needed to lie. God gave me direction and helped me to live by His commandments while putting me in a position where doing so seemed utterly impossible. That would get even worse. Those commandments - not to lie, steal, or murder, etc. – were damn near impossible to live by when surrounded by the wickedness of the world. It is even more impossible when your mission is to fight against that wickedness. It was and would always be like fighting with one hand tied behind my back.

Later that day, I pulled James aside. Making sure he knew what I had said, we agreed that we would shave his beard, lighten his hair, keep a lower profile, and start using a different name. Yes – now even I was participating in the name-changing game.

XXXI

Hail Britannia

The most difficult part of my plan to send James and Alucio to Hispania was transportation. I exercised significant control over the Roman fleet, and adding passengers was not a great issue...unless those passengers were identified as escaped slaves and religious dissidents. They would be in great danger, of course, but so would I and my mission.

One evening, when James and Alucio were to meet, James brought me a welcome visitor with a new plan. Seeing his priestly frock before I could make out his face, my heart skipped a few beats; however, when I recognized Joseph of Arimathea, I opened my arms and embraced him. The great uncle of Jesus sat with Claudia and me to tell us a story.

"I am a priest," said Joseph, "and a member of the Sanhedrin, that much you know. What you may not know is that I have been a successful merchant for many years. My business has been importing and exporting metals all over the world. I have a small fleet of ships that sail to and from Caesaria. I have shipped silver from Hispania's rich silver mines and gold from Macedonia. However, most of my career has been spent shipping tin, while not a precious metal, an essential one. Most of the tin used throughout the empire is mined in the Cornwall region of Britannia."

"Britannia," I exclaimed, "the land of the blue painted cannibals?"

"Ah, that is what everyone thinks. Probably because that is what they want Romans to think. They fought off invasion by Julius Caesar and have no interest in having to do so again. I love those 'heathens' and so did my nephew."

"Wait," said Claudia. "Are you saying Jesus knew the people of Britannia?"

"Yes, my dear," Joseph replied with a sparkle in his eye. "While Jesus was a builder and carpenter by trade, before accepting His divine role, He sailed with me on some of these voyages."

Claudia and I were stunned. "Jesus and the blue painted heathens", I mumbled, shaking my head.

"Seriously, Pilate, they are not heathens and are rarely painted blue. They are, in fact, a very learned people with a beautiful culture...and you don't know the half of it."

"Okay, spill it," said Claudia, eager to know more about the early life of Jesus. "What else should we know?"

Joseph obliged. "Jesus also spent more than a year in India. Shortly after the death of His adopted father. His father, Mary's husband Joseph, died shortly after Jesus turned thirteen. They had gone to Jerusalem for Passover and Jesus 'got lost' only to be found days later meeting with the priests in the temple.

"Upon returning to Nazareth, Joseph became ill. His last days were spent talking to his son, each helping the other on the next steps of their journey. Jesus, even at thirteen years, had knowledge and wisdom that comforted his father through his time of transition. He recited the traditional prayers with him:

'May it be Your will to heal me completely. And if I die, may my passing be an atonement for all the sins that I have committed, and grant me my portion in Gan Eden, and allow me to merit the World to Come, which has been reserved for the righteous. May it be Your will that my death be an atonement for all my sins.'

"Jesus knew how to prepare His father for his time of transition. Joseph, on the other hand, knew the transition that Jesus was facing, moving from childhood to adulthood was hard, doing so as the son of God would be even more so. He knew that I would be there to help Mary, but he worried that the pressure on Jesus to become the 'man of the house' would occupy his time when he needed to prepare for his birthright. A thirteen-year-old boy would be expected to carry the responsibility of the breadwinner. He would take a wife and assume all the other typical adult roles. Jesus was wise beyond His years, but this version of adulthood was not His path.

"After the funeral, I stayed in Nazareth and worked out the details of a long Journey for Jesus. I had a wealthy friend in the pepper trade who sailed out of the Arabian Gulf and across the sea to Malabar. At the right time of year, when the seas allow a direct rather than circuitous route, this journey takes only forty days. I arranged for Jesus to accompany my friend. There he could learn of Indian culture and get a better understanding of the people.

"As it turns out, He not only learned, He also taught, staying there for a full year while my friend returned to Judea and then made another trip the following year. My friend loved to tell me about finding Jesus teaching at the Temple and asking why they worshipped the sun instead of worshipping the One who created the sun and the entire universe. He questioned their use of idols and whether stones could answer their prayers. Many of the people loved Him and accepted His teachings. The temple priests not as much so. He barely made it out of India."

"So," I said, "our mission is not just to spread the message of Jesus to remote 'heathen' regions. We are actually bringing the teaching of Jesus back to places He has already been?

"Yes", said Joseph, "Places where He already knows and loves the people, people that He respects and cultures He understands and embraces."

Joseph sat quietly as we absorbed this new truth. It was strange to think that Jesus would have already met some of the people of Hispania or Britannia. It was even more strange to think of him living and teaching among the Indians. If these people already knew of Jesus, we were sending disciples, not to introduce Him for the first time, but to tell the rest of the story!

Jesus was a Jew by birth. He was a "son of David". His mother was a descendant of both David and Aaron. No one had a more Jewish pedigree. However, He had surprisingly diverse cultural connections. He had been uniquely prepared for the message his Father was conveying to His people – ALL of His people.

"I am preparing to take one last voyage," said Joseph. "You have managed to keep the peace here in Judea much better than I thought possible. However, this is not a peace that can last. Your time here will come to an end, and your ability to influence Judea directly will end with it.

"I am a very wealthy man. I can live anywhere; I plan on doing so in Britannia. I want to live out my remaining years among the people that I have grown to love in my travels. I could certainly use two new deck hands for my trip," he said, alluding to Alucio and James.

"That is amazing," I said. "Thank you very much. That will return Alucio to his family and homeland and give James a chance to spread the message of Jesus to Hispania. I wonder if you could do me one more favor. Could you connect me with your friend in the pepper trade? I think we know another potential passenger for his ship."

He told me how to find his friend who would be in Jerusalem for Passover. He promised to find a way to get word to him and prepare him for our meeting. He also suggested that I speak with Nicodemus, a close friend of his and a follower of Jesus. "Not all in the Sanhedrin are satisfied with the Temple leadership. Some recognize its exploitation and are trying to reform from within."

∞

Fall grew to winter and winter to spring. Claudia and I prepared for our trip to Jerusalem for Passover. This was the chosen time for Alucio to make his escape. We would not have reason to suspect he was gone until after our trip, which would give him and James a chance to board the ship with Joseph and his crew and slip away to Hispania unnoticed.

Since that first meeting with Joseph of Arimathea, a second group of travelers had emerged. Claudia had met with them and Joseph covertly. She reported back to me that there would be an additional five joining the voyage. Joseph knew the ports for trade and had one in mind where he knew people and felt this group would find safe harbor. Cornelius and I worked behind the scenes to provide further protection.

The ship would not set sail for another month, waiting for the Mediterranean to become more hospitable for transport. Hopefully, though, by the time we returned from Jerusalem, Alucio and James would be gone and safe aboard a cruise to Hispania.

The night before our Passover trip, Alucio came to me and Claudia. Tears ran down his face as he thanked us for helping him. "Even if I do not make it, I will die happy because you have given me the blessing of hope. I have hope to see my wife and my child, and I have faith that I will, whether in this life or the next! God bless you."

With that, Alucio slipped out of our room, out of our lives, but never out of our hearts. We would learn later that he did reunite with his wife and daughter. Along with James, they established a church on the coast of Hispania. I would never see Alucio again, but maybe one day I would meet Alicia, his daughter. But that is a story for later.

I would also never again see James the Great alive. Twelve years after planting the congregation in Hispania, James returned to Jerusalem. He knew this was dangerous. Word of his work had reached the new "King" of Judea, Herod Agrippa, grandson of Herod the Great and personal friend of the emperor at the time. Agrippa, the very man who had sold Alucio and his wife into slavery, took personal um-

brage at James working with the people of Hispania. He also wanted
to ingratiate himself with the Temple leadership, who saw ministering
to gentiles as sacrilege...and a threat. We will revisit that story later as
well.

While my path did not directly intersect that of James or Alucio
again, I had work left to do with Joseph...now not of Arimathea but of
Britannia.

XXXII

Nick at Night

Once again, Claudia and I found ourselves in Jerusalem for Passover, just our second such trip since Jesus died, the world turned black, and I found myself awakening in a tomb. You would think that this place would trigger trauma responses – anxiety, agitation, hypervigilance, and detachment. I had experienced these feelings here before, even prior to the death of Jesus. I had often had flashbacks of my experiences while serving in the Legion. However, since the resurrection, these responses no longer took hold of me. Now, anxiety gave way to calm as a raging sea, after a storm, turns tranquil. I was fully awake and alive, aware of everything around me but without fear. Detachment gave way to connection: connection to my true self, connection to others, and connection to God.

This change, my complete contentedness and joy, came from being able to see the "big picture", my place in God's universe, and the ability to "wash my hands" of control of things beyond myself. I still understood that I had responsibilities... no, I took even more responsibility for myself and for using my God given gifts to achieve my purpose. I just knew that the ultimate results were not in my control. There is something very freeing about clean hands.

Caiaphas and his "brood of vipers" still slithered through the city streets, making their nest in the temporarily repaired temple. However, their power among the people was clearly diminished. The Jewish people still gathered from around the world and still honored God at the temple in the way they had been taught, the way that made them feel cleansed and healed from their sins, at least temporarily. There was a subtle shift, though, and it seemed that more and more people were coming to understand that the priests were just people with positions of power rather than God's appointees. This, of course, drove the Sanhedrin crazy.

James, the half-brother of Jesus, had taken a leadership role in the movement inspired by Jesus. He had not followed Jesus during His time on earth but had come to realize, shortly after the crucifixion, that his brother was not the troublemaker he had considered him to be. He had his own encounter with the risen Jesus after the crucifixion and, like me, knew that he had a responsibility to continue with his brother's mission.

Peter introduced me to James the Just, as he was called, and found him to be very driven, accepting, and true to his moniker. He was perfectly placed to gain the trust of his Jewish neighbors and to lead them to understand Jesus as the Messiah of the Jews. He struggled, however, to balance his Jewish upbringing and ingrained admiration for the priests with what they had done and their obvious corruption. He was early in his ministry and would come to embrace the inclusivity for which Jesus died, but at this stage, he still believed his people, the Jewish people, were the "good sons" -the ones who had always remained true to God. He had difficulty accepting the equality of the Gentile prodigal sons.

I told James and Peter that, according to Joseph, there were temple priests and leaders pushing for change. They confirmed that some of the priests had been trying to change the system from within but were finding that wealth and power were change-resistant.

I mentioned that I had been given the name of Nicodemus as someone I should know. James told me that he knew of Nicodemus and had met him on several occasions, but that the need for discretion limited their opportunity to work together. "If Caiaphas knew that Nicodemus was a follower of Jesus, he would end his priesthood – one way or the other."

"Perhaps you can help me arrange a meeting with him," I suggested. Then I told James the Just and Peter of my plan for helping Thomas reach India.

∞

With the assistance of James, I was able to arrange a meeting with Nicodemus. He would not come to the palace and would not entertain me in his home. We had to meet under cover of darkness. Once again, Cornelius and I donned our cloaks and made our way through the city streets at night to avoid detection. It is interesting that, to follow the One who said "I am the way, the truth, and the light," I was often having to deceptively make my way through the darkness.

We walked out of the city gates and to the Mount of Olives, where Nicodemus had asked that we meet. We retraced the steps we had taken when Cornelius and I had first encountered the disciples after the death of Jesus and found Nicodemus in the same grove of olive trees. After brief introductions, he and his companion, a younger priest, escorted us further into the grove and where they lit an oil lamp around which the four of us sat.

"This is where I first met and spoke with Jesus," said Nicodemus. "My life changed after that first meeting. I could see that Jesus was more than a rabbi or even a prophet. His words challenged me, but I could not yet accept His call to follow Him.

"However, He lit a flame within me," he said, motioning toward the oil lamp. "I want to spread the light that now shines within me, but find myself caught in circumstances that require me to hide its glow; to make sure that I am not seen, even as we gather here to talk about Him. I think you may be the only person who can truly understand that."

"I most certainly do. I have been given such a blessing, allowing me a purpose within God's plan. Carrying out this purpose within the ranks of the Roman government and a culture that literally considers Caesar to be a god is daunting and perilous. I see how that would be the same for you in the Sanhedrin. The gates of the kingdoms of men are jealously guarded against the power of God.

"My way of conducting this mission is through cloak and dagger, hiding in the shadows while arranging for the light to spread. I think this may be your calling as well. We cannot directly force change, but we can work behind the scenes to set the stage for change.

"I am a man of God," grumbled Nicodemus. "Such clandestine behavior does not align well with my philosophy and values."

"Yet here we are conducting a secret meeting in the dark," said Cornelius, an audible smirk in his voice.

"More importantly, Jesus met with you in this same garden also under the cover of darkness," I added. "Perhaps He was telling you something. Your name literally means 'victory of the people,' and victory, in this case, requires stealth."

Nicodemus nodded his head almost imperceptibly as he looked at the oil lamp between us. The light flickered in his eyes as he whispered, "Perhaps so..."

After helping Nicodemus see the light in regard to keeping others in the dark, we went on to arrange a clandestine channel of communication. This system would allow Nicodemus to exchange coded messages with James the Just about pertinent issues in the Sanhedrin. Messages from the budding church in Jerusalem could likewise reach receptive rabbis within the Sanhedrin.

The conduit would be Lathraíos, the young priest and apprentice of Nicodemus, also present at our meeting that evening. Like Nicodemus, Lathraíos was a follower of Jesus and was perfectly placed for this role. Being descended from the line of Levi made him eligible for the priesthood, but having lived in a Hellenistic area, gave him great command of the Greek language along with Latin and Aramaic. He even knew Iberian as he had spent time in Hispania as a child. It was as if he were destined for this job.

XXXIII

"Sold into Slavery by the Lord"

Cornelius and I went to meet with Thomas, who remained skeptical: "This mission still seems crazy to me, but we drew lots among us to divide regions for our ministries. You told me that Jesus was sending me to India, and I did not believe you. I had my own encounter with Jesus where He Himself told me, still I argued. However, when I drew the lot for India, I decided I had to stop complaining. The universe conspired against me!"

Despite his "doubting" nature, Thomas exuded true faith, willingness to doubt, and still do what one is called to do. Faith is not the opposite of doubt, as courage is not the opposite of fear. Courage cannot exist without fear. Faith cannot exist without doubt.

There was a book called the "Acts of Thomas", one of the earliest written Christian works. It was written about the exploits of Thomas in India. It was not included in the Bible as it was written by others well after his death and was more of a semi-biographical account than a gospel.

Like many biographies, *The Acts of Thomas* contained hyperbole and seemed to stretch the truth to make a point or be more entertaining. Some in your time might consider it to be "fan fiction." However, it also contained many kernels of truth, including that "The lord sold Thomas into slavery." Through the centuries, people have found that line to be beyond belief and against the nature of Christ. And now for the rest of the story.

∞

After our time with Nicodemus, Cornelius and I met with Abbanes, the spice trader that Joseph of Arimathea recommended we see. True to his promise, Joseph had sent word to him as well. He was pleased to have an introduction to the Roman Prefect of Judea. "Dominus (Lord)! I am happy to meet you. Joseph had very kind words about you, and it is not often that I get to personally meet someone of your position."

"Thank you. Joseph also spoke highly of you and assured me that you would take good care of my servant and maintain discretion."

"Of course, Dominus, it will be my pleasure."

Abbanes had a ship leaving the following month out of the port in Leuce Come on the Red Sea. We paid him for his service and arranged for Thomas to meet him. The cover Thomas would assume on this journey was that of a slave, having been conscribed to cultivate spices in India.

After being "sold into slavery by his lord" (me, not Jesus), Thomas would go on to spread Christianity throughout India, and the churches that he planted thrived for centuries. A large Christian population still exists in India, thanks, no doubt, to Thomas. Thomas himself lived many years in India, but would not die naturally. As would be the case for many others, he died for his faith, killed with spears by guards of King Misdaeus at St. Thomas Mount in Chennai. He was buried in Mylapore.

XXXIV

‿❧

I Have a Dream

My remaining time in Judea would be short, yet there was much to do. While I was never embraced as one of the disciples, it seemed fate would have me as an outsider among Jews and Romans. I met with them on multiple occasions and would continue to work with them even after leaving Judea. Such meetings were, of course, always shrouded in secrecy. My relationship with them grew and changed from those first contentious meetings.

I had to overcome my role in the crucifixion, of course, but I also had to overcome the natural mistrust and bias against Romans in general and Roman rulers in particular. As such, I was not only a gentile but the most unclean possible example of a gentile. I was the embodiment of everything the Jewish people and the Jewish faith stood against. I was the face of what most assumed their Messiah was coming to extinguish.

∞

One night, shortly after meeting with Nicodemus, I dreamt again of Jesus. This time we met in a stable where we saddled horses, readying ourselves for a ride. I questioned where we were going, and Jesus replied, "We are going to survey our land."

We left the stable, and I found myself riding across the fields of my home in Abruzzo. I had flashbacks to my youth, riding this land with my father, checking the livestock, monitoring the workers. On this ride, we encountered a thriving land and much livestock, but there were no slaves.

We rode further, passing out of the family pastures and into the town of Cocullo where we saw people of all backgrounds living together in the shadow of the temple. As we approached the temple, I saw that it no longer had statues of Angitia or snake icons. Instead, there was a cross, the symbol of torture and death, yet it was placed in a position of veneration. Jesus said, "My death now provides hope, a new way of living, a new way of relating to others, a new way of relating to my Father. This temple from your childhood is now a church, a synagogue, where people worship God, the Father and Creator of the universe, and where God can commune with them because their sinfulness is forgiven. All sin was cleansed through my sacrifice, once and for all. Now, nothing stands between them and the God that loves them."

As we continued to ride, I felt a shift in the air around me, almost as if it were electrified. Abruptly, our surroundings changed, and we found ourselves facing another cross at another church. We rode past people in dusty streets who seemed to sense our presence but could not see us. The people in the streets were of all races and ethnicities, yet they interacted as if they were unified.

I recognized it as Jerusalem, but the church was not Herod's temple - that now lay in ruins. This church was small, modest, and almost humble. Jesus said, "I tore down the temple and rebuilt it in three days. The moment my body died, the old temple was destroyed. When I was resurrected, a new temple was established. This temple is one that originates with God, is carried in the soul of each of my children, and communicates through my Holy Spirit. It is a temple connected directly to God; through God, it is connected to all of creation, echoing throughout the universe."

Motioning toward the ruins of the Temple, He said, "People will continue to try to set up man-made temples, to use them for their own glory rather than the glory of God, and to advance their own agenda rather than for the Kingdom of God. "Remember that my church is wherever two or more are gathered in faith; it is not a building or even a formal organization." Motioning to the cross on the roof of the small church, He said, "There is nothing wrong with buildings or with people gathering together in congregations, but such buildings are not temples; they are not required to find God. Nor do they seclude God from His people, to be visited on special occasions. They are places where the faithful can gather. The rabbi of a church, whether called priest, pastor, reverend, or father, is not a conduit between God and His people. He or she is simply a person whom people decide has wisdom worthy of hearing, one who might help them in their walk. In many ways, you are now a rabbi."

He continued, "Be wary, though, for in the future, there will be attempts to control others by manipulating and altering my message:

"There will be people selected as pope, the leader of the worldwide church, who are corrupt and serve only their own wealthy and powerful families.

"There will be those who brand others as heretics and use their religious position to try to purge the world of those with whom they disagree.

"There will be people who use my name as an excuse to go on 'missions' to convert, by any means necessary, non-believers to their bastardized version of my message.

"There will be people who build mega churches that operate as big business rather than conduits of divinity.

"There will be power struggles within churches for who is to be in control. If it is not me running the church, then it is not of God at all.

"There will be debates over who is worthy to attend my church. None among you is qualified to make such a judgment.

"There will be some who categorize and rank sins and those who commit them. All are sinful, and only God can judge the severity of sin. I came so that all sin is forgiven.

"There will be those who say my salvation only applies to those who behave in this way or that – my salvation was freely given on a cross, once and for ALL.

"Situations such as these confuse my children, cause doubt, and drive my people away from me. That is not my 'church.' Yes, there will be charlatans, and the church, a human creation, will sometimes not reflect my glory. The good news, though, is that those who embrace the temple within and listen to God's whispers on the wind will know all of these are false prophets. They will walk with me and walk away from the Pharisees and Sadducees of their times. They will not tithe to line pockets but to spread my hope and to love those in need. If you are not adequately nurturing and growing the temple within, you are at risk of falling prey to modern temple priests.

"I need you to tell the others of this journey and what you saw. My message is not to one people, my message is to my people...all of my people. The work of my church is universal. You will not meet a person who is not one of my children. You cannot find a creature that is not my creation. Nothing is unholy or dirty unless made so by the sin of man. Sin is that which separates people from God, and nothing I created can separate you from me."

With that, we rode back to the stable. We tended to the horses, brushing them, providing them with water and food; we served them as they had served us on our long journey. The sun was setting as we walked back out into the fields of Abruzzo. I felt Jesus put His hand on my shoulder, but when I turned to look at Him, He was no longer there.

∞

The next morning, I told Claudia of my dream. Together, we came up with a plan to meet with the disciples. We did so under the nose of Herod Antipas. Claudia had befriended Joanna, a supporter of Jesus and wife of Chuza, the steward of Antipas. Herod was in residence in Caesarea at the time. Claudia and Joanna arranged a "girls' night", inviting the woman named Mary, whom we met along with the other disciples upon our initial introduction. Little did I know that her plan would take us right back to that same location.

∞

In Jerusalem for the Passover, Cornelius and I snuck out and met with the others in the same upper room in which we had met the first time. As it turned out, it was owned by Joanna and would grow to become the seat of the new faith during its formative years. If you consider the enmity Herod Antipas and his father had toward Jesus, literally from birth, there is great symbolism in their role in the birth of the Church.

There were now twelve of them again as they had selected someone named Matthias to replace the traitorous Judas. However, there were many more present, and all, including as many women as men, seemed to have an equal and valued voice. Joanna, Claudia, Mary Magdalene, Martha and Mary (sisters of Lazarus), and many other women were just as integral in the formation of the new church as the men. However, the seed had to grow in a time and place that was not hospitable to direct feminine authority. It was being planted, at least in part, to increase tolerance of others and recognition of the innate equality of all people. I found that interesting, given what I had come to say.

I recounted my dream and said, "We are all one people, all created by God and chosen by God. The temple of God is within all of us, Jew or Gentile, men or women, young or old…yes, even including Romans and Samaritans. It is our duty to nurture the flame of divinity, the holy temple, within each of God's people. We must do this without bias, preference, or judgement."

This caused dissension, division, and debate for several long minutes. I can assure you that it was not comfortable to be a Roman in that room. Then Simon, I mean Peter, (I can never keep that straight!) stood up and said, "I too had a dream." He recounted a dream, not surprisingly with a fishing theme, about hoisting nets full of every known animal. He threw them back as unclean, but when he drew up his nets again, they were once again full of the same menagerie. Then

God admonished him, saying that nothing He had created was unclean.

"It is time to start spreading our nets," Peter declared.

Cornelius spoke up, "I am a Roman Centurian, a witness to Christ's crucifixion and resurrection. My wife and her family are Jewish, and all believe in the resurrection of their Messiah, Jesus of Nazareth. None of us has been baptized. Are we not holy enough?"

Peter replied, "You are among God's beloved children and are the future upon which His church will grow."

Matthew said, "There is yet much debate to be had on how to bring such disparate peoples together. What about dietary differences? What about circumcision? I assume we can all agree on the ten commandments, but what about all the cleanliness laws, the moral laws, the social laws?"

I chimed in with "Haven't you people ever heard what Jesus said? 'Love God with all your soul and your neighbor as yourself. There is no commandment greater.' I would suggest that we make these two the standard. As for diet, circumcision, purity, and other laws, perhaps we let people make their own choices. They will know if something is sinful if it takes them further from God. He has established His temple in the souls of people for a reason. We can tell them our opinions, but we are not to sit in judgement. I for one have had more than my share of that!"

That last comment elicited some awkward laughs around the room from people who understood and appreciated dark humor. Despite my pleas and well-reasoned arguments, as you will see, these issues remained contentious.

Peter made a major leap forward, though, when he said, "Matthew and I will go to Palace Pilatus. I hear there are people there in need of a bath." The baptism humor helped to ease the tension, but I could tell there were still many in the room for whom this level of acceptance was a step too far. Change is never easy, and this degree of change was unprecedented; to this day, there has been no larger shift in society.

To this day, people still struggle with these issues, questioning who is worthy, who belongs in the church, and who is part of the kingdom. To me, these are questions only to be asked while looking in a mirror.

Later that night, Cornelius, Abigail, Claudia, and I, along with every other member of our household, were baptized.

XXXV

Short Timer

My time in Judea was coming to an end. I knew that was the case, though I did not know how it would end. Four years after the death of Jesus, his church in Jerusalem continued to grow and become more accepted, though still quite despised by most of the Jewish priests. However, I felt that I had accomplished my mission in Judea. It was time to take the show on the road.

One afternoon, as Cornelius and I patrolled Jerusalem on horseback, we heard shouts coming from outside the city gates. We quickly made our way through a throng of people as they scurried toward whatever horrifying reality show lay ahead. Once outside the city gates, we saw a man surrounded by priests from the Sanhedrin. They were shouting and holding stones. The man in the center of the melee shouted, "The heavens have opened! Look there is Jesus standing at the right hand of God."

With that, I knew that the end of days had reached this man. I spurred my horse toward the scene in a vain attempt to change the man's destiny. As Cornelius and I galloped, the priests pummeled. By the time I was on the scene, Stephen had given up the ghost. He lay on the rocky soil, blood and grey matter seeping from his open skull. Yet he smiled. I leaned over and whispered a prayer for him.

I looked at the priests with anger and disdain. "What is the meaning of this? You know you are forbidden from carrying out executions."

An agitator who seemed to be leading the vigilante clerics said, "My name is Saul, and I am a Pharisee. How dare you, a Roman, lecture me on Jewish law! The law allows us to stone a blasphemer in the Temple. He was in the temple uttering blasphemous words against God's anointed priests and the temple leadership. This stoning started there and ended here. We were within our rights!"

"Stoning, whether it results in death or not, must end at the walls of the temple. You men of God behave like beasts from Hell. This will not be tolerated." With that, I turned my horse, galloping to the Temple to do something I had longed to do for years, one of my last official acts in Judea, the removal of Caiaphas as High Priest.

∞

Just days after the stoning of Stephen, I found myself in another sticky situation, this one involving a Samaritan leading an insurgent group and claiming to be the reincarnation of Moses. From my perspective, this man had clearly broken many Roman laws. Worse, he was leading people astray, leading them to believe that the path to reconciliation with God and establishing His Kingdom was through violence and warfare.

Drawing upon my own wisdom, as well as my great understanding both of Jesus and Caesar, I made the choices I thought best given the situation. I took a small army of legionaries to meet the rebel leader and his followers at Mount Gerizim in Samaria. They were in the process of arming themselves and were not compliant with orders. In my mind, I had no choice; I ordered my men to attack and put down the rebellion. They did as commanded, resulting in many injuries and the brutal execution of the rebel leader and several of his men.

Bodies lay on the ground, their leaders looking over them while dying on crosses. While I had not personally carried out the carnage, I justified it as the proper action from both my position as prefect and as a follower of Jesus. I was wrong on both counts!

As I lead my troops back to Caesaria, I struggled trying to put aside feelings of guilt and shame, knowing that I had not acted in accordance with my values, with the part of God that existed within my soul. It just felt wrong, and I could not put the images out of my head. I had been at war before. I had executed men in the past. None of this was new to me or, at least, the old version of me.

When I got home, I immediately went to Claudia. I cried as I told her of my experience, flashing back to both the crucifixion of Jesus and my time in Jerusalem as an officer watching the massacre of the Essenes. I thought my new direction, my new mission, and my new faith would keep me from such pain and guilt.

Claudia comforted me but did not coddle me. "I love you with all my heart. You are a good man, but you are human. You make mistakes, and this is one of them, a big one. Perhaps this man was a corrupting influence who was putting his followers in jeopardy. Perhaps the world is better off without this man. However, that was not your call to make. You are here to make the world ready for Jesus, not to act as the judge and executioner of His people."

I fell asleep with a heavy heart and dreamed. Like Claudia, Jesus comforted me without coddling me. He put his arm around my shoulder, and I recoiled, loath to touch Him when I felt so unclean. We spoke as we walked through a beautiful field of what seemed to be infinite white crosses. We took care to walk on the paths between the rows of crosses, and I knew we were walking among the dead.

"The commandment says thou shalt not kill," He said.

I stood in shamed silence for a long moment, looking at the ground, unable to face Jesus.

He broke the silence and said, "The word I specifically gave Moses was 'ratzah', the version of the word 'kill' associated with murder. The commandment was really 'thou shalt not murder.' Murder is unjustified killing. Execution of a person so filled with wickedness that they will undoubtedly commit further evil acts is not murder. It is showing love for others by protecting them. In some cases, it is also protecting the offender from further staining their own soul."

"So, you mean, I was justified in carrying out the executions in Samaria?"

"Uh...no," said Jesus. "You had no knowledge of their hearts. You did not try them or hear their defense. Nor were you acting in self-defense. These men were not a direct danger to you. You allowed your men to act in anger and impulsivity. Sin is not just an act; it is the state of the heart in which the act was taken. I told my followers that if someone had even thought of adultery, they were an adulterer, if they even thought of murder, they were a murderer."

"So, you are saying that they were good men and did not deserve execution."

"Uh...no. I am saying that you will be judged by your own actions and the state of your heart, and they will be judged by theirs. Whether they were 'good' or 'bad' is irrelevant. Your actions did not come from love but from anger, from hatred, and from fear."

"How do I make it right?"

"You do not. I do. Your sinful behavior brought you feelings of guilt and shame. Those feelings separated you from God. Remember how you recoiled at my touch a moment ago. God does not want you to retreat from Him. He wants you to grow closer. However, growing closer to God sometimes involves pain. It requires that you chisel away parts of yourself until what remains is what God intends for you. I came to the world to give you grace so that you can reconcile with your creator."

He continued, "I forgive you, and through me you are forgiven. You must forgive yourself and learn from this experience. From this point forward, you may be involved in killing, though not murder. You will never again be required to personally cause death. You have had more than your share of blood on your hands. Your hands are now clean, and they will remain so."

"What about killing while at war?" I asked.

"It is in man's nature to have conflict. Most of these conflicts start from the same motivations as your own at Mount Gerizim – fear, anger, and hatred. Others are motivated by avarice or vanity. If one makes the choice to take part in war based on these motivations, then the blood they shed is on their hands. If they are conscripted into military service or otherwise have no choice but to fight, that is not murder. There are also battles fought against true forces of evil, fought to protect the world from these forces. You may encounter such a battle in your lifetime, and killing in such circumstances is not murder."

"How can a person know the difference and make good decisions when the world is full of deceit and manipulation?"

"First, approach every conflict as a pacifist, leaning on the general rule that causing harm to others is rarely, if ever, justified. Turning the other cheek is a sign of strength, not weakness. On the other hand, there is time to turn over the money changers' tables and directly fight against evil. That, too, is a sign of strength. Wisdom, which comes from God, gives you the discernment to know which approach is right. If the situation is one of the rare exceptions where fighting is the correct course, a righteous person will know it. They will feel it in their heart, my temple within."

"If only war were typically fought by the righteous," I muttered.

"Remember, you are only judged by your own actions. You cannot control what others choose to do. There will come a day when all wars cease, and the entire world is reconciled with God. However, just as a man must painfully chisel away his unrighteousness, so must the world. Pain and suffering are both symptoms of illness and signs of recovery."

We walked out of a long row of crosses and to a gate in the fence. Jesus opened the gate, and we walked through. As He closed the gate behind us, Jesus said, "Oh, and one more thing...Tiberius will soon recall you to Rome."

Before I could get clarification, I woke up in a cold sweat. My body seemed to be fighting off my soul's infection. Facing Tiberius would likely end this battle.

XXXVI

Reassigned

Six weeks after my graveside come-to-Jesus chat, I had an unannounced visit from Lucius Vitellius, the Legate of Syria, my counterpart to the north. Word of my dismissal of Caiaphas and the execution of the Samaritan militants had reached Rome.

"Tiberius sanctioned neither of these actions," said Vitellius. "You will explain your actions to Tiberius in person and be reassigned. You will not be coming back to Judea." Vitellius presented a proclamation signed by Tiberius ordering me back to Rome and authorizing Vitellius to assume command of Judea. I had known this time would come and that there was no need to fight.

Vitellius had brought a cohort of his own men as well as several servants. Much to my relief, he said that he preferred to have his own household staff. If I were to return to Rome, I would like to take my household with me. They could take up residence in Abruzzo, regardless of whether I survived my interview with Tiberius.

Over the next two weeks, Claudia supervised the packing of our belongings and preparations for our journey while I worked with Vitellius and made sure he had everything he needed to govern.

Little did I know that my recall was the first step in a thirty-year downward spiral for Jerusalem and Judea as a whole. This spiral would end in the demolition of the Temple, the slaughter of more than a million Jews, and the disbursement of most of the remaining Jewish population to the rest of the empire, either as slaves or refugees. This is referred to as the diaspora, and resulted in Judeo-Christian values and beliefs spreading throughout the known world. Again, it was clear that while the atrocities to come were not from God, He was able to use the sinful actions of humans to achieve His plan.

Likewise, He was using me to help prepare the most distant reaches of the empire to embrace these slaves and refugees and form communities of faith. My actions in Rome would delay the fall of the Temple and allow the followers of Christ to spread the seeds of the new faith throughout the entire world. My re-assignment, it seems, was not only in the hands of Tiberius. That is the nature of our relationship with the universe and its God. Things are always happening behind the scenes, steering us toward our destiny.

∞

The night before we set out for Rome, I tossed and turned, unable to fall asleep. Claudia seemed to have no trouble falling asleep, but after I woke her for the third time, she asked me what was wrong.

Flabbergasted, I asked, "What is wrong?! I am about to face Tiberius. We both know how such an audience is likely to go, especially for someone who was groomed and picked by Sejanus. We have both heard the horror stories."

Claudia said, "None of us know what will happen. I am just as concerned as you, but I am not worried. I know this is not the end of your road. You have too much left to do, and I have faith that you will have the time to get it done. Besides, even if your earthly road ends, it continues elsewhere. You and I both know that." As always, Claudia put things in perspective, easing my mind and allowing me to sleep like a baby for the rest of the night.

The next morning, we set sail from the port of Caesaria. At the same time, Tiberius was leaving the isle of Capri, one of the very few times he would set foot on the mainland of Italia during the last decade of his life. He would be waiting for me at the port of Misenum

near Naples and Sperlonga, the site of his near death during the earthquake so many years ago.

∞

Arriving in Misenum, we disembarked and lodged in the city. Always escorted by soldiers, Claudia and I enjoyed the baths and a fine
meal. As I thought this may be our last supper, I savored every flavor.
Every color was brighter, every aroma more salient, and I felt every
emotion more deeply. Claudia was not any more beautiful than she always had been, but I was fully awake and aware of the precious gift
God had given when He selected her for me.

Part of me wishes that I could have felt as alive every day of my
sojourn on earth as I did that day, recognizing my mortality and embracing the blessings I had been given. However, I also recognize that,
while the spirit can exist permanently in such a state, the flesh cannot.
The human experience can only withstand fleeting moments of such
joyous intensity, and such moments can only exist in duality with the
recognition that they can never endure, at least not on earth.

Claudia and I retired to our rooms, where we made love and then
slept the peaceful sleep reserved for those content with whatever fate
God may have in store.

∞

Cornelius led the contingent of soldiers escorting me to my meeting with Tiberius the next morning. Thanks to the steadfast faith of
Claudia, which helped to restore my own, I was in good spirits, allowing me to uplift the mood of Cornelius. Being tasked with escorting
me to my meeting with Tiberius was like being charged with taking a
friend to the gas chamber. I assured him that I was okay with whatever happened and that I knew God was using my circumstance for a
greater purpose.

As we approached the Tiberian Palace, we saw two riders approaching us. To my great surprise, one was Cassius. After an elated
and enthusiastic hug, he said, "I will escort you the rest of the way.
There has been a change in plans. Tiberius passed away in the night.

You will be meeting with Caligula, I mean the new Emperor Gaius Caesar Germanicus," he said with an eye roll I hoped was only perceptible to those of us who knew and loved the angel-voiced giant.

I was in shock. I had long lost any amicable feelings I had toward Tiberius, but his death was still a jolt. Was it better or worse that I would be facing his nephew and heir apparent, the crazy and sadistic "little boots?" I had not seen Caligula since the murder of his father eighteen years before, and I had so many questions. I wondered if he would remember me. Had his time with Tiberius amplified his psychopathic tendencies? How could such a damaged person rule the empire?

Cassius instructed me on how to address the new emperor and otherwise advised me as we approached my appointment with the new leader of the world, who insisted on being called Emperor Gaius. He would forever be "Caligula" to me and to the rest of humanity for generations eternal as they recalled his short and depraved reign.

Climbing up the stairs and entering the palace, I prayed for strength and courage to face whatever the outcome of this meeting may be. I also wondered at the mysterious ways in which the universe and God as its director worked, taking Tiberius the night before this meeting and substituting Caligula, the child I suspected of having a hand in his own father's murder. Cassius, Cornelius, and I had chosen not to share our suspicions. I had washed my hands of them instead. What would have changed if we had shared our suspicions? Do we bear any responsibility for the rise of Caligula?

On the judgement seat, Caligula did not look to be a grieving nephew as much as a cat who swallowed a canary, perhaps the very canary meant to warn the rest of us of grave danger. On his right hand stood a tall, muscular, and surly looking officer who Caligula introduced as the new Prefect of the Praetorian guard, Marcus Arrecinus Clemens.

"Thank you for coming, Pilate. It is with regret that your duties in Judea have to come to an end. I will re-assign you after I have had time to assess the needs of the Empire and the state in which my uncle left it." He dismissively clapped his hands and turned toward Marcus as if to ask, "What is next?"

With that, I did my best Roman salute, turned on my heel, and walked out before the little psychopath changed his mind. While that dismissive clap was certainly anticlimactic, I had no need for climax – I had avoided being proverbially fornicated. My official reassignment never came. Instead, a week later, I received word that my service was no longer required.

XXXVII

Thespians

I was free to return home! My mother, ever the strong woman, had efficiently run the family business for the past several years, and income would not be an issue. Thanks to Maters's management and the large and talented household staff, the farm had thrived, my mother herself not so much. As I rode up to the house, I remembered the last time I did so, along with Cornelius, on our journey from Syria after the murder of Germanicus.

Once again, my mother watched me from the front steps. Once again, I could see her excitement upon recognizing me. This time, though, she did not run down the stairs or jump with joy. She was no longer able to do so. I broke ranks with the small caravan of carriages carrying Claudia, the other household members, and all our belongings. My mother could not run to me, but I could run to her.

Throwing my arms around my mom, I stopped short of lifting her off the ground, sensing that she was no longer up for such manhandling. At sixty-two, she was nearly twice the life expectancy of our time. Of course, you must consider that a great many children never even made it to their tenth birthday. One way or the other, there were not large numbers of people over sixty, and I was blessed to still have my mother.

When the carriages arrived, Claudia gave Mater a hug, and we introduced the rest of the entourage. Abigail and Hannah were with us temporarily until Cornelius could arrange suitable accommodation in Rome, as he was now re-assigned to the Praetorian Guard. Claudia and I relished our role as godparents, so we secretly hoped this might take some time.

Mother looked perplexed when I formally introduced the other household staff. To her, our friends and family were socially misplaced in this circumstance. They should be busying themselves unpacking the carriages or otherwise staying in the shadows. Honestly, until just a few years prior, I would have thought the same.

My mother would eventually come to appreciate and embrace a new way of interacting with others, but change is difficult. Fighting against outdated norms and long-standing injustice sometimes involves heated battle, but more often than not, it is accomplished through loving patience and consistent modeling.

∞

Cornelius came to stay with us for a few days after we had settled in. He wanted to spend time with his wife and daughter, but he also needed to convey news from Rome. His role in the Praetorian Guard and respected reputation as a Legion Officer placed him perfectly as a conduit of such news.

Caligula had started off in his reign by magnanimously dismissing all the investigations Tiberius had launched into allegations of treason against Roman senators. He ironically railed against his uncle's paranoia and vindictiveness when his own would prove to be so much worse.

Of course, Caligula's main reason for magnanimity was garnering goodwill. Likewise, he started distributing the Roman treasury to the people, buying their support, even throwing coins minted with his image and images of his life to the crowds gathered outside of his palace. The people who got hurt, whether from hurled coins or frenzied coin collectors, seemed placated by their newfound and short-lived riches.

Leaders ever since have recognized the value of bribing their citizens. In the first few months of his reign, Caligula thoroughly ingratiated himself with the people and the powerful of Rome. It would prove a valuable investment, allowing him to get away with all forms of treachery and vice.

"Surely, the people see through this mask of sanity and decency," I said.

Cornelius shook his head, "It seems that people only see what they want to see. Behind closed doors, he is showing his true colors. He cannot delay gratification – he says and does anything he wants without filter. His sexual appetites are voracious and debased. His penis is the needle on his moral compass."

We both laughed at that. Dark humor often makes coping with true evil easier. We agreed to continue to watch the situation and pray that Caligula could change or would continue to keep his true nature behind closed doors.

In many ways, I felt bad for Little Boots. He was the product of a bloodline full of hate, greed, self-absorption, and violence; he had genetic predispositions to overcome. His playground as a child was littered with blood puddles and body parts, the mementos of dead and dying soldiers on the battlegrounds of Germanica. His mother had been tortured, blinded, and died of starvation at the hands of his uncle Tiberius. Both of his older brothers, would-be successors to the throne, died violently. All he had left of his family were his three sisters. His role models for leadership were the evil Tiberius and his even more demonic mother Livia, who were responsible for the demise of his other family members. We even had reason to believe that they had enlisted young Caligula to fingerpaint curses above his father's head in blood as he lay dying. Might he have even slipped his own father the poison, manipulated to do so by his uncle and great-grandmother?

However, even in the most horrible circumstances, we still have free will. We are not helpless victims controlled by the fates. We have personal responsibility; Caligula could still choose a better path.

The usually bright face of Cornelius turned dark as he said, "I do have other news from Rome. Cassius and I have been meeting frequently. He is frustrated with and willing to act against the imperial system. He wants to return Rome to a republic. He says he has seen too much evil arise from the concentration of power in too few hands and that, in the Republic, there were checks and balances to prevent such atrocities. He is right, of course, but idealism is dangerous in corrupt circles. I worry about him."

"On a brighter note," he continued, "even before we arrived, Cassius had heard a great deal about the followers of Jesus. He has not completely embraced the teachings of Jesus, but he is exploring and talking with me about what we saw in Jerusalem. I believe he will come around."

"I was cautious in what I wrote to him while we were in Judea," I responded. "I did not want my letters intercepted and read. However, I did share some of my story and that of Jesus with him in person. I will spend more time with him soon."

Cornelius stayed with us for a few days, but then it was time for him to take his young family to Rome as he had secured a small home for them near the Palatine Hill. They set off and took Junia, one of our former slaves, with them. Junia had been baptized by Peter, along with the rest of our household in Caesarea, and had assumed an active role among the followers of Jesus in Judea. Now that she was a freed-woman, she would work in the home of Abigail and Cornelius while also helping to form a church in Rome.

Cornelius had also come for business, to purchase new horses for the officers of the Praetorian Guard. We negotiated a new contract to supply horses on a regular basis. Breeding and training horses for the legion had been a large part of my family's business for decades, so this was a natural connection. However, it also gave us reason to communicate often. I sent two of my best hands with him. They could help with horse care and training while also functioning as messengers, spies conveying communications back and forth between Rome and Abruzzo…and elsewhere if needed.

Of course, we also had our good friend Cassius, who was now at the highest levels in the Praetorian Guard. Between him and Cornelius, they had eyes and ears everywhere throughout the empire and could place trusted assets as needed. Cornelius recruited like-minded operatives high up in the Roman ranks in both Syria and Judea.

In effect, we were forming an intricate spy ring, a web of informants and assets to ensure the growth of the budding church. Over the course of the next months and years, I would get frequent reports about palace intrigue, military movements, and legal machinations.

Like "Little Boots," we concealed our true motives; however, unlike Caligula, our motives were pure. We used these reports to help plan and orchestrate the safe movement of people and communications among the followers of Jesus throughout the empire. Spreading light rather than darkness.

∞

Over time, and not that much of it, it became clear that our prayers for Caligula to change or maintain some semblance of mental stability were dashed. The stories became more frequent, less sane, and more vile.

Early on in Caligula's reign, Cornelius sent word that the emperor was quite thankful for and impressed by a horse I had sent. In fact, he named the horse Invictus, "unconquerable," and took it for his own personal use. He loved the horse so much that he said he was going to name it Consul, the highest office in the Roman government.

One member of Caligula's constant contingent was a brutish thug named Protogenes. He carried two large binders with him wherever he went. Under one arm, he carried a binder labeled "sword." Under the other arm, he carried one labeled "dagger." The contents of these binders were purported to be the list of those for whom execution was being planned.

Caligula had frequent dinner parties with the rich and powerful of Rome. He would often get up from the dinner table, taking the wife, sister, or daughter of an attendee with him, returning sometime later to report on their sexual exploits. More than the sexual pleasure, he seemed to derive satisfaction from the power to do as he wished, just because he felt like it.

These dinner parties often involved plays and theatrics in which Caligula played the star role himself. It was as if he recognized that everything he did was just an act to simulate humanity. These plays gave him a chance to take that act even further. Dressed as a god, he would insist on being worshipped and adored. Dressed as a woman, he would engage in sexual exploits on stage. If people did not react as he wished, he had them tortured or killed.

Only a few months into his time as emperor, Caligula became very ill, almost surely the result of poisoning. He was unresponsive for weeks, and there was talk of his cousin, the young Tiberius Gemelus, ascending to the throne. Unfortunately for the world, Caligula recovered. More unfortunately for Gemelus, Caligula heard he was being considered as his replacement; of course, he had the eighteen-year-old murdered.

This near-death experience did not provide Caligula enlightenment, instead, it made him grow ever darker. He trusted no one and grew even more despotic.

It seemed the only people in his realm for whom he held any esteem or affection were his sisters - Drusilla, Lavilla, and Agrippina. They became his inner circle. In fact, he decided that he wanted an heir and that his heir should be a product of two royals, and he set out having affairs with each of his sisters. None bore him a child. He eventually had two of his sisters exiled for allegedly plotting against him, along with Lavilla's husband, whom he had executed.

This left only Drusilla, which is fitting since he had always had the most affection toward her. They had been caught together engaging in sexual behavior as young teenagers. After his attempted assassination by poison, Caligula named Drusilla his heir. The next year, she took ill and died, leaving Caligula devastated. He spent months in mourning and then had Drusilla deified, making her the goddess that he had un-officially worshipped for years.

Such were the private horrors of Caligula. Like Tiberius before him, Caligula's self-absorption and paranoia kept him fairly isolated. Most of his short four-year term as emperor had little impact beyond his palace. Until...

∞

One day, a group of Jews led by the famous philosopher Philo of Alexandria came to see Caligula to argue on behalf of the Jews in Egypt. They asked that he stop the discrimination against Jews that was rampant in Egypt. While, thankfully, Caligula did not respond to them with his trademark unpredictable violence, he did belittle them and their faith, asking why they did not eat pork. Then he asked a question that, it would seem, resonated loudly within him and upon which he would come to ruminate: "Why do Jews not worship me?" This rumination set about a chain of events that would change the course of history.

XXXVIII

Conspiracy

Perhaps the only good thing about Caligula was that he was too self-obsessed and driven by personal lusts to spend much time on affairs of state. He was a time bomb ready to explode and take the world with him, but he seemed content to create small explosions with limited impact.

I felt bad for the lives Caligula had taken and others that he had ruined, but my mission was not to intervene in every illicit act of narcissists, psychopaths, or others incapable of connecting with their fellow man. That was beyond my capacity – or anyone's capacity, for that matter. The population of the world at that time was 188 million, compared to eight billion in your time. However, per capita, there were probably even more such disturbed people in Ancient Rome than the roughly nine percent of your era. The world in which I grew up was an even better incubator for psychopathy. Unfortunately for you, though, with eight billion people and modern technology, evil people in your time have more opportunity to do great damage.

My opinion on the need for action against Caligula changed, though, in the third year of his reign. He had already pronounced himself as a god. He was enamored with the Egyptians, who had made their pharaohs gods, erecting pyramids in their honor. He started planning to leave Rome and rule the world from Alexandria, where he thought he would be treated as the god he truly was.

Part of me enthusiastically embraced Caligula leaving Rome – the smell of feces grows less repugnant at a distance. However, I had responsibility and a mission. It would be harder for me to monitor information or take any necessary action if the emperor were across the Mediterranean in Egypt.

Word came from Cassius that Caligula was commissioning a statue of himself to place in the temple in Jerusalem. His conversation with Philo of Alexandria had festered in him like an open wound. If the Jews would not worship him voluntarily, he would make it a requirement. Cassius, knowing the tensions in Judea, asked my opinion on the consequences of such a maneuver. We arranged a meeting.

The rumor mill being as it is, people in Jerusalem heard of Caligula's plan. I got word from our sources in Judea that unrest was fomenting even before I had the opportunity to meet with Cassius.

Cassius, Cornelius, and I met at the home of Cornelius to "discuss the equestrian needs of the legion." I informed the team of the rumors in Jerusalem.

I said, "Just the experience of putting up Roman banners in the holy city yielded hostility and death. I can hardly imagine the carnage that will ensue if Caligula tries to deify himself in the Holy of Holies. Not only will there be protests in Jerusalem. There will be insurrection from the Jews scattered throughout the entire empire! I do not choose to protect this empire; the fall of Rome will come, and sooner is better than later as far as I am concerned. However, as much as I may wish it, the time has not yet come. This will not end with the defeat of the empire. It will end with the slaughter of Jews and a clampdown on all religious freedom. This is the inevitable outcome."

Later, I told Cornelius privately that I had also seen the outcome of Caligula's plan in a dream and received divine instruction. I felt Cassius was not yet ready for that, and it may have dampened the kindling of his faith. It is our job to nurture the divine flame that already exists in each person. Forcing our own beliefs and "wisdom" on others is fighting fire with fire in the wrong sense – you risk extinguishing both flames. As a gardener in the kingdom of God, I cannot begin to tell you the number of souls who have grown more distant from God due to overzealous evangelism.

We agreed that the time had come to act. Cassius already had others who had expressed a desire to end Caligula's reign. To Cassius, this was striking down a corrupt system in favor of a republic where the corrupting influence of power was kept in check.

However, I could not help but notice that he also seemed to take it very personally. Pushing him on his motives, he admitted that he had personal animosity for Caligula even beyond his atrocious and tyrannical behavior. Despite his high rank in the guard, Cassius had become a target for the demeaning and humiliating bullying for which Caligula was known. Every day, multiple times per day, Caligula taunted Cassius for his high voice, referring to him as a voluptuous woman, mimicking his tone, and even kissing him as if he were a woman.

"Cassius," I implored, "explore your heart before moving forward. Make sure you are acting on righteous purposes and not seeking revenge."

"My friend, Caligula must be stopped, and this is the only way to end his reign of terror. I admit that Little Boots has tormented me and others, but I will be acting out of need, not desire. However, I will pray and consider your concerns."

I also asked that Cassius be the go-between and allow Cornelius and me to maintain our anonymity. We could not risk attaching the growing Jesus movement with what was to come.

For the next few weeks, I stayed with Cornelius, Abigail, and Hannah. It was as if God had placed me in the home with little Hannah, now a rambunctious and energetic eight-year-old, who brought joy and light to a time that could have become unbearably dark.

I knew what would occur if we did not take action against Caligula, yet I felt an incredible burden from my participation. As King Soloman said, there is a time to every purpose under heaven. One thousand nine hundred years from this point in history, another occasion for this type of action arrived. A deeply faithful man named Deitrick Bonhoffer and a group of conspirators tried to end the holocaust before it started. Multiple attempts to rid the world of Adolph Hitler failed, and the consequence was nearly unbearable. Based on my prior conversation with Jesus as we walked through the white crosses, I did not believe such an assassination would have been murder. In the end, though, it did not happen. Instead, God used this disgusting chapter in human history to demonstrate to the world that evil does exist and that we must never comply with it.

Likewise, I had no doubt that this battle in my mission was necessary and just. The problem with which I struggled was one of precedents. Assassination is nearly always man's effort to control the world and create the world in his own image rather than that of God and God's kingdom. There have been many historical examples of this. When John Wilkes Booth shot President Lincoln in the back of the head like a coward, he was trying to make the world safe for slavery – that is not God's plan! Whoever really assassinated John F. Kennedy did so to prevent him from making the underworld of the United States government more transparent. The murder of Martin Luther King was to keep God's people separated and divided.

Not only did I know that our action was just, I also knew that God would use it to His benefit and to the benefit of us, His children, one way or the other. Killing Abraham Lincoln was also the death knell for slavery. Even though it has never been completely solved, the killing of JFK alerted the masses to evil forces conspiring to control the government. Killing MLK put desegregation and racial unity on the fast track. Killing Jesus ended up ensuring that the whole world had a chance to know and understand God and His love for us.

I prayed often during this time, even more than normal. I listened intently for direction. But I also put one step in front of the other and did what I knew needed to be done. That and play hide-and-go-seek with a playful and precocious eight-year-old.

A plan was finalized. The assassination of Caligula would take place on January 24th of the year 41 A.D.

XXXIX

Caligula's End of Days

It was decided that the best time to act against Caligula was during the Palatine games celebrating the first emperor, Caesar Augustus. After the games, Caligula was to depart for Alexandria, where he would rule as a god. The indulgent eating and drinking, debauched orgies, and violent sporting events of this festival would provide many distractions for Caligula, a kid in a candy shop.

Cassius had a team of five guards that he trusted and who were committed to ensuring that the plot would be successful. Interestingly, his second-in-charge was also named Cornelius. Cassius had originally asked that my Cornelius be part of the execution squad, but I discouraged that – he was too important to the rest of my mission. I would, however, accompany the squad.

I knew that I would not have to spill Caligula's blood directly, but I still bore some responsibility for it. I could not look the other way. Besides, I wanted to be there with Caligula. Despite his demented nature, he was a child of God, and God wanted to heal him. I could not control what happened to his soul after death, but I had a role to play.

I thought about excluding Claudia from knowledge of this plan. I wanted her to have full and honest deniability. I also wanted to shield her from wounds to her soul that accompany the decisions that must be made in the heat of battle. Ultimately, my promise to her upon our betrothal took precedence, and she was kept aware at every step. She even had suggestions. It was her suggestion to add some extra fiber to Caligula's gluttonous feast before the festival, which ended up being a pivotal decision.

Claudia and I spent many days and nights praying about the momentous day to come. Of course, she was concerned for my safety. She was also concerned that my participation could become an anchor, tying me down to what would have to be yet another traumatic event in my life. We gave our concerns up to heaven and let them go.

∞

The night before the festival, Caligula invited the actors from the plays that would be part of the festival, as well as many of the Roman aristocracy, to his Palace. The feast and subsequent orgy would make Bacchus envious. It would also make Caligula hungover and in need of frequent bathroom trips.

Caligula mounted his seat the next day to watch the festival, taking pleasure in the bloodshed and hedonism, as was his nature. Midway through the day, his nature called in a different way. He had a sudden look of panic and left the amphitheater with an unusual rapidity and stride. As expected, he made his way to the Neronian Cryptoporticus, an underground tunnel leading to the palace and his private bathroom. I waited with Cassius and his team inside the tunnel.

Caligula pushed through the gates of the Cryptoporticus, uttering the password of the day. Seeing Cassius in the tunnel, even in his pained state, he could not help but taunt him: "Oh, thanks be to Jupiter, Lady Cassius is here to wipe my bottom for me."

With that, Cassius stood up to his full height, pulled his sword, and in his angelic high-pitched voice cried, "It ends here!"

He swung his sword down at the junction of Caligula's neck and shoulder, severing his collarbone, leaving the shoulder and arm hanging at an unnatural angle. I do not know if he intentionally struck a non-lethal blow, but the resulting agony in Caligula's face probably assuaged some of the pain and humiliation he had inflicted on Cassius.

The other conspirators jumped in to finish the job. After each had a blood spattering swing, jab, or slice accompanied by a soundtrack of their own laughter and the horrified screams of agony from Little Boots, I whisper yelled, "Enough!"

What was left of Caligula was a blood-drenched, mangled slab of meat draped in a toga. However, his lips still moved. I knelt at his side and looked into his eyes. At twenty-eight years old, Caligula was more than middle-aged in ancient Rome. However, in that moment, I saw the young boy with bloody hands. I had visions of the tormented life he had endured. I whispered, "May peace be with you and may God's love heal you."

With that, Caligula's end of days had come.

XL

I, Claudius

Sadly, the consequences of any action, righteous or not, are not under the full control of those who conduct the action. Cassius's dream of a Roman Republic did not come to fruition. God always answers prayers - the answer is either yes, no, or maybe later. For now, we would have to be satisfied with another autocrat, though one for whom Cassius had some affection.

While searching for Caligula's assassins, the Praetorian Guard stumbled upon Caligula's uncle, Claudius. Claudius was the outcast of the family, the one with whom Cassius had played as a child. The misfit child had grown up but was still relegated to the shadows, at this time, quite literally. He did not know what had happened, but knew something foul had hit the fan. Therefore, he was hiding behind some curtains in the palace.

Claudius had always been considered a bit slow and awkward, making him a perfect choice for emperor, at least according to Marcus, the head of the Praetorian Guard. Claudius could be a useful idiot, allowing Marcus, in the spirit of Sejanus, to assume the real power of the empire.

However, everyone had misjudged Claudius. He stuttered. He had a weak and sickly constitution. He was highly unattractive. He had no social skills or close friends. Cassius, even as a child and true to his nature, had seen beyond the superficial.   Long ago, Cassius had told me of young Claudius, the child alienated by his own family and divergent from their cruel and despicable nature.   He was correct.   Lacking much externally, Claudius turned inward to thought and imagination.

What he did have was intelligence and vision. While Claudius would indeed, in the end, turn out to be generally despotic as well, he was not inherently evil. Life had made him more accepting of individual differences and open to ideas that were not spoon-fed to him by Roman historians, manipulative oracles, or temple priests. Most of all, he did have some ability to empathize with others, including the plight of the common person.

Claudius would prove to be instrumental in allowing the growth of what was now starting to be called Christianity, even if he did not know that to be the case.

He would not, however, be a tool to be used by the Praetorian Guard, and he would not allow for assassinations. He knew he had multiple cancers within the empire. He recognized that his nephew was one of them, and for the elimination of Caligula, he was thankful. He had never had the intention to rule, but if he was going to, he was going to do so to the best of his ability. Step one was eliminating Praetorian Prefect Marcus Clemmons. The second was rounding up and executing the assassins.

∞

Knowing the gem that he had in his hands. The slightly slow, awkward, easily manipulated and controlled gem named Claudius, Marcus set out to execute anyone else who may have a claim to the throne, including the women and children of Claudius's extended family. Within hours of the assassination, Claudius was not only the best man left standing, he was virtually the only one. Therefore, the Senate, listening to the pleas of Marcus, who said that the security of the empire was at stake, took action to install Claudius. This tactic, getting people to ignore what is most important or to do what is not in their best interest by manufacturing an "emergency," is now used so frequently that it has its own name – "wag the dog."

To everyone's great surprise, once installed, the first action Claudius took was to order the execution of Marcus, implying that he had a hand in the assassination, even though this seemed unlikely given his good standing with Caligula and the power this relationship afforded him. Marcus never saw this maneuver coming. The only thing that silenced his screams and accusations of injustice was the blade that separated his head from his shoulders before his body was cast down the Gemonian Stairs.

XLI

⚬⚬⚬

My Personal Bodygaurd

Cassius met privately with Claudius after he was captured. He took full responsibility for the assassination and asked that his co-conspirators be pardoned. Of course, he never divulged any information about my involvement. The assassination was planned and carried out by a small group of guards who had seen the abuses of Caligula and felt compelled to rid the great Empire of his wickedness.

Claudius granted the pardon, calling off the search for the others. He thanked Cassius for his willingness to take responsibility, referring to his admission of guilt but implying much more.

Cassius asked that he be allowed to die by the sword that he had used to strike down Caligula. Claudius granted this request. He further asked to have a friend in attendance, which was also granted. He explained that he wanted to look upon the face of this friend of more than twenty years, with whom he had served in Syria, and whose life he had once saved. With the granting of that request, I got to witness yet another needless death.

Entering the cell in which Cassius was being held, I felt an overwhelming sense of loss that cut me to the core of my being as surely as the blade would soon cut Cassius. Tears began to well up in my eyes, but I was comforted by the angelic voice of Cassius. Seeing the look on my face, he laughed and said, "I asked for you to be here to comfort me, not the other way around."

Despite myself, I too laughed and said, "If you get your blood on me, I will kill you."

He looked at me as if wounded, but then started to laugh. Through tears of laughter, he sputtered, "I will try not to. Now hold me."

We both laughed raucously, and the executioner looked at us like we were crazy. I looked at him and said, "If we weren't all crazy, we would go insane."

Cassius looked at me, looked at the executioner, and said, "It is time."

Cassius bared his throat, and the executioner obliged, cutting deeply from one ear to the other. Blood spattered in diffuse waves, coating the cell like red spray paint. Everything in the room, including the executioner, was shades of sanguine red, yet somehow, I got not a single stain. I think Jesus and Cassius had a laugh at that one. Yet another wink from God that many people would choose to ignore. I did not. As his heart beat its final beats, I whispered in Cassius's ear, "Go in peace. May God bless you and keep you until we meet again."

I asked the executioner for the sword. I would never need to use it, but somehow knowing that I was carrying the sword of Cassius made me feel like I had my personal bodyguard with me for the rest of my days.

XLII

A Season for Everything

The next few weeks were a time of mourning and allowing God's plan to take hold. A huge part of me wanted to jump into the next big assignment or project. I wanted distraction from my sorrow. God wanted me to feel it and deal with it so I could carry forth the strength and the sword of Cassius without the weight of his death.

I spent a great deal of time with Claudia, and we were blessed by the company of Abigail and Hannah. Cornelius had decided that with the turbulence in the air, Rome was not safe for his family, so they returned with me to Abruzzo.

I also got to spend time with the elder Mrs. Pilatus. My mother continued to age with grace and beauty. We had a reunion with my aunt, uncle, and cousins, spending much-needed time talking about family history and current events. When they left, I asked Sarah and Tavi to go with them. Sarah and Tavi had been slaves in my household in Caesaria but married upon gaining their freedom, finally able to express their love.

My aunt and uncle were aging and would need more help in the final years of their life. No one was better suited for this role than Tavi and Sarah. Tavi was quite handy and able to fix anything. Sarah was nurturing and capable in all aspects of household management. Better yet, they were among the first followers of Jesus. Over time, I hoped they could share the faith with the family and others in Cocullo. As it turned out, they founded the church that ended up, over the many years, replacing the Temple of Angitia, the very church that I had seen in my dream ride with Jesus.

My inability to see God's vision for the next chapter in my mission gave me time with my mother. She had come to know and love Tavi and Sarah and was sad to see them go. Claudia and I had not provided her with a grandchild, but you could see that Hannah lit up every corner of her soul. She had long since stopped thinking of Abigail or any other member of our Judean household as a slave.

One afternoon, she took me aside and said, "I do not know what happened to you in Judea, but you are a different man. No, you are a better version of the same man I have always known and loved."

With some impatience, I responded, "I have told you what happened. I told you of Jesus dying on the cross. I told you of the earth shaking and the sky turning black. I told you of waking in the crypt and knowing I had been transformed. I told you about encountering Jesus on the road to Emmaus."

"Yes, but son, I assumed you were lying." We both laughed.

"Really, I knew you had experienced something, and I believed that you thought it was real. When confronted with something too fantastical to be real, it is human nature to assume a head injury, or an illness, or a very realistic dream. However, none of that explains why so many others report the same thing. Most importantly, it does not explain the change I see in you."

"Jesus said, 'You will know them by their fruits.' Sometimes my fruit is still pretty sour, but I do my best to treat others as I would want to be treated. If you do this, the rest is pretty easy."

"Maybe you should tell me the stories again. Maybe we should also get Abigail and the others."

The first thing my mother did after that conversation was meet with each of the slaves, both household and field slaves. She proceeded to free them, though she welcomed them to stay on as compensated household members. Some chose to leave and received her blessing in doing so. Most stayed and continued to help our businesses thrive; they saw that they were valued and loved. They saw that their service was honored. They recognized that their efforts helped the entire household thrive, the household of which each was an honored member.

Those weeks of respite yielded valuable and sustainable growth for me, my family, and God's Kingdom. It is funny how God uses your time away from "work" to work on you and those around you. There is a season for everything – embrace the season.

XLIII

⧉

Roots

Emperor Claudius had been raised in the shadows of his family to be seen and not heard...and to be seen but rarely. Rejected by his mother and tormented by his father, his only real companions were his books, his sister, and his trusted friend Herod Agrippa. Yes, Herod, as in that thorny family tree. Herod Agrippa was the nephew of Herod Antipas, brother of Herodias, and grandson of Herod the Great.

Fortunately, this friendship gave Claudius some sympathy for and understanding of Jewish faith and customs. He was also quite scholarly and had read all the great works of philosophy and religion. He was, therefore, open to diversity of belief and thought. Unfortunately, Claudius was blind to the fact that Agrippa suffered from one of the great downfalls of humankind...narcissism.

Herod Agrippa was in Rome when Caligula was assassinated, had counseled his friend Claudius, and had been instrumental in his ascension to the throne. It did not take long for Claudius to repay the loyalty and support.

I had been following events in Judea closely and, not surprisingly, Herod Antipas was scheming to regain the official crown. Also, not surprisingly, his schemes were not going well. In fact, they caught the attention and displeasure of his Roman puppet masters. He was exiled and forced to live out the rest of his days in Gaul. I would have loved to have seen the look on the conniving face of Herodias when they got the news and were given escort out of the country.

Claudius used this as an opportunity to appoint his friend Agrippa to be king over Judea. Reuniting the kingdom under one Jewish ruler placated the Jews, even if that king was still just a puppet king. Things were good...until they were not.

∞

The death of Caligula had ended the efforts to place his statue in the Holy of Holies. Herod Agrippa was able to settle the population, and the Jewish faithful felt hope: hope that he would return Judea to its Jewish roots; hope that they could be free of Roman oppression; and hope that they would once again have the status to which they felt entitled, God's chosen people.

Many of the Jews had incorporated Jesus into their belief system, either believing him to be the promised Messiah or at least a prophet. Many of these people understood that Jesus represented a change in what "chosen" meant. The Jewish people were indeed chosen. They were chosen in a specific era and for specific purposes. They were chosen to incubate the faith. They were chosen to help humanity of that time develop and live by a code of morals. They were chosen to be the shining light on the hill for others to see and emulate. Even though they fell short on their end of this covenant, they maintained God's love and would always be among the chosen.

They were not, however, chosen to be God's *only* children. They would have to accept new additions to the family. This was easier for some than for others. Unfortunately, Agrippa was one for whom this change was not only difficult; it was completely unacceptable.

∞

Agrippa was the golden child of the Kingdom. He was not only the grandson of Herod the Great, but his grandmother was Mariamne, of the royal Hasmonaean dynasty that ruled Judea until the time of the Maccabean Revolt two hundred years prior. When Rome stepped in to quash this revolt, they made Judea a client state, officially incorporating it under Roman rule. Thus formed the root of Herod the Great's prosperity and power.

Mariamne was Herod the Great's true love, to the extent he was capable of such a thing. Her beauty and charisma would have captured Herod's heart on their own, but her lineage also helped legitimize his own power. Mariamne was Herod the Great's most prized possession. Therefore, when he had to kill her, he could not let her go. Instead, he preserved her in a great tub of honey and visited her often.

Given this background, Agrippa was not only a branch of the tree of Herod, he was also descendant from the Hasmonaean family, a direct link to the last time the Jews had self-rule. Therefore, installing Agrippa was returning to glory days, or at least a shadow of those glory days, before the Roman occupation. Perhaps, some thought, he was even the promised Messiah, ushering in not a spiritual kingdom of God as Jesus was said to have done, but an earthly one with Agrippa at the helm. People who could not recognize the truth of the spiritual Kingdom were easily convinced that this was the case. Those people included Herod Agrippa himself.

The narcissistic nature of Agrippa himself made him susceptible to a god complex. He certainly was not willing to share his messianic role with a rabble-rousing rabbi, from Nazareth of all places. The church in Jerusalem had taken root and was growing, but Agrippa ushered in a time of drought for the church, and we had to find a way to get it water. Moreover, the entire country was increasingly unstable. While it was hoped that Agrippa would provide stability, my sources, both boots on the ground and the nocturnal whispers of my dreams, indicated that his character was not up to that challenge.

∞

James the Greater was still in Hispania during this time. Having left Judea near the time of my own departure, he had sailed with the Alucio back to his homeland, where he had hoped to reunite with his long-lost family; a family lost as a consequence of slavery, sold by

Herod Agrippa himself after the revolt of Judas the Nazarene, founder of the Zealots.

Since that time, I had received multiple communications from James. I was thrilled to find that Alucio's wife, Maya, was still alive and that their daughter, Alicia, a thriving young woman, had borne him a grandson and a granddaughter. They had established a small church there that met at the home of Alucio's son-in-law.

They were also collecting money to help fund other missions and set up churches throughout the rest of the empire. I had likewise been doing this as had Cornelius and his group in Rome. A disciple named Barnabas was also raising funds for this purpose in Antioch.

When a tree needs water, I realized, it could wait for rain and die, or it could spread its roots to find nourishment. It was time for us to spread our roots. God was already providing us the perfect person to lead this charge, someone with whom I had already become acquainted.

∞

During this time, word came to me from our contacts in Antioch that Saul, a Pharisee from Tarsus who had been persecuting the budding church, had himself been transformed into a follower of Jesus. Thinking back to my last days in Judea, I recalled the stoning of Stephen. I had a vague recollection of the name Saul. If memory served me correctly, he was an ass.

Apparently, now Saul was going by Paul and was preaching in Damascus. It appeared that he used his Jewish name, Saul, among his Jewish connections and Paul when addressing Romans and other Gentiles.

I sent word to Barnabas, who had taken up residence in Antioch to build the church there. I asked that he meet with and evaluate Paul. There was no room for charlatans and con artists in our midst. They would push people away and keep people from learning and understanding the teachings of Jesus and the relationship God wanted with His people.

Barnabas watched Paul from a distance and spoke to those who knew him. He interviewed Ananias, a disciple whom Paul had prosecuted, but who now fervently supported Paul. Ananias recounted the story of having had a vision in which Jesus told him to seek out Paul, who was to become the key messenger of Jesus to the Gentiles. Over his own misgivings, Ananias followed the direction.

Paul had been left blinded on the side of the road to Damascus after what he reported to be an encounter with Jesus. He reported a bright burst of light from heaven and hearing the voice of Jesus, who asked why he was persecuting Him. Jesus commanded Paul to go to Damascus and await instruction. That instruction came in the form of Ananias.

Ananias had reason to fear and loath Paul, who had spent the past five years persecuting anyone who believed Jesus was the Messiah. Paul, a devout and pious Pharisee, truly believed he was doing God's work, ridding the world of people who would lead the Jewish faithful astray. He conducted his mission with zeal and caused great harm to many friends of Ananias. However, Ananias, finding Paul blind and nearing death from dehydration, proceeded to heal him, baptizing him and welcoming him "as a brother." Paul's knowledge of the Jewish faith was unsurpassed, but Ananias helped Paul understand how Jesus fit into and transformed that faith, preparing Paul for the rest of his mission.

Based on the observations of Barnabas, I was convinced that Paul was the key to our mission as well. His background, his knowledge of the Torah, his command of different languages, his status as a Roman citizen, his ability to write, and, most of all, his firsthand encounter with Jesus made him ideal for the job. Much of this also made him the perfect lightning rod. Jews would hate his Roman citizenship. Romans would hate his Jewish faith and origins. Followers of Jesus would distrust and hate him for his persecution of Stephen and others. His brash personality did not change much from our first encounter. He was just as zealous FOR Jesus as he had been AGAINST Him. He would come to endure prison, beatings, shipwrecks, stonings, and ultimately beheading in order to spread the message of God.

XLIV

⟨∞⟩

Battle Strategy

I t was decided that Paul would go to Jerusalem to speak with Peter, John, and the other disciples and convey the need to do more to move beyond the walls of the holy city and redefine the meaning of "chosen people."

Despite our earlier conversations and the instructions of Jesus Himself, many of the disciples resisted the inclusion and recruitment of Gentiles. This "chosen people" misunderstanding ran deep and was core to the cultural and personal identity of the Jewish people. It is understandable that this would be difficult, but Jesus made it clear that to follow him, you would have to be willing to walk away from everything else.

God had directed me to assist in spreading the message of Jesus to the furthest reaches of the Empire. I had done as instructed, planning and directing missions to Hispania, Britannia, and India. James the Great had gone to Hispania, and the Jesus movement was blossoming there. Joseph and twelve of his followers had established a settlement in Southern Britannia, a town that would eventually be known as Glastonbury. There, myth, legend, theology, and history would blend in a beautiful mosaic to inspire Christians throughout the centuries. Thomas had made his way to India, where he was establishing churches that seamlessly blended the Indian culture and rich history with the truth of Christ.

Despite those great successes, the rest of the evangelic effort had sputtered and remained tethered within a three-hundred-mile radius of Jerusalem.

∞

The spread of God's message of forgiveness and redemption required cohesion and collaboration. It was time that we established unity among the branches of the church. To do this, I needed Paul and James the Just, brother of Jesus, to start to work together.

Like Paul, James encountered Jesus after his crucifixion. Like Paul, James was very well versed in the Torah and a devout Jew. However, James felt called to minister primarily to the Jews, reaching out to help them overcome their cultural and religious biases to embrace the teachings of his brother. He was uniquely qualified for this as he, too, had rejected these teachings during the life of Jesus. He understood the obstacles that the Jewish faithful, whether Essenes, Zealots, Pharisees, or Sadducees, would have to overcome to attain the redemption offered through Jesus.

Paul, on the other hand, was perfectly suited for his calling to work with the Gentiles. His command of different languages, his Roman citizenship, and his indefatigable spirit would prove to be indispensable.

These two needed one another, and the world needed both of them. However, Paul's background persecuting the church in Jerusalem and his adversarial nature made this first meeting contentious and seemingly doomed to failure.

Knowing that Paul and James represented the future of the church, I knew that they had to come together. They had to weave together the divergent views of Jesus that they embodied as well as the people that each represented. I arranged this meeting knowing that iron sharpened iron and that, while sparks would fly, the end result would be a honed focus and effective strategy.

∞

At first, Paul, true to form, was confrontational. Paul assumed that God's message to him must logically be what He expects from the rest of the apostles. They needed to get with the program. In an abrasive tone, Paul pointed his finger, saying, "James traveled to the edge of the empire, bringing the message, reuniting families, and setting up a new church. Yet you all sit here in Jerusalem, studying your navels, and waiting for the high priests to embrace you. That will never happen."

James replied, a bit too harshly, "It is not the priests we are trying to reach, it is the people the priests control and exploit. It is the sons and daughters of Abraham, the people that God selected to establish this nation as the beacon for the rest of the world to follow!"

"Being a Jew," Paul said, "I am one of those people too, but the point of your brother's death was to put that light within ALL people. God established, through Abraham, a great nation that would change the world. Mission accomplished. Jesus brought a new way, a new mission, one that was open to all, by grace, not by deeds, and certainly not by birthright."

Peter pointed out, "Were you not a Pharisee? Are you not now standing among us, a follower of Jesus? We do need to further embrace growth beyond Judea, but we cannot turn our backs on our friends and family here."

...And so it went. Debate sometimes bordered on argument. Always, however, debate was within the context of the golden rule as taught by their master – treating one another as they wished to be treated. Sometimes they had to be reminded. Sometimes they had to issue apologies when their human nature won out over their spirit nature. Through such discussion and debate over two weeks, the disciples developed a plan.

It was decided that a battle with two fronts was needed. James the Just, John Son of Thunder, and Peter the Rock would, for now, stay in Jerusalem working to build strong foundations among the Jews. Paul, Barnabas, Ananias, James the Great, Thomas, and others were charged with planting new churches beyond Judea. Cornelius and I worked tirelessly behind the scenes to ensure that these new churches had the opportunity to take root and grow.

As someone who had persecuted their friends, Paul was a target for the growing Christian faction in Jerusalem. As someone who had deserted the Sanhedrin and now spread "sacrilege", Paul was a target for the Temple leaders. If he stayed in Jerusalem, Paul would not live long enough to achieve the plans God had for him.

Paul decided it was time to return home to Tarsus, where he worked in the family leatherworking and tentmaking business. He did not, at the time, realize that God planted him in Tarsus to incubate, to grow as a person and as a leader, to become more humble and willing to listen more than he spoke. He started small church gathering groups in Tarsus and worked with Barnabas in Antioch, Damascus, and the surrounding areas to do the same. Through these activities and interactions, God was providing Paul the tools to reshape himself for the mission before him, to be the mortar uniting Jew and Gentile. Peter may have been the "rock" on which the church was founded, but Paul held the building together.

XLV

⸎

Back to the Crossroads

Paul was safe in Tarsus, preparing for future fights, like Rocky Balboa preparing to re-enter the ring, beaten down but never defeated. Meanwhile, James the Greater made his way back to Jerusalem for the first time in thirteen years.

Before his trip, he wrote to me to tell me of his excitement to reunite with his own family and to once again set his feet upon the soil of his homeland, to go back to his roots. He had great affection for his people in Hispania and planned to return to them after taking the tithes they had collected to the Jerusalem church.

I wrote back warning him of the grave danger into which he would be walking. Herod Agrippa not only had his own Messianic complex but had heard of the new church in Hispania. Worse yet, Agrippa, having sold the captives from Hispania into slavery to begin with, had a personal grudge.

I am not sure if my letter arrived in time for James to read it but, either way, he took the voyage. So did I.

It had been seven years since I left Judea, and I had not planned on returning. It was not a safe place for me for obvious reasons, and the powers that be in Rome would certainly not endorse my trip. Everything God had accomplished through me in Jerusalem thus far had likewise been accomplished through our covert communication channels. Nicodemus and Lathraíos had been integral in keeping the powder keg called Jerusalem from exploding. However, under the growing tension of the times, I felt compelled to go back in person.

Before undertaking the voyage, Claudia and I went to visit Cornelius in Rome. He agreed to go with me on the voyage and was able to come up with a cover story for his trip. Since the death of Cassius, Cornelius had increased in rank. At this time, Emperor Claudius had gone with troops on a campaign to invade and absorb Britannia into the empire, so Cornelius would not be terribly missed in the city. It was decided that Claudia would stay in Rome with Abigail Hannah, now eleven years old and going on twenty.

∞

Cornelius and I set sail for Caesaria, praying we could intercept James the Greater in Judea and prevent what I suspected would be the end of his mission to Hispania, the end of his life. We also prayed that we would make it at all as we were sailing at the very end of the season for seafaring on the Mediterranean. We were literally on the last official ship out of Rome for the year. Only the most dauntless pirates and smugglers would dare the seas in the winter.

I had grown very fond of James while he was with me in Caesaria. The love and courage he displayed knew no bounds and would become the model for the new covenant faith that would become known as Christianity. When shown injustice and brokenness, he was compelled to act. In doing so, he brought freedom to the slave Alucio, reuniting him with his broken family. He gave Alucio and his family hope and love that formed the seed of their faith, which grew into a strong tree, the first church planted beyond the Eastern Provinces. His life, his mission, and his witness were too integral to be lost.

Arriving in Caesaria, Cornelius and I noted a change in the tone of the city. It was still quite Roman and dominated by Roman influences in architecture, art, and culture; however, there was a subtle shift toward embracing more of the Judaism of the indigenous people. In my opinion, this was a positive shift, but, as Cornelius pointed out, these two cultures were often antithetical; at some point, this mixture would prove explosive. I hoped he was wrong, suspected he was not, and prayed that the explosion, should it come, be mild and far in the future.

We attained horses from the Roman garrison and galloped off toward Jerusalem. Sore and tired, we approached the gate of the holy city a day and a half later, traveling the seventy-three miles in record time... and were too late.

∞

As we neared the gate, we found James the Greater...his head displayed on a spike, a warning to "blasphemers" who contradicted the Temple Priests. Of course, the priests did not kill James, nor did they mount his head. This would be against Roman Law. However, the executive of Roman Law now was Herod Agrippa. In order to please the High Priest, secure his status as the savior of the Jews, and exercise his own retribution, Agrippa ordered his guard to execute James.

With mounting tensions and bloodlust in the air, we could not immediately go to the other disciples. Instead, we found Joanna, who arranged a clandestine meeting. We could take no risk of a chance encounter with a member of the temple priests who might remember me. Nor could we risk an officer of the Roman Legion becoming aware of our Jewish/Christian sympathies.

Under the cover of night, we met among the olive trees where I had first encountered the disciples three days after the crucifixion. This little olive grove was also where Nicodemus and I had our planning meeting, establishing means of clandestine communications which continued to serve our growing Christian cabal.

Peter was oddly absent from this meeting. John was still clearly devastated by the loss of his brother. His sadness superseded his anger, which simmered under the surface, ready to erupt with thunder upon provocation. Instead, I found myself, for the first time, face to face, dealing with James, the brother of Jesus. "So, you are the man who ordered the death of my brother."

An awkward silence ensued, but I did not look away or otherwise feign shame that I no longer felt. My sins had been forgiven. I did, however, offer my hand and said, "I am sorry for your loss and am so sorry to have to gather here with two brothers who have endured such tragedy." I made eye contact with John, who nodded and took my hand, which James had left hanging. They told me of the final days of James the Greater, who had arrived a week before me and Cornelius. He came bearing silver, mined from the mountains of Hispania, collected to fund the expansion of the church and to care for the needy in Jerusalem.

This brought up an insight in me that I shared with the others. Looking at John, I said, "I have heard that your brother James was the first disciple of Jesus." John nodded. "He was also the first to leave Jerusalem, taking the message to the Gentiles. His return brought the first tithes from a fully gentile church. Regrettably, he was also the first to follow Jesus to Heaven. He may or may not be sitting at the right hand of Jesus, but he is certainly the model, the example for all of us to follow."

Days before his untimely death, James the Greater had spent time with his brother and the other apostles. He told them of his adventures in spreading God's word. He told them of his love for the people of Hispania and of the beauty of the land in which he lived. He expressed the joy of knowing God had used him to reunite loved ones, to free people from slavery, and to reflect the light of heaven to others. He, too, had challenged them to spread the word to the Gentiles, saying, "The whole world needs to know Jesus and His message of God's love, forgiveness, and redemption."

James had planned his trip to coincide with Passover at the end of the prior week. He had escaped the attention of the temple and the authorities for the first days of his stay, but as Passover approached, it was noted by a priest that James was not taking part in the traditional rituals. He had not had his ritual bathing or come to the temple to have his sacrifice inspected. The other disciples continued these traditions and did not raise such suspicions or draw the ire of the priests.

John said, "I can still hear my brother's response to that self-righteous priest. In the clearest and most articulate way I had ever heard him speak, James told him, 'I am made clean by the blood of God's Lamb, sacrificed once and for all in this city thirteen years ago. Carry on with your traditions if they bring you closer to God, but my relationship with God requires no further sacrifice.'

"James did not enter or in any way dishonor the temple. He simply did not worship as a Jew normally would."

Noticing John's voice starting to break, James the Just continued for his friend, "The witness reported to the High Priest what James had said. That was enough for the High Priest, who had James held and taken to Herod Agrippa, who in turn held him for trial after Passover.

"At the trial, Peter spoke on behalf of James, saying, 'This man did not break Temple or Roman law. He is simply a man in this city, going about his business as would any non-Jewish citizen or non-believer.'

"Agrippa then asked James if he were Jewish, a descendant of Abraham, and a believer in the Torah as the word of God.

"James responded, 'I am', eliciting angry jeers from the priests and their followers gathered around the courtyard.

"Agrippa pronounced his verdict: 'You have broken the law of Moses and stand outside the Temple of God, proclaiming blasphemy. I find you guilty of inciting rebellion.' With that, he had James run through with a spear, ensuring a prolonged display of pain and suffering for the crowd.

"As James lay bleeding and moaning on the ground, Peter knelt at his side, crying and praying. Agrippa had his guard grab and hold Peter, making him watch as a henchman cut off the head of James."

"That evil Herod Agrippa arrested Peter, who is being held awaiting trial next week," added John with tears streaming down his face.

Seeing that his lifelong friend and cousin was unable to continue, James the Just picked up where John had left off. "Herod Agrippa is himself inciting rebellion. The people of Judea have been looking for a reason to try to overthrow Rome for a long time before my time. His ego is leading him, and the people who look to him for leadership, who believe that they are witnessing a new king rising, establishing Judea as God's physical kingdom. I am no fan of Rome, but the Kingdom of God is not a political or earthly one. This fever for political and social revolution, mixed with religious fervor, will inevitably result in death and destruction. Agrippa must be stopped."

"And Peter must be set free," said John.

James agreed, "Peter is a cornerstone for the growth of the true kingdom. My brother made this clear and even renamed him 'the rock'. Peter's steadfast leadership has proven it to be so."

With that, we began making plans to break Peter out of jail and assassinate Herod Agrippa. James strongly objected to the need for violence and reminded us that we need to lean into our faith and allow our faith to guide our works. John, Son of Thunder, was ready to strike like lightning to avenge his brother. However, he took a breath, begrudgingly agreeing that we should take some time to pray, meditate, and allow God to work in our hearts and the situation. We prayed and agreed to meet again in three days.

∞

The next three days and nights were restless and emotionally taxing. I was among all the same sights, sounds, smells, people, and places that had surrounded me in the last days of Jesus. Agrippa now slept in the palace I had occupied during that time, while I slept at the Antonia Fortress with Cornelius and the smelly soldiers of the Roman Garrison. Otherwise, the circumstances were strikingly similar: The death of a martyr, cries of blasphemy by protesting priests, the smell of roasted lamb, and pilgrims from the far corners of the empire. It brought back so many memories and so much pain.

Our time alternated between making plans and praying for guidance. Cornelius and I reviewed the layout of the prison holding Peter, got to know the rotations of the guards, and found a guard we thought would be sympathetic. He was of Jewish background and had a sister who often gathered with the followers of Jesus.

We also looked for chinks in the armor of Agrippa and his security detail. He was quite paranoid, having grown up among all the palace intrigue of Rome and having the Herodian lineage. He kept a very tight group of guards and did not give us much to work with.

I prayed for guidance, for some word from God. Before sleeping, I asked that Jesus come to my dreams and talk to me as He had so many times before. Awake or asleep, no guidance was coming.

∞

As the sun was setting on the evening of the third day, I found Cornelius. We ate together and discussed the plans we had been able to put together. Neither of us felt strongly about the chances for success of these plans. Neither of us felt a strong commitment to this course of action. Neither of us felt that there was a choice.

Once the sun set, we used the cover of darkness to set out on the road out of the city. We passed through the western gate and headed out to the Mount of Olives. There, huddled at the crossroads, under the olive tree, we found James and John. The stories of the last three days were all the same. No one had any moments of profound inspiration. No one heard the voice of God or had a vision of Jesus telling them what to do.

Cornelius spoke up and shared our prison break plan. No one objected, and all seemed in agreement that something had to be done. All seemed in agreement that the plan was not particularly promising.

I shared the assassination plan. James continued to voice objections in principle but did not have an alternative plan. All agreed that Herod Agrippa was a severe danger to the stability of the region, the safety of the Jewish people, and the viability of our growing faith. All agreed that the assassination plan was even less promising than the prison break plan. We agreed to further assess after the prison break.

We sat, prayed, and committed to moving forward. We walked back to the city together in silence, the mood somber and resigned. As we approached the city gate, we noticed a man walking along the wall toward the gate. He walked through and could be seen in the light of the torches at the gate.

James exclaimed, "That is Peter!"

The rest of us were incredulous, saying it could not be. James responded, "I have known that man since we were children, I would know that cocky swagger anywhere. Follow him with caution. Get him and meet me at Joanna's upper room. The guards know me too well; I can better avoid them on my own, and you all should not be found with me.

James and John split off to enter the city from another gate. Wary that the guards not notice Peter or pay attention to us, Cornelius and I walked slowly but kept Peter in our sights. He walked to the house of Mary, one of the followers of Jesus (Side note: this was yet another Mary, not Mary the mother of Jesus, nor was it Mary Magdalene. This Mary was the mother of John, yet another John, also known as Mark, who was to become the author of one of the "Gospels". Of course, we have also met two different disciples named James. There were way too few names in use in my time!)

Peter proceeded to pound on the door. We followed.

XLVI

∾∾∾

The Faith Not to Act

As Peter pounded on the door, my heart pounded within my chest. How could it be that Peter was here, just yards ahead of us, when he had been stuck in a prison cell, awaiting what would surely be execution at the hands of Herod Agrippa and his priestly acolytes? The door opened, and Peter entered.

Following in Peter's footsteps, we emerged from the shadows and proceeded to knock as well. A lovely servant named Rhoda came to the door but refused us entry, understandably afraid and skeptical of our intentions.

Andrew, one of the other disciples, who unbeknownst to me at the time was the brother of Peter, came to the door. He allowed us entry, leading us to a room where several others were gathered. They had been praying for Peter's release and safety when, to their utter amazement, Peter knocked on their door!

Peter told the story of his release. He said an angel had come to his cell, unlocking it, covering him in a cloak. The angel led him through multiple guarded checkpoints. The guards did not even seem to see them. They just walked through as if they were invisible.

We sat, drank wine, and celebrated. We listened in amazement to Peter's tales of the death of James, Herod Agrippa's treachery, mistreatment by guards at the jail, and his miraculous escape. After long, mesmerized minutes, I realized I had forgotten to tell Peter that James and the others would be waiting for him in the upper room.

Peter and Andrew left for the rendezvous while Cornelius and I followed a little later to avoid suspicion. As I walked next to Cornelius, I looked at him and smirked, saying, "I wonder who may have sent an angel", assuming that Cornelius had made a covert arrangement for Peter's escape behind my back.

"I had nothing to do with this. I assumed it was you!" replied Cornelius.

"There is no way anyone could have arranged this unless they had high-level connections," I said. "If it was not you or me, who could it be?"

"The only explanation is that Peter's story is true - an angel pulled off the prison break that we could not," he replied. "Perhaps the waiting during those three days of prayer and planning was not in vain. Maybe the fact that we did not receive an answer meant that we were to stand down. Perhaps our faith this time did not require works. Perhaps this time our faith required waiting and letting God act."

"Cornelius," I said, "after all of these years of friendship, you must have noticed that for me, waiting for battle is much worse than the battle itself."

"Trust me, I have noticed, my friend," said Cornelius. "Perhaps learning patience is part of your training."

∞

We decided to take the same strategy of patience with Agrippa. There is a season to take up arms against evil, but there is also a season to wait and allow God to work to overcome evil. Wisdom is listening to and leaning on God to tell you which season you are in. That is hard, and seasons of action are often easier to endure than seasons of patience.

Our patience, once again, paid off sooner rather than later. Herod Agrippa left Jerusalem after the week-long Feast of Unleavened Bread. Of course, he first ordered the execution of the guards who "let

Peter escape." Thankfully, the guard we had thought to enlist was not among them. He would go on to join his sister in the Jesus Movement and become a key connection for all of us, protecting and nurturing the sprouting faith.

Upon arriving back in Caesaria, Herod Agrippa came down with a stomach bug and died within a week. Cornelius and I looked at each other again, but knew that neither of us had a hand in this outcome - another example of having the faith not to act.

Our patience was further rewarded when it came to spreading the gospel beyond Judea. James and the others in the Jerusalem church had previously decided that the time was not yet right to make this their priority. Times had changed, and God had arranged circumstances to make it clear that the season for patience in this regard had given way to a season of action.

XLVII

Meeting of The Minds

There were many conversations had during these times of change. Nothing good can happen unless people are willing to come together, put aside differences, believe the best in one another, and listen to divergent perspectives.

The next steps in my journey and the Journey of Peter started with one such conversation, a meeting of the minds. James the Just, Peter, and I met in a tavern known to be a safe place for the disciples to meet. We sat at a table in the corner and drank beer from small jars of clay. There is an assumption that wine was the drink of choice in those days, but beer was also popularly consumed.

Peter sat with a dagger in his hand, not quite feeling safe after his time in the custody of Agrippa. As we spoke, he occupied his hands, carving something on the tabletop.

James said, "It is obvious that Peter is not safe here in Jerusalem."

"I agree," I said. "I am not sure any of us are safe here. There is even more trouble coming.

James responded, "This is our home, the home of Abraham. God saved Isaac from sacrifice right here, where He allowed the sacrifice of His own son, my brother! It is the holy land, the place promised to the descendants of Abraham. and the place Moses brought us when we escaped Egypt. I cannot leave the Promised Land."

"As a Roman," I responded, "I cannot fully understand your connection to this place. However, I think God wants you to live and spread His message.

"Of course," James said, we must spread the message of Jesus, but we must also remain present in our ancestral home."

I looked at Peter, wanting him to chime in, but he remained focused on his carving and seemed to be ignoring us.

"Jesus has given me a mission," I said with some exasperation. "I am to cultivate the growth of His kingdom, make it safe for you to plant the seeds of faith in the hearts of Jews and Gentiles alike. You are making that very difficult."

Suddenly, Peter plunged his dagger into the table, into the middle of his carving – two fish in a circle. In a quiet and relaxed tone, inconsistent with the knife sticking up from the table, he said, "You are both right." Clearly, he had been listening intently despite his seeming distraction. "James, you are the brother of Jesus, a descendant of David. The Jerusalem church will grow from the seeds you are planting here...

"...but Pontius is also correct – there is destruction and death coming to Jerusalem. However, like is often needed to maintain healthy crops, the seeds you plant will remain dormant only to grow back stronger and healthier when the time is right."

"So what about you, Peter?" I asked.

He remained silent for a moment, looking down at the fish carved on the table. Finally, he said, "I will go. It is time for me to build the church."

XLVIII

Journey to Another Place

Peter, the "Rock" upon which the church would be built, was no longer safe in Judea; instead, he would accompany me and Cornelius back to Rome.

We could not travel by sea, both because few, if any, captains would dare the seas for at least another two months, and because Peter's notoriety would make him a very difficult stowaway. Instead, we took the land route. This gave me time to discuss with Peter and Cornelius how the evangelical charge from Rome would take shape. All roads lead to Rome. All roads also emanate FROM Rome. To reach the masses throughout the world, one needed to be at that hub.

On the way, we visited Paul and Barnabas in Antioch, a town of which both Cornelius I had fond though somewhat haunted memories. There, Paul arranged an opportunity for us to meet with powerful Jewish merchants who had started to follow Jesus. They would be key to spreading our message along trade routes. Since neither Cornelius nor I was of Jewish origin, did not hold to a kosher diet, and sure as heck were not circumcised, the merchants did not want to eat with us.

They still met with us, but would not eat in our presence. I was open to compromise and could live with that. Paul, being Paul, could not. He confronted Peter and said, "You cannot give in to discrimination based on Jewish heritage! You are the fisher of men...ALL men.

You must be the example of how we are to live. Discrimination, segregation, or ranking of God's people for any reason must not be tolerated."

Peter accepted Paul's chastisement. He knew Paul was correct and did not allow his pride to cause him to stumble, though I could see the loving spirit nature of Peter restraining his hot-headed carnal nature from punching Paul in the face. I recalled that same reaction when I first met Peter. Thankfully, on both occasions, his spirit nature won the wrestling match. Peter made sure that Cornelius and I joined him at dinner, where we were able to map out routes and plan trips for the apostles who remained in Jerusalem.

Each of the apostles had their own disciples and would be traveling en masse, so this was not a simple feat. Andrew, for example, brother of Peter, went with his followers to Turkey and Greece, where he planted churches and would become the founder of what grew to be the Eastern Orthodox branch of Christ's church.

Andrew would be considered by many to be the first of the apostles to make such an evangelistic move. James the Great had done so in Hispania years before, though some historians still argue whether this could have really occurred. They question how James could have accomplished so much in a mere fourteen years, journeying from Jerusalem to Spain and setting up a church, establishing a Christian stronghold that far from the Holy City, only to return to that city to be executed. It seems impossible to some. I think these may be the same people who think infinite multiple universes are more likely than a creator. Regardless, it is fitting that the fishermen brothers set out, almost simultaneously, to two key hubs, where they could cast their nets furthest and bring the largest haul.

∞

We moved on, making connections along the way. We went slightly out of our way to Cappadocia as Paul informed us that a group of Jesus followers lived in the mountains there among a larger Jewish population.

I was amazed at the settlement there, having never seen geography like this. The alien features of the landscape made one feel divergent from the rest of humanity, perhaps fostering a bit of a mystical element in the people who gathered here. The church where we stayed and worshipped for a few days was one of dozens, maybe hundreds, carved into the sides of natural rock formations, many of which looked as if God Himself had formed tents for alien travelers making a pitstop through earth.

Passing through Galatia and Philippi, we met people who were already part of the Jesus movement, likely in large part due to the efforts of Paul. I had flashbacks to my journey as a younger man through this region. I recalled thinking that my mission was to convert backward people to the Roman ways. I laughed out loud at myself when this irony hit me. God has a great sense of humor.

XLIX

⟨❦⟩

Earthquakes and Aftershocks

The earth had literally shaken upon the crucifixion of Jesus; figurative aftershocks were felt throughout the Roman Empire for years. If Peter's move to Rome was an aftershock, it was a strong one, the results of which would alter the geopolitical landscape of the world and firmly plant Christianity as a new religion rather than a branch of Judaism.

There would forever be ties between Christianity and Judaism; they share the entire Torah as part of their doctrine, they share Abraham as the father of the faith, they share Moses as a prophet and guide, they share customs, holidays, and core beliefs. Their point of divergence is Jesus.

The entire Old Testament/Torah promised a Messiah, someone who would usher in the Kingdom of God, someone who would bring salvation to God's people, to put them back in their rightful place. Even from my "outsider's" perspective, it seemed clear that Jesus checked every box of who this Messiah would be. More importantly, Jesus fulfilled each prophecy about the Messiah. However, not everyone, Jew or Gentile, was ready to accept that their culture, their traditions, or their beliefs were secondary.

Jesus did not come to wipe out these traditions or cultures, He simply said they were secondary to God's Kingdom. They were secondary to and irrelevant to one's relationship to the Creator of the Universe. Don't get me wrong, God loves the diversity of humanity. God loves the variety of traditions. God created and loves each and every nuanced personality. All these things matter in terms of how God can use you to tell His story, reach others, to reel them into relationship with God. However, these factors do not give you any greater access to God's love or mercy. The pride of humankind makes accepting this "irrelevance" difficult. It is this sinful pride that keeps people separated from God.

Peter's move to Rome placed a bright spotlight on this shift. Jesus did not belong to Judea or even Judaism. The Jesus movement was not regional; it was worldwide and belonged to all people.

∞

We arrived back in Rome with Peter three months after leaving Jerusalem. Claudia and I stayed, along with Peter, temporarily with Cornelius in the city. There, Peter worked with and grew the small faithful gathering of Christians that had formed around Cornelius, Abigail, and the rest of their household. They met in private and could not openly conduct outreach ministries given Cornelius' position with the Praetorian Guard, a position which both protected them and segregated them. Like a canary perched in a cage high above the floor, their song could not be widely heard, but at least the room full of cats was kept at bay.

Peter had come to change that. He gave the small church gathering in the home of Cornelius a mission. They were to identify the other church gatherings that had sprung up in and around Rome. He wanted to know where they met, who led their groups, and how many gathered with them.

While they undertook this effort in secrecy, Peter went with Claudia and me to the safe refuge of our home in Abruzzo. There he met with the church that gathered in our own villa. The "church" was comprised of our immediate family, the household members who remained from our return from Judea, others of our freed former slaves, and many of their own family members and friends. What had started as eight people gathering for a meal and discussion once a week had grown to sixty-four regular attendees and others who came when able.

My mother relished her role as hostess and event planner for our gatherings. After spending her entire life watching others prepare her meals, she even enjoyed helping with meal prep. Seeing the transformation of my mother was a beautiful thing. As she aged, her physical vitality diminished, but her spirit thrived and grew.

Peter also attended the small church that had sprung up in Cocullo, which gathered in the home of my aunt and uncle. They were not yet Jesus followers; however, they had seen the joy that had returned to my mother's eyes. They were also quite fond of Tavi and Sarah, whom I had sent to help them in their home. They allowed the young couple to host a gathering, which was attended by some of the other household servants as well as others in the town. As with many such gatherings, part of the draw was to talk about spiritual matters, but the other part was free food, and Sarah's meals were a good inducement.

In the three years that Peter stayed with us, he became part of our little spy ring, helping in the horse trade between Abruzzo and Rome. While he was a fisherman by trade, he was quite adept at working with the horses; he seemed naturally able to sense their emotions and stay calm, and perhaps having to overcome his hot-headed temperament helped him in this manner. He was also naturally adept at any work involving his hands. It was not hard for him to maintain his cover.

Within a few months, Peter had identified dozens of small and isolated Christian groups meeting throughout Rome and the surrounding area. He visited them and their leaders, establishing relationships and giving their congregants first-hand accounts of his time with Jesus. He mentored the leaders, and I helped him establish an interchurch structure and flow of communication. Cornelius and I kept him safely off the radar of Roman authorities, who, fortunately, at that time, largely just saw early Christians as a sect of Jews. Therefore, they were treated with the same mild contempt, ignored rather than persecuted.

Soon, all the churches were communicating, working together to strengthen the foundation of the Roman church, and bringing new people into communion. These churches had many Jewish members, but they also included Romans and other ethnic groups, becoming the first "melting pot" of cultural and religious backgrounds to ever truly exist.

Divergent people with diverse backgrounds were brought together by common faith. All were welcome. This was an unheard-of shift, not just in Roman or Judean society of the time but of all societies of the time. You are far from perfect, even in the third millennium after Christ; however, you have the benefit of significant social evolution over that time. It is a natural tendency to feel most at home and secure among those with whom you share the most traits. In my time, the divides between "us" and "them" were much more salient, stark, and strictly enforced. Jesus had come to end that. There would always be sibling rivalry, that is human nature, but we are all children of God, as made clear by the message of Jesus, a message He died to deliver.

This blurring of lines was not just one of race, ethnicity, or religious background. It was also one of status, wealth, power, and even gender roles. Powerless slaves participated in Christian groups along with wealthy and powerful merchants. People of all skin colors and accents ate together, prayed together, learned together, and worshipped together. Women were often equal partners and frequent leaders in church communities, even though society, as a whole, remained very patriarchal in structure. These changes were often small and localized to specific groups, but they were seeds planted by the early church that blossomed over the decades and centuries to come.

As a matter of fact, these changes, almost imperceptible at the time, ended up, within less than three hundred years, becoming so powerful that the Roman Emperor converted and made Christianity the official religion of the entire empire. However, like an earthquake, substantial cultural change always involves pain and results in fissures in the land, thrusting into existence new mountains, forcing some land masses together while tearing others apart.

In the intervening years, the Empire struggled mightily against change and made a practice of killing off Christian leaders. The earthquake initiated by Jesus rumbled throughout the world, and Peter's arrival in Rome only magnified the shifting tectonic plates of first-century society.

L

Council Meeting

Despite my efforts and those of both Peter and Paul, there remained a rift in the early church about whether Jewish law applied to Gentiles, even whether Jewish law still applied at all. There were also questions about whether one got to heaven due to faith alone or whether it required works. I found this debate to be ridiculous, as did both Paul and James the Just, whose names were often uttered in these arguments.

They would both agree with me that this was a case of the chicken or the egg. Doing good things did not buy you a spot in heaven. Having "faith" did not automatically open the gates either; you can believe in grizzly bears and still not choose to embrace one. True faith is believing something AND embracing it. If you embrace Jesus, the result is always good works. Not so much if you embrace a grizzly bear.

Thankfully, Peter had turned the corner on whether one needed to become Jewish or accept Jewish customs in order to follow Jesus. He accepted my premise and the words of Jesus, that adherence to Mosaic Law was no longer required.

Others were still saying that laws requiring circumcision and kosher foods were applicable and should even be expected of non-Jews. I remember questioning one of my Jewish friends about whether he remembered his circumcision. To which he responded, "Of course not. I was a baby."

I replied, "Well, if I must be circumcised, it will certainly be memorable!" He snorted and nearly spit out the wine he was sipping. As he laughed, I added, "I cannot imagine the Jesus I know telling me that to get to heaven, I must go cut off part of my penis."

Such discussions led to a council of church leaders convening in Jerusalem. Eighteen years after the crucifixion, after three years organizing the church in Rome, Peter returned home to meet with the other disciples and church leaders in what has become known as the Council of Jerusalem.

James the Just and Paul both explained that Godliness requires faith, but that faith always results in good works, and that separating the two is impossible. They also further defined "works." Some were claiming that good works entailed keeping Mosaic Law, but they explained that good works were helping one's neighbor, feeding the poor, providing shelter, taking care of vulnerable widows and orphans, etc.

In some ways, this attempt to separate faith and works was like trying to separate the followers of Christ: In this corner, wearing the red trunks, we have Jewish Jesus Follower, and in this corner, wearing the blue trunks, we have Gentile Jesus Follower... Clearly, this was not God's plan. It was the antithesis of why Jesus died on the cross. Yet, from that day forward, Christians have continually found reasons to fight over such issues.

It was decided at this meeting that God loves us all, wants us all in His kingdom, and does not want us to focus on which of us is the most worthy. Thankfully, Peter was able to help lead the others to a consensus that such matters as circumcision and kosher diet were personal choices rather than a mandate.

Cornelius and I saw Peter off, not knowing that it would be our last time seeing him. After the contentious council meeting, he chose to spend time in Antioch and other places where faith communities had sprouted. Eventually, he did return to Rome, but by that time, Cornelius and I had already moved on.

LI

New Horizons

Shortly after Peter left, my mother's health started to decline. I first noticed it with mild forgetfulness, which thankfully did not descend quickly into outright dementia; she kept her memories and connections to the loved ones surrounding her. However, she was used to being capable of anything and had a strong independent streak. It was inconsistent with her self-image to have to rely on others. I think her heart and soul just realized it was time for her transition, and her body slowly started to give out.

For her last month, she had difficulty getting up and taking her meals, what little she would eat, in bed. Knowing the end was near, I made sure everyone who could had a chance to say goodbye. She kissed my cheek one night before I went to bed and said, "I am so proud of the man that you have become. Goodnight, my boy."

She did not wake up the next morning. When mom's end of days came, she was surrounded by family, including me and Claudia, my siblings, her sister and brother-in-law, many grandchildren and nieces and nephews, and the entire household - former slaves turned freemen and adopted family members.

Cornelius, Abigail, and Hannah were, of course, among those gathered to say goodbye to my mother. We spent many late nights talking about our lives, our work, our relationships, and our mortality. My mother lived longer than should have been expected, and I was blessed to have spent her last years with her.

When I left Judea, I was a very young and vibrant fifty-year-old. Twelve years later, I was still healthy and strong at sixty-two. Claudia, still the brightest light in any room, was now fully grey in her twenty-third twenty-ninth year. Cornelius was over fifty years old, and even Abigail, the baby among us, was over forty. The passing of my mother seemed to signal another changing of the seasons.

My spring was spent in the shadows of Romulus and Remus. My summer was in the heat of Syria and in my early years with Claudia in Judea. Fall came with the march up Golgotha in the wake of the cross and proceeded to successfully protect and promote the legacy of Christ. I was now entering winter. I would always have work to do, and my purpose would never change, however, it was time for the nature of my work to transform. I wanted a change of venue, somewhere that I could reflect, guide others, and prepare for the next cycle of my existence, whatever that might entail.

Hannah was now growing into a beautiful young woman. At sixteen, she was preparing to begin her adult life. As we were talking about what our future might hold, Cornelius said, "I do not want Hannah to marry and become stuck, a cog in the Roman wheel. It is time to move her away to a place where she can find happiness away from the Via Appia."

"Besides," he continued, "I am getting increasing signs that Rome is waking up to the impact that the budding of Christianity is having. We are no longer an insignificant Jewish sect. As we grow in number and influence, people in power are seeing us as a threat. Given our social and political positions within Rome, our activities to promote Christianity put us at particular risk. I am happy to die for our faith, if need be, but I want Abigail and Hannah to be safe."

"You and I both know the Empire, there is no place outside of the reach of the emperor. We certainly cannot return to Judea. Any day now, Jerusalem will erupt, a volcano spewing ash and lava over Judea and the Eastern provinces."

"Agreed," said Cornelius.

Claudia said, "What about Hispania? Alucio and James described it so beautifully, and there is a thriving community of believers there. It has been there and growing for nearly twenty years now."

Looking at Claudia, I countered, "We still have work here. Not only do we have the estate and all the work to be done here, but the world is not yet safe for those of us who follow Jesus."

"It never will be," said Abigail with a touch of resigned sadness in her voice. "The powers of this world will always be threatened by the things and people they cannot control."

"Let's take some time to think about it and pray for direction," I said.

∞

For the next week, Claudia and I went on long walks, rode around the estate, and talked about where we had been and where we were being called to go. I spent time alone with my thoughts and waited for the dream that I suspected was coming. And it came.

∞

One night, I found myself on the shore of a strange land I had never before seen. The sun was obscured by a layer of clouds, making my surroundings a strangely colorful grey. The primarily monochrome landscape made the pop of color stand out as if calling for appreciation and gratitude. The green grass lit up by a solitary break in the clouds, the royal purple of spear thistle on the shoreline, the pop of pink in the heather on the hillside – they were as welcoming as an angel's embrace.

Then I saw a beam of bright light shooting through a hole in the clouds beyond the top of the hill. I was reminded of the shaft of light that woke in the dusty tomb on Golgotha; I knew that rebirth awaited me at the other end of that light. I climbed up the hill from the shore. Once at the top, I could see a snow-covered mountain range in the distance. The foothills and valleys surrounding me felt comforting, like God's blanket spread out before me. The beam of sunlight lit up a solitary tree at the top of a hill. The tree lay just beyond a stream meandering down from the mountain, feeding and nurturing God's flora and fauna as it flowed. The sun was just starting to emerge from over a mountain range, rising higher in the east, turning the clouds from a warm rose gold to shimmering orange, like a bronze shield reflecting sunbeams.

I turned and looked back over the calm waters of the cove below and was surprised to see the reflection of two men. I was not alone. I felt a hand on my shoulder and heard a whisper in my ear: "Welcome home."

I stood for a moment, feeling the warmth of the sun on my back and the love of God running through me. I closed my eyes, basking in this moment.

I opened my eyes, looking back at the cove, I found only myself reflected in the serene water. Turning back to the landscape behind me, I knew this was our new destination. It seemed like the perfect mirror image of Abruzzo. The sun rising over distant mountains reminded me of watching it set over the temple in Cocullo. The lush green landscape, like that of our family villa, would be the fertile pastures waiting to be grazed by cows and sheep, and, of course, horses.

Waking next to Claudia, I told her what I had seen. We spent several minutes in silence, both reflecting on my dream, envisioning ourselves in these new surroundings.

Claudia broke the reverent silence, saying, "It sounds like the landscape Joseph of Arimathea described in his letters."

"It does, doesn't it? The sea at my back, watching the sun rise, it certainly seems like the furthest western reaches of the empire. It must be Britannia."

∞

Over dinner with Abigail and Cornelius, we told them our thoughts. "My concern, though is starting over," I said. I am not a young man, and the vision I saw was of a very secluded land where we would have to establish a new home and without the comforts to which we have become accustomed."

"It is a scary thought," agreed Cornelius, "but I am pretty sure you were the one who told me faith is not the absence of doubt but doing that to which you are called despite doubt. That dream sounds like a calling to me."

"I hate when you use my words against me, my friend."

Claudia said, "I am also getting older, and I am afraid that our window of opportunity to move beyond Rome, to see the world, and to live a new dream may close on us if we do not take the chance soon."

"As I recall", Abigail said, "Joseph of Arimathea was about your age when he left for Britannia."

"Am I really THAT old?!" I exclaimed. I was asking a serious question, but, for some reason, they all laughed at me.

So, it was decided that we would spend the next six months wrapping up business in Rome and Abruzzo. We would plan and orchestrate a westward caravan with our combined households. The land route would allow us to visit others not seen for many years along the way, see the result of our work over the past twenty years, and maybe even continue our mission to cultivate God's Garden.

∞

In the years leading up to our departure, Claudius Caesar had invaded and established Roman rule over the southeastern reaches of Britannia. Cornwall, however, where Joseph had settled, was still beyond Roman control. Perhaps that would afford us the opportunity to escape the clutches of Rome. We could live out our remaining days outside of Roman rule.

I knew that too many years had passed for Joseph to still be living, but I hoped some of the twelve others, and their family members who went with him, might still be in Britannia, safe from the ravages of Caesar's aggression.

Likewise, I hoped to be able to see Alucio and meet his family in Hispania. Perhaps I could even meet some of the others who had settled in Gaul. While I was feeling my age, I was certainly still up for an adventure!

LII

The Adventure

Six months of letter writing, giving instruction, selling off belongings, and otherwise settling matters in preparation for the journey before us seemed both much too long and far too short. I wrote letters to people from India to Britannia and everywhere in between. I sent love from Claudia and me told them how the church had grown in and around Rome as well as throughout the empire. I called out the amazing work of each apostle as they accomplished their mission. I told them of our travel plans and destination. I told them of my concerns for when Claudius Caesar passed away and suggested ways in which they might prepare themselves for the sweeping changes that would come.

Cornelius and I had been watching as Claudius got older. Having never been a beacon of health, we did not expect that Claudius would last much longer, even without the usual mortal intervention of would-be successors. Next year, he would be sixty years old, and he appeared at least ten years older than that. During his reign, Jesus' followers had been relatively safe, at least outside of Jerusalem. However, our growing influence was coming into more conflict with the Roman way of life.

Worse yet, it appeared that Claudius had a succession plan. That plan named his adopted stepson Nero, biological son of his wife/niece, as his heir. It seemed to Cornelius and me that Nero had far too much in common with Caligula and that this boded poorly for the future of the empire and especially for its Christian citizenry.

The future would bear out our concerns. Nero would execute his own mother, the only person who had kept him in check. He burned down much of the City of Rome in an effort to take over land he wanted to expand his palace. He blamed Christians for the fire and used the fire as a reason to start killing off Christian Leaders.

Both Peter and Paul were executed by Nero, who failed to understand that their martyrdom only served to spread the faith he was trying to exterminate. Instead of silencing the voices of Peter and Paul, Nero amplified them.

Peter was crucified upside down, at his own choice, as he did not feel worthy to die as Jesus had. He was buried under what is now St. Peter's Basilica, literally becoming part of the foundation upon which the Catholic Church was built.

Paul also died in Rome. He was decapitated at the hand of Nero. Like Peter, he was also buried in Rome. The two public pillars that propped up the fledgling church are both forever entombed in the very City whose rulers killed them in a vain attempt to kill God's message.

The oppressive rule of Nero was the final straw setting off the Jewish revolt, which resulted in the permanent destruction of the Temple in Jerusalem and the scattering of millions of Jews and Christians throughout the empire. Like amplifying the voices of Peter and Paul through martyrdom, the unintended consequence of destroying Jerusalem was further hastening of spread of Christianity. Even the worst people and the most tragic circumstances are used to bring people closer to God.

∞

My letters, more than twenty in all, contained what would have been considered treasonous statements. Thankfully, all the recipients took my final instruction seriously and burned the letters. I suppose if one of these letters could have been hidden away to be rediscovered two thousand years later, it would have helped clear my name, but it is not about me.

With no children to leave the estate to, my brother bought out my portion of the property, providing us with the capital for the trip and to re-establish ourselves. He would continue the family business and maintain the staff members who chose to remain.

Cornelius submitted his resignation two months before our departure and sold his home in Rome. He and the family came to stay with us for the final month, which turned out to be quite providential since the logistics of organizing our adventure proved to be even more complex and time-consuming than anticipated. Remember, this was before the advent of Google Maps, Expedia, or even AAA Triptiks.

Our entourage had also grown significantly from what we had originally foreseen. Between our household, Cornelius and Abigail's household, extended family members, friends, and church members from Rome, Cocullo, and Abruzzo, we had seventy-seven people making the journey, twenty-three men, thirty-one women, and twenty-three children under fourteen years of age. Not all these people would reach Britannia.

LIII

❧

Mount Pilatus

On March first, the first day we felt it possible, we started our new adventure heading north on the Apennine Way, passing through Cocullo where we said goodbye to my family members and the members of the church there. We also picked up some of our fellow adventurers. Our goal was to make it to Augusta Raurica in Germanica (now Augst, Switzerland) within thirty days, covering a minimum of twenty miles per day. If we kept this pace and stayed only a few days at each of the four major planned stops along the way, we would be in Britannia before the end of September. It was a long and arduous journey, but also a pilgrimage, a mission trip, and the adventure of a lifetime.

Augusta Raurica was an established stop along the very important western trade route and the northernmost stop before we were to turn west toward our friends in Hispania. These trade routes started as roads for military campaigns, another example of how God can use the evil of man to build connections among His people.

On the twenty-fifth day, we reached a snowcapped mountain next to a huge blue lake with crystal clear icy water. It was one of the most beautiful places I had ever seen, and I am not sure I would have moved on if we had come a month later when it was ten degrees warmer. I was so in love with the area that Claudia started jokingly calling the mountain Mount Pilatus. Somehow, that name stuck, perhaps being communicated to others through our letters to the friends we made in the area.

There is now a legend that I died on that mountain, committing suicide out of shame for "killing Jesus." Of course, that was not true. I had no shame for my actions as I was forgiven. However, I would not have been opposed to drawing my last breath from the clear mountain air.

The legend, however, started as a disinformation campaign. Six people from our party would be leaving us at the next stop - a former slave couple, their children, and two grandchildren. They would spread the rumor of my demise, hopefully helping to keep us safe from the long arm of the Empire. A similar disinformation campaign has me dying and being buried in Gaul in a city you now call Lyon.

Thanks to Dagrun and Alba, we had rooms awaiting us at our next stop, Augusta Raurica. The couple, who had been slaves for nearly fifty years before my mother freed them, had worked at our family estate. In recent years, they worked as paid staff rather than slaves, their love for my mother transcending injustice and anger.

They were sold into slavery, victims of the wars in which Germanicus earned his reputation and moniker, the wars witnessed by young Caligula. When abducted and enslaved, they were a very young couple, both in their teens. I remember the first time I noticed them in our home. It was that momentous day when I became "an adult". The beautiful young Alba served me, and Dagrun caught me looking at his bride. I remember thinking then that we could be friends were it not for social roles.

When my parents first encountered the young couple, they were being sold at the slave market in Cocullo. Recognizing that they would have been separated, and Alba would likely have ended up as a sex slave, my parents purchased them, participating in and financing the evil system that enslaved the young couple to begin with. To their credit, my parents kept them together, and my mother eventually freed them. That, of course, does not justify their original enslavement or the wickedness of a society that would allow it.

That was more than fifty years ago. Dagrun and Alba spent almost their whole lives in forced servitude. Their children and now grand-children had never known freedom. I was happy I could now do my part by helping Dagrun and Alba return to their home and to the fam-ily from whom they had been stolen.

We stayed for three days in Augusta Raurica, talking to locals, es-tablishing friendships, and discussing faith. I will always have fond recollections of the tiny town and its Germanic locals.

As we packed up and prepared to leave, Dagrun and Alba made their rounds, saying goodbye. Alba hugged Claudia for a long mo-ment, both crying and sharing emotions that required no words.

I turned to mount my horse. His muscles quivered, and as he whinnied in expectation of another ride. Great white plumes of breath erupted from his black muzzle. As I put my foot in the stirrup, I felt a hand on my shoulder. I turned to see Dagrun, who smiled through tears. He said, "You do not get to ride off without saying goodbye, my friend."

Hearing those last two words, I too teared up. I hugged Dagrun tightly and said, "Goodbye, my friend. Take care of Alba and the rest of the family until we meet again."

I would never have the opportunity to return, but I did receive cor-respondence from Dagrun and Alba. They established a church there, exposing travelers from across the empire to Christianity.

LIV

ᢒᢒᢒ

Detour de France

Leaving Dagrun, Alba, and their blossoming family, we turned southwest for the next leg of our journey. We would follow the Via Domita to meet up with a group with whom we had frequent correspondence over the years. The letter always came addressed to both me and Claudia; actually, Claudia and I, since she was always addressed first.

We hoped that we could make the journey in just two weeks; however, following the trade route back toward the Mediterranean coast, we were delayed by broken carriage wheels and flooded rivers. The melting ice from the mountains at our back made it necessary that we take a detour, which cost us four days.

Travel was not easy, but the extended route afforded us an opportunity to see more of God's beautiful creation and meet more of God's beautiful people. We got to see much of Germanica and Gaul (France to you).

After four days of traveling along roadways through mountain passes and valleys, we reached another glorious lake surrounded by mountains. Making our way west, around the shoreline of the lake, we came into the small city of Genava – in your time, the very large city of Geneva. There, Cornelius was able to arrange accommodations. The city was, at the time, an important military town for the Roman legion that used it as a hub for occupation and governance of the region. Ergo, Cornelius had connections.

We had no connections in Cularo, the small town we came to two days later. Fortunately, we found the Allobroges people who lived in this area, later to be known as Grenoble, to be quite hospitable, at least once they realized that we were not fans of Rome either. We even had a couple of new travelers from this tiny town join our troupe, but more on that later.

The Allobroges people, whose name means "foreigners," were now considered Gallic but had come to the area centuries before, having Celtic origins. They understood what it meant to be travelers, strangers in a strange land. Cornelius and I got some sideways glances at first, but we were able to find rooms for the families with children that night, and the rest of us camped right outside of town.

Most people we met in Genava and beyond adhered to the pagan Roman religion and beliefs. However, those in Cularo shunned the Roman Gods and continued the Celtic worship of their ancestors. Whatever the belief system of the people we met, we loved them, accepted them, and shared with them. Our goal was never to change them; God's people are perfect as they were made. Our goal was to show them the loving God we knew - first through our actions, then through our words, he latter if, and only if, the person we met was open to discussion. As we got closer to our destination, a week later, many people we met were already Christ followers, a testament to the people we were going to see.

∞

Nearly twenty years ago, Mary Magdalene had arrived in Massilia (Marseilles, France in your time) accompanied by Lazarus and his sisters, along with some others, former slaves and some who had been healed by Jesus. Sensing the danger they faced in Jerusalem in the wake of the crucifixion, Mary had spoken with Claudia and Joseph of Arimathea, arranging passage out of Judea. Lazarus and his sisters were quite wealthy, as was Mary herself. It was decided that they had the ability to establish themselves in Massilia, a thriving port city where they could blend in. The city had a reputation for being unruly and, at times, defiant of authority. Mary Magdelene, as expected, fit in well.

LV

⊚❦⊚

The Magdalene

Approaching Massillia, walking the banks of the Rhone River, I sensed what pagan pilgrims may feel, looking on the great temples of Apollo and Artemis, which sit high on a ridge, dominating the vista. Many desperately sought healing or redemption, while others sought blessings for new marriages, business ventures, or military service. Many, even then, recognized that these were wishes, not hopes or prayers, that may be answered by the god and goddess enshrined above the city. Their wishes, as opposed to true hope, were devoid of faith.

However, any person willing to take such a pilgrimage recognizes that there must be something that rules the universe; in order for creation to exist, there must be a Creator.

No matter how ardently one may argue, the world in which we live simply cannot result from random chance. If the Big Bang launched all of creation, what existed prior to this point? Likewise, is evolution not more likely to result in humanity if guided by a Creator, especially when the math shows it to be impossible without one...or infinite other universes of different outcomes.

These pagan pilgrims were not backward or sinful; they sought holiness and connection to God in ways they could understand, given their time and place. As I walked toward the Rhone Delta, I prayed that this time and place would become fertile soil for the growth of true hope, faith, and spiritual connection rather than desperate wishes to beautiful but soulless statues.

Massillia was surrounded by great ramparted walls, protecting its citizens from the hostile world beyond. It was necessary to have some knowledge of who was coming in and out of your city and to have early warning of approaching armies. Back in my day, there were wars and threats of wars; there were people with evil intentions; there were hostile regimes that wanted to assume power and control; there were terrorists with divergent world views who thought the way to win the debate was to kill the opposing debate team. Oh, wait, I think all of that, sadly, remains the same in your day.

We entered the Greek-inspired city dominated by marble structures supported by a mix of Ionic, Doric, and Corinthian columns. This city was built on the riches of the rare metal trade, which initially brought Joseph of Arimathea to its shores and subsequently to the planting of one of the first Christian communities – this one led by Mary Magdalene.

Asking around like the typical tourists, we found that Massillia had a thriving synagogue and many Jewish worshippers, some of whom had embraced the teachings of Jesus, though the leaders of the synagogue viewed the stories of Jesus as the Messiah with something between incredulity and indignation.

The synagogue in this city, as elsewhere, operated not as much as a "church" but as a fellowship hall, bringing the community together for meals and social events which were attended by Jews but were also frequented by curious Gentiles. Unlike the Temple, this and most other synagogues promoted the free exchange of ideas and were healthy hubs of faith and philosophy.

With the frequency of people traveling for both commerce and personal reasons, this particular synagogue operated as a hostel, allowing weary sojourners an inexpensive place to lay their heads and nourish their bodies. As such weary sojourners, we took full advantage.

Arising on our second day in Massillia, we broke our fast with mostly Greek-inspired fare, which, honestly, was a delight after having spent time in other parts of Gaul where pig, dog, and horse were often the main dish. While I did not observe the rules of a kosher diet, I agreed that much Gaulish food was ghoulish food. Instead, we had barley bread dipped in wine, cheese, and tiganites (a magnificent cross between a pancake and a donut).

At breakfast, we met Lazarus for the first time. He was somewhat of a local celebrity, being a man who died and was brought back to life by Jesus. Our new friends at the synagogue had contacted him and arranged this meeting.

After introductions to Claudia, Cornelius, and Abigail, Lazarus said that he and his sisters lived here in town and that both Martha and Mary had married and started their own households. "Uncle Lazarus" himself had lost his wife years before and had not remarried or had children. He maintained a separate home near the synagogue where he could interface more readily with the Jewish community and its budding Christian offspring. However, most of his personal time was spent with his sisters and young nieces and nephews.

Claudia jumped in to ask about Mary Magdalene to which Lazarus responded that she was still a very active leader in the Christian community but had taken up residence far beyond the city walls, saying that she did not wish to be surrounded by the icons of Greek gods and goddesses or to participate in the Roman lifestyle. She loved the people but not the culture surrounding them, being especially averse to all things Roman. Instead, she desired the peace and tranquility of God's creation. Living in a cave away from the city allowed her to commune more easily with the Divine without the distraction of what she considered profane.

"She has chosen a life much like John the Baptizer, a life into which Jesus Himself frequently escaped during His times in the wilderness," said Lazarus. "She comes into the city to preach several times a year, and people journey out to see her. She conducts baptisms and tells others of the teachings of Jesus."

"I would love to spend some time with you and your church members while here in Massillia," I said. "We can go to see Mary of Magdala when we leave for the next leg of our journey," I said, despite the looks of impatience coming from both Claudia and Abigail. They were anxious to see their friend Mary, someone with whom Claudia and Abigail shared a deep spiritual connection.

We all have a spiritual connection with Mary of Magdala; she was one of the closest people to Jesus and His ministry. She was one of the few people to see Him die on the cross, a cursed blessing that would forever connect us. She was the first to see him resurrected, chosen above all others for this honor. She was the one who brought the other disciples back to Jesus after His death, when they had lost faith. Without Mary Magdalene, the other disciples may still be wandering in the wilderness.

Mary Magdalene was also one of the first victims of the far too human nature of organized religion. Early churches were not the giant cathedrals of Europe, they were small dinner parties of people interested in God's truth, not people's power. For a time, this changed, and you are still in recovery. The separation of church and state was first conceived when Jesus said, "Give unto Caesar what is Caesar's." For a time, the church would try to become Caesar, collecting earthly wealth and power by pretending to control access to God's Kingdom. A great example of this is the "selling of indulgences", a common practice in the "Dark Ages" when priests would take money for the forgiveness of sin. Jesus Himself would have turned over the tables outside of cathedrals during this era.

Mary's life and ministry happened before this time, in a time of purity, before women were relegated out of equality in the church and into the backseat where the earthly leaders felt they belonged. Her teachings were collected in the "Gospel of Mary," one of the first writings on Christian belief. It spread widely throughout the early

Christian church, but it would be left out of the bible compiled three hundred years later. In fact, virtually all copies of the gospel were gathered and destroyed, labeled as heretical. Thankfully, there were early Christian monks who recognized the truth Mary's Gospel contained, and a couple of copies survived the censorship of Rome.

∞

Lazarus said, "I would love to host you at a dinner party this evening at my home. Mary, Martha, and their husbands and children will, of course, join us. They will be excited to see you again and hear the stories from Rome, India, Britannia, and elsewhere. We often hear from the church in Jerusalem, but to hear about Thomas, Philip, Paul, and the others is a treat. We will organize a sunrise meeting at the seashore in a few days, and you will see the vibrance of our church. Perhaps you will share your stories there as well."

And so it was. The dinner party was fun and lively. Lazarus would forgive me for joking, "These kids are loud enough to raise the dead." He did give me a slight glare before breaking into a broad smile and clapping me on the shoulder.

I told my stories and the stories that had been conveyed to me by others. "But," I said, "you must keep my name confidential as the source of these stories. For our safety, we must keep my identity secret. Unfortunately, I cannot speak to your congregation, but you can share the stories as you wish. Just refer to Cornelius and me as messengers from Rome."

In this way, I was able to spread information that would become a mix of history, tradition, and legend. As these stories spread, of course, they changed somewhat, but the core truths always remained, and people knew these stories in large part because of my efforts and those of Claudia, Cornelius, Abigail, and many others.

Martha and Mary were growing older with grace and retained the beauty and spirit that I had witnessed in our early meetings in Jerusalem. Martha, the elder sister, was even a grandmother now, and

Claudia and I almost refused to give the little boy back to his young mother at the end of the night.

∞

Sunrise on a Mediterranean beach is a thing of spectacular beauty. The sun's glory rising in the east created a dark orange highway over the calm seas, seemingly conveying the spirit of God's warmth and love directly from heaven to nourish our souls. The dark, still depths of the sea teemed with life, unseen just under the surface. Fishermen manned ships in waters just beyond the shoreline, harvesting fish to nourish our bodies.

Standing on the convergence of land and sea had always, even before I could express it, felt holy to me. There, I experienced a convergence of body and soul and a connection to every other living creature and with their creator.

We gathered on the shore to worship, to recognize the wonder of creation and the cycle of life and death, of spirit and body, of man and woman. We recognized that none of these dichotomies represented duality. Rather, they are in a perpetual dance between the partners, swaying to the music of singularity. Neither partner can exist without the other; the two parts together reflect the wholeness of God.

I kept these thoughts to myself, but they are what I would have said to those assembled on the beach; the beach where Joseph of Arimathea landed his vessel and gifted Gaul with Mary of Magdala and her compatriots. It was Claudia who made this part of history a reality. I had worked with James the Great, Joseph of Arimathea, and Alucio to arrange the Mediterranean cruise to Hispania and Britannia, but it was Claudia who arranged the extra shore excursion in Massillia.

At least five hundred people gathered together that morning. Lazarus and his sisters each took a role, telling people the teachings of Jesus, leaning heavily on his words from the Sermon on the Mount, particularly regarding worry. During this time, the people of the region were becoming more oppressed by Rome, and there was increasing hostility. People needed this message. Worry and anxiety paralyze people, blocking the flow of love both among people and within them. Worry blocks the natural dance of Godly duality.

They then took turns telling stories, the abbreviated versions, of course, recognizing that no matter how good the preacher or how riveting the sermon, no one wants a service much longer than an hour.

Mary then weaved my stories together to show people that, regardless of what happens around them or even to them, God has a miraculous way of making all things work for the good.

Lazarus saved his story for the penultimate moments of the sermon, saying how he had been alive, then dead, then lived again. He told the story of Jesus's death and resurrection from my perspective. He reminded all that the body, like a boat, is just a vessel and that it carries immeasurable treasure - an eternal soul that longs for unity with God. Finally, he spoke of Mary Magdalene and how she had been possessed of seven demons and had been cured by Jesus, and how the same could happen for all of those whose souls are under assault. They just need to ask and look inward, beyond the needs and limitations of the flesh. He reminded people that Mary Magdalene would be joining them for a service the following month and conveyed a message from her to the crowd.

We would not wait for her to come to visit. We would go to her.

LVI

❧

Inward Ascent

Even with horses and carriages, it would take us two days to reach the grotto in which Mary was now living, a cave high up in a mountain surrounded by deep forest. As we left the city, we were barely above sea level, but we would ascend, climbing higher with each step. Heading inland, the city's bright roadways, arches, and columns gave way to a winding route that became increasingly forested; trees gathered ever closer and denser to the point of blocking the sun. We spoke less and less on this journey.

As always, I felt the love and support of Claudia at my side, but our journey deeper, darker, and higher was one we took parallel to one another, each on our own journey of inward ascent. The sounds of hoofbeats and wagon wheels became white noise, strangely adding to the silence as we traveled in solitary togetherness.

After more than eight hours of travel, my reverie was interrupted by Cornellius, who rode up next to our wagon. He suggested that we stop for the night before making the final ascent up into the mountains that lay ahead. Both the people and the horses were tired, and it would be good to rest before making our final approach.

Three members of Lazarus's church had made the journey with us, conveying messages to Mary and ensuring that we could locate the grotto. They affirmed that the final approach to the grotto would be difficult, and a fresh start in the morning would be best. They also added that, while Mary lived alone in her cave, she was one of many who lived in the area. A group of druid monks had inhabited the forest and its caverns for many years. It was starting to get late in the day for proverbially knocking on the doors of strangers.

Sitting and talking around the campfire that evening, we discussed the ancient order of druids, their pagan beliefs, their lifestyle, and their history. The druids, like our new young compatriots from Cularo, were of Celtic descent, a culture much of which would be lost to history. The druids were Celtic priests and mystics, ministering to the spiritual needs of their people for multiple millennia. However, in your time, the druids are shadow figures cast upon the walls of history by the flickering flames of time. The kernels of truth we know are hidden within blurred and exaggerated forms that we dismiss as strange, backward, and inconsequential. Modern biases tell us that there is nothing to be gained by learning from "those people", people not of our own culture or belief systems.

Much of this loss was intentionally orchestrated by the Christian church, which, for centuries after my time, grew more in alignment with its human organizers and less with its spiritual foundation. Jesus had warned me that this was going to happen, but He also told me that faithful people will see through this. That, the free will that makes us human, will always yield some profane to accompany the sacred. In fact, the soul's battle to distinguish these forces, to find the light in the darkness, is what prepares us for reunion with the God that created us. The church is flawed; church people are not any more Godly than their secular counterparts; however, that is no reason to throw out the Baby with the baptismal water.

∞

I decided that Cornelius and Abigail would accompany me and Claudia, along with our guides from Massillia, to meet Mary; there was no reason for our entire convoy to make the journey up the mountainside. Later, Mary could come down to meet the others who would wait at the base of the mountain.

A winding trail switched back upon itself several times, extending the climb of only a few hundred feet to over two miles, taking more than an hour. Finally, we emerged from the tree canopy, and the world opened up, revealing an expanse of creation that seemed endless. The green forest below, flecked with early autumn red and gold, merged with the blue and white of the sky above – unifying at a horizon for which we must strive but can never attain.

Above us, we heard a shout of greeting and looked up to see Mary of Magdala, standing at the mouth of a cave. Getting closer, I could see that time had changed her, but in no way dimmed her beauty. Instead, it transformed her beauty. The last time I saw Mary, she was under thirty years old with sensual curves that could be seen under even her modest wardrobe. She had always worn her long, dark hair down, letting it flow over her shoulders and down her back. She did so now, though most of the black hair had turned white, giving the impression of an alpine waterfall spilling down her back. Her face was now thin, revealing an angular and muscular jawline that had been hidden in her youth.

The later stories of Mary being a penitent prostitute are, of course, completely untrue. As the church grew in a patriarchal society, it had trouble dealing with femininity, especially feminine leadership. These issues were much less pronounced in the early church, which embraced the message of Jesus that all people, whether Jew or Gentile, rich or poor, or man or woman, were all the same. There was an emphasis on unity that became harder to maintain as the church struggled to conform to social mores rather than be the beacon of change Jesus had ignited. Even in this relatively early meeting with Mary, these issues were emerging.

After exchanging correspondence with the messengers from Massillia, Mary dismissed them, inviting the four of us into her grotto. The sudden transition to the darkness left me completely blind. Mary waited patiently as our eyes adapted to the dark cavern. Further in, Mary had oil lamps glowing, which augmented the natural light that beamed in through openings in the wall and ceiling of the cave, forming nature's version of stained-glass windows, letting in light filtered through the multicolored leaves of the mountainside.

We sat around a table with the oil lamp in the middle, casting a reddish glow on our faces as we spoke. Of course, Mary was excited to hear about the ministries of the other apostles. We gave her all the good news first, saving the death of James for last. I saw a tear form and run down her cheek, creating the visual effect of a stream of blood flowing from a spring at the corner of her eye.

"His death may have been the first, but I am certain it will not be the last," said Mary. "I have been shown that only one of the apostles will die naturally, and he will do so in prison. The coming persecution will start in Rome and quickly spread to Jerusalem, where hundreds of thousands of Jews, including many of our fellow Jesus Followers, will die horrible deaths. The Sea of Galilee will turn red with blood, bloated bodies floating on its waters. Men, women, and children will die, and others will be forced into slavery."

I replied, "I have also had some such disturbing visions, though, clearly yours are more detailed. I have given warning to James the Just and others in Jerusalem. I have done what is in my control, and I pray that God's will be done, even in the face of the pending horror."

"It is inevitable that, in order to continue to grow, to avoid persecution, and to become more acceptable to Roman culture, the church will become more aligned with secular society. I see this trend already, but it will become clearer in the wake of the death of Peter and Paul in Rome. I see them both buried under the city. I see the church growing from their bones and becoming powerful despite, no, because of their deaths. There will be many other martyrs to come, and "Christians" will stand against Rome. However, I see a future emperor who will embrace Christianity, making it the official religion of Rome. This will be great for the followers of Christ, but will not stop the impending death of the Roman Empire. It will also lead to more Romanization of the church, which will result in warfare, hoarding of riches, power struggles, and the marginalization of women. These things do not come from God, but many will blame God for the follies of corrupt men."

Mary continued, "I have been writing my visions and thoughts for others in the future, but I know these will be suppressed and hidden by those in the church to come that want to enshrine themselves, tightening their grip on earthly power and wealth. That is okay. I have accepted it. It is a season we must go through. It will pass."

"Then there will come another season, one in which the pendulum will swing in the other direction. People will rebel against the church that fanned the flames of human division rather than God's unity. This will drive people away from the church and from God. There will be empty seats in buildings devoted to God. It will seem that the message of Jesus has been extinguished, but it will just be dormant. Energy cannot die, and the Holy Spirit is the energy that connects us all. We will reconnect to each other and to God through the spirit."

Claudia spoke up, "The things you describe are horrible. Did Jesus really die only to have others bastardize His teachings? Does the world so fear Truth that it has to murder the messengers who speak it? Do men really have to try to control and dominate each other and women for their own power and glory?"

Mary laughed and simply replied, "Yes."

After a pregnant pause, she added, "But all of that is transient. We live in a material and temporal world. God's Kingdom is one of spirit and is beyond time. Our struggles here prepare us for there."

"As for the male domination of women, I will point out that no man dominates you, my dear," giggled Mary.

I found Mary's ability to maintain levity and light while discussing heavy and dark issues absolutely invigorating. She had given up all need to control and seemingly all attachment to the material world.

"Women of the future will read my words, and there will be a shift to embrace their God given strength and power. Between now and then, there will always be women of strength and character who change the world. There will be female warriors, inventors, philosophers, teachers, and leaders. They cannot be held down when God wants them to rise. The men who will control the church, though will not recognize that the original Hebrew word for God, Yahweh, is both masculine and feminine. To our ancestors, the founders of Judaism and Christianity, God was not a man. Likewise, the Hebrew word for spirit, as in Holy Spirit, 'ruach', is feminine, whereas the Latin/Roman translation 'spiritus' is masculine. Looked at as a whole, the three aspects of God are not Father, Son, and Holy Ghost; they are Creator, Created, and Connector.

"You tell them!" shouted Abigail, eliciting an uncomfortable laugh from Cornelius.

"Well," said Mary, "there is a flip side to that coin. Jesus was the Son of God, and as such was clearly masculine. God's nature is both entity AND relationship and cannot be fully understood outside of relationship, much like light cannot be fully understood unless seen in context with darkness." (I will add that I find it fascinating that scientists in your time have found that light, like God, cannot be understood unless observed as both particle and energy - photon and wave - entity and relationship).

Mary went on, "Jesus bridged the gap between us and God, allowing us to be in relationship with God the creator, God's Son, and God's Spirit. I am sensing that, when the pendulum swings and women regain a sense of power, many will lock onto the material world, rejecting Jesus and becoming alienated from God."

She continued, "There will be many women who mistake God's power working through them with power and control springing from self. They will use my name along with the names of ancient "goddesses" as though these pagan ideas are their source of power rather than the spirit of the God working through them. They will conflate magic with miracle, self-empowerment with soul-nourishment, and solitude with independence. Refusing to be dominated by others will lead some to become unable to dance freely in partnership with others, where giving and receiving must be in balance. Given the wounds that many women will have endured through centuries of male domination, this may be understandable, but they will inflict further injury upon themselves. We must achieve balance between male and female to have healthy relationships and societies."

"Speaking of Pagan," said Cornelius, "are you not living among Druids, pagan monks?"

"I am." She looked Cornelius in the eye and asked. "Did you not live among people worshipping Roman Gods and Emperors? You and your household became a beacon, attracting pagans to God. You even learned from some of them, everyone is part of God, whether they recognize this or not. God works in them and through them, whether they call themselves Jew, Christian, Hindu, or even Druid."

After reflecting on this, Cornelius asked, "But didn't Jesus Himself say that he came to bridge the gap between us and God? I believe His words were, 'I am the way and the truth and the life. No one comes to the Father except through me.' How can you reconcile your lack of judgement with the words of Jesus?"

"Jesus reconciled all of us to God. It is not my place to judge others. In fact, my job is to actively withhold judgement. I cannot fully comprehend the mechanism by which Jesus reconciles us. I strive to fully walk as Jesus did, with love and grace for everyone I encounter, flaws and all." Then Mary laughed and added, "But, trust me, I still see lots of flaws."

"Me too," I said, "especially if I am looking in the mirror...or at Cornelius."

It seemed that we spoke for hours. As the day got later, we all made our way down to the forest and Mary ministered to the rest of our entourage. She stayed with our group that night, shared a meal with us, told stories around the campfire, and even sang a few songs. Waking with the sunrise, Mary stayed with us until we were on the road again. Her final goodbye, as we traveled west toward Hispania was a poignant and knowing. "Until we meet again, my friends," she said with a wink and a smile.

∞

Within months, Lazarus would be dead again, beheaded by a Roman soldier. His sisters and their families carried on the congregation that met on the Mediterranean shores of Massillia.

Not long after that, Mary herself would notice a lump on her breast. Even back then, we knew what this meant. Soon, she gave in to the illness that would come to be called cancer. Her immortal soul rejoined Jesus, but her spirit remains in Marseilles. Her grotto on the mountainside is open to visitors from around the world who want to better understand her, her connection to Christ, and how to follow her example as the first female Christian and a key disciple of Jesus.

To this day, pilgrims journey to see her skull displayed at a local cathedral. Somehow, even her mortal remains shine with the strength, intelligence, love, and spirit flowed out of her during her walk on earth.

LVII

∞∞

Camino de Santiago

The next part of our adventure would take us more than three weeks, trekking across the south of Gaul and the full northern expanse of Hispania. Our group had diminished in numbers as we left some in Massillia and a couple of others in parts of Gaul, where they reunified with families or had other connections. However, we also picked up some new travelers who wanted to accompany us to Hispania or Britannia. All were welcome, sharing part of our journey, but three were to become permanent members of my family.

∞

The first two additions, as mentioned earlier, we had picked up in the pagan town of Cularo. Atticus and Coria, nineteen and thirteen respectively, were orphans. Atticus had raised his sister for the past five years, since the passing of their mother. They had some friends in Cularo, but otherwise were without connection – no family, no church, no purpose. This lack of connection is what drives people to the fringes of society and sets them up for long-term failure. In your day, the most salient result of this lack of connection is the growing homeless epidemic.

I think the primary reason for Atticus's decision to join us was the sparkle I saw in his eye anytime Hannah walked by. I also noted that she seemed to enjoy walking by him with some frequency, as if dangling bait before a hungry fish. Awe, young love...

Corria, on the other hand, seemed to be in a perpetually perplexed and conflicted state. She and Atticus were very close, brother and sister, but also guardian and child. She seemed to look at Hannah with affection and admiration...when her brother was not around. When Atticus was around, she became morose and sardonic. She alternated between vying for their attention and rejecting them as if they carried the plague. Coria clearly struggled with the normal coming-of-age conflicts, but they were aggravated with the worry that she might lose the closest thing she had to a parent. Atticus was amazingly patient and precociously perceptive to the needs of his sister.

Claudia and I watched this dance of youthful relationships like you might binge-watch a great Netflix series. However, Claudia clearly relished the opportunity to distract Coria from the drama of coming of age or spend time with Hannah as she pretended not to notice Atticus. I enjoyed getting to know Atticus, bonding in the way boys, I mean men, do with a mix of competition, aggression, and laughter.

∞

The other new addition was Lulit, a former slave, whose very fitting name meant "Pearl." She was indeed precious, bringing joy and positivity to all around her. She was also full of "pearls" of wisdom, which she shared infrequently but impactfully. It was as if she took everything around her in and processed it at a deeper level than most. In so doing, she distilled the world around her to its most basic and beautiful truth.

She had resided with Mary of Magdala until Mary retreated to the solitude of her grotto. She felt a need to be part of a household and connected instantly with Claudia. While helping to care for Lazarus gave her occupation and income, she missed the company of a strong woman, and Lulit saw something of the Magdalene in Claudia.

Mary had taken Lulit out of Jerusalem when she was just a teen, having been set free by her owner. Upon becoming a follower of

Christ, her "owner" recognized the impossibility of owning another's soul, the harm this practice was having on his own soul, and the damage it was doing to the broader human spirit.

Lulit's smooth mocha skin and nearly black eyes contrasted starkly with Claudia's fair complexion and green eyes, but their indomitable spirits made them two peas in a pod. Over the rest of our journey and the years to come, Claudia and Lulit would grow closer as friends and then almost as if sisters. They grew to love one another, watch out for one another, and feed one another's spirit. Watching this always made my heart smile.

∞

The forty-seven remaining pilgrims headed west on the Roman road, transitioning somewhere about halfway from the territory of Gual into Hispania. The transition point between the regions was breathtaking. After a long climb through wooded alpine trails, we came to a summit overlooking miles of lush forest in varying shades of dark green. Just for an occasional pop of color, God planted deciduous trees whose leaves were now starting to turn, creating red and gold arboreal islands within a sea of green.

Trees are always the same despite their differing hues, heights, or hardness. Trees are startlingly active. They set down roots to gather water. They spread their leaves to gather light. They seek the company of others, connecting branches or roots with other trees. They do all of this while hosting countless other species within the protection of their canopies.

Likewise, people are always the same regardless of heritage, though we did notice distinct changes in cultural practices between Gaul and Hispania. Thankfully, these cultural shifts also altered the food available at the crossroad towns in which we stayed. We did not encounter any horse meat, and much less roast pork. Instead, we found fish, chicken, a wide variety of vegetables, and beans. My favorite, scallops, seemed to be on the menu everywhere along the way.

We met so many people on this penultimate leg of our pilgrimage. These people shared their stories with us. Each was unique in personality, cultural heritage, and background, but we all seemed bonded by the pilgrimage itself. Somehow, walking this part of our route felt holy, though not in the way of Paul's Road to Damascus experience or my own encounter on the road to Emmaus. It was more an inward holiness, time spent reflecting and listening to God with the ears of the soul.

We journeyed down this road together, sometimes in union and sometimes in parallel, but always toward our destiny. We were each processing where we had been and where we were going. As the answers came to each of us along the way, we became more true to ourselves, and that allowed us to become more connected to one another.

Over the centuries, this road would come to attract millions of pilgrims from around the world. They would each walk hundreds of miles, listening to the conversation between spirit and soul on the journey to the final resting place of James the Great, not yet known as Saint James.

To God, time is not a thing, so as we traveled the "Camino De Santiago" or "the Way of Saint James", I felt connected not just to my own entourage, not even just to God. I felt connected to the shepherd who would later rediscover James's remains, to knights of the Middle Ages who felt compelled to honor St. James, to the lost and lonely souls of your time who want to reignite their purpose and sense of divinity. Soul and spirit are beyond time and place, and to millions, this road is a bridge to the infinite. I have heard that there are places where the veil between heaven and earth is thin; this is such a place. Little did I know that we were heading toward another such place.

∞

Sometimes I found myself wondering where we would end up. I questioned whether we had given up too much. We had a life of luxury, not opulence, but certainly luxury. We turned our backs on these material comforts, feeling called to a new life, but what would that life entail? As we traveled down the roads of Hispania, I pondered these things and shared my thoughts with Claudia, my permanent pilgrimage partner.

She said, "Look around. Do you see all the flowers that line the trail? Do you hear the birds singing their songs all around? They remind me of one of my favorite things that Jesus said."

Sarcastically, I said, "If lilies and birds...blah, blah, blah...why should I worry? How many times are you going to tell me that one?"

She punched me in the shoulder...hard...reminding me of a similarly lovely day when I first kissed my bride-to-be. "I will stop telling you when you start living accordingly!"

She then hopped out of the wagon, agile as a twenty-year-old, and walked to a tree near the road. She reached up and pulled out two fruits, bringing them back to the carriage. As we ate the figs, she looked at me with her forever-smiling eyes and said, "God will provide. After all, He gave me you."

I spent a few moments in silence, absorbing the resplendence of nature around me. I noticed fields of wheat in the distance, a grove of wild almond trees on a hillside, a well-tended olive grove, and melons growing on the edge of the ditch flanking the road. There were even heads of cauliflower perched atop stalks like walking sticks. There were finches singing in the trees, and a peregrine falcon, a "pilgrim" falcon, swooped through the sky in search of its next meal. I could see a fawn peeking at us from the edge of the forest, its mother partially obscured further back in the trees.

Ahead of us, but in parallel reverence, were Hannah and her new suitor walking next to the carriage of Cornelius and Abigail. Hannah and Atticus walked hand-in-hand, looking through the eyes of young love at the beauty of nature provided by God.

Then I looked at my Claudia, who had walked beside me through the wild undulations of life. Claudia had been at my side from young love walks, admiring nature, lying in the grass looking at clouds, to the torturous times dealing with the evil forces of this world, and now to the long pilgrimage out of Rome and into the unknown.

After contemplation, I replied to Claudia, "God always provides." All my worries dissipated, but that did not remove my obligations to care for and keep my fellow travelers safe, at least to the best of my ability. In fact, that lack of worry helped me – it is what made it possible for me to meet these obligations. My eyes could remain alert to everything around me, good and bad, because my attention was not wrapped up in fears and anxiety.

The spiritual aspects of the journey did not completely mitigate the physical and mental hardship of the travel itself, with steep mountains, rough terrain, whiny children, sleep-deprived parents, and the constant din of our little wagon train. Every night when I lay down with Claudia, I fell immediately into a deep sleep where my dreams processed our adventure and revealed glimpses of our future. Every morning, I awoke to sore muscles and a desire to just stay in one place. Every day, I found new reasons to be thankful that I did not give in to lethargy.

However, nearing the end of our journey, I was also nearing the end of my patience. We would often get up early and travel until lunchtime, nap during the heat of the day, and resume in late afternoon to get us closer to our destination before setting up camp.

One evening the sun was setting on the western horizon, we could see that we were within ten miles of our destination, the small town in Galicia where James the Great had settled with Alucio and his family, the same small town to which we had conveyed James's remains to be buried six years ago. I made the call that our westward wagon train would continue even though travel in the dark was treacherous. We were just too close to spend another night on the road.

As the sun went down, the sky gave way to deepening shades of pink, purple, violet, indigo, and then black. With each darkening shade, another group of stars became visible. By the time the sky was devoid of color, it was lit up by what appeared to be a magically endless field of stars, points of light ripe for the harvest. There was no moon out that night, but the brightness of the stars guided us and lit our path.

LVIII

Wisdom, Knowledge, and Beauty

We had sent word announcing our travel plans in hopes that we might stay with the other followers of Jesus who lived in the small enclave, thanks to James and his original disciple, Alucio. Both men had now passed from this earth, but the tree of faith they had planted here was now a small grove that was to become a thriving forest over the next two thousand years.

In order to quell the panic such a horde of travelers may create, Claudia and I entered the village first, leaving Cornelius to watch over the rest of the pilgrims. We walked to the small cottage that had been described to us and, upon knocking, were greeted by a man of approximately twenty-five years.

In the typically gregarious fashion of the region, he opened the door wide and called out to his wife. Sophia entered the room, her belly swollen with new life, and her smile as bright as the field of stars that guided us to her doorstep. She threw her arms around me and kissed my cheek with so much love that I felt a bit awkward with our esposos in the room.

Sophia and her husband, Turibas, were a stunning young couple – beautiful, healthy, and strong. In an era where health and hygiene were not always on the front burner, these two looked like celebrities from your time. It was as if I were standing with Jason Momoa and Jessica Alba. I could not wait to see the kind of perfect being to which she would give birth.

Then, two children, a boy and a girl of approximately five and three, respectively, entered the room. The boy said, "Mama, you woke us up." I could now see that the apples did not fall far from the tree and that the young couple had taken seriously the admonition to "go forth and be fruitful."

Picking up the three-year-old and hugging her son to her hip, Sophia said, "Let me get my mother. She has waited so many years to meet you." Turning to Turibas, she looked at her belly and asked, "Would you mind going to get Mama?" Sophia's doting husband smiled, rubbed her belly, and kissed her, a little too passionately, before turning to exit the home. Despite my discomfort, I must admit that I found the enthusiasm with which these two seemed to live life to be infectious.

A few moments later, Alicia, daughter of Alucio, walked through the door along with Turibas and another handsome young man who looked to be in his late teens. Alicia looked like the slightly older sister of her daughter, Sophia, especially when she smiled. Before speaking a word, Alicia hugged Claudia and then me. She introduced herself and said, "I see you have met my daughter Sophia and her family. This is my son Sapio, my youngest. He looks just like his handsome father, who is traveling himself at the moment; he is working to start a sister church near the coast."

I teased Alicia, asking, "Did you choose to name your children wisdom and knowledge because you were worried that no one would see through their good looks?"

She laughed and said, "Stop or you will make their heads even bigger, especially this one," she said, pointing at Sapio. "He is already way too vain!"

"On a more serious note, thank you for allowing me to meet my father and spend his last years with him. Thanks to you, my children had an amazing grandfather who taught them so much about how to live. He spoke of both of you with great affection." Then, turning to Claudia, she said, "My father loved you dearly and described you as an angel sent to earth by God Himself. I wish my parents were here to see you, but as you know, my father passed away a couple of years ago, and my mother not long after. Their spirits were intertwined on earth, even when separated by slavery and living in two different worlds. When his time came, so did hers. Now their hearts forever dance together in heaven."

The brief dark sadness in her eyes succumbed to the brightness of her smile as she went on to say the functional equivalent of "Mi casa es su casa." She explained, though, that the community had grown so quickly that they could no longer meet in one another's homes. They had built a church, not a synagogue, but the very first, as far as I know, Christian Church. It was not Catholic or Protestant. There was no fighting over obscure theology. The people of this community just met together, told stories, sang songs, and broke bread together. For the next two weeks, this church would be home to forty-seven weary travelers. I have never been to a church youth group retreat or "lock-in", but I imagine the vibe is similar.

We even had several youths in our midst, and Cornelius and Abigail had the unenviable task of watching over Hannah and her young suitor. Claudia and I got to watch the growing young love and fully enjoy the energy it brought without the stress of enforcing boundaries. I could tell there would be a wedding in our future. Turning to Abigail, Claudia joked, "We better make the wedding soon or the baby may be a bride's maid." Abigail laughed, though somewhat nervously. Cornelius was not laughing.

Some of the other teens among us also made friendships, some with romantic tension. Likewise, I saw that some of their parents and other adults in our group found a social niche in this community.

By the time we arrived, our original seventy-seven travelers had dwindled to just forty-seven, and before we left, we would lose sixteen more. I was fairly certain that young Sapio would not stay unattached for long.

The night before we were to leave, everyone gathered in the church. Turibas and Sophia led the group in prayers, and we feasted together. Turibas told us about meeting James the Greater when James first arrived nearly twenty years ago; Turibas was just a child. He described him as tall, strong, and effusive. People naturally noticed him and gathered around him like moths to a flame. He spoke of getting to know James in his youth, of wanting to emulate him, of seeing him as a father figure when his own had been lost in one of the wars with Rome. He gestured to the small garden outside where they had buried James and said: "His spirit is still with us. His love for God and his teachings from his time with Jesus remain with us. We are joined here tonight by pilgrims brought to us by their love for James and their search for a new home, both physical and spiritual. We will carry forth the spirit and principles of James; our doors will always be open to the pilgrims of this world."

∞

The next day, we resumed our trek, this time heading toward the northern coast of Hispania and the port city of Brigantium. This portion of the trip would only take us two days. After our much-needed rest and having the perspective of five months of terrestrial travel, this was a piece of cake.

Arriving on the evening of our second day, we were inspired by the light from the Farum Brigantium, the ancient lighthouse known to you as the Tower of Hercules. The lighthouse, modeled after the Tower of Alexandria, was built in my lifetime and remains standing in yours. I pray that future generations will do a better job of recognizing their connection to history and appreciating the collective footsteps that make their individual journey possible.

We could see the light from that beacon on the shores of the dark Atlantic Ocean. It called to our weary assembly. Since leaving Abruzzo, we had covered 1,987 miles, making great time, even with some amazing layovers along the way, we arrived in less than five months. The rest of the trip would be aboard two ships that would carry us, along with a payload of silver to trade in Britannia.

LIX

The Celts

Rather than sail into Londinium (London) or Richborough, which were now heavily dominated by the Roman military, we chose to sail into the small harbor in what you now know as Caerleon, Wales. The Romans had taken over and occupied almost all southeast Britannia by this time, but the west and north were still occupied almost exclusively by the Celts. In addition, the area that would later become known as Glastonbury, where Joseph of Arimathea and his disciples had settled, was much closer to this western port.

There were, however, a couple of problems with this harbor. First, while it had been an active trade port for hundreds of years, it had largely only served the Celtic tribes that resided in Britannia, Gaul, and Hispania. Therefore, it was smaller than a typical Roman port and would not accommodate larger ships. We were relegated to two small sailing vessels for this trip and hugged the coastline as much as possible to avoid high seas. This made what could have been just two days at sea take us almost a week.

The second problem was that the people of this small port town were not used to unknown foreign visitors. The Celtic inhabitants were already on edge, battling the Roman power grab. In fact, the small Celtic town would become a Roman fortress and port within the next twenty years. The residents, who would be driven out in the coming years by the Romans, were not happy to greet strangers, especially since many of us actually were Roman.

As we sailed into the port, we first saw a hillfort, a fortified town built onto a hillside. As we got closer, we could make out people on the shoreline. Even closer, we noticed that the people were armed and their bodies, mostly naked, were painted with blue and black symbols. Having given some forewarning of our arrival to our friends in Britannia, I knew we would eventually be accepted, assuming we were not victims of friendly fire before we could introduce ourselves. I must admit, however, from my "civilized" Roman perspective, the people lining the shore appeared crazy, and I started to question Joseph's credibility in his expressed affection and admiration for them.

On our final approach, I laid down the sword of Cassius, and we all raised our hands to show that we were not wielding weapons. I was the first to disembark and walk up the beach to the older man who appeared to be leading the greeting party. I introduced myself and told him who we were.

His stern, hostile, and stonelike countenance gave way to a broad smile and a firm grip on my hand. He turned to his horde and issued what appeared to be a standdown order in Celtic. I could not understand what he said, but the tension eased immediately, and the men started walking back toward the village, as if leaving work and heading to the pub for a pint.

"Please forgive our inhospitable welcome," he said in perfect Latin. "Our lookouts watched your approach and signaled a possible invasion. When we go to war, we are a very intimidating foe. I think you might find us a bit more pleasant when we are fully dressed and cleaned up for dinner this evening. I insist that you join our banquet. Don't worry, contrary to all of the rumors, we do not eat our fellow man...most of the time."

I joined him in laughing, but I think he considered his joke more humorous than I did.

∞

Despite the Roman rumor mill and hyperbole about the cruel and carnivorous Celts, I found this village to be one of the most quaint and relaxing places in which I had ever stayed. In the chieftain's banquet hall that evening, we found ourselves in the company of families clad in colorful wool and decorative jewelry, being served delicious wine and mead from ornately decorated jugs and eating fresh food from the farms that surrounded the hillfort. The main course was lamb, which was no longer part of my diet; I had too many bad experiences with the slaughter of lambs. However, they also served salmon and roasted vegetables with an intoxicating mix of savory herbs that overwhelmed the senses.

The Chieftain's name was Volisios, and I relished my conversation with him that night and others over the next three days. I gave him information that would delay the advance of the Romans into western Britannia. This would allow Volusios and his lively and colorful tribe to move north, salvaging their way of life, the traditions of which remain to this day and have a wide influence throughout your culture.

I learned from him as well. I learned about his clan, the history of the broader Celtic culture, the Celtic way of life, and their beliefs, which, apart from being polytheistic and "pagan," were not all that different than our own. In a world that only understood God in pieces, it was the norm to have a god of war, a goddess of the harvest, a god of wine, a goddess of fertility, etc. They did not, as many suggest, worship the trees or pray to them as if they had magical powers; they worshipped the maker of the trees and prayed to this god. They were trying, as were all of us, to understand the greatness of God through the limitations of the human mind. It was like the blind men trying to understand the elephant, each just getting a part right – "it is like a tree trunk, no it's like a fan, no it is like a snake..." The bottom line was that they believed that they were part of the God created cosmos and treated the rest of the world with the respect due to anything created by God and for God's purposes.

The very little you know about the Celts is through archaeological evidence and assumptions based on that evidence. The Celts left no written record, and the remaining parts of Celtic tradition and culture have been woven together like the wool of a tartan with fabric from other cultures.

I will not tell you ALL the secrets I learned, but it certainly put things into perspective. Most of the non-Roman people we had met over the past few months were Celts. Before Rome tried to dominate and subjugate all of Europe, even before Greece had done so centuries earlier, the Celts had already established an empire. Their empire was one of common language, customs, and trade. Still, they valued their freedom too much to enable the political and military alliances needed to create an empire in the grand sense. The language Volisios and his people spoke was familiar to me because I had heard derivatives of it in Augusta Raurica, in Cularo, outside of Mary's Grotto, and even with Sophia and Turibas. Volisios explained that the Celts in Hispania had integrated with the Iberians and spoke a dialect blending the Celtic and Iberian languages.

There was occasional infighting between the Celtic tribes, but they worked together and traded with one another over all of what you know of as Europe and even parts of western Asia. In fact, when Paul wrote to the Galatians, he was writing to a Celtic community in the area you know as Turkey.

In short, the Celtics had a sophisticated culture with shared language that thrived throughout Europe. They were not cannibals, or heathens, or a small group confined to Ireland. Nor were they a basketball team. The Celts were powerful and influential, and remain so today.

I was so thankful to have gotten this time in the village of Volisios. It chipped away many of my prejudices and beliefs that separated me from fellow humans, beliefs that separated me from the man God intended me to be. Ultimately, such prejudice, literally prejudging, was a sin as it separated me from God.

Our brief sojourn among the Celts also prepared Claudia and me for the final mission of our lives, we just did not know it at the time.

LX

Let it Be

A week after landing in Britannia, we finally made it to what I had
assumed would be our final destination.

We had all been looking forward to the end of the line, our new
home. As such, the small town that sprang into existence less than
twenty years ago was a sight for sore eyes as it sprang forth once again
out of the mist.

The morning clouds surrounded us as we wandered south over
miles of rolling hills and dales. We rose out of the clouds as we as-
cended one such hill. From this vantage point, the largest hill on the
horizon, topped with a cluster of buildings, looked like Noah's Ark
traversing a fog-covered ocean. The roofs of several houses in the valley surrounding the hill popped in and out of the mist like playful dol-
phins.

The town founded by Joseph looked just as it had been described, a
bastion of hope on a hillside, the hill now called Glastonbury Tor. The
church at the summit of the hill was much larger than the other buildings and reminded me of the lighthouse in Brigantium, summoning us
to safe harbor.

Diving back beneath the churning tide of fog, we were guided by
the hazy outline of the ark-like mount and its holy beacon. The fog
thinned as we traveled, as if rising from the ocean depths to shallow

waters near the shore. On that shore, we could see dozens of houses taking form. We started to hear cows and sheep in the fields around us, discerning their forms as we approached the town.

Still closer, we found ourselves among a band of horses. A black stallion stood in the mist, watching, silent, observant, and protective. We heard children playing and several ran out to greet us with refreshing exuberance, the joy and curiosity of childhood.

A young girl, eleven or twelve years of age, appeared to be the leader of the group, the other children deferring to her age and wisdom. "Hello, who are you?" she asked, holding her hand up in a non-verbal command. Deferring to her clear authority, I pulled our horses to a stop.

In a serious, woman-to-woman tone, Claudia answered, "We are pilgrims. We have traveled the world to come here to see you. I am Claudia, and this is my husband, Pontius. Can you introduce us to your parents?"

The girl said, "I am Tess and these are my friends." She looked at them and commanded that they introduce themselves; they did so in deference to their leader. "Follow us," Tess commanded.

She turned and started to walk, her little troop following like ducklings, so we fell in line as well. As we approached the largest house in an alcove at the base of the hill, the sun seemed to magically burn off the remaining fog, bathing us and our surroundings in warm light, illuminating the colors of nature – God's own quilt embracing us in His warmth and protection.

Out of the house appeared a woman, about my age, adorned with simple elegance, her hair pulled back and covered in a purple scarf.

"Welcome to Mount Aran. We have been expecting you," Mother Mary said.

∞

I had met Mary once before at one of my early meetings with the disciples, though I had never had the opportunity to speak with her. I had also seen her sobbing during my sentencing of Jesus and had watched her at the foot of the cross. I had never been introduced to her as the mother of Jesus. Looking at her, I was able to put two and two together. As she had twenty years ago, Mary looked much like her son, enough for anyone to recognize them as family members. When I first met her, though, this similarity was based solely on physical likeness. Now, I saw in her something of the divinity that I had recognized in Jesus as we spoke privately in Herod's palace, standing in the place where Herod had ordered the slaughter of the innocents. I saw the same otherworldly knowledge and spark of God behind her eyes as I had seen in Jesus when he asked me, "What is truth?".

I did not know Mary would be here. Her presence was, by design, never mentioned in letters, and few would have been privileged to this knowledge. I had had no time to prepare for this moment. I was not ready to fully acknowledge the horrific pain I had caused this woman. Honestly, I might have been less inclined to take this journey had I known this moment was coming. I thought that all of the guilt and shame I carried in my soul had long been assuaged, but standing before Mary, I froze like an animal faced with a mortal challenge. My response options were fight, flight, or freeze; my soul chose the latter for me.

Mary stepped down from the small porch next to her doorway, walked directly to me, reached up, and embraced me. I fell into her arms as if I were an inanimate bag of beans, lacking bone, muscle, or even mind...my body was no longer in my control. My soul embraced Mary and felt love, forgiveness, and full connection to God. In this moment, my soul was perfectly clean, free of any sin that could possibly separate me from God. Tears streamed out of my eyes and my body was wracked with sobs, my soul directing my body to cleanse itself with my tears, expelling any internal impurity and washing the grime of the world from my eyes.

I remained in Mary's arms for a moment that felt like eternity. I started to regain composure, bone and muscle back in place, my mind aware of its surroundings once again. Looking around, I could see that everyone was exactly where they were when I left them, but I had indeed left them, to where the human construct of time lacks meaning.

Mary hugged each of our group and seemed to find special delight in the children, picking up the toddlers, holding babies up in the air, even kissing a pregnant belly – young couples can always find a way for affection and amorous activity even among a throng of tired travelers. The young mother-to-be squealed with surprised excitement, feeling her baby move inside as if recognizing and trying to embrace Mary. Likewise, Mary was full of life, and her spirit animated everything she touched, everything in her presence.

∞

Soon we found ourselves, quite winded, sitting in the church at the top of the hill. In some ways, this building seemed less like a church and more like a house, a home filled with love. In other ways, it seemed like the Vilisios hillfort, high on a hillside, protecting its people. One way or another, built of wood and having a thatched roof, you would not recognize it as a church. It lacked your presupposed steeples, spires, or stained glass. It did not even have pews!

Stepping inside felt like a warm embrace that lifted and lightened the spirit. Mary and several others from the village welcomed us to the church and took seats among us on the floor. Mary did not seem winded at all, even at her age, she must make this climb regularly. Each of our fellow travelers introduced themselves and their families.

Lulit introduced herself last, always listening before speaking. As she started to speak, Mary interjected, "Of course I remember you, my Pearl. Looking at the rest of the gathering, Mary said, "I have known Lulit since not long after the death of my son. Then she accompanied us on part of the journey out of Judea. These were times of terrible loss and uncertainty, made more tolerable by Lulit's precious spirit.

"I may be the mother of Jesus, but I am human. During this time, I could not escape sadness except by giving in to anger. I felt that all love had died with my son. My life felt meaningless, hopeless, and without purpose. Days, weeks, and even months passed when I felt helpless to pull myself out of the darkness. I might still be in that dark state were it not for Lulit."

Lulit initially looked down with embarrassment, uncomfortable with praise from Mary. However, this bashful moment passed, Lulit looked directly at Mary and with complete self-assuredness said: "Thank you. I am so honored to be back in your presence, which, whether you knew it or not, always brought light to those around you."

Lulit remained silent for a moment, then added, "I am grateful for any part I played in providing you, the mother of our Lord, comfort during the dark days after His death. You are human, and part of the human condition is trauma. This world is full of pain and lost souls. All you need to do is care, listen, and let God do the rest. What is lacking for struggling souls is not a word you can share or a gift you can give. The pain, loss, and trauma of this world disrupt the connection between soul and spirit. Without this connection, one cannot have healthy human relationships or commune with the creator. Healing comes when space is created, a quiet space wherein this connection can be re-established."

I thought about this and recognized the wisdom of these words. I, too, had been a lost soul. No words or material items could have fixed that. What ultimately prevailed was my connection to others, such as Cornelius and Cassius, connection to my closest loved ones, such as my mother and, ultimately, Claudia, and most importantly, connection to God. I had to be hit over the head to re-establish this connection to God; others will as well, but this is where healing comes from.

In your time, some new age hippie types will call this "connecting to source." That is not wrong – just, like the "wise men" looking at the elephant, it is incomplete. God is indeed the source of creation, but God is also part of and within that which was created, and God is the energy and spirit that unifies everything. Nothing is complete without all three aspects of God. The eternity of God exists and can only be fully understood in relationship, in love, that transcends time and space.

∞

Our hosts introduced themselves as well. Two were half-brothers of Jesus, Joses and Simon, and their wives. Another was Salome, the half-sister of Jesus, and her husband. Others had been among the followers of Jesus in Judea, some of whom were men and women whom He had healed. These were the original disciples of Joseph of Arimathea who traveled with him in the early years after the Crucifixion. They apparently formed the inner council for the town but had intermarried and otherwise grown the community, forming the thriving town with a population of about seven hundred.

Simon said, "Uncle Joseph named the town Mount Aran, which means Mount Bread in the local Celtic Language. He was there when Jesus fed the multitudes with just a few loaves and fishes." Claudia elbowed me to remind me that she had been there too. Simon continued, "He had heard Jesus tell followers, 'I am the bread of life.' He was even there when Jesus broke the bread and poured wine the night before His crucifixion. It made sense."

One of the teenagers in the room exclaimed, "I thought it was because the hill looks like a loaf of bread!" I mentally slapped my head. We are just one generation from completely losing the context and meaning of our heritage. Joses gave his son a look that conveyed a touch of anger and a great deal of perplexity.

Mary spoke, and the rest of us got quiet, in awe of the woman who gave birth to Jesus, had raised Him to manhood, and had watched as He transcended this life. She explained that as Jesus was dying on the cross, He commended her to the care of a man at the foot of the cross. Some have since said that it was John, son of Zebedee, brother of James the Great, and the intimidating apostle with whom I shared many memories. Others said it was her other son, James the Just. In reality, this was misdirection and intentional ambiguity so people would not track her here to Britannia.

Mary had been cared for by her uncle Joseph since childhood. Her uncle Joseph had been a father figure and guide for Jesus after Mary's husband died. Her uncle Joseph would go on to bury Jesus in a family-owned tomb. He would then take Mary away from the danger of Jerusalem in the wake of the crucifixion, at a time when she was caught in the darkness of loss and in need of such a father figure.

My direction to be cautious of what we placed into the written record kept Mary and her family members safe, but it has led to much debate and infighting since. People would get along better and be happier if they could embrace the joy and mystery of the unknown. Instead, many think that they must know all in their efforts to control their surroundings.

Now, Joseph of Arimathea had also passed into the spirit realm, his mortal remains buried outside of the church near the Hawthorn tree he planted upon reaching their new home. While this was their new home, one he loved and had always connected with spiritually, he wanted to have a piece of his childhood home with him as well. This variety of Hawthorn tree, native to Judea, was this remnant of childhood, one he would share with his adopted kinfolk in Britannia, who still wonder how Judean Hawthorn trees came to be part of their landscape.

Mary said, "Our little village is our home and will be safe, however, the Roman armies are ever advancing westward with the goal of gaining control of all Britannia. This region is particularly significant to them because of the importance of tin mining. It is just a matter of time before they infiltrate. You are all welcome here, but for some of you, Roman authorities may prove particularly troublesome."

She paused to look at me from the corner of her eye before continuing. "We have spread a bit over the past years and have ties to other settlements to the north, places that will remain free of Rome for some time yet. We can arrange introductions. Some of you may choose to stay here, and we will help you establish new homes. The rest of you will need to prepare for one more road trip."

∞

We spoke some more and made tentative plans. Then we broke bread together, first in a ceremonial re-enactment of the last supper of Jesus and then in jovial communion. The initial ceremony had not yet become widespread, but some variation was practiced by many in Judea, Rome, and elsewhere. One of the people who had been present at the last supper offered a loaf of bread, repeating the words of Jesus on that fateful night. Then Mary held up a cup of wine. Light shimmered off the golden goblet in her hands as it did from the tear in her eye as she said, "This is my blood given for you."

The chalice was passed around, and each of us drank from it. I took note that this goblet, the "grail," was not just gold-plated but solid gold. Something that might have been found in the Herodian Palace, not the home of a fisherman...not even in the home of a tax collector...not even in the home of a wealthy merchant such as Joseph of Arimathea.

I thought back to the upper room where I met with the disciples. I remembered Joanna, who owned the house in which the group met; Joanna, the wife of Chuza, Herod's chief of staff. Connecting the dots, I realized that this was the very cup that Jesus had held, and I suspected how it came to be in His hands. As it came to rest in my hands now, I felt as if I myself was in that upper room then. I was among the disciples being prepared for my journey through this world where I was to bring bread and wine, body and blood, to others.

I watched as both Lulit and Claudia drank from the cup, and I recognized that they were now permanently connected, brought together by God to continue God's work in a new place, the place to which we would travel in the coming days. I did not know what life still had in store for me, but some of my responsibility lightened in that moment, watching them together. Claudia had always had her own purpose, but part of my purpose was protecting her.

For now, we would enjoy our time in this place, this holy place. In fact, our home for the next week would be this very church, where we were sheltered and fed by Mother Mary herself. The meals were always delicious, but her words of wisdom would stay with us forever, feeding our spirits even in times of trouble.

LXI

Dark Waters

After twenty members of our party decided to stay with Mary, the final eleven members of our troupe headed back north toward what you know as the Bristol Channel. Two guides joined our party, which now included Claudia and me, Cornelius and Abigail, Hannah and Atticus, Lulit, Coria, as well as three other members of the group who had been with us from the very first step of this journey.

The guides took us to a hidden harbor, even smaller than Caerleon, where we found two fishing boats that seemed rather sketchy to me. The guides assured us that these boats were seaworthy and had made the journey on which we were about to embark multiple times.

It was now October, the weather was growing colder, and the dark waters of the sea churned more each day, so I was not sure I trusted their judgement. Nevertheless, we sailed west out of the small harbor and then north upon reaching what you refer to as the Irish Sea.

The cold, wet October wind seemed to relish its ability to startle us, creeping up and jumping out with unexpected blasts, a sneak attack from a winter waiting in the shadows of the dark sea. At times, the boats tossed and turned, and our stomachs churned. Cold water sprayed over the bows of the tiny ships, pooling at our feet, and threatening to capsize us.

Despite these fearsome fall shenanigans, God had brought us here and did not plan on our Journey ending at the bottom of the sea. While nature was a childlike prankster, the real terror of this season, as always, came from man. I had faith that we would find our new home soon, a home where we were not subject to the horrors of Roman oppression, a home where we could live out our mission without wicked and tyrannical rulers. The changing seasons of this new land would be much better than the season of brutality I knew was coming elsewhere in the world.

While nature was a childlike prankster, the real horror in the world came from man. My dreams had been haunted with visions of brothers and sisters dying on crosses, some upside down. Others were beheaded, skinned alive, or torn apart by animals for the amusement of Roman mobs.

In the coming years, we would lose Peter, Paul, James, Matthew, Philip, Thomas, Andrew, Simon, Matthias, Thaddeus, and Bartholomew. All of them murdered, victims of humans trying to maintain power and control. This ego-centrism, self-absorption, self-aggrandizing, and self-worshipping are the ultimate sin, elevating oneself to the position belonging to God, trying to push the Creator out of creation. The only part of this creation that a human can push God out of is their own heart and soul. They empty the temple God created and replace God with an idol unto themselves. This void, the great chasm created by pushing God out, is Hell, and nothing good can spring out of depravity.

Of the original disciples, only John, brother of James, would die of natural causes. One might think that all these martyrs were men, the prototypical warriors willing to die for God and country. However, women were not immune to the persecution either, and many of these women were warriors as well. Theckla, a follower of Paul, is just one example of many faithful women who would die for the kingdom of Christ. She was torn apart by animals after other attempts to execute her failed, her faith overcoming her executioners.

I knew that men and women murdered for their faith lived on, their souls were eternal, and nothing done to them on this earth could kill the spirit God had breathed into them. However, my mission was to spread Christ's message of love and redemption to all God's people, and dying a martyr was not in God's plan for my life or the life of Claudia. God's plan for us brought us here...

∞

As I had that thought, I spotted it – a small village on the shore of the tranquil loch into which we had sailed upon exiting the wild Irish Sea. The village was backdropped by the highlands of what you now call Scotland. The smoke rising from several of the small buildings of the village seemed to be a signal – "Welcome home."

LXII

❧

Leaven

The little hamlet and the lake on which it lay were named Loch Leaven by the first pilgrims from Mount Aran. The founders had paid homage to their home at Mount Aran, referring to the yeast which makes bread rise. The village grew from Mount Aran, was further north, was at a much higher altitude, and signified the spreading of the faith; therefore, the rising bread theme was both meaningful and humorous. Since that time, the name was misspelled as Leven, and much debate has transpired over the origins of the name of the Loch and the "Leven trout" which swims in its waters.

The Loch Leaven community had set up a church/gathering hall to serve them and travelers who came through their village from Mount Aran and neighboring Celtic trading partners. The building was at the western edge of the hamlet nestled up to the alpine river, forming the western boundary of the town as it made its way out to the loch. The community hall had a hearth to keep us warm through the winter and on which we could cook our meals during our first months in Loch Leaven.

You might think that at this latitude and altitude, we would be LOCHed in for the winter, but winter was surprisingly mild. Most days were about forty degrees, and the stream next to the church gurgled by happily, frigid, not frozen.

It was not a good season to be out building new homes, but it was ideal for exploring and planning. Cornelius and I took trips out into the vast wilderness beyond the village, scouting for the best place to build our new homes, a place that would allow us to grow some crops and raise livestock, a place where we could easily come to town or spend time with each other, but could also enjoy some peace and solitude; spending nearly a year traveling with others and living communally makes one appreciate personal space!

The morning on which we found the perfect spot, Abigail and Claudia came with us. We traveled west along the loch and then south into the foothills. Claudia stopped for a moment as we approached the summit of a small rise topped by a lone tree, its bare limbs seeming to quiver in the cold breeze. She turned in a circle and said, "This is it...We are home."

Standing next to her, I too surveyed the landscape. What I saw was more vision than vista. From this vantage point, I could see the smoke rising from the Loch Leaven Village where we would go to meet with friends and conduct business, trading goods and services. I could see the shore of the loch and the boats we would dock there, nets full of fish. There were sheep grazing all around us on the hillside. Horses trotted in the corral next to the barn, silhouetted against the mountainous backdrop. A small herd of long-haired cows huddled, keeping one another warm, their humid breath billowing forth clouds that merged with the fog still hovering over the meadows below. I could see the future home of our beloved friends, Cornelius and Abigail, across the glen. Between our homes, partway up the hillside, was a smaller house. From our vantage point, I could see the thatched roof and the garden behind the house where children chased chickens. I could hear the joy of their laughter and the squawking of the hens and chicks.

As usual, Claudia was right; this was it...this was home.

∞

Over the spring and summer months, everyone worked together, building our new little enclave, an outgrowth and expansion of the Loch Leaven community. Some of our fellow travelers chose to make their homes inside the main settlement where their background and skills would allow them to work and contribute to the town. Cornelius and I laid out our plots of land, designed our homes in consultation with Abigail and Claudia, and led teams of neighbors and friends to build the houses.

Coming together to build houses is not just a matter of building roofs and walls, it is community building community, it is taking "love thy neighbor" seriously. We appreciated the hard work of our new friends and neighbors and would return the favor many times over the coming years. This is how leaven works; it takes a good deed done in love and multiplies it like fishes and loaves.

I noticed how well Hannah and Atticus worked together building our house and the house of Hannah's parents. One would hold a nail while the other wielded the hammer. Atticus would lift and place a stone while Hannah applied mortar. It did not shock me when Cornelius came to me late one afternoon, as we walked back down to Loch Leaven, and asked him to help design and build another home. "Atticus and Hannah plan to marry and will need a home of their own."

"I know exactly where it will be," I responded, thinking back to the children chasing chickens in my vision. Cornelius might think those are his grandchildren, but Claudia and I would have other thoughts!

∞

By the end of summer, we were in our new homes. While the new house may have lacked the grandeur of the Abruzzo Villa, the cozy cottage nestled in a charming community somehow felt more like home. The livestock and crops raised here would never rival those of my childhood home, but we were not feeding an empire. Nor were we interested in status. We wanted to feed ourselves and contribute to the well-being of our friends and neighbors.

Cornelius and Abigail hosted Hannah and Atticus while they waited for their new home to be finished. The young couple also waited, rather impatiently, for their wedding day, planned for later in the fall. Atticus's sister, Coria, chose to live with us and Lulit. At fourteen, Coria, did not want to be a third wheel in her brother's relationship. She had also developed an almost mother-daughter relationship with Claudia, a relationship young Coria needed, a relationship that my Claudia relished. Aunt Lulit would complete a little triad of feminine family members who would love and support one another and often gang up against me for years to come.

LXIII

Weddings

To be honest, I have never been a wedding guy. This is, in part, because while I love people, I am most comfortable in small gatherings or watching at a distance. The other part, though, is that weddings always seem to be disingenuous, and this was amplified in my era. People always have mixed emotions at a wedding. Some may feel legitimately happy for the couple but also harbor jealousy for their joy. Others may secretly feel it is a bad match but never openly say so; even when told "speak now or forever hold your peace", they do neither. Still others harbor secret feelings for one or the other of the newlyweds, jealousy barely concealed while sober and sometimes fully revealed after a few drinks – "in vino veritas." Some new in-laws hold their noses at the addition of a new family member with barely concealed undercurrents of rejection.

In my day, though, this was even worse as most new couples rarely married because of the love and joy they experienced with their betrothed; they married to enhance their social position. I was blessed that Claudia magically made both possible. However, my wedding was no exception to the cringeworthy nature of nuptial ceremonies. In fact, while Claudia and I focused on one another, making our wedding privately joyful, it was a public spectacle put on by Sejanus for political purposes. The party hosted by Sejanus was not to celebrate the marriage but to hob knob, solidify political relationships, advance his aspirations, and assuage his ego. Sadly, at that point in my life, that seemed normal, acceptable, and even admirable.

The wedding of Hannah and Atticus was a paradigm shift to me – marriage for the sake of embracing and spreading love with no secondary gain required. I had watched Hannah grow from an infant completely dependent on Abigail and Cornelius to a strong and confident young woman of intelligence, beauty, and virtue. She was marrying a young man with whom she had found happiness and true love, with no strings. When they met, Atticus was an orphan whose net worth was the value of the ragged clothes on his back. He was saddled with caring for his younger sister, who, without him, would have had little choice but to turn to prostitution if she were not sold into slavery. He took responsibility for his sister, never treating her as a burden. He was a young man of character whose values *were* the value he brought to the marriage. This young couple was brought together by God and were connected by love, not materialism or power. What a breath of fresh Scottish air.

∞

On the wedding day, Claudia joined Abigail, Lulit, and Coria, sequestered in our house with Hannah for what seemed like endless hours or primping. To us men, this seemed like complete overkill; Hannah was gorgeous by nature and glowed even brighter in the presence of Atticus. Why bother trying to improve upon God's creation? Besides, it's not like we had overpriced wedding photographers in my time.

Kicked out of my own house, I checked on Atticus, who was getting ready at Cornelius's house. He was already dressed, his chestnut brown linen tunic over dark blue breeches and a matching cloak pulled over his shoulders. The cloak was fringed in a design that looked like gold ropes woven together, which corresponded to the color and design of the gold clasp holding the cloak together. I had not fully noticed how impressive this young man was until this moment.

He always carried himself with dignity but never with pride. While pride comes from the ego, dignity comes from the soul. Dignity is often more subtle, running deep like the waters of the loch, while pride is usually more superficial, like a shallow stream coursing over a bed of rocks. Pride often garners more attention, but dignity drives destiny.

Atticus had three friends attending to him, so I decided to take a walk down to the loch, where I found Cornelius. We spent our time talking about the change of seasons, both of us knowing we were not just talking about the trees starting to turn gold and red on the other side of Loch Leaven. We were not just talking about the extra chill blowing off of the water. We were not just talking about the heat of summer having passed us by. I put my arms around my best friend's shoulder and said, "Our little girl is starting a life of her own. She is ready and she has chosen well."

Cornelius replied, "She has indeed, and so did we, my friend," speaking of both our wives and our adventures. "If we had stayed in Rome, she would never have met Atticus."

"If we had stayed in Rome, I doubt we would even be around to see our grandchildren."

Cornelius let my ownership claim on his future grandchildren slide. "If we had stayed in Rome, I would not be standing here with you looking at this little piece of heaven."

We turned and surveyed God's land. The land that the Creator entrusted to us. The land we now called home. The land upon which we felt spiritually connected to all people: past, present, and future. The land where our roots would remain entwined with the rest of God's Creation long after our earthly travels ceased.

"I guess it is time to join the rest of the wedding party," said Cornelius.

"Yeah, but which of us is giving Hannah away?" I said, elbowing him in the ribs.

LXIV

New Life

For fifteen more years, I watched over our little slice of heaven. Claudia and I sat on our porch and watched as more and more children chased chickens outside the little house down the hill from our home. In all, there were five, three girls and two boys, the oldest being a young man who perfectly blended Hannah's dark brown hair with the green eyes of Atticus. Tall, handsome, and athletic, he walked with his mother's grace and watched over his siblings with his father's sense of responsibility. His younger siblings also blended their parents' features, but each in a slightly different way. The youngest, a little girl with streaks of red in her hair, reminded me of Claudia – a force to be reckoned with.

Cornelius and I worked together, and our families thrived as did the little town of Loch Leaven. Our village grew only to a modest three hundred people, but others spread out, little interconnected colonies, outposts of freedom and faith on the western frontiers. Rome NEVER intruded on our little corner of the world. In fact, we intruded on Rome. Christianity grew here among the Celts, the "barbarians" and "heathen" who Rome had sought to conquer, enslave, and exploit.

Instead, these people would end up as the "barbarians at the gate," ushering in the fall of the Roman Empire. While this was still three hundred years in the future, my dreams were filled with forecasts of the coming fall, the "dark ages" to follow, and the renaissance more than thirteen hundred years in the future. The other empires that would rise – the Mongol Empire, the Spanish Empire, the Russian Empire, and even the British Empire. They each happened in their own time and place, but my dreams were beyond these boundaries, and I saw them rise and fall from my bed in our little Scottish cottage.

I witnessed all kinds of atrocities in these dreams, ranging from young women burned alive because they did not follow social expectations to old men in white robes pretending to represent God while hoarding gold stolen from distant lands.

I saw other men in white robes, which contrasted starkly with the tan skin of their hands, the only part uncloaked beyond their angry eyes. They claimed to be virtuous while hanging young men with slightly darker tan skin from trees.

I saw entire cities wiped out by explosions as bright as the sun. A great wind emanated from the blast, obliterating all in its wake. I saw nude people running from the blasts, fire having consumed their clothing and charred their skin.

I saw people herded together in great wagons seemingly pulled by ghosts. They were brought together like cattle in prison camps, experimented on by insane physicians, killed in gas chambers or with weapons I did not recognize or understand. Their bodies were discarded in huge piles as if garbage in a landfill.

But above all, I saw love, which over time, became more the norm than the exception. I saw that people started looking at each other and seeing what they had in common at their core rather than how they differed on the surface. I saw a new kind of empire, one that rose on the other side of the great ocean. I saw that this empire did not grow out of some violent lust for power as had the others. Don't get me wrong, there was vicious violence and lots of lust... but the people primarily sought freedom and the liberty to live according to their beliefs. There were land grabs, but in comparison, this empire grew by spreading influence; by growing wealth even beyond its borders; by being a 'beacon on the hill' and providing hope for a better life to the billions (yes, billions!) of people on earth.

Unfortunately, this new empire was not immune to the evils inherent in human society. The people of this empire got to a point in their evolution where these atrocities caught up with them. Rather than celebrating the evolution of their society and recognizing God's hand in this evolution, they started devolving into the hatred and tribalism rampant in my day that ultimately led to the fall of Rome. I wondered if this devolution would halt the spread of unity and love that was clear in some dreams. That is the nature of dreams, or at least mine, you cannot tell beginning, middle, or end.

My dreams did not haunt me as they had in the past, especially as one might expect given their content. I was an observer, watching from a place beyond the pain and suffering inherent in this world. I knew that those suffering in the scenes playing out before me were, even now, in the same place...united with their creator, surrounded by love. We are all from God and will, unless we refuse His love, reunite with Him. It just takes time.

∞

One morning, I woke up from such a dream. I lay in bed next to my beautiful Claudia as she snored like a contented cat purring in my ear. I kissed her cheek and said I was going for a walk. Her smile said, "I love you and have fun...now let me sleep."

The sun had just crested the hills on the western horizon, starting its climb. I too climbed, heading up the hill beyond the eastern wall of our cottage to my favorite tree: the tree perched atop of the hill, overlooking the loch, the town, the stream, our house and the houses of our beloved adoptive family members; the tree I had first seen in my vision of the place; the tree that overheard Claudia when she said "we are home." Yes, this tree was special, even magical. Protected under its canopy, I could see everything that mattered to me from one place, all the gifts God had given me. I fell asleep.

I woke up in the same spot. I woke up like a child after a restful sleep, invigorated and ready to take on the day. Looking up, I saw sunlight filtering through the thin multicolored fall leaves. It was like looking up from a crib to see the most stunning mobile, placed there by God for my viewing pleasure. Then I noticed I was not alone.

The cows had made their way up the hillside and were grazing just feet away. Somehow, my favorite horse, a large black stallion, stood next to me, pawing the ground, looking over the beautiful landscape, and telling me he was ready for a ride. I felt something warm next to me and found a lamb curled up by my side, my hand stroking its curly wool coat.

I stood, stretched, mounted, and rode off into heaven – my heaven.

LXV

My Revelation - The View
from Here

While my life ended, my story continues. I will not tell you the details of what I found awaiting me in heaven. That is for you to discover when you come to your end of days. Besides, what you find will be different than what I found.

Of course, I woke up holding a lamb. Of course, I woke up in the place on earth I found to be closest to heaven. Of course, I rode into heaven on my favorite black stallion. These things made sense - for me. They made my transition perfect - for me.

I now recognize that most people who are brought back from death report a near-death experience (NDE). These are, at their core, exactly the same. Around the edges, though, they are nuanced. These nuances reflect how the soul interacts with the divine, making the transition from earth to heaven easier and personally relevant.

The free will experienced on earth continues in heaven, but rarely does anyone choose evil. Why would they when they are surrounded by joy and happiness?

Speaking of happiness, the same three things that make for a happy and whole life on earth are equally integral in heaven. In heaven, we experience love, play, and work, but, unlike the material world, these things just flow seamlessly.

In heaven, you are surrounded by and infused with love. I will not tell you if you reunite with earthly loved ones, but I will tell you that the experience of love is perfect in heaven, where love can be free of the bondage of the self. Yes, obviously, there are animals in heaven. The carnal aspects of the human condition often hinder perfect spiritual connection among people, but many people overcome these barriers with animals, experiencing the joy of selfless love. God would not take that away in heaven!

In heaven, we experience the contagious joy and laughter of play, playing as a child plays. As we age on earth, scars form from our encounters with others and from our own imperfect attempts to sculpt ourselves into what God intends us to be. These scars bind the child within, death sets that child free.

In heaven, you will also continue to work. This work is not a "job" in the traditional sense; it is a purpose. You cannot have heaven without purpose. The purpose one feels in a job is to support oneself and one's family. At its best, the purpose of a job goes further, has deeper personal meaning, and makes the world a better place. The purpose of heavenly work is to bring creation into perfect alignment, to mold the clay of creation into the form of heaven.

My specific purpose in heaven is an extension of my mission on earth: to help people navigate through the false circles of power and wealth of earth and discover the true infinite power and treasure of heaven. In heaven, there are no human constraints, no constant pulling from one task to another, no reason to prioritize the needs of one person over another.

I am capable of being in multiple places and at multiple times, anywhere from the "Big Bang" to the end of infinity. Accordingly, I walked with some throughout their entire lifetime, the unseen "guardian angel" guiding their footsteps through a treacherous world. Others I was with for only a season. Still others, I was only needed for a moment. Oh, the stories I could tell! I leave you with an episode of one such life.

Epilogue

The artist looked at his medium. His job, as he saw it, was not to create something. It was to reveal God's creation, what the block of marble was always intended to be. Other artists had examined this huge block and could only see its flaws. Decades ago, one such artist had taken up the hammer and chisel, attempting to create sculpture from the rock, to mold the rock into what he wanted it to be. He failed.

The rock was now lying in the church yard like an empty tomb, ignored by passersby who could not recognize its significance. Flawed by nature, wounded by someone trying to make it into what was never meant to be, the marble might never have reached its potential. However, the artist had endured battles of his own: battles with his own demons and battles with monsters masquerading as the pious and powerful. His battles allowed him to see what others could not - the soul trapped within the stone. In fact, the artist had known this block of marble, had played on it as a child, had grown up with it before the powers of the world swept him up into their service.

At just thirteen, the artist was taken in by the richest man in the world, the patriarch of the most powerful family in the world. The patriarch, despite his own flaws, saw and wanted to nurture the artist's God-given talent.

The patriarch's family used their power to control the church, selecting and puppeteering popes, leaders of a faith that he did not share, a faith that even these popes failed to follow. His philosophy was humanism, placing humanity at the apex of all creation and imbuing people with godlike status.

As a teenager, the artist watched as the church resisted the puppet master and the pendulum swung against the art, literature, and all forms of creative expression he sponsored and endorsed. In the streets, statues were smashed, paintings were ripped apart, and books were burned. Women wearing excessive jewelry or fine clothing were subject to being publicly stripped of their belongings, assuring compliance with "sumptuary laws." Such deadly swings of the pendulum are the natural consequence of people being used by the powerful; those narcissistic enough to want to recreate the world in their own image.

The artist looked up to his wealthy and powerful benefactor and was treated as a family member. He even agreed with aspects of the humanist philosophy, seeing that the human mind and body were indeed the pinnacle of God's creation, but unlike his benefactor, he did not worship man. He worshipped the God that created man.

The marble before him now was to be his message to the church and the humanists. There is no dichotomy of God or man; God is revealed through man, who was made in God's likeness. He used his God given intellect to design a system that allowed him to hoist the twenty-six-foot-tall block of marble to a standing position. He built scaffolding around the block and draped it with curtains, allowing him to work unobserved as he brought forth what God had revealed to him in the rock.

Week by week, he used his tools, a wide variety of hammers, chisels, and drills, to chip away at the block. Day by day, extraneous pieces fell away. Moment by moment, the interaction between the soul of the statue within and these material forces wielded by the artist allowed its true form to emerge. Slowly, a youthful man sprang forth, not a boy but not yet a man, fully masculine but with a subtle and graceful femininity in his form, poised to fight but with love in his eyes. Every taut muscle, perfectly formed out of imperfect stone, was full of action potential, yet David's physical force would be forever frozen on the precipice of motion.

The artist would become the bridge between art and science, religion and secularism, Christianity and humanism. David would become the most recognizable statue of all time. Those who look upon the naked form of young, one-day King David, ready to defeat Goliath, would forever be inspired to take action against the evil and injustice rampant in the material world. They would be inspired to put their faith in the goodness and divinity of the Kingdom of God.

My job was to make sure these messages came through, to walk with Michelangelo as he chipped away at his own imperfections, as he navigated his own treacherous times and poisonous people, much as I had fifteen hundred years before, much as I have for countless others throughout time.

Caesar's Family Tree

THE ROMAN EMPIRE
IN THE FIRST CENTURY

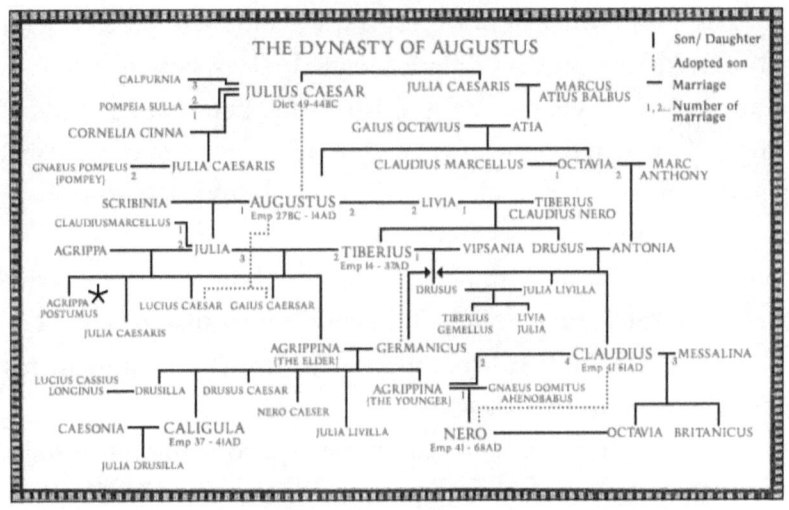

THE DYNASTY OF AUGUSTUS

	Son/ Daughter
	Adopted son
—	Marriage
1, 2.	Number of marriage

CALPURNIA
POMPEIA SULLA
CORNELIA CINNA
JULIUS CAESAR
Dict 49-44BC
JULIA CAESARIS
MARCUS ATIUS BALBUS

GAIUS OCTAVIUS — ATIA

GNAEUS POMPEUS (POMPEY) — JULIA CAESARIS
CLAUDIUS MARCELLUS — OCTAVIA — MARC ANTHONY

SCRIBINIA — AUGUSTUS Emp 27BC - 14AD — LIVIA — TIBERIUS CLAUDIUS NERO
CLAUDIUSMARCELLUS

AGRIPPA — JULIA — TIBERIUS Emp 14 - 37AD — VIPSANIA DRUSUS — ANTONIA

AGRIPPA POSTUMUS — LUCIUS CAESAR GAIUS CAERSAR
DRUSUS — JULIA LIVILLA
TIBERIUS GEMELLUS — LIVIA JULIA

JULIA CAESARIS

AGRIPPINA (THE ELDER) — GERMANICUS
CLAUDIUS Emp 41 61AD — MESSALINA

LUCIUS CASSIUS LONGINUS — DRUSILLA — DRUSUS CAESAR
NERO CAESER
AGRIPPINA (THE YOUNGER) — GNAEUS DOMITUS AHENOBABUS

CAESONIA — CALIGULA Emp 37 - 41AD
JULIA LIVILLA
NERO Emp 41 - 68AD — OCTAVIA BRITANICUS

JULIA DRUSILLA

*
CLAUDIA PROCULA INSTERTED HERE BT AUTHOR.

Family Tree of Caesar including Claudia Procula

www.pbs.org/empires/romans 2006 Public Broadcasting Service

End Notes

This book is the product of both inspiration and meticulous research. Once I started this process, Pilate invaded all aspects of my life as would any typical Roman leader – infiltrating, dominating, and commanding. Often it felt as if my thoughts were not my own; Pontius whispered in my ear while God spoke to my heart. The story had to come out, and I was just its conduit.

Over several months, I immersed myself in books, movies, articles, websites, and YouTube videos well beyond my ability to list. While not exhaustive, the sources listed were significant in helping uncover the details of Pontius Pilate's story.

Of course, I re-read parts of the Bible. I also read classic sources related to Pilate's journey, including: Robert Graves' *I, Claudius*; Irving Stone's *The Agony and the Ecstasy*; Paul Maier's *Pontius Pilate*; Conn Iggulden's *Nero*; and Mary Beard's *SPQR: A History of Ancient Rome*. However, the following lesser-known works provided great inspiration and context:

- Meggan Waterson provided a well-researched perspective on the life and influence of Mary Magdalene in *Mary Magdalene Revealed*.
- *Laura Morelli's Giant: A Novel of Michelangelo's David* provided insight into both the artist and his masterpiece.
- *Paul vs. James* by Chris Bruno helped me explore the debate over the age-old faith/works debate as well as the dynamics between the personalities of these two keystones of Christianity.
- *The Search for the Twelve Apostles,* by William Stuart McBride, helped piece together what may have happened to each of the apostles.

- I was somewhat angered in reading *After Jesus Before Christianity*, by Erin Vearncombe, Brandon Scott, Hal Taussig, and the Westar Institute; however, they provided great insight into the early church.
- *Killing Jesus* and *The Last Days of Jesus* by Bill O'Reilly helped me understand the timing of Christ's last days on earth and the geopolitical dynamics of Jesus in the Roman Empire and the Jewish Leadership.
- *Signs and Secrets of the Messiah* by Rabbi Jason Sobel helped me understand the mystical elements of the story beyond what is evident in the Bible itself.
- Lyndon Penner helped me walk the *Way of The Gardener* in his book of the same name. He helped me visualize and understand the Camino de Santiago.

Movies and television shows helped me visualize the surroundings and humanize the characters in *I Wash My Hands*. These included: *The Last Temptation of Christ*; *The Passion of the Christ*; *Rome*; *Martin Scorsese Presents: The Saints*; *Jesus Crown of Thorns*; *Mary Magdalene*; and, of course, *The Chosen*. However, I also spent countless hours watching some well-done YouTube videos including:

- *Who Was the Real Pontius Pilate? Historical Proof and Legends*, by Matt Whitman and the Ten Minute Bible Hour.
- *Lazarus of Bethany*, by Patristix
- *The Story of St. Thomas: Apostle of Belief*, By Bible Unbound
- *Bible Secrets: The Real Jesus*, by the History Channel
- *Historical Evidence of Jesus*, by The Table
- *Joseph of Arimathea (& King Arthur)*, by Patristix
- *Jesus In India, Tibet, and Persia, Account Missing from the Bible*, by rainbowlightstudio
- *The Story of Peter, The Crucified Disciple*, By Bible Unbound
- *The History of St. Peter, With David Suchet*, by Our History

- *The Twelve Apostles*, by Parable – Free History Videos
- *James the Just – His Teachings and Tragic Death*, by James Tabor
- *Nicodemus: The Night Visitor*, by The Incredible Journey
- *The Essenes & The Dead Sea Scrolls*, by Let's Talk Religion
- Who Wrote the Dead Sea Scrolls
- *Essene Beliefs Overview*, by Ken Johnson
- *From Jesus to the Christ*, by Frontline
- *A Camino de Santiago Story: To the end of the world*, by Hank Leukart
- *Michelangelo*: Artist and Genius, by Biography
- *Michelangelo – A Revolution in Art*, by hazards and catastrophes
- *How Did the Roman World Work?/Mary Beard's Rome: Empire Without Limit*, by Odyssey – Anxient History Documentaries

Thank you to all the people producing books, films, and other resources to keep us connected with our history. Without understanding our own "old testaments" we cannot be prepared for our path into the future.

When not writing, P. Drew Warren is the Chief Executive Officer of Community of Hope, a non-profit dedicated to eradicating child and family homelessness. With degrees from Stetson University and Florida Tech, Drew brings a unique blend of experience in mental health, higher education, and nonprofit leadership to all aspects of his professional and personal life. Drew has served as a therapist, professor, and college president and is a passionate advocate for children and families, believing that through community, we discover purpose, connection, and hope. Drew is a devoted husband and father who enjoys exploring nature, reading thought-provoking books, and playing basketball to recharge. His writing blends this experience with insights from his faith, his deep love for others, and a willingness to explore darkness to help others see the light!